HOW YOUNG THEY DIE

Also by Stuart Cloete:

HOW YOUNG
THEY DIE

A Novel about
the First World War

Stuart Cloete

TRIDENT PRESS : NEW YORK

How Young They Die was previously published in Great Britain by William Collins Sons & Co., Ltd., as *How Young They Died.*

Copyright, ©, 1969, by Stuart Cloete
SBN: 671–27041–9
Library of Congress Catalog Card Number: 73–80654

Published simultaneously in the United States and Canada by Trident Press, a division of Simon & Schuster, Inc., 630 Fifth Avenue, New York, N.Y. 10020.

Printed in the United States of America

To
TINY
who was not yet born
and the old soldiers
who still survive
the war we fought for
God, King and Country

This book is fiction. The only real characters are such figures as Kitchener or Sir Douglas Haig. Some regiments have fictitious names; the others were almost certainly not where I have put them, except for the Battle of Loos where my battalion was destroyed. The description comes from survivors and histories of the war.

Contents

Part One

THE VIRGIN

1 : The Anatomy of Fear

JIM HILTON stubbed out his cigarette. The floor of the railway carriage was a mass of stubs. Men's stubs. Not one marked red with lipstick—like Mona's. He kept thinking of silly things. But this was what he had wanted: to get to the front, to the war. He had been afraid it would be over before he got there. Active service. Why had he? His mother had asked him that.

"Why do you want to go, Jim? You're so young."

He had been seventeen then. He would be nineteen in July. In a way it had been patriotism—your King-and-Country-need-you kind of stuff. He thought of the posters with Kitchener's blue staring eyes, his big moustache, his pointing finger. But it had been more than that. It had been the fear of missing the greatest and most terrible event the world had yet seen. The fear of missing it had been greater than the fear of facing it. Until today when it was actually happening, when every second was taking him nearer to the war. He knew there was only one thing to be afraid of—that was of being afraid. And they were getting close to it now, to the place where fear must be faced. Like a thing, like a dragon. Like something solid. Not the Germans, they had nothing to do with it. James Hilton had forgotten the Germans. He wasn't even sure it was the Germans he was going to fight. It was fear that was the enemy. His and all men's. That was why they did such absurd and reckless things. Because they were afraid of doing them and could not live with their fears. The danger was up there where the noise was. Only it wasn't noise yet; nothing you could isolate. A kind of vibration. Up there. Up the line. He was hearing it again as he had in August

'14, only now he was a soldier, not a kid on holiday in France. How would he manage?

Fear had an anatomy. A curious thought. It had genitals, a bladder and bowels. That was where you felt fear. Not in your head. It was between your legs. It affected your excretion. It emptied you. It turned your bowels to water. It was disgusting. He shied away from his thoughts.

His mind went back to Mona and the flat. To her body. To the feel of her in his hands. He looked down at them in surprise and stuffed them into the pockets of his trench coat. How distant it all seemed—Kathleen, Gwen, Mona, his mother. He thought of the battalion that had gone to its death without him; of the reserve battalion; of the week's embarkation leave divided between his pretty mother and Mona in London; of going back to pick up the draft. Thirty-four other ranks. The Channel crossing. France again, and now Belgium.

The cold wind blew in from the Flanders plain. The rattling windows of the railway carriage could not keep it out. First class. But not going anywhere now, just shuttling up and down from the base to the railhead. He looked at the other men in the carriage. They were coming back from leave. One was a captain in the King's—about thirty. He looked tired. What was he thinking? He knew what it was all about. But you couldn't ask. He'd never been able to ask anyone what it was like. Sometimes they talked to each other, chaps who'd been out. In it. You picked up a bit by listening. You read about it in the papers. But they told you nothing and the chaps said it was all a lot of bloody lies. They said why don't they write about the wet and the cold and the bloody lice. You saw the casualty lists. But none of it was real. This was reality. "We don't want to lose you but we think you ought to go." King and Country. Kitchener's first 100,000. Songs and slogans.

He expected the captain in the King's was married. Children. He wondered what it would be like to be married and leave your wife and children. He could not visualize it. The other two officers were lieutenants. Field gunners. Both a good bit older than he was. Men. Twenty-five or twenty-six at least.

They knew, too. It was like being a virgin out with a lot of married women. They knew something you didn't know. Some secret. Some truth. He wished he could ask them.

The captain took a round yellow tin of fifty Goldflake from his haversack, lit one and passed the tin around. "Have a stinker?" he said. Thanks. Thanks. Thanks. Three voices. That was me, he thought. The captain, looking at a shelled farmhouse they had just passed, said, "There's a canteen near here. They'll stop. They always do. We can stretch our legs and get some tea."

"Done it often?" one of the gunners said.

"Four times. By the way, my name's Legget. Charles Legget. Christ!" he said, "I was at *Chu Chin Chow* last night with my wife. Hard to believe, isn't it?"

Hard to believe. Impossible to believe. That other life, so near in time and distance, was something led by a different man. Two lives that bore no relation to each other. That was what they all felt, the bloody lot of them.

"A good show," the gunner said. Then he said, "I'm Barnes, and this is Jackson. We're both with the Sixteenth Division. So are you, aren't you?"

Legget nodded. They were all looking at Jim now. Six eyes. Their faces were brown and hard, like wood. They had met fear. They knew about it. Their mouths were half smiling; it was just their eyes that were sort of dead, as if they were looking through him into yesterday, into the leave they had had. Into girls. Women. Legget into his wife and kids.

"I'm Hilton," he said. "James Hilton. I've just come out."

Barnes smiled at him. "Bit nerve-racking at first."

"A bit."

"You'll get used to it. There's a first for everything."

"How long have you been out?"

"Six months this time. I never like coming back."

The others laughed.

"What division, Hilton?" the captain asked.

"Sixteenth."*

* This is an arbitrary number. I do not know where the 16th was in April '16 or its composition.

"So we're all in it. What battalion?"

"Tenth."

"That's in my brigade. Expect we'll go up the line with the rations after dark."

Fear was creeping nearer now. "Up" was fear. "Rations" was fear. "Dark" was fear, as it had been in the nursery. "I've got a draft," he said. "Thirty-four other ranks."

"Any trouble? Any of them get drunk?"

The gunners laughed again.

"No trouble. I've got a good sergeant. Regular," he said. "He was at Mons. He's got a DCM."

"Then do what he tells you till you find your feet."

Of course he'd do what Sergeant Hargreaves said. He was old enough to be his father.

Apart from the one ruined farmhouse they had passed, the country looked peaceful; flat, lightly powdered with snow. There was no further trace of war. A covered cart plodded down a road bordered with leafless poplars. Poor little Belgium. Overrun in 1914. Once again the cockpit of Europe. It was not so long ago that he had been learning about it at school. The ball in Brussels on the eve of Waterloo. The officers drifting quietly away to mount the horses that had been brought to the door. Fighting in what was now called full dress. Khaki had only come in with the Boer War. History. Facts. His mother. Mona. Girls, women. Christ, it was cold! The wind came off the North Sea, the Arctic, over the snow-covered Flanders plain with nothing to check it. That was geography. He looked at the holiday resort photographs over the seats. Ostend. Brussels. The blue cloth upholstery was gray with dirt, black with grease where heads had rested against it. In peacetime there was a kind of white lace antimacassar stretched below the pictures. He looked again at the floor littered with cigarette ends, matches and scraps of paper. How many men had traveled in this carriage? Where were they now? How many had been killed, maimed? You could not keep away from it. He wondered what the other men were thinking, remembering, hoping.

One of the gunners said he hoped some of the horses were for them. Forty men, eight horses. Jim's draft had a truck to themselves. When they stopped he'd go and see how they were getting on. All strangers except the sergeant. He had known him in the reserve battalion. Thank God Hargreaves had been out before. But this was trench warfare. Still, he'd been in action. He'd seen Germans. Killed them. Been wounded by them. He knew the secret of death. What an extraordinary thing the human mind was! What an absurd simile! Bride and matron. And these other chaps in the carriage. Brother officers. Part of a great khaki family. Part of England. He was in it but not of it. Not yet. Still a bloody virgin. He could feel they were sorry for him in a way, wondering how he'd take it. How he'd make out. Well, God damn them, that was what he was wondering himself. Stiff upper lip. "If you can keep your head when all about you . . ." But would he? Could he? He had never seen an accident. Never seen a dead man or anyone seriously hurt. Wounded. Never seen more blood than came from a cut finger.

He kept looking at the men he was traveling with. Their uniforms and trench coats were old. Battle-stained. Their caps crumpled. He felt as if he'd just stepped out of a bandbox. They. He knew their names but in his mind they were They. The matrons. The veterans. They had had more women. Seen more life. They had seen death. They were men and he was still a boy. Was that what made a man—women and death?

"I must say I liked the music," the dark gunner said. That was Barnes. They were still talking about *Chu Chin Chow*.

"I've got a record in my gear," the other one said. Jackson. But he was thinking to hell with *Chu Chin Chow*. Vera had given him the record, "so that you'll think of me when you play it, darling." He'd think of her all right—wondering who she was sleeping with now. Wondering who else she'd given records to. He was sure it was one of her tricks. She was full of tricks— wonderful little female tricks. The way she undressed so slowly. Her black underwear. Black on blonde. Blonde all over. Genuine. There was something about blondes. They look so clean. Gold and white. You were sure they were pure. That you were

15

the first man. The only man. That you could not get anything from them. That was a joke, that was. And Monique, a Belgian refugee. He'd bought her some black satin garters in the Burlington Arcade, with a gunner grenade on them. Rolled gold and imitation diamonds. What a bloody fool he'd been about Monique with her French accent! He wondered how many regimental garters she had. "Zere is only you, *chéri.*" Only me, William Alfred Jackson. That was a laugh. Only me when I'm there, he thought. Only someone else when he's there. Half the bloody Army List probably. But what could you do? Some girls got you. They were good in bed. They understood men. They were beautiful. Christ, how lovely she was! Dark. Slight. And Vera, all ivory and gold. Not white, her skin had a tinge of cream. Jersey cream. He laughed.

"Joke?" his half section said.

"Thinking of a girl."

"Aren't we all? The girls we left behind us. Sleek, clean, scented little bitches."

The captain said, "I'm over all that, thank God. I'm married. Settled down. A couple of kids—a boy and a girl."

"That's worse," the dark gunner said. "Leaving them, I mean. They're real. Girls aren't real. We invent them. We use them and they use us, but it's not real. Never real even when you are in them."

"You're right," the other gunner said. "But it still bloody well hurts."

The Burlington Arcade with its little expensive shops—jewelry, ties, lingerie, silk stockings, shoes. The tarts looking at themselves in the windows, their gloved hands touching their hair, their hats. Smoothing their hips, standing with their high heels together. Pretty little tigers waiting for their woman-hungry prey. Sam Brownes, spurred field boots, khaki slacks. Men in a hurry for love before they died. How much could they fit in? Jackson saw it all in his mind. He heard the high heels clicking, he saw the furs. He smelled the perfume—sickly, strong, like the odor of something in heat. But it was the men who were in rut. In hurried rut. "Hallo, darling! Come home

16

with me, darling. I can make you happy." Was release happiness? Young stallions.

But he had not met Monique there. He'd met her at a party. She left the man she was with—an old major in the ASC—and rubbed herself against him like a cat. No, she hadn't done that—only given the impression of doing it by doing nothing at all except look at him with enormous black saucer eyes and drop her mascaraed lashes. He'd gone home with her to a flat in the Earls Court Road. That was the way it had begun on his last leave—a month's sick leave after a wound in his arm. She had written quite often in a tight, sloping French hand. Letters that told him nothing. But how alike all men's experiences were until they found what they were looking for, like the chap in the King's—a wife who made a home and gave them kids. And that was the end of it in a way. But only in a way, because a home was a kind of cage. Look at the number of married men who'd joined up at once. Patriotism, yes. But to get away from it too. To break out of the cage. Well, at least in the army you had no worries. Everything was arranged for you. You didn't even have to pay for your own funeral.

The Flanders plain continued to pass them by, drawn backwards by the train. Bare hop poles that no one had taken down, more lines of poplars, telegraph poles. All verticals, straight as pencils standing up on the white paper of the snow. Four men in a carriage. Other officers in other carriages. Men and horses in trucks. *Quarante chevaux—huit hommes.* Tarpaulined guns lashed down in flat cars. Ammunition. Rations. Blankets. Army supplies of all kinds going slowly up to war. Slowly up to be consumed, swallowed by the army, the insatiable monster that lay extended—waiting—from Switzerland to the sea. A strange animal that only consumed the brave—British, French, German. It lived on their flesh. They were at once its creators and the host on which it fed, a great blood-sucking parasite. The brave who fought to protect the women at home. Wives. And the girls who took the life stuff from them into their bellies and syringed it out again in the bathroom. The profiteers who grew fat on the byproducts of all this waste and carnage.

17

None of these men was actually thinking this, but they knew it instinctively. They knew they were caught in the machine of history. Caught by the accident of their birth, of their conception. A few years earlier or a few years later and history would have passed them by. Which of their fathers could have guessed as he lay with their mother that the fruit of his seed would ever rot in foreign soil? It was all an accident. All life was an accident. An accident of time, place and circumstance. Perhaps there was no God. Only Mr. Luck and Mr. Bad-luck. Mr. Luck was a blighty, a wound that was bad enough to get you out of it and keep you out. Mr. Bad-luck was not death. No. Mr. Death was almost a friend. They all knew him so well. Mr. Bad-luck was the crippler, the blinder, the taker-away of a man's legs or his balls, or both arms. That was Mr. Bad-luck. He was the chap to propitiate and pray to. Not God. What the hell had God done for anyone?

No one thought about the future. Not the next leave, or even the end of the war. After all, it had to end some time. Because no one could think even as far as tomorrow. They could think that far now, but once they detrained and began to march through Ypres and up the Menin Road it was over. Then, if you thought at all, you thought backward, retracing your steps. Home, mother, father, brothers, sisters. Dogs, horses, cats. Pets you had as a kid. A garden in the moonlight, the smell of roses on a summer's evening. You thought of girls, of a hand on a black silk stocking, of the soft flesh above it; of pink-nippled breasts, of soft throats; of dancing, music and soft lights; of wine, rich food—*pâté de foie,* caviar, smoked salmon, cold grouse. For the men life was simpler. Steaks and cunts; tits, fish and chips. Beer—bitter, half and half. Guinness. Port and brandy for the blowsy girls who were waiting to take them in their arms or, more like, for a half-crown upright in a dark doorway. Girls who thought it indecent to undress. Women, steak, beer at home. Women, *vin rouge* or *blanc* and omelettes over 'ere. And what if you did get a dose of clap? You were out of it for a bit, weren't you? Not that they treated you decent in them VD hospitals, but whatever they did was better than the line, and a lot safer than a self-inflicted wound. No court-martial for clap.

They went past a ruined village. The blackened roof timbers pointed like fingers to the sky. You could hear the guns now—a dull boom that merged with the vibration. You could not tell where one began and the other stopped. You heard the vibration and felt the noise. This was the feel of danger, the mother of fear. It was getting dark. But not the horizon. That was rosy, salmon with gunfire. No flashes. They merged with the sound and the vibration. It was all one thing. It was curious to think that fear was salmon pink. Such a pretty color, a woman's color. It ought not to be pink, Jim thought.

"I hope some of the horses are for us. We're very short." Jackson said.

Cigarettes were passed around again. Jackson went on about horses. "Thrush and grease. It's standing in those bloody horse lines up to their hocks in mud that does it."

His friend apologized for him. He said, "He used to be a horse gunner. RHA. Horse-mad, like all of them. But he's a godsend to the battery. Ours are the best kept in the division."

"You've got to love them," Jackson said. "I've taught our drivers. 'Make much of them, boys,' I said. We've brought up the guns through mud up to the axles. Just with talk. No whips." He glared around as if the others had accused him of something.

The train slowed up with a crash of couplings.

"Tea," the captain said. "The canteen."

The train stopped and they climbed out on to the steps and jumped to the ground. The canteen was forward near the engine. A long hut, the whole front a counter lit by acetylene lanterns hanging from wires in the roof.

"Going to see to my chaps," Jim said, turning his back on it.

"I'll come with you," Jackson said. "See if the horses are all right."

"Not in charge of them, are you?"

"No. They've got some remount men. But I'd like to have a look at them."

Jackson climbed into a truck where eight horses stood facing one another. He went in among the frightened animals. "Steady!" he said. "Steady!" They quieted and cocked their ears as if they knew he was a man who loved them.

The remount men came up.

"Nice lot you've got here," Jackson said.

"Traveled well, sir, the lot of them. Sixty in all."

Jim met Sergeant Hargreaves and his party. He was marching them forward in column of fours. He shouted, "Halt!" He saluted.

"Everything all right, sergeant?"

"No trouble, sir. I'm taking 'em up to get a cup of char and something to eat if they've got it."

"Rations holding out?"

"Yes, sir. Bully and biscuits. Water. But I thought we might get a sandwich."

"March them on, then."

"Party quick march!"

They moved on. Tramp, tramp. Left, right, left, the ammunition boots crunching the cinders of the track. One sergeant, one lance sergeant, two corporals and thirty rank and file. Reinforcements, replacements. A lot of wastage in war. Sick men, dead men, wounded men. Wastage that had to be replaced. Men to fill gaps. Pegs into holes. Round pegs. Square pegs. Any bloody peg into any bloody hole. The war would shape them to fit. Jim wondered whom he was replacing.

The gunner caught up with him, the rowels of his spurs clinking as he ran.

"Horses all right?"

"They've stood it pretty well. One went down when the train stopped but we got him up. Nice lot," he said. "And some of them are for us. I got that out of the NCO in charge. He showed me his requisition form. I squared him to get the pick."

The counter was lined with officers and men. Motherly looking women in blue uniforms and white aprons were handing out cups of tea in big white enamel mugs with blue edges, and thick ham sandwiches. The men were happy. Like schoolboys stretching their legs. Urinating twenty yards or so away with their faces to the train. There was a white-painted sign with an arrow marked "Latrine," but that was for other things. The women knew what was going on but they weren't girls. They were mothers and these were little boys. Great big little boys with bayonets at their belts. Because they were living in the now of it and not thinking of tomorrow, they were happy with their tea and ham sandwiches.

A bit different from the men Jim had seen at Victoria coming off the leave train. Hunchbacked with kitbags, tired, unshaven, dirty, the bottoms of their overcoats ragged where they had shortened them, hacking them off with their jack-knives. A queer blank look in their eyes as if they could not believe any of it was real—not all these bloody people in civvies. Young girls, flappers, women with children, men in bowler hats. Christ Almighty, who'd have believed it? They had their rifles slung over their shoulders by their webbing slings. They had full packs and kitbags. One of them had a shiny brass-mounted *Pickelhaube* tied to the top of his pack. They allowed the red-capped military police with white pipeclayed belts and white spats over their puttees to direct them, but the police were careful with them. These men were fresh from war, from killing and being killed. They'd not be buggered about by these bastards who had it so good sitting on their arses at home. If one of the chaps had been roughed up they'd have turned on the police. It had happened before. They had no love for stay-at-homes, soldiers or civilians. Bugger them, having the girls and the beer and the steaks and WC's with a pull and let go. A mixture of regiments—Line, Guards, cavalrymen, Highlanders, Riflemen, Gunners—but they were all fighting soldiers and they knew it.

These were the same men. Friendly as pups. Some of them would die, but they'd do it together. They were men, comrades in the most bloody awful adventure the world had ever seen.

Jim found the captain of the King's Liverpools and the other gunner. Comrades, too. A little temporary nucleus that had formed in a filthy first-class carriage and would shortly break up to form again into more permanent, organized shapes with their own units. Already Jim saw that this was the pattern of war. Change. Men coming and going, their paths crossing. In peace-time you stayed put. At school, at home. Society was relatively fixed.

The engine blew its whistle, a sad, wailing sound that broke the night in two. It ended the canteen interlude; it divided time into the before-the-whistle and after it. There would only be so many such pauses before the balloon went up.

"Entrain, everybody, entrain. Get fell in. . . ."

The engine gave a number of little hysterical hoots. As the men clambered back on board, one of the motherly women in the canteen began to cry.

2 : The Sound of War

THE TRAIN started soon after they had settled themselves in their corners. Legget said, "We'll not get to Poperinghe before dark. Supposed to be safer that way."

The guns were louder now. Jim's mind went back to the first summer of the war. To 1914. And the scene he had had with his Uncle George. It all seemed rather funny, looking back on it. What a kid he had been then—only eighteen months ago! His uncle had been telling him off for kissing Kathleen. They always came to his uncle's place at Laurent Plage for the summer holidays. Good for his French, his mother said. There had been a smell of sweet peas in the air—his mother loved them—and the hum of bees.

He had done more than kiss Kathleen. She was sixteen, with long, straight blonde hair, wide-set gray eyes and slim legs—bare legs. A sort of Alice-in-Wonderland girl who had been bored to death until he came. Her parents had taken a nearby cottage for the summer. He'd only been back from Denby three days and two of them had been spent with her in the woods, going down to the sea to bathe, walking barefoot in the hot sand of the dunes. School was over and done with. He was going to Oxford. He was almost a man.

Kathleen had been waiting for him behind some shrubs.

"Well, what did your uncle say?"

"Said I must leave you alone."

"What a good thing he only caught us kissing!" She laughed. "We'll have to be more careful."

She had on a short white cotton dress, a white ribbon in her hair, sneakers. When she ran, her hair flying over her shoulders, her knickers showed. She looked back at him in invitation. An invitation to what? How far could he go? He wished he knew more about these things.

On June 28 the Archduke Franz Ferdinand, heir to the Austro-Hungarian Empire, had been murdered at Sarajevo—a well-planned affair with seven assassins stationed at various points on the probable route of the procession. But no one had paid much attention to that event at Denby. Not with the cricket match against Lancing coming off the following week. That had been a month ago, but no one bothered with dates in the summer holidays, certainly he didn't as he wandered with Kathleen in the pine woods. Their hands had sought each others and more. Soft tendrils of exploring love. What was a dead Archduke to them?

It was full summer, hot, fecund, heavy with the weight of the sun. Honeysuckle in flower, newly fledged birds precariously perched, a yellow-hammer proclaiming his presence with repeated calls of "A little bit of bread and no cheese. No cheese . . . No cheese . . ." Larks by day, nightingales by night.

His uncle's talk of the seriousness of the situation had meant nothing to Jim. He was in love. Calf love, people called it, but it was an extraordinary sensation. He had no appetite. He could hardly sit through meals. All he wanted to do was to find Kathleen and be with her. Hold her hand, stroke her hair, kiss her and touch the soft skin of her thighs. It was two days before he noticed that all the men and boys were gone from the village. Called up. General mobilization. Also, for the first time— dislike.

The French had not been sure that England would stand by them. Perhaps the treaty, the Entente Cordiale, was just a scrap of paper too. How perfidious could Albion be? Then it came. England declared war and the Gowans, Kathleen's parents, said they were going home as soon as they could make the arrangements. This took two more days. Two days of blissful heartbreak for Jim. An idyll. The first phase of a mystery he knew was going to be important to him. Girls. He had heard boys talk about them at Denby. Hollis had some dark, stiff, curly hairs in a matchbox that he bragged about. Other chaps talked about their sisters' friends who came to stay. And there it was, a boy's strange composite picture of women and girls. Glimpses of a peasant's breast as she suckled a child. Nude statues and pictures. Stories he had heard. Talk. The knowledge of animals that came from holidays in the country. The surprising sight of a young man lying on a girl in a hedgerow. And finally Kathleen, the only girl he had ever really touched. That was on the last day in the forest. She had said, "No, no, don't do that!" But she had moved to let him.

She had smelled of soap and milk and talcum powder. Clean, with a sweet, acrid scent of fresh sweat that reminded him of gorse in full flower under the sun's heat; as if the sun had distilled her too, as if girls were flowers. Under her arms were a few short golden hairs. The down of a young pigeon before flight. About them in the forest clearing there were butterflies: Red Admirals, black velvet splotched with white and scarlet, brown peacocks with purple eyes on their wings, frilled tortoiseshells, orangetips . . . Butterflies—pairs joined in courting flight. Everything, because of her, was more beautiful. Brighter, sweeter, dearer, poignant with young love.

A cuckoo called. He said, "It's late for a cuckoo."

"Yes," she said, lying back on the short rabbit-cropped grass, her hands behind her head, her pale gold hair spread on the greensward carpet. Her face and frock were dappled with tree

24

shadows that moved like hands over her in a sudden breeze. He knew what he wanted to do. But he did not dare. And he was not certain. At least he was certain only of desire. He was not ready yet. But he knew he would be soon, that this was a prelude, the tuning-up of the orchestra that was man.

Her gray eyes had mocked him. "Kiss me," she said, and they kissed. He lay on her, his body on hers, urgent, unknowing, flooded with unskilled desires, his hands fumbling, the fingers of a blind man feeling for dropped gold. Her lips opened to his— moist, cool nectar. Her body arched under him and she broke away.

"Come!" Kathleen had said, taking Jim's hand. "Let's run!" So they had run like deer through the woods, for the joy of it and the youth in them and the blood in their veins. Oaks, beeches, silver birch, wild cherry, the leaves of years a carpet to their feet. Above them a green canopy of leaves, above the leaves a blue sky, and all silent but for the hum of insects and the wing clap of a frightened pigeon. Alone as Adam and Eve, running because they were afraid of their own beating hearts that cried for nakedness.

All over the world it was going on, this young mating and near-mating. This love play and courtship. This showing and hiding. This coming and going. This "so far, and that is all for now." Like the birds of the air, the rabbits and foxes of the forest. The badgers.

Then the Gowans had gone in a high, two-wheeled peasant cart with a canvas hood. Dr. Gowan, his wife and Kathleen, his beloved. Gone on iron-tired wheels down the white dusty road to catch the cross-channel steamer from Boulogne. And Jim had had his first parting from a girl, his first uncertainty.

The other partings had been from his mother when he went to school, but she was not uncertain. Mothers were always there. This was a microcosm of the million partings that were taking place in Europe. Just a single minuscule displacement of war, a parting of two innocents who had never really come together. No more than two leaves drifting on the same current for an hour or a day, irrelevant to each other except in their own context, except as symbols of greater and more tragic partings.

Next day Jim had ridden his bicycle to Pont de Briques where Belgian troops in full retreat were disembarking from a train. Exhausted men in dark uniforms with packs made of red and white cowskin. It was here he saw blood for the first time. Lightly wounded men with bandaged heads and arms. Men wounded in the leg helped by their comrades. Belgium had been overrun. Poor little Belgium. He had ridden home quite slowly. Love and blood. Kathleen's satin thighs, and the bloody bandage on the head of a boy no older than himself.

Hardly knowing what he was doing he had walked over to the Gowans's cottage, as if she was still there—or the ghost of her. As if he could tell her what was in his mind. Nothing was in his mind except that he missed her and was going to be a soldier. He had always wanted to be a soldier like his grandfather— there was a painting of him at home—but there had been no money for it. Now there would be no need of money.

The door of the cottage was unlocked. The place had been tidied up, cleaned. There was no trace of any of them. He went into the small room Kathleen had used. He thought he could feel her there, in the emptiness of it, as if she'd left her shape impressed on the air. This was where she'd slept, dressed and undressed. These walls had seen the whole of her, all of her. Naked. The room was like the casket of a jewel, but the jewel was gone. He wondered if she had left anything behind and began to look everywhere. Nothing. Nothing at all. Till in the last closet, right at the back on a shelf, he found a handkerchief that was not quite clean. A token. A talisman. He'd take it to war with him like the knights of old who wore their ladies' favors. Tennyson, Kipling, Sir Walter Scott, the stuff he'd been brought up upon, the poetry of Empire, was all mixed up in his mind.

The war took hold of him. If only he could get into it. He saw himself as a hero, irresistible. He saw Kathleen in his arms. Soldiers were men. Men had women. Girls. Kathleen. This was his chance to be a soldier if the war did not end too quickly.

How he hoped it wouldn't! Hoped that the war would wait for him. If only he was older. Just a year or so.

As soon as he got home he ran into the house. "I saw them," he said. "Belgians. Some of them were wounded."

His mother turned quite white. His uncle said, "They could have held out longer."

"There were French soldiers guarding the level-crossing. Old men in képis with long blue coats buttoned back over their red trousers. They had fixed bayonets, Uncle George." He saw them again in his mind—long thin bayonets glistening like rapiers in the sun.

Next day they put Gipsy into the trap and drove into town to see the first British troops disembark. The Expeditionary Force under General Sir John French. Some Highlanders, Seaforths and Argylls, had already arrived and had been quartered behind bars in a school to save them from the French women who were curious to see what they wore under their kilts. The bars of the school playground were lined with women and girls watching a couple of Pipers march up and down, their kilts and sporrans swinging as they played. The 60th Rifles were disembarking and some light cavalry—the Hussars and Lancers—who would form the cavalry screen that would protect the marching troops. Horses were being slung by cranes out of the hold on to the dock. There were horses everywhere. Beautiful blacks, bays, browns, chestnuts, led by troopers with steel spurs and puttees tied over their boots. The horses had swords fastened to the near side of their saddles. Lances. Rifles in buckets. The lovely smell of horse sweat and man sweat, and the sound of the iron shoes on the *pavé*. What a thing to see! British troops where only a hundred years ago Napoleon's army had been encamped waiting to attack England.

On the drive home he had been silent. There was plenty to think about. Ten days ago he had been at school. Now a new world was spread out before him. The curtain of childhood had been pulled back. He had known love. Just the golden fringe of it. Warm, moist, silken. He had seen war. Again, just the beginning of it. Bloodied Belgian soldiers. British troops disembarking, marching to battle. It occurred to him that this was the difference between men and boys. Love and war. It was like a sum. You added them to a boy and he became a man.

Yet everything was the same. The white dusty road. The mare's hooves clip-clopping along. The trees. The grass verges. All the same but different, because he was different. Something had been thrust upon him. He did not know it was history. All those beautiful chargers, troops, squadrons, regiments. The rumbling gun carriages of the horse artillery. The men riding and marching, all going southeast toward the Germans. Like a river running into the sea, into the turbulence of it. To war. His blood, hot from the memory of Kathleen, had had no chance to cool. It was as if two fevers had struck him, one after the other. Fragments, odd lines of poetry came back to him: "Clothed in white samite, mystic, wonderful"—Kathleen showing her legs when she ran. "Guns to the right of them, guns to the left of them . . . noble six hundred!" "It's Tommy this and Tommy that till the band begins to play . . ." The pipes of the marching Highlanders. Nothing under their kilts. The smell of the sweating men and horses—the little pigeon hairs under Kathleen's arms, the soft skin of her thighs. He felt her handkerchief in his pocket. They had gone back to England. He'd go too; join the army and see Kathleen. Life was about to begin. He was going to enlist in the cavalry. It was just a matter of getting back. He paused. There was a sound he had never heard before, a kind of vibration. GUNS. Guns were firing in the distance. It was the sound of WAR.

What a long time ago all that seemed. His temporary commission in the Wiltshire Light Infantry, the training period under canvas in camps, in huts; Aldershot; the battalion leaving without him because he was too young. That at least was what they said. But it hadn't been that. And because they hadn't taken him he was alive today. The division had been cut to pieces at Loos. It just went to prove something—he wondered what. He'd seen Kathleen a few times, taken her to the pictures a few times. But it had been different in London. Then she had been sent to a boarding school, his letters had not been answered. And now there was Mona. He thought of how Maurice had introduced him to her: Maurice Colton, his best friend, who had been killed at Loos with the others.

3 : The Virgin

"So THIS is your friend, Maurice," Mona said, holding out her hand. She was dark with bobbed hair and big brown eyes.

"Jimmie," Maurice said. "I've told you about him."

Her hand was soft. She was small and slim. About twenty-two, Maurice said. Dressed in a dark-red silk frock with a wide black suede belt. Slim legs, black silk stockings, high-heeled black suede shoes. Slim arms, slim neck. Slim, slight, small. Nothing to be afraid of.

She said, "Jimmie." Her voice was soft, a little husky. When she smiled she had pretty teeth set in a little red mouth. Not mean, just small like the rest of her. All of her pared down like a blood horse. He was sure she could run like Kathleen. Only dark, not fair. When she said his name, he said, "Yes," as if it was roll call. He almost answered, "Here!"

"He's shy," she said to Maurice, as if he wasn't there. People were always doing that, as if he was a child. It embarrassed him.

"I told him it would be all right—with you."

She laughed again, crinkling her nose like a rabbit, and sat down. "Give him a drink. Me, too. All of us."

Maurice switched on a standing lamp with a rose shade tasseled with crystal beads, fringed like a skirt. The dusk of the room was warmed with its pink glow—the pictures, the carpet, the armchairs, the big sofa. On the mantelpiece there were photos of men in uniform. Officers, in soft leather and silver frames—one of them was Maurice. The gas fire was not lit. It looked like a little pile of white skulls, with dark eye sockets. How calm they all were, as if they weren't going to do anything! But they were. That is what they had come for. Jimmy could not bear to watch them any longer or even look at the room. He'd get to know it later. Somehow he was sure of that.

He went over to the photographs. He could hear Maurice fixing the drinks, squirting the soda. But he couldn't get away from her. There she was in the mirror above the frames. Framed in it, sitting curled on the sofa with one leg under her, showing a slim white thigh between the red dress and the black silk stocking. A black suspender ran upward from the stocking top like a snake; a small black satin bow covered the rubber end where it clipped on. Just like the garters he wore to hold up his socks. At least they seemed to fasten the same way. Her eyes caught his in the glass and she smiled at him. Just the eyes, not the mouth. Maurice came into the picture—because it was a picture framed in gold, not real at all—carrying two glasses. She took a cigarette out of a silver box. Maurice lit it for her. He couldn't stay here for ever, with his back to them, staring. Because it wasn't a picture, it was real. As he turned Maurice bent over her and kissed her. His hand disappeared under the red silk dress. She laughed again and stood up.

"What a man!" she said.

She brought him the whisky and soda Maurice had poured. They all had drinks now. He needed one.

Jimmie had turned back to the photographs.

"My friends," Mona said.

Then he saw their backs in the picture—in the mirror—a man in khaki and a girl in red. A wide black suede belt and a Sam Browne. They went through a white door. Before it closed, she said, "Put on some records," pointing to a gramophone he had not noticed. He went over to it and wound it up. He played "You Great Big Beautiful Doll," "My Little Grey Home in the West," some Gilbert and Sullivan, "You Great Big Beautiful Doll" again.

The picture of Maurice on the mantelpiece was the one that

30

he had. He supposed he'd given her a photo one day. He'd had some taken for his mother. That was funny in a way. The way photos were distributed to mothers, girls, wives, friends. Maurice had said, "Mona Moon is not a tart. She only sleeps with friends. You have to be introduced. A bit like a club. If she doesn't fancy you she won't have anything to do with you. A chap called Frazer in the Buffs introduced me. Then I talked about you and she said, 'I think I'd like him, don't you?' Of course we all pay her."

"How much?" he'd asked.

"A fiver. But don't give it to her. Just put it on the mantelpiece. We telephone for appointments."

Then they came out. She had changed into a dark blue dress with white polka dots. Of course she'd had to undress. How silly of him not to have thought of it.

She said to Maurice, "You'd better leave us now. We'll meet you for dinner."

He was glad of that. If he made a fool of himself like that other time . . . the only time.

"See you later, then," Maurice said, picking up his little leather-covered swagger stick.

The front door closed quietly. They were alone.

"Alone at last," Mona said. "And how about a cup of tea? I can always do with a cup of tea." She went into the little kitchen to put the kettle on.

For a moment Jim thought of bolting. Back in the room she said, "We've lots of time—a couple of hours."

It seemed a very long time to be alone with her.

"I hope you don't mind but Maurice told me about you. He thought it would be better if I knew."

"About that . . ."

"The woman at the Empire," she said. "I'm not surprised, really."

"I thought I was no good."

"You'll be good with me. But we'll have tea first." She went out to make it.

He had two cups and a Bath bun. When they had done she

31

took the tray away and stooped to light the fire. It started with a loud pop. The little white skulls turned blue and then red. There was something very exciting in the way she bent over. He could see the back of her legs and the tight curve of her buttocks under the spotted dress.

"I think I'll take my dress off," she said, and began to unbutton it. "I don't want another one rumpled." A moment later she stood in front of him in a thin black *crêpe de chine* chemise through which her nipples showed.

"Now you," she said. She undid the buckle of his belt and took off his jacket. She pushed him into a chair and knelt at his feet to take off his shoes. "I'll get you a dressing gown and then you can take off the rest." She fetched a blue silk dressing gown that had a white dragon embroidered on it. Chinese. "Now let's be cosy by the fire." She pulled him down to her. She took his hand and put it on her breast. She lowered it to her loins. Her own hands found his body, light as butterflies on it. His arms went around her as she lay back. Then it was over.

"You see," she said, laughing. "You're a man now and one of my friends. One of my very best friends. Only don't fall in love with me. I want you to think of me like a sister."

"People don't sleep with their sisters," he said.

"They're not supposed to, but the Pharaohs did in Egypt. And Byron did, or so they say. I'll get you another whisky." She got up and came back with one. They each had a cigarette.

Then she said, "Now we'll go into the bedroom."

She closed the door, took off her shoes and stockings—this time they were held up with red satin garters—pulled her chemise over her head, and before he realized what she was doing had removed his dressing gown.

"Come!" she said, flinging herself on the tumbled bed.

Now he saw her. All of her. Her dark tufted armpits, the triangular mat of her groin, geometrically neat, the full perfection of her invitation. He thought of Gwen, the woman he had picked up at the Empire, of Kathleen Gowan whom he had never seen, as he bent over to stare at her belly, her navel, the masked junction of her slim thighs. A man. He had done it. She smiled up at him and pulled him down onto her again.

It seemed as if only a few minutes had passed before she rose on her elbow and said, "We must get dressed if we don't want to be late."

They took a taxi to the Berkeley where Maurice was waiting for them. He'd been to the club and had just arrived, one of the hundred or more officers in khaki. Some had the red tabs of the staff. And a few foreigners—a Frenchman in pale blue, a Belgian cavalry officer just going out, with a black forage cap that had a long gold tassel dangling past his nose. They all had women with them—women, girls. Short-tight-skirted, vivacious, excited by so many soldiers, by uniforms, by obvious virility.

Maurice ordered dinner: *hors d'œuvre, consommé,* lobster, pheasant. They finished up with ices and drank champagne. Mona raised her glass for a toast: "To Jimmie!" she said, laughing at his blushes. No one seeing them—two young officers with a pretty girl sitting at a softly lighted table—would ever have taken her for what she was. Engaged to one of them, perhaps. The sister of one of them.

Jimmie had spoken very little. The wonder and surprise of his experience, of this world of woman that he had just entered, the virgin world that he had lost, closing the door of it behind him. This was the tree of knowledge. He'd eaten of its fruit. It was there between those thighs, hidden by the white napkin and the spotted dress.

4 : The Captain

JACKSON, LT. WILLIAM ALFRED, RFA, had gone out with C Battery of the Royal Horse Artillery in August '14 as a driver. Those were the days—the six-horse, six-gun batteries galloping into action with the cavalry, wheeling, unlimbering, firing—over open sights sometimes. What a thing that had been to see! What comradeship! What horses—matched teams, quiet as kittens, bold as lions! Or did it all only seem so much better now, looking back at it from the mud and muck of today? He thought of the cavalry regiments in the line: The 5th, 9th, 12th, 16th and 17th—Lancers. The 4th, 15th and 20th—Hussars. All dead now or dispersed. The old BEF nothing but a memory. From driver to gunner. Corporal, sergeant, and then a commission. Second Lieutenant RFA. Lieutenant. But field gunners weren't horse gunners, and he was a ranker. Not that anyone ever said anything about it, but he wasn't one of them. Good school, university and all that. He was a board school boy, but he'd been a good scholar, especially at math. So he didn't talk much. Only about horses and guns—the things he knew. He had never been abroad before the war. He had never read books or listened to music. But he was good-looking and it was his looks and style of a regular soldier that had got him girls like Vera and Monique. Girls with silk and lace underclothes. In peacetime he'd seen officers with their like but he never thought he'd have one under him. And there was another thing about them: they had taught him a lot. How to speak nicely, how to order meals. Manners. He picked things up quickly, he did. He'd learned about women, too. Class didn't make them honest or moral. No bloody fear. They'd hop into bed with another chap before you could say Jack Robinson, if they got a chance. All women were bitches if it came to that, so you might as well have a pretty one that dressed nice and smelled nice, as a common one.

That was where they differed from horses. Common horses—cold bloods—would always let you down if it came to a push, but women—well bred or common—were all the same. But with both horses and women it was the hands that did it. The patting, the petting, the stroking. The making much of them, the talking soft to them. He thought of the way he used to comb Monique's long, black hair.

"You comb a lot of 'air, Alf?" she'd said. "You must 'ave, you do it so nice."

"Yes," he'd said, laughing. "A lot." Christ, what a lot of

34

hair! Chestnut, black and brown. Neat bangled tails. A lot of tails—hundreds in his time. Thousands.

They'd been with the 5th Cavalry Brigade under Sir Philip Chetwode. Mons. The Aisne. Heartbreaking to see the exhaustion of the horses. Heartbreaking. He thought of the horses in the trucks behind them. The remounts. There were a dozen light vanners with a dash of blood he'd like to get hold of—not heavy enough for wheelers, but team horses—and two chargers. Walers, from the look of them. He needed a second horse and so did the major. Matched teams? That was a laugh. By God, it was cold! You could hear the guns clearly now. They seemed pretty active.

Lieutenant Barnes, Charles Algernon, RFA, was thinking about young Hilton. A kid. About twenty. But he looked as if he'd be all right—if he lasted the first month. So many didn't. There were tricks to learn if you wanted to stay alive. Then he thought about Jackson and his bloody horses. Still, he was lucky. Worrying about the horses kept his mind off things in a way. Then he thought about women. Actresses. Lily Elsie, Gertie Millar, Gaby Deslys, Gladys Cooper. Christ, there were some pretty women in the world! He wondered if they were any better than the others, all cats being gray in the dark. But why have it dark when there was something beautiful to look at? Not that he had anything to complain about. He'd picked up a nice little bit of fluff the first day home—a redhead—and by the time he'd had to leave her he was all shagged out. He felt a bit guilty about his people. He hadn't been home to see them. He wouldn't tell them he had had leave or been in London. Tunbridge Wells. So close, really. But it was a question of time. Besides, if he'd let that little redhead out of his sight she'd have buggered off with some other chap as like as not. Well, it was all over now. Those kind of days were like flowers pressed in a book. Beautiful when you put them in, but irrelevant. Nothing to do with the book itself. When you saw them again—all dry and faded—you wondered why the hell you had kept them.

The shortage of ammunition was a bugger. It was also a scandal. When the infantry wanted retaliation, what could you give them? Half a dozen rounds at most. Well, they'd soon be back for it now. For how long? Till you went sick or were hit, or killed. No one spoke any more about the war ending.

Captain Charles Carsdale Legget of the 7th King's was thinking about his wife. Frances. They had been married five years and had a boy of four and a little girl six months old whom he'd just seen for the first time. He was—had been—a stockbroker, with a nice little house in Golders Green. He was glad it had a garden for the kids. But they did not want any more children. Two were enough. My God, how careful they had been this time! But it was funny how after five years, even when you had been away almost a year, passion did not come back. Where had it gone? Was it him or her, or both of them? It was habit now. Urgent certainly, after so long, but still habit. Something you remembered rather than felt. He had said when they were talking about girls that he was over all that. But was he, he wondered? There had been two girls at the Savoy he had kept looking at when they had had lunch there. Well-dressed girls. Girls, not mothers. He wondered if that was it. If a woman, when she became a mother, stopped being a wife. He loved his kids but he missed the other thing.

He looked at the young chap in the Wiltshire L.I. Hilton. A second lieutenant. Subalterns did not last long as a rule—about a fortnight was the average. Captains lasted longer. He smiled bitterly. Captains didn't go out on patrol or on wiring parties. They had learned to take care of themselves. By the time they were captains they were already survivors. That was a man's aim today. To survive. To do your duty and survive. That was why they were here. All of them. To do their duty. Nelson's "England expects . . ." And still to live. It sounded sentimental, so much so that no one ever mentioned it. Embarrassing. He'd keep with the boy if he could till they got to brigade. He seemed a nice boy. They'd be at Poperinghe soon after dark unless the train pulled up for some reason. Considering how far back they were, the guns seemed very loud.

Then he did something he had never done before. He took out his field service notebook and wrote down his home address and telephone number, very carefully with an indelible pencil on three separate pages, tore them out and said, "I want to give you chaps my home address. If ever you are in London . . ." He did not say any more. It was as if he expected them to call him up and arrange a party.

They took the pages reluctantly. This was not in the book of rules. It looked as if Legget had had some kind of premonition. The two gunners looked at him as if he was already lying on a stretcher. Jim said, "Thank you, sir," very politely, and put the paper in his pocketbook.

"Don't call me 'sir,' " Legget snapped, as if he regretted his action and would have taken the papers back if he could.

5 : Goodbye Mrs. Hilton

IRENE HILTON found another letter from Jimmie when she got home. That was three letters and four field service postcards with everything but "I am well" crossed out since he had left a month ago. There was no more news. He was still at the base. What base? Where? But expected to be sent up the line before long. Things, as she must have seen from the newspapers, were very quiet. It was cold. There had been snow. But the hut he was in was warm and comfortable, with a Queenie stove which they kept red-hot. He had made a friend—Jack Campbell of the Irish Rifles. Their cap's badge was a harp—did she know that? The canteen was very good. He had bought some trench boots and sheepskin fingerless gloves with the wool inside. And thank you for the muffler and the parcel. That was about all. Much love from her loving son and don't worry. I shall be all right. . . .

It reminded her of the letters he had written from school. She tried to be cheerful about it and pretend he was still at Denby. He was right, things did seem quiet on the Western Front. That was where he must be. Quiet for the winter. Quiet till the weather improved. According to the old history books, troops had always gone into winter quarters for the bad weather—a kind of hibernation.

She sat down at her desk to write him a letter. She wrote twice a week. Her letters conveyed no more to him than his did to her. They were living in two worlds. He was in the military world, poised on the very edge of war. Of the trenches, of no-man's-land, of bursting shells and gunfire. All words to her. The pictures in the papers did not really convey the truth. She was in London, the world's capital, frenetically gay, bright, laughing with near hysteria. Ambivalent. Laughing and crying. She felt like that herself, caught between despair and happiness.

It might be cold and snowing in France but it was a lovely day in London. She decided to change and go for a walk. Blow the cobwebs away. She dressed carefully, thinking how lucky women were to be able to escape into a world of costume and decoration. They were all actresses at heart.

In Kensington Gardens the forsythia was pouring its yellow gold over the shrubberies. The daffodils were out. Flowering crabapples, thorns, plums, all bright in the sunshine. Though the big trees—elms, planes and sycamores—were still bare, they showed a faint haze of green. The promise of summer. When it warmed up and the leaves came out the war would move into high gear once more. It was a lovely day for a walk. Nurses and children, well-dressed women and older men were out. A few wounded in their blue hospital uniforms and scarlet scarves sat on the seats watching the human traffic pass with wondering eyes. They were out of it. Bloody marvelous. Neither soldier nor civilian. In limbo. Not adjusted yet. But the April sun was something those who could get out were not going to miss. It was a kind of present.

Heads turned to look at Irene Hilton as she passed—a pretty, fair woman in a black coat and skirt, a silver fox scarf and a small straw hat with a short veil that came down to her nose. It was a bit early for a straw hat but she had felt like wearing it. After all, it was quite hot for an English spring. Appreciating it all—the warmth, the flowers, feeling really alive—Irene walked toward Hyde Park Corner, weaving her way between prams and toddlers. The war, even with her son in it, was a long way off today.

For ten years, since her husband had died, she had not been a woman—those years had belonged to Jimmie—not really a woman, that is, and then only for short periods. Yesterday everything had changed. Now it was goodbye Mrs. Hilton and enter Lady Gore Blakeney, wife of General Sir John St. John Gore Blakeney, Bart. What a name! They were being married next Wednesday. She wondered how Jimmie would take it. She thought of John coming to her house in Melbury Road yesterday. "Come to tea," she had said. Tea, crumpets and seed cake. She had let him in at four-thirty, a big red-faced man with red tabs and a red and gold cap. Rows of medals, top boots, spurs. So big and so out-of-doors in her small drawing room with its Queen Anne furniture. He had smelled of tobacco and whisky and shaving lotion. He was, as they said, a fine figure of a man. She had known him for more than a year but it was the first time he had come to the house. Dinners, lunches, theatres, whenever he was in London. He had made what were called advances to her but had never got very far. He had never said anything or proposed anything. But she had learned a lot about him. A widower with no children. Very well off. He had been in the Greys and had seen service in India, Egypt and South Africa. Men liked him. But she had had to have time to think.

She had worn her pink tea gown. Pink silk under a froth of lace. And no corset. As soon as they had reached the drawing room he had taken her in his arms. He had kissed her before but never like this. He had bent her backward, pulling her to him. She had felt his hand on her waist and had relaxed in his arms. After that there was no stopping him. Not that she had tried. He'd only taken off his belt, jacket and tie. She'd said, "The crumpets will get cold!" He'd said, "God damn the crumpets!"

After it was over she left him to tidy herself and give him time to recover. When she came back, the man had gone. Only the general remained. He got up when she came in.

Standing at the door, framed in it like a picture, she said, "Well, John, what now?"

"You don't expect me to say I'm sorry?"

"No, John. But you've got to make up your mind. I'm not going to be your mistress. Either you marry me or you don't see me again. I can't trust myself with you. A few more times and I'd have no way out."

"I've wanted to marry you for a long time, Irene."

"Then why didn't you say so?" She stamped her foot.

"I was afraid to ask you. I'm twenty years older than you are."

Jim's father had been much older than she, but she did not tell him that. She said, "With your boots and spurs on, John! Just like the Duke of Marlborough when the Duchess came to his tent after the Battle of Blenheim."

"How could I get them off without a jack? Besides . . . besides you were in the mood. I could feel it."

"A very indelicate remark, Duke, if I may say so." She had sat down. "The tea is still warm but the crumpets are cold."

Then they laughed and talked and had warm tea and cold crumpets. And more talk, and she gave him a whisky and soda. He took her hand in his and said, "I want that."

"My wedding ring? It's never been off my finger."

"I want it."

"It won't come off."

He pulled her to the bathroom, moistened her left hand under the faucet, rubbed some soap on it and pulled the ring off.

"But why, John?" How odd that one man should put a ring on and another, twenty years later, should pull it off.

"Why, you silly girl? For size, of course. Lunch tomorrow"— that was today—"and I'll have a bloody great ring for you.

Something vulgar like those the Johannesburg women had at the Mount Nelson in the war." The Boer War was still "the war" to him.

She looked down at the black kid glove on her left hand where the ring made quite a bulge. And he had called her "silly girl." How wonderful that was, to be called silly! And a girl. He'd take care of everything now.

Then he said, "Get dressed and I'll take you to dinner and a show. *Chu Chin Chow.* I've seen it before and I don't want to go to a show I've got to look at. I want to look at you."

She left him to change. She put on her new white dress, like a bride.

They had lunch at the Savoy, that was where he had given her the ring. He had to leave early to go to the War Office and she took a taxi to the Broad Walk. A taxi into the sun. She was a woman again, a man's woman. Not a lady. Ladies did not seduce generals in their own drawing rooms. She asked about the wedding ring. "Don't want it, do you, my girl?" So that was it. The new broom.

She thought about Jim again. Almost nineteen and at the war. He had wanted to go. She couldn't have stopped him if she had tried. But what luck it had been his battalion leaving him behind in England. Nearly all of them had been killed. Loos had been a disastrous battle. Only a few hundred left out of a division. The colonel had said he was too young. But what was the right age for a boy to be killed? Who decided? Tears came into her eyes. It was no use crying. She signaled to a taxi. He had been so gay and happy when he said goodbye. The young warrior. All she could do now was to hope and pray, write letters and send parcels, the way she had done when he had been at school.

Back at his headquarters in the Northern Command, Major-General Sir John Gore Blakeney was changing for mess. Putting on his blues. Undress blue uniform, high-collared tunic, red-striped overalls over Wellingtons with box spurs. Williams, his batman, was emptying the pockets of his khaki. Watch, loose change, pocketbook. He had them arranged on the chest of drawers in exact military alignment. The change sized—half-crowns at the bottom of a neat pile. When the General looked at him he had the wedding ring between his fingers and was lining it up with the silver.

"Know what that is, Williams?"

"A ring, sir. It looks a bit like a . . ."

"That's what it is, my lad. A wedding ring."

"Yes, sir." What the hell was the old boy up to now? He was older than the General, had been his servant in India and South Africa, but he always thought of him as the old boy. Gay old bastard. Fond of the ladies. Well, why not? He was, too. All cavalrymen had a way with women. Women and horses. Understood them.

"I'm getting married again, Williams."

The old bugger. Just fancy that, getting spliced at his age!

"Next Wednesday. Pity it's wartime and we can't do it properly. Regimental band, arch of swords and all that."

"It is indeed, sir." Next Wednesday. Say a week or so for a honeymoon. He'd get some leave while the General was away and find something for himself. A bit of fluff, not too young. About time for some greens. Say thirty. Not too big. He didn't like big women or big horses. More of them to go wrong.

"You're the first to know," the General said.

"Thank you, sir." And so I bloody well ought to be, seeing as 'ow I've bin a sort of mother to 'im. . . .

He'd tell the staff at dinner. They'd drink his health. Wednesday. He could get away all right. Brighton. The Metropole. He'd taken women there before. Not openly, of course. Just arranged to meet them there. But this would be different. A honeymoon. All square and above board. Major-General and Lady Gore Blakeney in the book.

Irene and the General were married at the registry office in Marylebone. The General in mufti, much to his servant's disgust. A dark lounge suit with a striped regimental tie. " 'Ole and corner, that's what it is," he said, "but nice of you to 'ave let me come as a witness, sir." The other witness was Ellen, Irene's parlormaid. All secret because the General did not want any publicity. No "General Sir John St. John Gore Blakeney, baronet of Albany and Blakeney Hall married etc., etc." He did not want talk. Why not in a church? Why not? Because he wanted to get married, that was why, and it was no one else's damn business and he was in a hurry. It was wartime and he was busy, and he was not a social kind of chap. Invitations, presents, thank-you letters and so on. He just wanted to get on with the job. Get married, get Irene to bed at the Metropole, and after the honeymoon get back to his division and let her organize her affairs, move to Albany and do the place up to suit herself.

The day before the wedding he had said, "Tell me about the boy, Irene. It's funny to have a soldier stepson I've never seen."

Of course she'd told him about Jim often enough before but he hadn't listened. At that time he'd only been interested in her. Now that he had her he also had Jimmie in a kind of way and wanted to know more about him. He was a very possessive kind of man. How she hoped they would get on. She fetched her photographs. They were in a dress box. She hated albums. Jimmie at one year, naked on a bearskin. Jimmie at three. Jimmie at prep school. Jimmie at Denby. Jimmie in his first uniform. She could see that to John they were just pictures of a baby. Child, a boy, a young officer. "Tell me about him," he said. "He's a nice-looking boy. How tall is he?"

"Six foot and he weighs seven stone ten. He's dark like his father. His hair has a slight wave. His eyes are hazel, almost green in some lights." What could she tell him? How could she describe his voice, his charm? How did a mother describe a boy? "He's not finished growing yet," she said, as if the General didn't know. "His father was a very powerful man."

Lying in bed at the hotel, Irene went back over the scene in her mind. What an inadequate description she had given of her son! Till that moment she had never thought of him objectively, of the way he must appear to other people. Tall, dark-haired, hazel-eyed, gangling. A boy-man, like a colt or a half-grown pup. He had good teeth, a nice smile, a strong, almost Roman nose. A pleasantly modulated voice. That was what other people would see. Girls. Women. And beautiful hands. A man's hands were important to women as instruments of love. They played a woman as if she was an instrument and made music from her. The sweet, moist music of desire. She wondered if all women thought of their sons in this way. Of their touching women, getting into them? She wondered if all women had these vague, almost incestuous feelings of curiosity so profound that it was almost envy of these unseen, unknown girls whom their sons would possess. Was that why so many women hated their daughters-in-law?

John had hired a hack and gone for a ride on the Downs. She wondered if he'd want to make love when he got back. Since her marriage she had done nothing but wonder about things. She felt safe, warm, relaxed, gloating in a new, strange, exciting sea. She thought about her brother-in-law, George Hilton, and of being in France with Jimmie when war broke out. The garden at Laurent had been particularly beautiful in the summer of '14. Rambler roses, tea roses, big flat Malmaisons that looked as if they had been sat on and which perfumed a whole room if you picked a vase of them; sweet peas in clumps growing up peasticks—white, pink, lavender, her favorite colors; dahlias, hollyhocks against the wall; blue spikes of delphiniums and godetias, Indian pinks, phlox. How beautiful, how peaceful, it had all been!

And Jimmie with his little love affair, a boy and girl just coming into flower as it were. Tentative, beautiful in their still childish slimness. Like reeds swayed by the breeze of passion. At that age it was still a breeze, a zephyr of guessed delight. Tentative, an exploration of the land adults knew so well, an Eden, of great heights and dark valleys of despond. They did not see them yet or understand, as they wandered hand in hand on the periphery of life. She was both amused and amazed at the way his uncle had taken it.

44

"I know us, Irene," he said. "Where women are concerned, Hiltons are the devil."

"Your brother wasn't—at least not with me."

"He respected you too much, but before . . ."

"And perhaps afterwards, when he was away from home?"

"I dare say."

"And I suppose that's why you never married. This Hilton business—you didn't want to be tied up to a woman you respected?"

"Damn it, why must you always twist everything I say, Irene?"

"I'll tell you something, George Hilton. No married woman wants to be respected—she wants to be loved."

"Well, some men can't love those they respect. It inhibits them."

The scent of the garden had come in through the open French windows of the verandah. Perhaps they should not have come to the continent this summer. Her friend, Brigadier-General Gore Blakeney—that was what he had been then—had said, "Don't go, Irene. There's trouble brewing; any spark will start it. Look at the Agadir trouble in 'eleven. But the Germans weren't ready then. Roberts had been warning the country for years, but no one listens to him. Too old. Too small a man." But she'd just laughed at him. They'd always gone to stay with Uncle George for the summer. For the change, for the boy's French, because she liked a break in the routine of her life. It prevented involvements. And George amused her. She knew when she wasn't there he had women staying with him. A woman always knew. Feminine touches, furniture moved. A man never moved anything. A forgotten hairpin in a dressing-table drawer—a black one, a bronze one. Little things. Perhaps her coming prevented him from too deep an involvement too. She could imagine him saying, "My sister-in-law and her son always come for the summer."

Then the murder of the Archduke. French mobilization. Sir Edward Grey's statement. Ultimatum. The German march into Belgium. The fall of the forts. Liège, Namur, Antwerp. The sound of the guns. The arrival of the British Expeditionary

Force—one division of cavalry and six of infantry. The old contemptibles. Britain's contemptible little army, the Kaiser had called it. Jimmie mooning about in love. His wanting to join the cavalry. His story of seeing the wounded Belgians disembark from the train. All in summer, with the nightingales singing in the moonlight as if their hearts would break. Who'd have thought then she'd marry John Gore Blakeney?

When they got back to London he'd been in uniform. Resplendent. A major-general, a different man. All values were changed by war. She supposed that she, as much as a London shop girl, had been affected by the glamor of the uniform. Medals, boots, spurs. What extraordinary creatures women were—hating war and loving soldiers! And he'd been so different. No longer the retired soldier, the country gentleman with a place in London. Decisive, back in harness, taking his rightful place in the machine of Empire. It was really through him Jim had got his temporary commission, though the boy had never known it. "He'll only enlist, Irene. Might as well see if I can get him a commission." He'd written a chit to someone. Jim had been told to present himself to a Colonel somebody at Hounslow. The clubman had turned into a man of power overnight. She was impressed. She had gone with Jimmie to get his uniform at Moss Bros., and then he had left her to join his regiment. Now she was alone, her son grown up, flown from the nest on khaki wings. That was when she had made up her mind to marry John, not consciously at first, but she knew what he felt about her and she had led him on. An old soldier to replace the young one she had lost. A marriage of convenience, she had thought then. How wrong she had been!

Riding over the Downs the General was thinking what a wonderful life he'd had—hunting, shooting, fishing, war. What friends! Splendid men, beautiful women, wonderful horses. He let his memory flow past him like one of the cinemas the young people liked so much. He thought of his first wife, Susan, a golden slip of a girl who'd ride anything. It had been a great blow when she died. Only twenty-four. He thought of his

46

childhood at the Hall, then Sandhurst and the regiment. His first twelve-bore—a Holland & Holland. His first charger, an Irish gray, 16.3—Blue Boy. His first tiger, lion, leopard, elephant, buffalo. Nile perch over 100 pounds. Tiger fish. Trout, salmon in Norway. North-West Frontier seconded to the Guides. Omdurman seconded to the 17th—he'd managed that very cleverly. That was the highlight of his life, the cavalry charge. The trumpets, the wild neighing of the horses, the thunder of galloping hooves. Shots, screams, yells. The rasp of steel as your sword came out of the scabbard, the feel of the horse under you, the pair of you exciting each other, the men leaning over the horses' necks, their lance points bright in the sun. Point into a Fuzzy-wuzzy's throat and on, the speed of his horse pulling the sword out as he swept past. The Fuzzy-wuzzies on their backs, trying to stick the horses' bellies as they galloped over them. Mounted men with scimitars, shouts of "Allah! El Allah!" Great black flags with Arab words in white on them. Dust, sweat. A wheel into line, the lances and swords flashing in the burning sun above the sand. By God, that was glory! He was breathing hard as he thought of it, his hands taut, holding an imaginary sword as he sat forward in his saddle. But machine guns had ended cavalry charges. Elandslaagte had been nothing. The charge to Kimberley had been exciting but there had been no resistance and the horses were tired. So he had probably ridden in the last great one.

He often thought about Waterloo and the way the British squares had stood up to the French cuirassiers. Someone—a German, he thought it was—had said that if the horses' reins could be cut five yards from a square, the cavalry would break it. But in men's hearts—even in the bravest—there is a faint hesitation at facing a hedgehog of bayonets. This hesitation communicated itself to the horses. They still galloped, but no longer with wild leaps that would impale them on the bayonets and break a square. There was something in it, too. A man's heart and brain talked to a horse through his bridle hand and his knees. But what a sight it must have been! What a thing to participate in, to be part of! Part of thousands of squadrons.

47

The Greys had done well at Waterloo, and in the Crimea, though the Light Brigade was all anyone ever heard about. Tennyson should have written another poem about the heavies.

What good horses he'd ridden! What pretty women he had loved! What fine heads he had shot! What men he had known, served with and commanded! Well, he was a lucky chap, he supposed, to have a division to play with, and a young and beautiful wife to grace his bed. By God, he had no complaints—apart from not being in France with the regiment. Fit as a fiddle. No aches and pains except in wet weather from an old wound or two.

He wondered if Williams would stay with him when it was over. Go to the Hall with him. He might, because he seemed to have come to some kind of agreement with Irene. That was generally the trouble when a man got married—his man was jealous of his wife, afraid of his perks and refused to take orders from a woman. Not used to it. But they seemed to have hit it off. He must ask Irene about it. He liked Williams saying, "I've 'anded you over to 'er ladyship, sir." That was a good sign.

He laughed and leaned over to pat his horse's neck. A gray mare too old for the army but she must have been a good one in her time. If there was any choice of horses he always took a gray. His chargers at the divisional HQ were gray. So were those of his staff and lancer escort. He'd managed to wangle it. People pandered to his idiosyncrasies. He amused them. Old Gore Blimey of the Greys. The men liked him, too. They could see him coming, with his staff and Lancers, the bloody lot on white horses. He was not of those generals who liked to surprise his men and catch them out.

He thought of Irene still in bed, turned the mare and galloped back to town. It was only half past eight. A bath. Breakfast. Irene . . .

Lying in bed looking out over the sea, Irene wondered how Jimmie would take her remarriage. She had already composed half a dozen letters in her mind. Anyway there was no great hurry about it. She'd break it gently by saying she'd been seeing a lot of the General, as they called him. That certainly was true.

6 : Miss Moon

MONA COULD not get Jimmie out of her mind. It was nearly a month since he had said goodbye to her. But it hadn't been like the other goodbyes—the other men to whom she'd said goodbye so cheerfully. So bravely, they thought. It was easy to be brave if you didn't really care. She thought of the dinner with Maurice at the Berkeley the day they had met. Of how she had kept looking at him from under her lowered lashes. My God, she thought, I told him not to fall in love with me but I'd better be careful myself. A boy. Only eighteen. But mine, mine. Even then she had felt fiercely possessive about him. I was his first, she thought. I taught him. She had pressed her thigh against his. When Maurice got up to speak to a friend at another table, she said, "Come to me any time you're in town. I'll fit you in somehow, and don't worry about the money." She was still astonished at her remark. But why shouldn't she have her fun, her own pet, her pretty boy to play with? But it had been quite an experience, a boy who had never had a woman before. A virgin, wide-eyed as a girl. She'd told him her story later. How her father, an officer in the artillery, had been killed at Mons, leaving her penniless and unequipped for work. Of how she had been seduced by a promise of marriage and then had drifted into this because she liked men and liked making love to her friends. Not like those whores who hated men, all men except their pimps, and did it just for money. Her friends swallowed the story because they wanted to. The real story was quite

49

different. Her father was alive, a dental mechanic in Balham. She had gone wrong at sixteen and climbed her way upward from bed to bed, always leaving a lover for a richer man, or someone who could teach her something new, till at last she could almost pass as the daughter of a regular officer. She saved her money. One day she would buy a little business or marry, or both. But the war had been a godsend. Except that you had to keep on making new friends. So many got killed.

Out of the corner of her eye, as they went out of the flat, she had seen Jimmie put some notes behind the photographs on the mantelpiece. A nice boy. She'd told Maurice how nice he was. She'd never forget that dinner. The look of wonder in his eyes. It had been an extraordinary experience for both of them but she really thought she had been more deeply affected than he. She felt like a mother toward him, an incestuous mother only four years older than her son. Maurice looked pleased with himself because he had known she would like him. Poor Maurice.

Then they had had coffee and *crème de menthe* and the party had died gently, happily certain of rebirth. They had to catch their train but had taken her home first. A triangle in which no one had been betrayed. And now Maurice was dead and Jimmie had gone to France. She supposed it was France. The BEF. She wondered where he was, how he was, what he was doing. The telephone beside her rang.

"Yes?" she said.

"That you, Mona?"

She wondered who it was. "Yes, it's me."

"Well, it's Jock McDougal. I'm back. Three days' leave. I'm coming round."

"Back! My Hielan' Jock . . . ," Mona said. "I hope you're wearing drawers."

"A Highlander in drawers?"

"Suppose you get killed or wounded? More decent, I'd say."

"It may be decent but it's not healthy. The hardiness of the Hielan' race is due to keeping their . . ."

"I know, I know. I've heard it all before." And so she had.

Seaforths, Argylls, Black Watch—the bloody lot. "When can you come? I'm not dressed yet."

"That'll save a lot of trouble."

"Half an hour then. And take me out to lunch."

"Twelve-thirty, ma wee lass," he said.

Captain Jock McDougal of the Seaforth Highlanders. He could talk English perfectly well but he liked this Scottish business. Sometimes she could hardly understand what he said. Where was the book of Burns's poems he had given her? She found it and put it on the table. People were always giving her books of poetry. She only liked Ella Wheeler Wilcox. She put away the photographs of two other officers, got out Jock's picture and gave the silver frame with the regimental crest on it a polish. A silver stag's head surrounded by a kind of wreath. She'd put James Besant, Dragoon Guards, and Major Harold Burnaby, West Kents, in a drawer under her lingerie. She called it "lingerie" not undies—it sounded more genteel. She called her flat a *bijou*—French for jewel. She called napkins "serviettes." She never left out too many men's photographs at one time—she didn't want anyone to think she was promiscuous. It was a club, very small and select, though not as small as she pretended.

Lucky she'd had a bath. She put on a dark rifle-green coat and skirt, a little black toque, and got out her black fox fur. You could still wear furs in April even if it was warm. After all, you never knew, did you? And there'd be no bloody nonsense till after lunch. She was hungry. The Café Royal or Frascati's, she thought. Then she sat down to wait for her Hielan' lover, her black silk ankles crossed, her small feet very neat in black patent leather shoes. Her dark hair looked nice with the dark green suit. A black leather handbag and black kid gloves. Ready. Ready for lunch, and anything else later on. She lit an Abdullah cigarette. She liked Egyptian cigarettes. One day she'd marry one of her friends and settle down. She'd better do it soon. There was a lot of competition even now; so many men being killed and that meant more girls for less men. Marriage, security, a little house, kids, responsibility—Christ, how respectable she would be! She had it in her. She was a born little housewife. She got up to wind the gramophone. She put on "Alexander's Ragtime Band": "Come on and hear . . . Come on and hear . . ." Marriage. But suppose he was killed? But that wasn't what she was afraid of—he might be maimed, blinded. She might find herself tied to a cripple for life, because she knew herself: she knew if she did it, she'd do it, in sickness and in health, and all that. This was her fling. This was collecting a nest egg in what was really a very enjoyable and exciting manner, but it was the nest that she really wanted. She wasn't a loose girl; she wasn't even very highly sexed.

The bell rang and she went to the door. How many bells were ringing in London in wartime? How many men, straight from the mud and blood of the battlefields, were waiting for women to let them in? Into their flats, into their bodies, so that for a few hours they could have love or its illusion. Harold Burnaby had said that to her once. She never answered the door without thinking of it. Love, or its illusion. Into their flats and bodies. It was crude, brutal. She liked euphemism. Play-acting, playing pretend.

7 : Mona Plays House

MONA WAS quite well known at Fortnum's for the parcels she sent to the BEF. She enjoyed going there. She loved Piccadilly. Hatchard's bookshop established in seventeen-something. She bought books there to send to her friends. An old man in a frock coat, who looked like a Russian Grand Duke, advised her what to buy. Rowland Ward with his stuffed lions, buffalo heads and spotted leopard skins. And then Fortnum & Mason's, the best shop of its kind in the world, she'd been told. Select. Jackson's was another good grocer. Also select. The difference between a select and an unselect grocer was that the former didn't smell of cheese and bacon and had a dozen blends of tea. Besides, the people were so nice. Polite. "Yes, madam, No, madam. Shall I charge it, madam?"

The parcels today were for Jimmie, Jock, Billy and Montague. Pound cake, sardines, potted shrimps, herring in tomato sauce, chocolate. Four of each, one in each parcel. She wrote down the addresses.

"You do send a lot of parcels, Miss Moon," the girl said. "You do have a lot of friends, don't you, Miss Moon? I suppose it's a kind of war work."

"In a way. I want to do my bit to help the boys."

"If only everyone felt the way you do, Miss Moon. You know we often talk about you. Most people only send parcels to two or three men. But since the beginning of the war you've sent them to more than fifty, Miss Moon. We had an argument about it and I counted them up."

"A lot of them have been killed, or are back in hospital."

"It's terrible, Miss Moon. You've got a list, I suppose?"

"Oh yes, I have a list. I work through it and then start again."

"No favorites?"

"Oh no. That wouldn't be right, would it?" It wasn't true of course. Jimmie also got parcels every week from Jackson's, but she didn't want Fortnum & Mason to find out. It would spoil their image of her. "You'll pack them nicely, won't you?"

"Of course, madam."

The two girls smiled. They understood each other. Such a nice girl, each thought the other. So kind, so thoughtful. Dorothy was the name of the Fortnum girl. She'd lost her fiancé. That had brought them together. They both wore black. Mona had told her she had lost her fiancé too, and a brother. Sometimes she wore a wedding ring, called herself Mrs. Moon and posed as a war widow.

If she did her hair differently, Dorothy would be quite pretty. Mona wondered if she should tell her. She wanted to ask her if she was a virgin. She wondered how old she was. Twenty-five or so. A bit older than she was. If she didn't get a man soon, she wouldn't. She wondered what her legs were like; she'd never seen them properly. Always behind a counter. Legs were so important and silk stockings so expensive. No girl could have good legs in cotton or even lisle. Mona looked down at her own. She stood with her heels together to see them better. High heels, of course. And a short, tight, hobble skirt. She had to pull it up to get into a bus or taxi. Men liked to see girls' legs in silk stockings. They liked the feel of them in their hands. Slippery silk, the legs soft and firm.

That was the way it generally began—in the taxi. You could tell a lot from the way they did it. She wondered if Dorothy knew. If she ever had when she was engaged and how far she had gone. You could never tell by just looking at a girl. But if she really liked men she wouldn't be working in a shop, not with her looks.

She thought of her parcels being done up, packed and sent off. Over the sea. Up the line. Of them being opened. A present from Mona. "Mona?" "A friend." "Is she pretty?" "Oh yes." She liked to think of men talking about her, loving her. It was extraordinary to think of it; to think of them in dugouts under the ground, eating Fortnum pound cake. It brought them nearer to her. Her war work. Her list. Name, rank, regiment and battalion. That was all, but they got there.

She signaled a passing taxi. The driver was an old man with a walrus moustache. " 'Op in, miss." He wasn't too old to lean out of his seat and look at her legs as she got in. They were never too old for that. Pretty little piece. Past it, but he could still look, couldn't he? He caught her eye and winked. Saw a lot, taxi drivers did. Couples kissing and messing each other about. Even doing it. They knew a lot, those bastards did. Cynical. And why shouldn't they be, with what they heard and saw—in their taxis and cruising? And what they told each other. Mona laughed. It must be terrible to be too old. She thought of all the places they took couples to: The Troc, Quaglino's, the Café Royal, the Piccadilly, the Elysée, Scott's, the Savoy Grill, the Hungaria. All the same; all one place with different names.

54

Orchestras, uniforms, men, girls; a west end whirlpool; furs in winter; high heels, perfume; food, music, dancing, voices, laughter. Her places.

Sometimes she went to Victoria Station to see someone off. Most men didn't like it. They had other people to see them off. Mothers, wives sometimes. Girls they were going to marry and didn't sleep with. She was "instead." She knew that. It didn't even hurt any more. But what terrible things you saw there. Men and women clinging together. The men getting into the train, the women turning away alone, trying to be brave. Waiting till the train pulled out to wave grief-wet handkerchiefs. You saw men crying too. Men, NCO's, officers.

You saw them coming back on leave, unshaved, dirty, exhausted. Feverish to wring what they could out of life in a week's leave. Dancing, drinking, seeing shows, making love. Seven days and seven nights, with sleep a waste of precious time. Men with rifles slung on their backs, side arms; puttees clogged with pale dry mud. Crumpled service caps on their heads, all badged with a regimental insignia—stars, horses, tigers, deer, crosses, knotted ropes—that was the Staffordshires. Each with a story. A sphinx for Egypt, and so on. All of them out of it for a while, getting a nice cup of tea at the Red Cross canteen. And then, when the leave was over, going back into it, clean as new pins with shining buttons and polished boots, reckless with bravado.

Mona supposed she knew more about it than most girls because her friends talked more freely to her. Uninhibited was the word. Swearing, effing and buggering. Christ and bloody every other word sometimes, and she let them. It did them good. Took the tension out of them, like going to bed with her. She wrote to them and sent them parcels. She felt she served a purpose, was really doing the kind of war work she was best suited to. And she was making a nice bit of money too. A couple of hundred pounds in a month sometimes. But if they didn't spend it on her they'd spend it on someone else. Some cheap little tart, a flapper who'd give them no value in bed or out.

What a lot of men she knew! Had known. Her flat was like a corridor; either it led them back to itself in a circle of time, or it led them nowhere—into a casualty list of dead, missing and wounded. If they were wounded she could not trace them unless they wrote from hospital. She tried to see them if they were near London. She was always busy with one thing or another. There was shopping. Swan & Edgar's, Selfridge's and Harrod's. She tried to look nice, with her hair freshly dressed, good gloves and shoes. Quite the lady she looked, always in black because it was neat, ladylike and mourning. In a way she was always in mourning. Much more so than most other girls.

There'd been a letter from Jimmie yesterday. He'd been reading her book of poetry. Just fancy that! She looked at the bookcase where he had found it. "You can have it," she'd said. Bound in pretty, soft red leather, small enough for his pocket and light to carry—Shakespeare's Sonnets. But she'd never cared for it. Bill Havelock had given it to her. He'd been killed like so many others. He'd wanted to improve her mind. Educate her. If he'd lived he might even have married her. A husband, a little house, babies. A pram, washing on the line. And all this would be in the past, forgotten. The way the men would forget their battles.

Henry had written to say he'd be in London today. He'd telephone first just to make sure. She didn't think men were as jealous as women. Not unless you were married or kept. Then it was a matter of money. If he paid your rent you ate his food and wore his clothes and you belonged to him.

She arranged some pheasant's-eye narcissus in a vase. They lasted well. The Roman hyacinths she was growing in water were nearly out. She loved their scent. They looked like onions in their long vases and their pale roots lived on nothing. Just water. But they never flowered again, not even if you planted them in a pot of earth.

She went into the bathroom to see if everything was ready for a guest. Shaving soap and a brush. Two razors, a new toothbrush. Clean pajamas and a dressing gown behind the door on a white hook. Homelike. A man could come here with nothing and find all he needed. Whisky, brandy, sherry, gin, bitters; a sparklets siphon in its silver net of metal. If she ever had a house, she'd have a cat and a dog—a fox terrier, she thought, like the one on the gramophone records—and a yellow canary and some goldfish in a bowl. Plants, too. Red geraniums and a rubber plant. A little garden with roses and a laburnum.

The telephone rang. She picked up the receiver.

"Miss Mona Moon?"

"Speaking." She wondered who it was but it was nice of him to ask for Miss Moon.

"It's me. Henry. Henry Dent."

"Oh Henry, I've been expecting you."

"Well, I'll be there in twenty minutes."

She went to the little kitchen and filled the kettle. Tea, and scones. She looked in the drawer by her bed to see if she had aspirins. Then she sat down at the dressing table, did her hair and made up her face. She ran a buffer over her nails till they shone like pink, varnished shells. She had pretty hands. Soft, long-fingered. She added a little mascara to her eyelashes, a touch more of lipstick, and she was ready for Henry. For anybody. In a black satin housecoat with gold buttons all the way down the front and black high-heeled satin mules.

There was only one picture in the bedroom—a good color print of *The Bookworm*. A naked girl with dark hair lying on a bed reading. She lay on her stomach. On the table beside her was a vase of yellow and red tulips. Mona told everyone she had posed for it; that she had in fact inspired it, being so fond of reading.

The front doorbell rang and she went to it on clicking heels.

"Oh Henry," she said, "how long it has been!"

"Six months, Mona. Six bloody months. I only got in today. I had a Turkish bath to sweat the dirt out of me before I came."

"I've been thinking of you ever since I got your letter, but you must have got away early."

"You're a good girl, writing."

"I try to write to my friends. That's the least I can do."

"And the parcels. Cakes!" he said.

She laughed. "Sit down, Henry. I've got the kettle on."

He was a tall, fair man; a major in the Engineers. He had on field boots and spurs. Later, after tea, she'd unbuckle the spur straps and pull off his boots with her back to him, the boot between her thighs. She enjoyed doing things like that. Feminine things. That was what women were for, to wait on men. To please them. To make them comfortable and happy.

When she brought in the tea tray, she said, "How long have you got?"

"Seven days."

"Are you going to stay in London?"

"I'd like to stay here."

"Stay here?" she echoed.

"We'll go dancing, Mona. See some shows. The Bing Boys. *White Horse Inn. The Maid of the Mountains.*"

Well, why not? There was no one else in town. Not any of her real friends, that is. She'd cook for him. They'd play house. Play married. Play Mrs. Henry Dent. She put on her wedding ring.

8 : Breakthrough

OVER THE narrow seas, so near to England that the gunfire could often be heard on the South Coast, was the world of war. Here millions of men were stuck like flies on the immense flypaper that stretched from the Channel to the Alps. A double line of trenches, both drawing their lifeblood from their homelands. Statistical men; the numbered hundreds, thousands who, individually, were sons, fathers, husbands, brothers, lovers. But these relationships didn't show up on the casualty lists, those neat categories for men living and dead, marching past in columns of newsprint—killed, wounded and missing—as they had marched past on their last parade behind a band playing "Tipperary." But "Tipperary" was music many of them would never hear again. The roll of honor. The muffled drums whose echo would end only when the last of those who had known them had died, taking their memories to the grave. It was difficult to believe that the war was so near to England, or England so near to the war. Jim Hilton had been in France a month, wasting time at the base, but the others had been in England yesterday; had stepped out of beds warm with women this morning and were struggling to reconcile the two situations. Which was dream and which actuality? They all knew this short phase of their lives was approaching an end, that this journey by sea and rail was the hyphen that joined Home and War. Very soon they would detrain and part, the two gunners remaining together, Jim and the captain in the Liverpools going up the line to their units. What had they in common? Khaki. The King's commission. Youth. The captain at thirty-two was still young, a man in his prime. Hilton was a boy. What else? Like every other soldier—every man, officer and NCO—they were volunteers. Kitchener's first hundred thousand. Motives: adventure, the mystery of foreign parts, the call of strange women; danger —a magnet to youth that must risk life to prove manhood; change; boredom; fear of missing this great event, this enormous exclamation mark in history. All this in varying proportions for every man at war.

But those were not the real reasons. The real reason was patriotism. Something all of them were too embarrassed to mention or even think of. The King. The Empire. Glory. Duty. The Union Jack, the flag on which the sun never set. England, home and beauty. Great Britain, Queen of the Seas. They had been brought up on her history. Kipling. Tennyson. Boys' books by G. A. Henty. And now they were part of it, drawn into the vortex by the suck of heredity and education. Spinning around and around, into trenches and out of them, knowing nothing of what was going on outside their own sector, no reasons, no strategy. Just obeying orders. *Theirs not to reason why . . .* The Germans were abstract. Thousands of them had never seen

59

a German, would be killed without ever seeing one. But the Germans were evil. Dragons to St. George of England. Belgian atrocities. Women with their breasts cut off. Hostages shot. Edith Cavell executed. They were on the right side. God was English. British, anyway.

Right must triumph in the end. But would any one of them ever say so? No fucking fear. Not bloody likely. They were 'ere because they were 'ere. That was why.

"Oh my, I don't want to die, I want to go 'ome . . . ," Jackson chanted, staring into the darkness and the rose horizon beyond it. "That's what I'd bloody well like to do—turn about and go home."

That's what they would all have liked to do. They wondered if they ever would. When I get back—if I get back—Jim thought, I'll be different. I won't be the same. He hadn't been the same after Mona. He wouldn't be the same after this. Life was like a flight of stairs. You went up but you never came down again. You went on and on, landing after landing. You never got back where you had been before.

The train slowed up and stopped.

"I expect we'll stay here till it's dark," Legget said as he settled down in his corner to sleep.

Fancy being able to sleep at a time like this, Jim thought. He thought of the last month. After a fortnight in the Bull Ring he'd wangled a few hours' leave and gone to Rouen with Jack Campbell, the Irish Rifleman. He had been out before, was a Catholic, and they'd gone to the cathedral first. It was protected by a wall of sandbags. Useless, unless it came to street fighting, which seemed unlikely at the moment. Only God could protect a cathedral. Just as only God could make a tree, or a steak, or a dead man for that matter.

Inside it was cold, gloomy, a columned cave dedicated to God and lit with the fire of stained glass where the sun pierced the windows with red, green, yellow, blue and orange darts. Figures outlined with lead. All centuries old. Joan of Arc, the Maid of Orleans, the *Pucelle* of France, had been burned in Rouen by the English. The cathedral was musty, fragrant with incense and the odor of sin. How many adulteries and fornications had been confessed here? How alike they must all have been, because there was no variety in it. So little difference in lying with a woman or a maid, joined or not joined in wedlock, but locked in sweat, arms and legs entwined, striving. How could the confessions of the twelfth century differ from those of the twentieth? Or the act, except that today the bodies were clean and without vermin.

Jack Campbell had taken his arm. "Let's get out of here," he said. They went out in step, soldiers walking like one man, their heels hard on the stone tiles. Past women bent in black-shawled huddles, praying for their dead, past candles guttering in remembrance, past sanctuaries fenced off with gilded rails, past statues of saints and virgins, past Jesus bleeding for ever on a stucco cross, past saints and disciples, past sacred pictures, past a great font—like a baby's bath—of stained marble.

"It's that way," Campbell said, pointing along a canal, tree-lined, the trees decorated with pigeons as if they were fruit. "But we'll have dinner first. Lobster, an omelette, a bottle of wine, and brandy with the coffee. And then I'll take you there. She's still going strong, I hear."

"Take me where?"

"To Madame Fanu's place. It's easily the best."

So Jack wanted to go to a brothel. Well, why not? They had just come from a cathedral. Religion and sex were intimately related. The old phallic cults, fertility rites. Temple prostitutes. A chap at school had lent him a book about these things. "But don't get caught with it, Hilton." Women had been in his mind when he was thinking of people confessing the sins of the flesh over the centuries; of his sin with Mona. With Kathleen. For lust in the mind was supposed to be as bad as the act. The sins of his eyes; of his hands. Hands were eyes, too, in a kind of way.

They had lobster thermidor and a bottle of Graves, and an enormous *omelette aux fines herbes,* and *crêpes* squirted with lemon over the sugar, coffee and brandy. They and other officers, in groups, in pairs, a few with girls they had picked up—smartish shop girls who wanted good food and the things they could not afford to buy for themselves—silk stockings and underclothes. Girls whose men had left them, suspended in the limbo of war. It was six of one and half a dozen of the other—a deal, an exchange of commodities in the marketplace. Food, wine, clothes—for the feel of a naked girl under them. Cash for nookie. The men, knowing each night might be the last, were reckless. There was no need to save anything—neither money nor love-stuff. Strong young hands on silken knees under the red-checked tablecloths. Hands in a wartime hurry. Here, there, everywhere. All over the world. No difference in it. Not for hundreds, thousands of years.

There was one beauty—dark, with blue eyes—with an Army Service Corps captain. Probably his mistress since this was a base. He was dressed for it. A poodle-faking bastard, with a crease in his trousers and a pressed tunic. He was having a good war. Jim found himself wishing she would betray him with some fighting soldier. But French girls were practical. She had at least found provisional security and was making the most of it.

Jack looked at his watch. They banged on the glass for the waiter, a decrepit man who looked as if he was a veteran of 1870. He came sideways, like a black crab wrapped in a white sheet. On the plate with the bill was a card: MADAME FANU—Amusements, Rue Jeanne d'Arc. He snarled up at them ingratiatingly, showing yellow fangs, and said, "Jig-a-jig. Very good." This was the extent of his English. He needed no more. And they had been going there anyway.

They paid him in grubby notes, saying, "Keep the change." Full fed now, wined, dined, ready for "amusements." It was not far and easy to find, with a red light over the door identical in color with the little lamps burning in the cathedral. But much larger. A light to guide Mars into the arms of Venus. They were let in by a hairy, one-armed monster. *"Mutilé,"* he said. *"Mutilé de guerre."* "A hero of the Marne," Jack said. He remembered him.

The hero took their caps and placed them on a shelf beside the others—Gunners, Royal West Kent, Leicesters, Buffs,

Welsh Fusiliers, Northumberlands, Durham Light Infantry. Cap badges from half the regiments in the BEF.

A captain of the Gordon Highlanders was playing the piano when they went into the big palm-spotted lounge. Girls dressed in bright kimonos, their hair loose on their shoulders, were serving champagne. Madame Fanu, dressed in tight black satin, corseted in armor, her hair dyed orange, came on small running feet like a mechanized toy to greet them.

"Enchanted to meet," she said. "Brave allies who bleed for France! I make amusements. A little wine, messieurs? A dance? The spectacle, and alors l'amour! Les girls are good. Clean, intelligent, of the first quality." Taking their hands in hers, walking between them like a little black hen, she led them toward a big blonde girl with the hips of a percheron mare. Jack had gone upstairs with her. He had waited for him. He was not going to chance getting a dose. When Jack came back, he said, "I'm sorry now I didn't pray in the cathedral." He'd done some bobs, crossed himself and lit a couple of candles. Too randy to pray, no doubt. Going to the cathedral at all had been a kind of compromise.

A small dark girl had sat on Jim's knee while he waited. He bought her a drink and patted her bottom. She seemed to expect more and began to touch him. He slapped her hands gently. "Naughty," he said. She laughed. She seemed nice enough and was quite pretty, but he had not come to that yet. Sooner masturbate. Better class of woman. It was like drinking out of a dirty glass, only more so. Not that he was the only man with Mona, but she gave you that illusion. And the chaps weren't lining up for it.

The train started again and crept on through the night. That put an end to his dreams of Mona.

Poperinghe was dark, the station dimly lit with lights that had been painted over with Reckitt's Blue. Like London, like Folkestone. Like every bloody station in Europe.

"Well, we're here," Jackson said. "The party's over."

They got up, stretched, put on their belts and haversacks and slung their field glasses over their shoulders. Prismatic compass.

Pistol. Like a Christmas tree decorated with things hanging from straps.

Legget said, "Goodbye, my lads, and good luck!"

They all laughed. "Goodbye, goodbye! Cheerio! Good luck!" They climbed out of the carriage, the gunners' spur rowels clanking. There were a lot of men on the platform, a dark mass, their faces ghostly in the dim blue light that turned the red caps of the military police to purple.

Sergeant Hargreaves had fallen his men in, numbered them and reported, "All present and correct, sir." Jim's companions were gone. They had been met with horses. Even the captain in the King's had gone. But there were other drafts. Shouts, orders. "Farnham? Where's Farnham?" "Here, sir." "Fall in! Get fell in! Stand easy!" There was the bang of brass-shod rifle butts on the platform, a smell of khaki cloth, of men, of fear. And all the time the noise of the guns at the back of the other sounds. There was a "Come on, we're back here now, let's get on with it and push off" feeling. An uneasiness. They wanted to get to their units, to get back into the machine with NCO's and officers they knew. They'd feel safer there with their mates. They wanted decent hot food and an issue of rum.

This was Poperinghe, the base for the Ypres Salient that surrounded them in a rosy arc. The guns sounded much louder than they had on the train where the noise of the wheels had dulled them. The ground acted as a kind of sounding board. You felt it coming up through the soles of your boots.

Jim found the Railway Transport Officer—the RTO sign faintly illuminated—and reported his draft. The RTO was a fat major who seemed flustered.

"Tenth Wilts L.I.," Jim said.

"I've got a guide for you. Get the Tenth Wilts L.I. guide, corporal." The corporal went out of the office shouting, "Tenth Wilts L.I. guide!" A man came up and saluted.

The corporal said, "There you are, sir. He'll take you up."

Hargreaves gave the orders. "Attention! Slope arms! Quick march! March at ease!" And they were off.

The town was very quiet, very dark. Here and there glimpses

of light—thin strips of it—could be seen shining through the closed shutters.

"Something going on up there, sir," the guide said. "They put a few shells over while we was waiting for the train. Lots of people about generally, sir." He sounded as if he was apologizing for a dull evening. "Lots of people. Business as usual. But Wipers had been getting it, sir. Full of civvies, an' it's burning." So that was the enormous glow in the distance. "Women and children killed, sir," the man said. "But we don't know much. Bin 'ere all day waiting for the train, sir. An' they don't tell us nothing."

There were other troops moving. Small, compact, black bodies of men tramping through the night. Some limbers rattled by with a clink of trace chains and hammer of hooves. Two big GS wagons.

Something going on up there. A city burning. The dull, thudding roar of gunfire that went in through your ears and came up through your feet from the ground to meet in your middle. In your guts and genitals.

Sergeant Hargreaves came up from the rear. "The Jerries are attacking, sir," he said. "That's the rumor." He laughed. "Latrine rumors, we calls 'em. But it does look as if there's a bit of a show on." Sergeant Hargreaves was excited. He did not show it, but he was. War. Action again after all these months as a bloody instructor with the reserve battalion. He'd gone back in '15 with a blighty and they'd kept him there. Musketry and bayonet-fighting instructor. By God, he thought, how we could shoot! The bloody Jerries thought we had hundreds of machine guns. It was Bobs who'd seen to it. Lord Roberts who'd turned the whole regular British Army into sharpshooters. Fast, accurate, disciplined. Not many of us left now, he thought. The retreat. My God, that was a bugger, but the cavalry had covered them. Not that he cared for horse soldiers. A sidey lot of bastards, with all their swank and spurs. Riding by, looking down on you as if you was dirt from the back of a bloody great 'orse that did all their marching for them. Still, they fought well. He'd been with the 1st Battalion then. What a show they'd put

65

up! Officers gone, the sergeants had taken over. Clever, the Jerries was, picking off the officers first. He thought of dead mates. His friends. His officers. By God, how it all came back. . . .

They were in open country now, on their way to the transport lines up a side road. Off the *pavé*, thank God, but it was slushy with trampled snow. He was always afraid of a shell on *pavé*. They burst at once. And cold—Christ, it was cold! The fields on either side of them a sheet of white, no hedges, just some poplar trees here and there. Thin black things, not proper trees. But there in front of them was a wood, a dark patch. That was where the lines would be, a bit of shelter in the trees for the horses. Cut the wind a bit for 'em. And hid 'em a bit from the guns. Even if it wasn't true, you felt safer in a wood somehow.

The guide led them past the horse lines to some blacked-out huts. "That's the QM's office, sir," he said, and fell back. He'd done his job.

Jim went in. The hissing glare of the pressure lamps dazzled him. The quartermaster was a captain with a row of ribbons that included the dark red Long Service. "Reporting with a draft, sir," Jim said. "James Hilton. Thirty-four other ranks."

"Well, you've come at a bloody fine time, young feller. I'm Captain Green. Bin out before?"

"No."

"Well, they've broken through and you're to go up at once. That's the orders, but I'll give 'em a hot meal first. Christ Almighty," he said, "they used gas. French Colonials broke on the left. Bolted and worse. Black chaps. Shot their officers, ran away. Raped the nurses at the casualty clearing station. The Canadians are holding from what we hear, but the flank is open. Gas. Some of 'em stopped here. Gasping and choking. Couldn't go no further. Frothing at the mouth, drowning in their own bloody spit."

9 : The Battle

THIS WAS a hell of a business. There was going to be no quiet baptism of fire, as they called it. They were going into the middle of a bloody battle. He heard the quartermaster say, "Two bandoliers of ammunition, iron rations, field dressings, sergeant."

"Iron rations and field dressings all checked, sir."

They began issuing the pale khaki bandoliers of ammunition. The men had been given some hot food. Skilly: meat, potatoes and cabbage boiled into a kind of mess for hours. Bread, butter and plum and apple jam. Tea.

"How about our issue, sir?" Sergeant Hargreaves looked at a big earthenware jar of rum. "They're green, sir, most of 'em. Put some guts into 'em."

"All right," the quartermaster said, "it's a long trek. Shelling all the way. Got any stretcher bearers?"

"No, sir. None trained."

"Well, take a couple of stretchers anyway, and a box of gear. First aid?"

"Yes, sir. I can manage most things."

"Mons? Le Cateau? The Aisne?"

"Yes, sir. First battalion."

"I was with the Second. RSM Green." He laughed. "Old sweats, eh?" The two men looked at each other with a kind of special understanding. "Issue, boys. Rum ration. Get your bloody mugs ready." He began to pour the rum out into a little after-dinner coffee cup. It held one sixty-fourth of a gallon. That was the ration. Dark, overproof. Jamaica.

"The French on the left of the Kanuks broke." The quartermaster told the story again. "French niggers. Shot their officers

67

and raped the nurses at the CCS, but they've been rounded up. Gas," he said. "The buggers."

Jim was beginning to get the picture. The Germans had launched a gas attack on the junction of the French Colonial forces and Canadians. The Africans had bolted. The Canadians, who held the extreme left of the British line, had bent back, pivoting to prevent themselves from being outflanked. They had suffered badly but had held on. Every available man had been sent up to help them. Ypres, which till yesterday had been a lovely old town with a military band playing and a market of peasant produce for the troops in the grande place, was a shambles. The Cloth Hall had been destroyed. The Germans had used their big siege guns for the first time since the fall of the Belgian Forts—17-inch howitzers that fired a shell weighing a ton. Reinforcements, marching through the streets, had been crushed by falling masonry. The gas was chlorine, terrible stuff that drifted on the breeze in a yellowish cloud six feet high.

Green said, "I'm going to issue you extra nose-wipes, Mr. Hilton. One each. Wet 'em and put 'em over your faces."

"Wet 'em with what?" Hargreaves said.

"With wet. Don't waste water. All the water bottles full, sergeant?"

"Yes, sir."

"Well, don't use it. Pee on 'em. I don't know if it's any bloody good, but that's what they say. Think they'll be all right?" The quartermaster nodded at the draft.

"Yes, sir. I've got four wot's bin out before and the others are good boys."

"The officer?" the quartermaster whispered loudly.

"He'll do, sir."

All as if he wasn't there. Christ, what a business. . . .

"Here's the guide," the quartermaster said. "You'd better move off."

"Get fell in!" Hargreaves shouted. "Attention! Numbers! Slope arms! Form fours! Right turn, quick march!" And off they went.

Jim had to run to catch up with them. "Sorry, sir," the

68

sergeant said. "But I had 'em in my hand, as it were. They don't know you yet. I'll hand over in a minute. Can I 'alt 'em and talk to 'em?"

"Of course."

"Talk rough, sir?"

"Go ahead."

"Halt!" Hargreaves's voice was a rasp. "Left turn! Now listen to me, you bastards. This is it. I didn't start this bloody war. I didn't bring you into it. But we're in it now. Right into a bloody battle. Second battle of Wipers, that's what they'll call it when it's over. The Frenchies ran away, the Canadians are scuppered and we're goin' up to 'elp. An' you know who we are: the Wiltshire L.I., the Fifty-first* Regiment of Foot, and we'll bloody well show 'em 'oo we are. Remember our battle honors. Malplaquet, Minden, Ramillies, Badajoz, Waterloo, Inkerman, Alma, Mafeking, Ladysmith." He paused. "Now," he said, "Jerry's using gas. Gas is new. It's new to me, too. So when the officer gives the order, get out them nice new nose-wipes, pee on 'em and stick 'em over your noses."

So he was to give the order, "Halt! Pee on your nose-wipes! Put on your nose-wipes! Do it by numbers!" Oh Christ!

Hargreaves went on, "When the officer is killed, you follow me. When I'm killed, you follow Lance-Sergeant Smith. When he's killed, you follow the corporals. Any questions?"

"Sarge, what do we do when all the corporals is shot?"

"Brew up a bit of char and choose someone." He turned smartly around, saluted and said, "Will you give the order to move on, sir?"

So it was his baby now. Thirty-five other ranks—thirty-four and the guide—and they'd follow him rather than an old soldier like Hargreaves with a DCM. What a lot of bloody rot! But Hargreaves had said, "They'll follow you, sir. They likes the look of you."

"Attention!" he shouted. He hoped his voice sounded more confident than he felt. "Slope arms! Right turn! By the right—

---

* There is no such regiment as the Wiltshire L.I. The 51st Foot are King's Own Yorkshire L.I. Numbers are now obsolete.

quick march!" And they were off again, a fat little snake of men marching toward Ypres, toward the guns, the salmon-pink horizon that all but surrounded them, marching into the Salient.

Sergeant Hargreaves came up to him. "When they've got used to moving, get 'em into single file, sir, and march at ease."

"Thank you, Hargreaves." Thank you, God. Thank God for Hargreaves. Men he did not know, marching into country he had never seen, into battle that he had never experienced. When they'd gone about a hundred yards, he said, "March at ease!"

"March at ease!" Hargreaves echoed.

Hargreaves was just behind him with the guide. They would not need him till they got to the reserve and support lines. No mistaking the front. The lance-sergeant and one corporal were in the rear, the other corporal was with the leading file. The iron-shod heels on the men's boots rang on the cobbles, the famous *pavé*. Ypres was still being heavily shelled and they had to go through it. A shell burst on impact two hundred yards ahead of them.

"Single file, sergeant," he said. "Four paces distance between men." The fat worm turned into a slim serpent. The ring of the boots was muted as step was lost.

He saw the buildings of Ypres lit up by the flames in black silhouette. Shells burst red, orange, yellow and salmon pink. They marched past smashed limbers and dead horses that had been dragged to the side of the road. This was the ultimate reality but it was utterly unreal. They passed a dead man, abandoned on a stretcher. His first dead man. But it did nothing to him. He was dead and that was all there was to it. Left, right, left, right—the *pavé* was hard and uneven beneath your feet. They were alone on the road. No other troops. You'd have thought there'd have been a lot of men. Reinforcements going up the line. He said so to Hargreaves.

"I expect they've all gone up, sir. We're the last. You saw the transport lines. Practically no one left. Cooks, clerks—the bloody lot."

"And we're the dregs. The bottom of the barrel, sergeant?"

"That's about it, sir. But we'll turn the bloody tide." He

70

laughed. Hargreaves was a born soldier. Gunfire excited him. He turned back to the men. "Let's sing!" he shouted. "Sing, you bastards!" And he started in a fine baritone: " 'Wash me in the water where you wash your dirty daughter and I shall be whiter than the whitewash on the wall . . .' " The men took him up. Then they turned to "Mademoiselle from Armentières," then to the old one "She's got hairs on her didydo, right down to her knees." "Barnacle Bill the sailor . . ." The soldiers' repertoire. How many soldiers had sung on their way to battle? Whistling in the dark might be another name for it. They'd been going an hour. Ten minutes' halt.

"Halt!" Jim shouted. "Fall out. Ten minutes."

"Empty your bladders and lie down," Sergeant Hargreaves said.

Obedient as children, the men did as they were told. They stood where they were on the side of the road and urinated. They lit cigarettes and lay down. Hargreaves sat down beside Jim.

"It's going to be all right, sir. We've got 'em. You can feel it. But I wish we had some Lewis guns. Of course we may find some. I've got some gunners."

"But the battalion?" Jim said.

"We'll never find it, sir. I've seen this kind of mix-up before. We're on our own, sir. You, me and the chaps. We'll find some guns and go for 'em on our own. Bloody Jerries," he said. "You'll see what I mean when we get up there, sir. A bloody mix-up. Units all mixed up with chaps they don't know, officers they don't know. We're lucky, we are, being all together, like. Wiltshire L.I.," he said, as if it was a magic word.

The ten minutes were over. Jim blew his whistle. The men got up. "Come on, boys," Hargreaves said, gentle as a mother. No orders now. They marched on to another halt, but they weren't singing. They had passed too many dead. Wounded and gassed men were staggering past them down the line. They were in the town now. There were dead civilians in the street. Old men, children, women, their skirts torn, their white underclothes showing in the livid light of the burning buildings. Hargreaves came up to him. "Don't stop for the shelling, sir. Go right through it. If we stop we shan't get them moving again. Just march on good and steady. I'm going to drop back now into the middle. The two of us mustn't be hit together. Good luck, sir. Just pass the word if you need me." He gripped Jim's wrist hard and was gone.

They marched on past more bodies, past houses torn in two with curtains still in the windows and pictures on the walls. Homes. The shelling seemed to have slowed up but Ypres was still burning. Jim heard Hargreaves shout, "Fall out sharp, you bastards! Get close to the wall!" He obeyed with the others. Hargreaves knew what he was doing. He had hardly reached the wall of a house that seemed intact when they came—battery after battery of Canadian guns at full gallop, the horses wild-eyed, the drivers leaning over their necks, the guns and limbers jumping and rocking first on one wheel and then on the other as they went over the shell holes in the road. All illuminated by the burning town. The noise of the pounding hooves, the whirling iron-tired wheels, the desperate men and horses. The officers galloping beside their teams. Canadian gunners going into action to stop the breakthrough. To wheel, unlimber and fire over open sights into the advancing German hordes. Galloping through their own wounded, through anything that was in their way.

Hargreaves had him by the shoulder. "We can move on now, sir. Fine sight, wasn't it?"

So this was war. A little girl with torn underclothes, dead, a doll in her hand. Burning houses. Six-horse gun teams mad with fright. Guns and limbers jumping into the air like children's toys. He blew his whistle.

At the crossroads a military policeman—red cap, white armlet and gaiters and all—was directing traffic. He saluted ironically. "Going to the party, sir?" he said. A mad world. Past the Cloth Hall. It was burning, much of it was down. Out through the Menin Gate—what was left of it—and on. On up the open road, the burning town behind them and all hell broken loose in front of them. Signal flares like fireworks going up in the darkness above the glare of the gunfire. Three red balls, two green ones, golden rain. The white magnesium flares of Very lights, each with a meaning: a call for help; a signal to advance.*

10 : Cold Steel

THERE WERE more wounded and gassed men coming down the line. Men without rifles, walking in groups and helping one another, gasping. It was impossible to see them except in silhouette against the false sunset of the British gunfire. The German gunners had stopped shelling; they did not know where their infantry was. Some gun teams, unhitched, passed them at a canter with rattling chains, going back to their lines in the rear.

Jim was shaken by an explosion that seemed to come within a few yards of his party. "Howitzer," Sergeant Hargreaves said. So they were up to the big guns. The going became difficult. The road had been plastered—pocked with shell holes; littered with debris, a smashed horse-ambulance, smashed limbers, dead horses, more dead men on the roadside. They were no longer marching, they were merely going forward. A string of men in single file picking their way, stumbling in muddy slush up to their ankles. The snow was marked with holes—black shell craters—like a tablecloth gnawed by a thousand rats.

There was series of sharp explosions in front of them, and a sheet of spitting flame. "Field guns—whizzbangs," Hargreaves said. Like taking a bloody kid out for a walk, he thought. Got to explain everything. But he seemed all right. The men were

* This is a description of the second battle of Ypres which took place on April 22, 1915, not in 1916 as described. In April of that year there was a battle sometimes called third Ypres, though this name is usually applied to Passchendaele in June 1917.

steady too. Thank God, no one had been hit. Always shook up green troops, someone getting hit. And only four of them had been in it before—four not counting the guide. Four to thirty-four. Not much of a stiffening. He'd tell him to halt them now. Rest 'em a bit this side of the guns. No good getting in front of them. The screaming noise of the low-trajectory shells would upset the lads, and there was always the chance of a short.

"We'd better halt 'em, sir," he said. "Rest a bit. We're getting close."

"Pass the word down." It was passed down.

"Halt! We're stopping 'ere. 'E says 'alt." The string of men closed in, the elastic stretched by the bad going contracted. They squatted in the snow. The field guns went on firing, battery by battery. Salvoes. Between the noise of the guns—fitted, as it were, into the interstices of sound—came the chatter of the machine guns.

A gunner officer came over to find out who they were.

"Tenth Wilts L.I.," Jim said. "Know where we are?"

"Buggered if I know where anyone is," he said. "Nor do they, thank God. Thought you might be Jerries. The left is open. The French ran. Gas. The bastards. We only got here a couple of hours ago."

He was a Canadian, one of the chaps who'd passed them at a gallop through the flames of Ypres. "You passed us," Jim said. They lit cigarettes. The men were smoking too. For an instant faces were lit by match-light. It was extraordinary to be standing here just behind the guns, talking. Hargreaves came up.

"I've been talking to the gunners. We shan't find the battalion, sir. Real muck-up. We're on our own."

"What shall we do?"

"Go on till we find some of our chaps and join them. Any regiment. Be glad to 'ave us." And he'd be glad to have them; to get the men among others who were used to it. Poor buggers—what a beginning!

"You must have passed our teams going back," the gunner said.

"We did."

74

"We lost three men and some good horses."

"We were lucky," Jim said.

"I guess you were, chum. You got in on the lull."

"Shall I tell them to load and fix?" Hargreaves asked.

"Yes. Load and fix bayonets," Jim repeated.

"Load and fix bayonets!" Hargreaves shouted. There was a rasp of steel as the bayonets came out of the scabbards, and the sound of magazines being loaded.

"We'll get along," Jim said. "Get them started, sergeant."

"Come on, lads. We're off!" Hargreaves ordered.

"Good luck, chum," the gunner said.

"Thanks. Same to you." Good luck, as if they were going into some sort of game. They moved on. They passed the guns and ducked instinctively as another salvo went screaming over their heads. On. They came to a blown-in communication trench and followed it, going along the top parallel to it, a kind of black gut through the thin snow. Their guide had given up trying to find the way. The situation had changed too much since the break-through. He just marched with the others.

"You'd better have a rifle and bayonet, sir," Hargreaves said. "We'll find plenty before long." Then he said, "Six inches is enough, sir."

"Six inches of what?"

"Bayonet, sir. Don't shove it in too deep. Six inches is enough. It'll stick in the ribs if you go too deep. But if it does, fire a round into the body. That'll clear it."

A rifle and bayonet. Hargreaves was expecting him to stick it into someone—not a straw-filled sack on a gallows—into a man. A German. Find one. Plenty about. A dead man's shoes. He wondered what he would have done if there'd been no old soldier with the draft. On. Scrambling through barbed wire cut by shellfire into wire brambles. Over a trench, or what was left of one. A challenge.

"Halt! Who goes there?"

"Tenth Wiltshire L.I."

Jim saw an officer with half a dozen men, their bayoneted rifles at the ready, come toward him.

"What the hell are you doing here?" the officer said. It was almost dawn. The sky was a pale wood-pigeon gray.

"I've got a draft. We're looking for the tenth battalion."

"I'm Lomis," the man said. "Captain, Fifth Dorcesters. And you won't find your push. Nobody knows where anyone is. You'd better join us. We came up to reinforce the Canadians."

"Join 'em, sir," Hargreaves whispered hoarsely.

"Where are you?" Jim asked.

"Dug in over there. Come on." Lomis led them to a new trench running at right angles to the old line. "We're the extreme left flank," he said. "Lost a lot of men. Good thing you came."

A minute later they were in the trench with the Dorcesters. In the line. Nothing in front of them but snow and Germans. "They know we're here," Lomis said. "Felt us out. They'll attack any time, but they won't shell. No one is shelling much except the heavies." The fog of war. Another name for a fuck-up. Nobody knows where anyone is—British, Jerries, the bloody lot.

It was lighter, almost dawn. There was a curious silence. A hush. Machine-gun and rifle fire on the right, but here nothing. Just men waiting, and the white snow, polka-dotted with black shell holes.

"I wish we had some wire in front of us," Lomis said.

Sergeant Hargreaves put a rifle with a fixed bayonet into Jim's hands and slung a bandolier of ammunition over his shoulder.

"It's loaded, sir," he said.

"Good sergeant you've got," Lomis said.

"Old soldier. Regular."

"Pity we've not got more of 'em."

Then they came. A dark mass of men advancing over the snow. It was light enough to see the glint of their bayonets.

"Hold your fire!" Lomis shouted. "Wait for my whistle!" They waited. It seemed like an hour. Just a few minutes that seemed like an hour.

The Germans knew where they were. Or just about where

76

they were. But they did not know how strong they were. They came on. Lomis blew his whistle. They opened fire. Jim aimed, fired; pulled back his bolt to eject the empty shell and fired again. Again. Again. The magazine empty, he loaded a new clip. The Lewis gun a few yards away was spitting lead. Another Lewis started up. It must have had a stoppage.

There weren't too many Germans. A company or so. Two hundred. Three hundred. A battalion would have overrun them. With this lot they had a chance. A lot went down. Killed or wounded. Jim went on firing mechanically. Aim, fire, load. A new clip. The rifle barrel was getting hot in his left hand. The Lewis guns were still firing. No stoppages, thank God. He heard Sergeant Hargreaves shouting, "Steady, the Wilts! Steady! Fire low!"

The Germans were still coming. A lot were down in the snow but more were still coming. They were a hundred yards away. Fifty yards. Thirty. Getting ready to charge. Their officers and NCO's were shouting—you could see their open mouths. Lomis blew his whistle again. Jim could not hear it—he just saw him put it into his mouth. "Up, boys! Up and at 'em!" He jumped on to the parapet and spun around, dead. Jim jumped up. All around him on either flank his men were up. There seemed to be no other officers. What now? What did one do now? Only a minute to make up his mind. The Germans, their rifles at the high port, were running toward them through the snow. His infantry training came back to him. He saw the paragraph in the little red book—the color of dry blood—in his mind.

"Charge!" he shouted, and ran forward. The men swept on with him, cheering. He was part of a khaki wave. The Germans he was facing seemed enormous. Giants. Christ . . . He drove his bayonet at a man's belly. The German parried. Barrel met barrel in a blow that stung his hands. He brought up the butt under the German's chin. He went down and Jim spitted him in the throat.

The Germans—what was left of them—turned back.

"Halt!" Jim shouted. "Open fire!" The men did what he told them. It surprised him. They went on firing in a desultory

77

manner till the Germans got back to their position and their machine guns opened up.

"Get back!" he shouted. They came back, bringing the wounded and the dead. Hargreaves came up to him.

"Good work, sir!" He patted him on the back. Turned out bloody well, this boy had. And the men, too. Blooded now. Soldiers. Steady.

To his own horror, Jim began to cry. Hargreaves held him to his chest. "It's over," he said. "You won't never go through this 'ere again. Bloody 'ard luck, sir. 'And to 'and first day up the line."

Yes, it was over now. Jim shook himself like a dog coming out of water. He'd killed a man hand to hand. He'd shot he didn't know how many. Used half a bandolier of ammunition.

"Far as I can see, sir," Hargreaves said, "you're the only officer left. And it's a mixed bag you've got. Our chaps, Canadians, Dorcesters, King's, East Lancs, some Gordons . . ."

"What do we do, Hargreaves?"

"Hang on till we get relieved. That's wot we do. Take it easy, sir. Have a fag." He put a lighted cigarette into Jim's mouth. "I'm going to have a look-see. Casualties. Rations. Dig in a bit more if we can without getting down to water. That's the trouble 'ere. Water's too near the surface—won't go down in this clay soil. They may shell us now and attack again. We'd better be ready for 'em."

11 : Relief

FOR THE time being the line, this little section of it at any rate, was quiet. There was no sound except for the men talking as they cleaned their rifles. Wiped them and pulled them through with a rattle of bolts. Christ, it was cold! They had no overcoats, no blankets. They had come up in fighting order, leaving their packs with the quartermaster. They had no food, only their iron rations—bully and hard biscuits—which they could not touch without orders. Water in their water bottles. No rum.

How much ammunition was there left? How many men had been hit? This was a lull. An ominous silence like the center of a hurricane. It would hit them again before long.

Jim moved down the line. Sentries had been posted. They crouched, staring out at nothing; at the white, pock-marked snow, at the bodies. At the carrion crows that had arrived out of nowhere to feast. He stopped to speak to the corporal of the East Lancs.

"You chaps all right?"

"We're all right, sir. Couple of men hit but they're not bad. Come and look at 'em, sir. I got 'em in the next bay." He spoke as if they were exhibits.

His first wounded. They seemed cheerful enough, glad to be alive. One was hit in the leg, the other in the arm. Both were bandaged and sitting on ammunition boxes that had been scrounged from somewhere to keep them out of the mud.

"Cold, sir, ain't it?" the man with the arm wound said.

"It's cold all right." What did you say to wounded men? He met Sergeant Hargreaves coming back.

"We did pretty well, sir. Only twenty men hit. Six killed. I've shoved the dead over the parados. Out of the way."

"And the wounded?"

"Stretcher bearers done what they could for 'em, sir. One's bad. Hit in the stomach. Pity we've got no blankets to cover 'em. Teeth chattering."

"We'll go along the line, Hargreaves." They went on together.

"It's not very nice up there, sir. A lot of dead."

"I thought you said . . ."

"Yes, sir. But these are Frenchies. Been dead a long time, too. They dug right through some of them. I moved the wounded down a bit; fixed up a kind of hospital bay."

The wounded were grouped together, smoking. Quiet. Waiting. Waiting for what? Only the man hit in the stomach was groaning.

"You all right?" Jim said.

"We're all right, sir," the men said. "Might be worse. All blighties except for 'im." They nodded at the groaning man who held his belly with both hands.

They stopped at a Lewis gun post with its team, its drums of ammunition ready.

"How are we off for ammunition, sergeant?"

"Enough for a while, sir." How long was "a while"?

"For another attack? And bombs—what about bombs?"

"Enough SAA if it doesn't go on too long. And we're fairly well off for bombs. I've picked a man for your runner, sir. Get him on the way back. One of our chaps from the Tenth that got lost. You know what I think?" Hargreaves said. "I think there's a real muck-up. Jerries, too. No one knows where anyone is. That's why they're leaving us alone. We're on the edge of the breakthrough. The Jerries don't know how far their flanks extend and they're pushing on."

Perhaps that was it.

"Shall I tell 'em to eat their iron rations, sir?"

"Yes. They'd better."

The sentry in the bay they were in turned and said, "Look at that, sir!" "That" was a greenish-yellow mist coming over the snow. Gas. No one had seen it before but they knew what it was.

"Wet your bloody handkerchiefs! Pee on 'em!" Sergeant Hargreaves shouted. "And stick 'em over your noses. Pass the word down the line. Stand to!" he bellowed. "Stand to" was echoed from bay to bay.

The men lined the trench masked like bandits. It was difficult to urinate on a handkerchief held in one's hands. The urine steamed in the cold, like hot water out of a tap. Jim clapped his wet handkerchief on his face. Through it he could still smell the gas faintly—chlorine. It made his eyes water and he coughed. The Germans had gas masks.

Then the breeze dropped. The cloud stopped moving. Heavier than air, it sank to the ground.

Hargreaves removed his handkerchief. "All right!" he shouted. "Take 'em off! But don't stand down."

There was fighting going on all around them. Machine-gun and rifle fire; some field guns. Heavy shells that sounded like express trains passed overhead in both directions.

"We better go and see to Captain Lomis, sir," Hargreaves said. "Get his papers and things before we put him over. I've got the paybooks of the other dead."

Lomis had been shot in the heart. The congealed blood on his chest was almost black. His face looked peaceful. "Never knew what 'it 'im," Hargreaves said, as he took off his silver wrist-watch and removed the blood-stained pocketbook from the top left-hand pocket of his tunic, a silver cigarette case from the right, and a silver St. Christopher medal on a chain from his neck. "We'll hand them over when we get back," he said. "Go to his next of kin. Tonight we'll go out and see what the dead Jerries have got in their packs. That should tide us over. Good food, they have. Tinned meat, black bread . . ." There was nothing else in Lomis's pockets except a fountain pen and a small silver knife. "Take his whistle, sir," Hargreaves said. It was fastened to a lanyard that went over his shoulder. "She'd like to have that."

She. How right he was. For every man there was a she— mother, wife, girl. "I'll take his pistol," Hargreaves said. "The field glasses go back to 'er, too. Little parcel," he said. "Effects, that's what they call 'em. Dead man's effects."

Little groups of men had gathered around the tiny fires they had managed to make. God only knew where they had found the wood. They were brewing tea—iron ration tea packed in little canvas bags, mixed with sugar.

"If we only had some rum they'd be all right, sir. It's the cold. They'll catch cold, the lads will." He spoke as if he was immune to cold, danger and hunger. Of course he wasn't. He was as cold and hungry and frightened as the rest, but he was hardened. Disciplined.

The men were eating bully and big hard square biscuits like Spratt's dog biscuits. Smoking. It would be a bugger if the tobacco gave out. "Careful with your smokes," Hargreaves said. "Make 'em last."

The men grinned at him. He said, "Pass the word for Private King, Tenth Wilts."

"King, Tenth Wilts!" Five minutes later King turned up.

"You wants me, sergeant?"

"Aye. Here's your officer, Mr. Hilton. King's an old sweat, like me, sir. Sergeant once; reduced to ranks for being drunk."

Jim laughed. "Well, none of us'll get drunk today, King."

"Take care of him," Hargreaves said.

The long day passed without activity. Evening. Night. More gunfire in the night, both sides strafing the roads where the troops and supplies were moving. More signal flares: two red balls; two green; one green and one red; golden rain. A fireworks display. Jim fired his first Very light from a short brass-barreled pistol. It went fizzing up into the sky, burst in a white star that came floating slowly down, illuminating the black bodies lying on the white snow carpet. There was no movement. No enemy flares. No burst of machine-gun fire. No sign of life.

Corporal Ames, one of the draft who had been out before, took a couple of men and some empty sandbags he had found to see what rations they could find in the dead Germans' haversacks. There was no possibility of concealment against the snow with a half moon playing hide-and-seek in the clouds.

But they went carefully—well apart—going a few yards, dropping into a shell hole and waiting before they went on. They had orders to get back if even a single shot was fired. Hargreaves had been sure the Germans had gone on. The attack on the Dorcesters had been a feel-out to establish the extent of the breakthrough on their left flank.

Jim watched the men turn the bodies over, open packs and haversacks and stuff what they found into the bags they trailed behind them. The bags left black trails in the thin snow, rather like the trails of giant snails in a garden. At last they turned and came back, the bags over their shoulders. They had not taken rifles, only bombs in their pockets.

It was a good haul. Cans of meat, black rye bread, small cigars, two bananas and one orange. They were all set for food. Enough for now, anyway. NCO's from the various units took what seemed to be their share. The men laughed as they lit their cigars. Grub. Smokes. If they'd had their overcoats and a bit of rum they'd have been happy.

This was a reaction. They were still alive. It was quiet. For the moment no one was trying to kill them.

Jim spoke to Ames.

"Shook them up a bit, sir, them not being used to stiffs. But I said if you're hungry that's where the food is, in them packs. And they soon settled down to it. Good thing it wasn't daylight, though. Blood don't look so bad at night, if you know what I mean, sir. Not red."

Jim said, "Well, you did a good job."

"Can't say I liked it, sir. Specially going out. Not knowing if the Jerries was there. We must have showed up very nice. Very nice indeed."

There was a challenge from behind them. Jim turned. Hargreaves shouted, "Stand to!" and counterchallenged, "Who goes there?"

"Friend."

"Advance, friend, and identify yourself."

A figure detached itself from the dark mass and came over the snow. The men closed in on Jim, opening and closing the bolts of their rifles. Because the reply had been given in English did not mean that these men could be trusted. Lots of Germans spoke good English.

"Relief. Captain Johnson, Seventh Rutlands." There was a string of men behind him. The relief, thank God!

"Not much to take over, sir," Hargreaves said.

"Who are you?" Johnson asked.

"Hilton with a detachment of Tenth Wiltshire L.I.," Jim said. "And a couple of hundred mixed other ranks. Dorcesters mostly. I joined them. Couldn't find our lot. I'm the only officer

83

left." He was talking fast. "We were attacked. Beat them off. Lomis was killed."

"Well, you're out of it now. I'll take over. No wire in front of you, I suppose?"

"No," Jim said.

"We've got some."

. "Ask if he's got any rum," Hargreaves said.

"I suppose you can't let us have some rum?"

"Not for two hundred men. But you'll get some soon." He laughed. "Get your chaps out. We'll take over. More troops are coming up. Expect we'll counterattack and close the gap."

"What about my wounded? I'm short of stretchers."

"I'll lend you some. Stretcher bearers!" he shouted. "We're lending these chaps some stretchers. I'll send a couple of chaps with you to bring them back, Hilton." The men were filing out of the trench.

"You'll find guides down the line," Johnson said. "Real muck-up. They're getting the regiments sorted out by degrees."

Jim waited till the last man was out. Stretcher cases. Walking wounded, helped by their mates. Nothing would be as bad as this again. Nothing could be.

"We're well out of that, sir," King said.

Well out, indeed.

12 : The Sergeant

SERGEANT HARGREAVES—Hargreaves, Alfred Henry, DCM, No. 5467, Sergeant KOWLI—in his paybook—was pleased with his young officer. 'Ilton was all right. Make a good officer if he lived. That was the bloody trouble—the best didn't live long.

He thought of the officers who had gone out with the regiment in '14: Colonel Hugget, Major Blackwell, Captain Hard-ross. Wilson, Blenkinson, Mason. Dead, the bloody lot of 'em. Except for Morgan. He was commanding a battalion somewhere now. He had come through. He'd been a lieutenant then. Captain Fitchit had lost a leg. And the other ranks? NCO's and men? Not many of us left neither. But what a regiment it had been, all of a piece, like—officers, NCO's, men. Ran like a bloody watch. Beautiful, beautiful. Slope arms! One, two, three! Three separate sounds as the rifles went up onto the shoulders, alignment perfect. The parade ground, that was where you made soldiers. Discipline. Close order drill. Spit and polish. No courage without pride, no pride without cleanliness. When you went into action it showed. An' musketry. By Christ, how they could shoot! Regulars. Men with seven years', fourteen years', even twenty-one years' service. The regiment was their home. Their life. Professional soldiers. These new chaps in Kitchener's Army were different. They'd all volunteered. That was a bloody extraordinary thing when you came to think of it. Leave a cushy job in Blighty, leave the money, the booze, the girls, the comfort. For King and Country . . . bloody odd. But they were a fine lot. Take them chaps first time under fire—nervous, yes, 'oo wasn't? But steady. An' wot a start for the poor bastards! Fresh out from home straight into a bloody battle. Gas. Just fancy that! Lucky they'd been clear of it in their sector, but it had been a near thing. A bloody near thing. Bloody funny peeing on your nose-wipe, too. That was a story to tell. Holding your cock into a clean khaki nose-wipe and waiting for the water to come. Like blood it was, hot on your hand. But they didn't know that, not those Kitchener chaps. Not yet. Blood ran hot and then turned cold.

"Come on, you!" he shouted to a soldier staggering in front of him. "Soon be there, me lad." But would they? And where the hell was "there"? " 'Ere," he said, "give me your bandook." He took the boy's rifle.

"Thank you, sergeant." Polite, too. They were on duck-boards in a communication trench of breastworks that had not been knocked about too much.

Christ, and I thought I knew something about gunfire. Hargreaves's mind went back to September '14, to the French in red and blue uniforms. Cuirassiers in polished tin bellies, like the bloody Horse Guards. Then the retreat. Mons. That was when he had got his DCM. Not half surprised he hadn't been, when it came through. What, after all, 'ad he done? Brought in his officer, Mr. Willis, who'd been 'it in both legs. Wot was so bloody wonderful about that? Couldn't leave 'im there, could I? Carried 'im fireman's lift, put 'im down, shot a couple of Huns wot was getting too close, and then picked 'im up again. Not too 'eavy 'e wasn't. Small, light chap. Light as a girl. Not that you carried girls that way.

Jerk 'em up a bit. "Come on, you bastards," he shouted. "We're the Wiltshire L.I. You put up a bloody good show. You're soldiers now. Just show it. 'Ere, give me that bloody rifle." He had three now, his own and two others.

Girls. You carried them in front of you with one arm around their tits and the other under their thighs. My, wouldn't they squeal if you lifted 'em onto your back! He thanked God he wasn't married. Got all the greens he wanted without any trouble-and-strife.

What the boys needed was rum and a band. Bloody wonderful what a band could do to tired men. "Sing, boys!" he shouted, and began himself. " 'It's a long way to Tipperary . . . to the sweetest girl I know . . .' " The men picked it up. Soldiers. Like a lot of bloody babies, they was, nursed along by the NCO's. Bloody nurses, that's wot we are, the lot of us. Wiping their arses. Don't know if they're coming or going 'alf the time. An' stupid. So stupid they never knew when they were licked. Not the Wiltshire L.I. Never been licked. Corunna. Minden. Malplaquet. Waterloo. Never licked. Just died where they stood. Stupid.

Squares, in them days. Red squares like rocks, with the French cavalry beating against them like waves. That was what it said in the regimental history. Christ, he was tired! Tired, but not beat. Never beat. It would be better when they got out of this bloody trench onto the road. Then he could get 'em to march proper. In step did a lot to a man. His feet going with all the other feet, to the sound of them. Christ, how many bloody miles he had marched in the last ten years! 'Undreds. Thousands. Foot soldiers. PBI. Poor bloody infantry. His Majesty's Foot. But it was foot soldiers wot won wars. Rapid fire. The bayonet. Cold steel. Up an' at 'em. You sort of went mad then, your rifle at the ready, the bayonet up and pointing to the left. Charge. He'd been in a couple of charges. A slow trot. Thrust, parry, thrust. Lunge, the left foot forward, the bayonet going in of its own, as it were, with the weight of the rifle behind it. . . .

By God, they were out of the trench and in the open at last, the men bunched on the side of the road. Now he was out he wished he was in again, with the protection of the trench walls. Never satisfied, that's wot you ain't, 'Argreaves.

The men stood like sheep, waiting to be rounded up.

"Where's the officer . . . Mr. 'Ilton!" he shouted. "Are you all right, Mr. 'Ilton?"

"I'm all right, sergeant. There should be a guide here. Tell the men to sit down while I take a look round."

Look round in the dark. Ypres was still burning and you could see shapes against the glow of the burning town. Black shapes of men and horses. Transport limbers and wagons. Jim Hilton left the men and, seeing an officer with a flashlight looking at some papers, he went up to him. He was a staff captain.

"Who are you?" he asked.

"Tenth Wiltshire L.I., and a mixed lot of other units."

"Then sort them out. I've got guides for 'em."

"Come on, boys. Sort yourselves out," Hargreaves shouted.

But they'd done it already. Unit by unit, they had found each other, like families that had got mixed up at a picnic. Picnic was the word. A bloody picnic muck-up. But they'd be out of it for a bit, that was for sure. Rest. Reinforcements. Training. Building up the depleted battalions. But they were alive. Survivors. Bloody lucky. Luck, luck. Everything was luck till a shell or a bullet came along with your name on it. You were safe till then. That was why men carried lucky charms. St. Christopher medals, little crosses, rabbits' feet, and Christ knew what else. Hargreaves had nothing. His identification disc was enough. His medal hadn't done Lomis much good, had it?

Hargreaves stood in the middle of the group. "Soon be 'ome now, boys. The guides are 'ere. Rum. Tea. A nice 'ot meal all waiting for you." Home, what a bloody silly word. . . . Here was Mr. Hilton with the guide.

"Wilts L.I."

"Fall in—we're off!"

"Get fell in," Hargreaves said.

Hilton went to other groups of men who had been with them. "Goodbye," he said, "and good luck!"

"Goodbye, sir, and the same to you." Not a bad chap that young officer. Not 'arf. 'Eld us together, didn't 'e? Lots of guts . . . an' straight from 'ome. . . . Just a kid, too. . . .

The Wilts L.I. shuffled off two deep behind Hilton and their guide. "March, God damn it!" Hargreaves shouted. "Left, right, left. Sing . . . Where's that bloody mouth organ? 'Ere, give me your rifle and blow." He had four rifles now, the hard, indestructible man. The old contemptible, one of the last of them.

"Oh my, I don't want to die, I wanter go 'ome," the men sang. Well, the poor buggers were going home. To a rest camp. The next best thing they'd get to it over 'ere. Left, right, left, you bloody bastards. Heroes, soldiers, men of the Wilts Light Infantry. Another little battle, one that would never appear on their battle honors, was behind them. But they'd done well, bloody well. Hargreaves was proud of them. The dead of the regiment, from Minden to Waterloo, would be proud of them. He straightened his back, four rifles and all, as the men started to sing "A Broken Doll," marching into the burning town behind their guide and baby officer, with Hargreaves, the sheepdog, bringing up the rear. The Light Infantry was marching again, the remnant of a regiment that could not die.

You had to kid 'em along, curse 'em along, shame 'em along, praise 'em along. That was the job of a noncommissioned officer, the backbone of the army. The officers to lead, the NCO's to drive, ready to take over when the officer went down.

Ypres continued to burn. Thank God they'd picked up the civilian dead—women, little girls, kids. The sappers had filled in some of the shell holes so the transport could get by, but houses, homes, were still being reduced to rubble.

Pretty, it was. Very pretty indeed. A bloody great bonfire. That was it—the bonfire after the picnic.

13 : The Battalion

THE GUIDE led through Ypres. It was still burning, with odd salvoes of shells still falling in the town. But Jim was too tired to pay attention to anything. Just keep moving. Keep them moving. They were marching away from it, out of it. Out of the war. Out of the smell of lyddite and smoke. The smoke had a special smell of burnt furniture, wool mattresses, painted paneling. It wasn't like woodsmoke. It wasn't like anything he had ever smelled before.

They passed troops moving up the line. Poor bastards. They passed limbers taking up rations. Red-caps on point duty. A house fell with a crash behind them. They never looked back.

"That's the asylum over there, sir," the guide said, as if they were on a Cook's tour and he was showing them the sights. "That's where we'll pick up the buses."

Buses. Stop marching. Sit on your arses in a bus. And buses went fast, much faster than men on foot. Soon they'd be out of it. Riding out of it, in buses. He turned to the leading file. "They've sent buses for us."

"Buses," the men said. Bloody buses. One of them said, "Got any change, sir? We've got no change." There was a laugh.

"Come on, lads. Not far now. Step out—left, right, left." That was Hargreaves in the rear.

"Not far? 'E's been saying that for the last six bloody hours. An' 'ow far is 'not far,' sarge?"

But their step was firmer on the cobbles. Left, right, left. Boots, boots. That was Kipling, but that was all Jim could remember of it. And then the buses loomed up in front of them. Double deckers painted khaki, like great dark beasts in the night. Bloody great elephants on wheels.

Sergeant Hargreaves and Jim counted the men in. Twenty-eight other ranks. They'd left their wounded at the aid post. The boots clattered up the metal stairs. Ten little nigger boys, and then there were nine, eight, seven. That was what war was. Another guide came up with more 10th Wiltshire L.I. straggling behind him. Part of the battalion that they'd never found. Even in the dark you could see white bandages on some of them. The line of buses filled up and the convoy moved off slowly without lights. Jim and Hargreaves sat together near the door.

"Where are we going?" Jim said. "Do you know?"

"Some 'uts near Poperinghe, they say. A rest camp. They got it bad, our push did. More'n two 'undred casualties. Fifty dead, I 'eard. Only six officers left."

They dozed. They slept, exhausted, leaning against one another, swaying as the bus bumped over filled-in shell holes. When they stopped, the men woke, rubbing their eyes. "We're 'ere, mate."

Men with flashlights were moving about. You could see the rows of huts. Someone shouted, "Cooks! Where's the bloody dixies?"

"Get fell in, get fell in! Fall in, fall in for rations. . . . Mess tins ready!"

Jim saw the quartermaster. Captain Green seemed like an old friend; he seemed to have known him all his life. He seemed to have been parted from him for a month.

"Well, Mr. Hilton," he said, "a nice mess you got into. Lose any men?"

"Six. One was badly hit in the stomach. None killed."

"Didn't give him water, did you?"

"No, my sergeant stopped me. Hargraves."

"And the battalion's had a bad time," Green said. "Round figures: two hundred casualties, fifty dead and ten officers killed, wounded and missing. But we shan't know the details till tomorrow. No hurry either, with half the division gone. Those paper-wallahs'll have enough to do without our returns. Colonel came through though, thank God."

"I must see to my chaps," Jim said.

"Don't worry. They've been taken care of. Food, quarters, blankets. What a start-off for a new draft. And you, too."

"I don't know what I'd have done without Hargreaves."

"Lucky to have him," the quartermaster said. "I'll take you to the mess. I expect you can do with a drink and some food."

There were a dozen officers in the hut. It was lit by hurricane lanterns hanging from wires, the windows blacked out with brown army blankets. Only four of the officers—one of them a major—were clean. They had been left behind, in reserve, at the transport lines. The others were in much the same state as himself. They were seated at a trestle table eating stew. They hardly looked up when he sat down.

The major came over to him. "I'm Major Hardy," he said. "Second in command. You brought us a new draft, I hear."

"Yes, sir."

"Don't call me sir in the mess. Hilton, aren't you?"

"Yes."

"Been expecting you. Damn glad to see you. Quite the old soldier now." He laughed, patting his shoulder. "I hear you did very well. Took over a bit of line and held it."

"Thanks to Hargreaves," Jim said.

"By God, so he's back with the regiment? I thought he was still an instructor at the reserve battalion."

"He couldn't stand it any longer and asked to come back."

"Get on with your food. I'll get you a whisky and soda."

King had found Jim's valise and spread it out on a chicken-wire bed. Hargreaves said, "He'd better be your batman, if you're willing? I'll get you another runner."

"Willing? I'm very pleased." The two men looked at each other. The young officer and the old soldier.

"If you're not wanting anything, I'll say good night, sir. I'll be back in the morning with some tea."

"Good night, King."

Other officers were turning in all around him. Undressing. Putting on pajamas. It was like being back in a dormitory at school. A new boy. Other boys. Men. All with names. All people with lives of their own, with civilian pasts, and he had nothing—just school. But he'd seen death now, and he knew what fear was. Well, he'd found out about them at last.

He was too tired to wash. He put on his pajamas and crawled into his sleeping bag.

In the morning King brought him some tea in a white enamel cup and took away his uniform and belt to clean it. "No 'urry today, sir. No parades. No nothing. Just make and mend."

Jim got up, shaved, dressed and went to the mess hut. There were several officers having breakfast. Major Hardy said, "Colonel, this is Hilton."

Jim went over to his chair and they shook hands. Colonel Robinson was a man of forty with both Boer War ribbons. He looked tired and drawn.

"Glad you're with us," he said. "We're very short of officers. I'll post you to D Company. Put it in orders later. We were hit pretty hard. Haven't got the lists out yet, and a few more men have turned up since last night. Introduce him to the others, Hardy."

Jim was introduced. Smith and Herring, both captains. Jarvis, Barine, Mantel, Telfer, Jacobs, MacBey, French, Morland . . . These were to be his companions. A queer idea occurred to him. Till death or wounds did them part. He got on with his breakfast—bacon and egg, toast and marmalade, tea. He was thinking about the dead captain's effects. Lomis had been married. He'd found a picture of his wife in his pocketbook. She was not very pretty. Just a fair, ordinary-looking English girl, with a baby in her arms. He'd have to write to her. He had seen her husband killed. He was the last man, the last officer at any rate, to see him alive. Like a crime story. A witness. And by God, it was a crime. You wondered how God allowed it. The War Office would notify her. The War Office sent wires to the next of kin and the names of the dead, wounded and missing, rank by rank, regiment by regiment, to the papers.

Hargreaves had said he would hand in the paybooks of the dead.

Just as he was pushing his plate away and getting up, Leslie Dashwood came into the mess.

"My God, Dashwood! I thought you were killed at Loos."

"So did I, chum. Bloody miracle that was."

"What luck to find you here."

"I've just arrived, old boy."

He sat down to breakfast. He was a captain. Jim wondered if he could get into his company.

Then he settled down to write to Mrs. Lomis.

DEAR MRS. LOMIS,

You will by now have heard of the death of your husband in action. I was with him as he led an attack against the advancing Germans from the open flank where they had broken through after the gas attack on the French colonials and Canadians.

I am writing to express my sympathy at your great loss and to tell you his death was painless and instantaneous. He was shot through the heart.

I found your address among the papers, which included your photograph, in his pocketbook. Although I only knew him a few hours I liked him. So did his men. He was a good man to serve under.

Yours sincerely,

J. F. HILTON
2nd Lt., KOWLI

PS. I am riding over with his effects to his battalion head-quarters. You will receive them in due course.

He thought of her receiving the little OHMS parcel. His watch, silver cigarette case, penknife, whistle, field glasses, the blood-stained pocketbook, the St. Christopher medal he had worn on a silver chain around his neck. She had probably given it to him to keep him safe.

In the afternoon he borrowed a horse and rode over to the Dorcester lines with the captain's things in his pocket. One of the men recognized him and came up.

"You all right, sir?"

"I'm fine. How are you?"

"Fine, sir. But we was lucky, wasn't we?"

"I've come over with Captain Lomis's effects. Things out of his pocket. Where's your orderly room?"

The man said, "I'll come with you, sir."

Jim dismounted and, leading his horse, followed the soldier. The orderly room was a creosoted clapboard hut. He said, "Mind holding my horse?"

"Not at all, sir."

Jim gave him the horse and went in. It was the usual orderly room. Some clerks sitting at tables. An orderly-room sergeant. An officer, a captain, at another table facing the door, looked up as he came in. Jim halted and saluted.

"James Hilton, Tenth King's Own Wilts Light Infantry," he said.

"And what can I do for you?"

"I was with Captain Lomis when he was killed. I brought his things. His effects." Jim fished them out of his pocket and arranged them in a kind of pattern on the blanket tablecloth. How pathetic they looked: A silver wristwatch with a pigskin strap. The silver cigarette case. The St. Christopher medal on its chain. The pocketbook with blood on it. The field glasses he had strung over his shoulder. "I tried to clean it," Jim said, "and there's some blood inside too. On her picture. She's holding a baby. And her last letter."

The adjutant said, "My name is Fell." He smiled. "Nasty business war, isn't it?"

"I've written to her, Captain Fell," Jim went on quickly. "Shot through the heart."

"Heard about you, Hilton, from our chaps. You took over, didn't you? A very mixed lot too. A good show from what I was told."

"My first time up the line. My sergeant really ran things."

"I heard that too. But the men thought a lot of you. 'He led us,' they said. 'Just a kid.' " Captain Fell laughed. "The colonel's at Brigade or I'd have introduced you. He'll be sorry to have missed you."

He got up and held out his hand. "Goodbye, Hilton, and drop into our mess any time."

Jim shook hands, saluted and went out to his horse.

"Sorry to have been so long."

"That's all right, sir. Not going anywhere, are we, sir? I'll tell my mates I saw you. They'll be glad to hear you're all right."

"Thank you. Give them my regards." He mounted.

The soldier saluted. "Good luck, sir!"

"Same to you."

And that closed the incident, a little story with a beginning, a middle and an end. A stone chucked into a pond but the ripples would go on. The fair-haired woman and the kid were ripples.

14 : Make and Mend

THE BATTALION rested for a fortnight to absorb new drafts and officer replacements. Close order drill. Inspections. Route marches. Musketry. Bomb-throwing. Lewis gun practice for the gun teams who sat on their bottoms with the gun taken down on a blanket, the metal pieces spread out like a meal in front of them. They were supposed to be able to reassemble it with their eyes shut. Some could and some couldn't.

Jim got in some riding with Dashwood. It was nice to be on a horse again. The MO—Captain White—often lent him his mare. Dashwood, as a company commander, had his own charger—a little short-coupled bay gelding, too small for the cavalry. Ellen, the doctor's mare, was a nice ride. Well bred, a bit herring-gutted and rather hot, as was so often the case with a chestnut.

Jim felt the time had come to ask Dashwood about Loos. He said, "I'll tell you some time, old boy, but I don't want to spoil this."

They were riding over flat, more or less undamaged country. Peasants were working in the fields, plowing with big, thick-necked Flemish horses. They passed low, four-wheeled carts; farmhouses; cattle, dogs. A white cat sat washing herself on a wall. Early May. Some fruit blossom was out, apple and pear.

"You know, Leslie," Jim said, "I was very upset when the battalion left me behind." What an understatement that was!

"They said you were too young, didn't they?"

"Yes, but that wasn't it."

"What was it, then?"

"It's quite a story. When I joined the battalion in September 'fourteen we were in billets at Maidenhead. New officers and men arriving every day. No organization. No battalion, in fact. Fisher, the RSM, was in a bowler hat, his Boer War and long-service ribbons sewn on his waistcoat." How it all came back! "Well, I was put in a bedroom at the Rose and Crown with Benjie Brown, the adjutant."

Dashwood nodded his head.

"Then, as soon as I'd put the light out, he said, 'Hilton, I'm going to get into bed with you.' I jumped up and got the big jackknife that had just been issued to me with my blankets, opened it and said, 'If you try it I'll stick this into you.' I'd never been like that, not like some chaps at school. No one had ever touched me." No one except for Gwen, the woman he'd picked up at the Empire. And Mona. He did not count Kathleen; it had been too tentative.

"I knew then that I'd bitched myself, Leslie, but I wasn't going to be the adjutant's bugger-boy. That's the real reason I was left behind. You never guessed it, did you?"

"No, I didn't."

"No one knew. I never spoke about it. But it's funny the way things turn out, isn't it? If I'd let him, I'd have gone out with you and probably been killed with the others."

"Bloody odd, old boy, the way things turn out. But you know he died bloody well, Benjie did. Almost the last officer left on his feet. I saw him leading what was left of A Company, with half his jaw blown off. A good soldier. Regular, First Battalion. Home on leave from the East when war broke out."

"I know all that, but he had queer habits. Funny thing, though, to be like that at home when the place was lousy with girls."

"Picked it up in the East, I expect. But I'll never forget his charging with those chaps. Nothing but a little swagger stick in his hand."

It was not till they got to the rest camp that Dashwood began to talk about the Loos battle.

"We had been marching for eighteen hours," he said, "with only ten-minute halts. The cookers had been left behind so there was no hot food. We were soaked to the skin. But they told us the Germans were smashed, retiring in disorder. All we had to do was to follow them up. Christ!" he said. "Haig even expected to put his bloody horses through the gap.

"That was on September twenty-fifth. We should have known something was wrong from the lines of ambulances and walking wounded we met going down the line, Jim, but we'd only been out a fortnight. We deployed below the ridge. That was us, the old Twenty-first Light Division, and the Twenty-fourth. No maps. No food, no rest. Bugger all. There was a ground mist and when it cleared our guns were in full view of the Boche. They blew them to glory. Now we had no guns to attack at eleven ack emma, over no-man's-land, without artillery support, smoke or gas. The wire in front of us wasn't cut, but we didn't know that then. We were enfiladed from both flanks. The ground was covered with dead Devons, and Highlanders, lying every which way or in long lines where the machine guns had caught them and cut them down. Like grass with a scythe. My God," he said, "those Highlanders lying there, lots of them with their kilts up showing their white bottoms. Like girls. Made me think of girls with balls, and remember we'd never heard a shot fired in anger. Never seen a dead soldier. And they weren't all dead; some of them were crying for help. Screaming for water. It was terrible, Jim, leaving them. We weren't used to it then.

"In the old German front line where we assembled there were German dead. Gassed, swollen. Some of them blue in the face, others yellow. They had been dead two days in the heat, and they stank. By this time we'd had no sleep for forty-eight hours, and only bully and hardtack to eat. There was a bit of bombardment but the Germans didn't know where we were. Then we went over.

"The Germans held their fire and allowed us to extend, line after line of us. They let us come. And then suddenly they opened up. We didn't have a chance. Charge. God damn it, they were still a thousand yards away. We passed more wounded and dead from the previous day's attack. Men fell in hundreds but the lines moved on. There were concealed guns firing over open sights, but we reached the wire. Heavy, ungalvanized steel stuff that our issue clippers wouldn't cut. Crisscrossed, strong, on pit props and thick pine stakes. The wire was four foot high and twenty feet across. Men pulled at it with their bare hands, they went mad, frenzied. They ran up and down looking for a gap, and all the time they were being mown down. Killed like rabbits in a cornfield.

"Then we turned and began to walk slowly back. The Germans never fired another shot as we found our way over our dead and picked up what wounded we could.

"We didn't know the whole story then. We'd used gas, so the Jocks attacked wearing gas helmets. Attacking half blind with their own sweat. One of the pipers marched up and down playing 'Scotland the Brave.' Brave, by Christ! That was the twenty-fourth, Jim. The gas didn't work because the wind dropped. Chlorine is heavier than air. It just sank to the ground. This was mining country. They had dugouts hundreds of feet underground. The gas—our gas—lay in the hollows and shell holes so the wounded who crawled into them for shelter died of it.

"They told us the Germans were beaten. Beaten, hell! And all this to take the pressure off the bloody French. Well, there it was."

"All those chaps," Jim said. "All those men." Not just our own outfit, the others—Durhams, Bedfords, Oxfords and Bucks. West Kents. Two divisions cut to ribbons, lying in swathes like hay behind a mower.

Maurice, Benjie Brown with his jaw shot off. Christ, and how near he'd been to it!

"You can see why I don't like to talk about it," Dashwood said. "Never got over it. Those lines of dead men. The pick of Britain. Kitchener's hundred thousand. King and Country. Enlisted for three years or till the end of the war. So either we end or the war ends, and for an infantry officer the betting is on the war lasting longer than he does."

Only twelve months, Jim was thinking. The battle had come. Twelve months after they had all joined up. September '14 to September '15, and it had been the end of them. Maurice and he—a David and Jonathan friendship. Closer than brothers. Closer than girls. Men could be like that, though people always suspected them of homosexuality. It was hard to make friends now. Dashwood was four years older than he and was separated from him by the Battle of Loos. It was memories that joined or separated people. Sometimes, when he was making love to Mona, he'd thought of Maurice. He knew she was grateful to Maurice for giving him to her. A kind of present. It occurred to him that for some girls a virgin boy must correspond to the feelings some men had for a virgin girl. She had more or less said so.

So here they were in a wooden hut talking about war, about a battle. His link with it was Maurice who'd introduced him to Mona, and Benjie Brown who'd wanted to bugger him.

Dashwood poured out a drink. The two candles on the table, stuck into cigarette-tin tops with their own grease, burned clear and still—pointed yellow flames with a blue center. Pointed as candles on an altar, sharp as pricks. His mind went back to the dead Highlanders. Bare white bottoms, like girls with their skirts up, Leslie had said. To the piper, playing his pipes. Skirling in a hell of exploding shells and chattering machine guns. How horrible death was! Ignominious, revolting. Utterly without grandeur at the end, unless you could go down fighting hand to hand. To lie there, just emptying your blood and bowels into the mud like a leaky barrel. Alone.

Dashwood's mind was still on the battle.

"I'll never forget looking for a gap in the wire. My God, it was murder! Green troops against uncut wire. And there had been a chance earlier on. The Germans really were pulling out. But there had been no men ready. I've got the figures, Jim. Twelve battalions, ten thousand men attacked. In four hours we lost, in round figures, four hundred officers and eight thousand men. Lucky, wasn't I, Jim? Lucky to have survived a battle that was the end of some of the finest men England has ever seen. Volunteers who joined up as soon as war broke out. Now you can see why I hate the bloody staff. Christ," he said, "sometimes I think I'd sooner shoot a general than a Jerry."

"Maurice?" Jim said. "You didn't see him go?"

"Yes. Maurice, Joe, Gordon, the bloody lot of them. I saw them fall, one after the other like ninepins. And you'd probably be dead too, if you'd let poor Benjie have his way. Makes you think, doesn't it?"

All those men. All those marching boots. How many route marches he had made with them! Two thousand left out of ten thousand. Out of two divisions. And this was the war he had been afraid would be over before he got there.

15 : The Cloth Hall

BEHIND THE front line was the support line. Then came the reserve line, then the rest area of tents and hutments. And all this on both sides, English and German, with no-man's-land—wired in as if it was a park—between them, grass-grown, shell-holed with shorts, dotted with rotting dead, all killed at hazard in little, useless forays in the night. The trenches fringed with rusty wire, line upon line of metallic brambles that bore dead men as fruit. Dead men—grotesques—hung out like laundry to dry. This was the design. The tapestry of war, continually embroidered by the bursting shells. A world of men that was fringed, decorated, by women on its outer edges. No children on this curious frontier. Just women, pressed into the mold of danger by their cupidity, purveyors of drink, food and their own bodies, the camp-flowers of a stationary war. Only farther back were children and virtuous women to be encountered. But here, as opposed to the war area, there were no men. Only boys not yet old enough to die, old men too old to die except in bed, and cripples. The mutilated. Men who had passed through the war as a grasshopper passes through the hands of a thoughtless child who pulls off its legs.

So men, going up the line, passed through these strange zones of grandmothers, widows and husbandless wives waiting for news, at once eager and fearful, of virgins and children and old and broken men into the zone of *vin rouge,* omelettes, whores and harpies, and on toward the world of young men and guns.

Their rest over, the battalion moved up to Ypres, in reserve, to dugouts in the ruins. They rested all day and went on carrying parties at night, picking up fence posts, wire, water and sandbags at the dumps where the transport left them, and carrying them up the communication trenches to the front line. It was a way of breaking in green troops to the sights and sounds of war. They would do seven days of this, then seven in support, followed by seven in the line.

It was late afternoon when they reached Ypres—what was left of it: a city cracked like a walnut by shellfire into jagged edges, serrated against the sky, the great fingers of the Cloth Hall's surviving masonry pointing accusingly to heaven. Houses —whole streets—were rubble; others had had the fronts torn off them, exposing their secret papered entrails. A bed, still made up after all this time, hung its rotting blankets half out of a second-floor bedroom. Shreds of window curtain blew, tattered flags of domesticity, in the cold wind that still swept the

Flanders plain. Gas brackets, their globes intact, remained riveted to shattered walls. It was all more shocking than total destruction, for here were the remains of private lives; homes, furniture, places that had been loved; refuges that in the end had provided no security. Solitary chimneys. An entrance arch. A door swinging eternally with every gust upon its hinges. The paved streets pitted with the pox of war. Shell-holed. Most of the holes had been repaired for the transport that had to pass through the town each night to reach the front. How they hated it! For every shell burst on percussions—on a raised house, on masonry, on the *pavé* of the streets. Sometimes the limbers of two or three divisions were held up. A traffic jam in a bursting hell of shells while dead horses were cut from the traces and dragged aside. With the dead and wounded men and beasts removed, the others had nothing to do but wait in their drivers' saddles, hoping for the best, cursing, praying. Red-caps stood at every crossroad directing traffic. The roads were named, marked in black on white signpost arrows: Poperinghe in the rear; St. Jean, Potige, Wiltje up the line. This was the Ypres Salient—a great bite taken out of the German line, a half-circle with guns firing into it from three sides. And Ypres itself a bottleneck under almost continuous fire by day and night because every man, every tin of bully, every round of ammunition—from small arms to heavy howitzer shells—had to pass through its narrow gut.

It was strange to be quartered in what was left of the town, to take a chance and stroll out into the sunshine among the ruins. That was what gave them this eerie quality. When he'd been here last there had been women and children dead in the streets. It made him think of the stories he had read of ravaged and looted cities of older wars; of the sixteenth century, of Wallenstein's black-cuirassed riders looting, raping and killing. Then, too, there had been dead women and children in the streets. Then, too, the hooves of galloping horses had struck sparks from the paving stones. But if that was history, so was this.

He found what had been a convent. A statue of a virgin, decapitated, her white marble head lying under what was left of

102

the choir stalls. He picked up some leather-bound books and put a small one in his pocket. He'd post it home to his mother.

In the Cloth Hall that had been the city's pride there were coats of arms, brilliantly painted on a black background, that had been blown off the walls. He picked up a couple as souvenirs. Soldiers had always collected souveniers; they were only souveniers because they were of no value. Once soldiers had fought for loot and women: church silver, bullion, savings of gold extorted from civilians by torture; and every girl and woman raped; children dashed to death. By God, you had to live in history to appreciate its horror.

He found a little courtyard garden against a south wall. A rose was in flower. He picked it. Who had picked the last rose from this bush? A young woman? What lovers had kissed in the moonlight here?

The heels of his boots rang bright on the pavement of this dead city, and it wasn't just the city that was dead. There were dead buried in the rubble. You could smell them—sickly, sweet, putrid—an odor that mixed with that of the red rose in his hand. A military policeman saluted him. "A nice quiet afternoon, sir," he said. "But take cover if they start shelling."

"What about you, corporal?"

"Oh I've got me own little 'ole, sir. When they start, I pops in like a bunny rabbit. When they stops I pops out again."

Jim nodded.

"You should have been 'ere when they shelled it first, sir. Open town, sir. Full of civvies—women and kids. That was when they used gas on the French and Canadians."

"I was, corporal. It was my first day in the line. I saw the Canadian guns come up. Full gallop—what a sight!"

"Split arse, sir. Poor buggers, them Canadians. Gassed. But they 'eld."

"Good luck," Jim said.

"Same to you, sir."

It was Jim's turn on the roster to take up a carrying party. Tomorrow they were going in to support. They marched through the town past an enormous seventeen-inch crater, forty feet across, which it had been impossible to fill in, and on through the main gate to the point where the transport dumped the stuff that had to go up the line. The horse transport could only go so far. The battalion sent down their own men for rations and water, but parties from the reserve were used to take up new duckboards, boxes of small-arms ammunition, bombs, rolls of barbed wire, iron screw piquets that looked like crazy corkscrews. All awkward things to handle at any time, and worse in cold weather through muddy going. Greasy mud up to their knees if they got off the duckboards.

There were no proper communication trenches. The clay ground was too wet to dig in. The water was within a foot or so of the surface. Here and there were breastworks, but most of it was over the top and hope for the best. The men in their goat-skin coats looked like a flock of sheep in the light of a cold half-moon.

The first line was not a trench. It consisted of sandbagged breastworks eight feet thick, supported by wattle hurdles and sheets of expanded metal.

The Germans had all the high ground. The rain that fell on them drained off into the British lines. They kept pumps going as if the line was a sinking ship, a ship sinking into a sea of mud. They pumped it out two-handed. Suck, suck, and it all seeped back again. In some places the men were up to their knees in water. Jim wondered how they stood it. Well, he'd soon find out. Tomorrow they were going in to support; next week they'd be in the front line themselves. In some places the Germans were only fifty yards away, but they were always higher up.

When Jim got back he found a big pile of the men's letters on the mess table. Fenchurch, the orderly officer, was waiting for him.

"How about giving me a hand, Hilton?"

"Of course." Jim sat down and began to read.

The men's letters had to be censored by an officer—in the company headquarters dugout in the line, in the mess when out of it. Written on cheap French paper or sheets torn out of notebooks, in lead or indelible pencil. The officers worked their way through the pile of unsealed envelopes. Hardly reading them, simply checking them for place names or military information that might be of value to the enemy. Despite all precautions, news still leaked out. The letters were very similar. Their writers were well, or had a bit of a cold. Thank you for the parcel. Can't wish you were here but I wish I was with you. Guess why. A decent meal—steak and fried spuds, sausage and mash, a nice kipper, fish and chips, a pint of bitter. And a bit of nookie. I am in the pink. Hoping this finds you as it leaves me. Sometimes SWAK on the flap of the envelope in spite of the fact that the letter would be sealed with a company officer's spittle. Many of the letters were badly written and crudely expressed, but they were all what the French would have called cries from the heart to their women at home from lonely, dirty men up to their ankles in mud. Pathetic, magnificent in their restraint, stoic, uncomplaining, they formed a kind of literature of their own.

Jim Hilton tried not to read them. It was easy enough to pick out anything that was information in the military sense and black it out with this new kind of punctuation that came in the middle of a sentence. When the letters were read you put them in their envelopes, sealed them and wrote your name in the top right-hand corner where the stamp should have gone. J. Hilton, 2nd Lt. J. Hilton, 2nd Lt. J. Hilton, 2nd Lt. . . .

But there was one letter he did read. He had glanced at it like the others and then the phraseology had struck him. This was the letter of a literate man, passionately in love with his wife. Private Goodby, A. No. 265785. It was a love letter. Goodby spread his offering of love as if it was butter on the small gray-squared paper. Why did the French use notepaper ruled like graph paper? The letter had a Song of Solomon quality, a lyric description of a woman's secret perfection written to her so that she should see herself naked, mirrored in the looking glass of her husband's mind; so that she should feel his lips and hands upon her body, know the ache of his parting.

In a way Jim was ashamed of reading it, but Private Goodby had known his letter would be read. He had weighed it up in his mind, the pros and cons of it. And he must have thought: to hell with it. In war the personal became impersonal. The subjective, objective. What mattered was that she should know. What did it matter if, on the way to her knowing, another man—who did not know her and never would—should read what he had written? He might be killed before he saw her again and could tell her himself. Besides, it was easier to write some things than to say them. And the faceless officer who would censor the letter would have plenty on his own plate. He might be killed, too. Life was short and, by Christ, in war if you did not do something you felt you had to do today, there might be no tomorrow in which to put things right.

What Private Goodby felt about his Enid was what he had felt about Kathleen, but much stronger because Goodby was a man and had known her in the biblical sense, whereas he had been only a boy with Kathleen, but it still hurt him to think of her. So he understood what Goodby was getting at. Mona was different. She was a passionate friend, a friend with whom you made love; and she had other friends with whom she also made love. There was nothing unique about it.

What hell it must be for a man like Goodby to be parted from the woman he loved, especially if she was as attractive as she seemed to be. Pretty women were honey pots. They got lonely. He gathered she had been a dancing teacher and that she and Goodby had won ballroom-dancing competitions together before their marriage.

16 : Patrol

THE WEEK in support passed without incident. There were no casualties, only boredom, cold, fear and lice. It was a Frenchman who had said it wasn't the bite that annoyed him, it was the promenade. If only the little buggers would stay still and just feed. When it was warm enough to strip, the men took their gray flannel shirts off and went through the seams, squashing their little friends between their thumbnails.

You got to know the different shells. 5.9 crumps—high explosive. Woolly bears—5.9 shrapnel that burst like long black worms. Whizzbangs, field guns that you never heard coming. The big howitzer shells sounded like trains passing overhead. You could often hear the gunfire, and waited for the shell to come.

They stood watching dogfights between planes. They watched the ack-ack exploding like white cotton wool in the blue sky. Jim saw one plane hit. It burst into flame and came down, twisting and turning like a burning leaf, behind the German line.

At dawn and dusk they fixed bayonets and "stood to."

They had been on two wiring parties, driving in wooden posts with mallets muffled with sandbags, and stringing wire within a hundred yards of the German line. "We've been nearer to Fritz than that, ain't we, sir?" Hargreaves had whispered. When the German flares went up, they flung themselves down. A machine gun traversed over them two or three times in a desultory sort of way. The men had been very steady. But it was a hell of a place, the water standing wherever there was a depression. There could be no real trenches here, just parapets built of sandbags, riveted with hurdles and expanded metal, walls six feet thick of headers and stretchers that even a whizzbang could blow to hell. They all slept in little cubbyholes like dog kennels, cut out of the parapet and roofed with a sheet of corrugated iron. It was still bitterly cold and they were all wearing goatskin or leather jerkins. Jim had a pair of sheepskin-lined fingerless gloves fastened to a tape that went over his shoulders, that he had bought at the Expeditionary Force canteen in Pop.

At the end of the week they took over the front line from the Leicesters who handed over picks, shovels, very light pistols, flares and sandbags. The front line was only eighty yards from the German wire. Sentries stood in every fire bay; they were relieved every four hours. So were the officers: four on and eight off, in the company dugout, a cutting on the road that led through Potige to behind the German lines.

"They don't shell this road much," the Leicester captain said. "Not as far up as this. They're after the transport. But there's a fixed rifle that fires down it every now and again. Very well sighted, too."

There were chicken-wire beds in the dugout, a table scrounged from somewhere, two armchairs covered in *petit point* and a gilt-framed mirror. A home from home. Live ammunition had been driven into the wall to make pegs for hanging clothes and equipment. They had two stable lanterns, also taken over from the outgoing battalion. The mouth of the dugout was masked with a blanket curtain. This was where the signalers sat, tapping out Morse to battalion headquarters, and the runners relaxed till they were needed. Theirs was a poor job; they were only used when the telephone wires were cut by shellfire. After the signalers and the runners came the cook and the officers' servants, who between them produced endless pots of tea and meals on a couple of hissing primus stoves.

Jim was alone in the dugout, censoring letters and listening with half an ear to the signalers talking on the other side of the second blanket that separated them from the company mess, uninhibited in their token privacy.

" 'Ave a good time, Jacky?" Jackson Field had just got back from leave.

"Not 'arf."

"Wotcha do?"

"Eat and fuck. Christ, when I got 'ome she was cookin'. Shepherd's pie, it was. The spuds nice and brown-like on top, just out of the oven on the bloody table.

" ' 'Ullo, Alf,' she says.

" ' 'Ullo,' I says. 'I'm back.' An' I shoves 'er back on the table and 'as her.

" ' 'Mind the bloomin' pie,' she says. 'Why can't you wait?' she says.

" 'I bin waitin' fourteen bloody months,' says I, and fucks 'er.

108

Christ," he said, "it was good too, and I 'adn't 'ardly looked at 'er. 'Er and 'er bloody pie. An' then we 'ad it. Still 'ot, mind you. An' she gives me the bloody news."

Then Dashwood came in. "Patrol tonight, Jim," he said.

"What's the drill?" Jim asked.

"Go out after stand down. Black your face. Take two chaps, or three, with you, and have a look at the German wire."

"Weapons?" Jim said.

"Just bombs, trench knives, clubs. Guns are no bloody good on a job like this. Hard to crawl with 'em."

The word was passed down the line. Officer patrol going out. A narrow track was cut through the British wire. Jim marked it with a length of white tape and hoped to God they'd find it when they came back. Mulholland, King and Goodby were going with him. Mulholland was telling them what to do.

"When the flares go up lie doggo, sir, face to the ground. If we run into a Jerry patrol chuck your bombs and bolt. They won't use their Emma Gees with their own chaps out."

They stood in between the breastworks like nigger minstrels with their blackened faces in the light of occasional German flares till it was time to go. Once out, they crawled through the wet grass till they got to the German wire. Then they crawled along it. They could hear the Germans talking. They even heard the wheels of the German transport. Because the ground was better drained, they could bring their horses much closer than the British.

A flare went up, a magnesium star fizzing up and floating slowly down. Lie doggo. They lay frozen, still as mice, till it sank to the ground and died.

Then they went on. And on. Interminably. Soaked to the skin from the long, wet, unmown winter grass.

The wire was perfect. No weak point that they could find as they looked up at it silhouetted against the sky. Jim was in front with Mulholland on left rear and Goodby on his right. Mulholland gripped his ankle. He stopped.

"That's about it, sir. What about turning about now and

going 'ome?" He gave a soundless laugh and they turned. Only fifty yards separated the lines at this point. Not much more than twenty between the British and German wire. They waited for another star shell and went in, creeping along their own wire till they found the tape that marked the gap.

"This is the most dangerous part, sir," Mulholland whispered. "A jumpy sentry and we've had it." Then he said quite loud, "Patrol coming in. King's Own patrol coming in. Officer patrol," and stood up.

Dashwood was there to meet them. The men in the traverse crowded up.

"German wire's perfect," Jim reported.

"I knew it would be. It's just that Brigade gets these ideas. They want to report something to Division. Got to do something, I suppose."

When Jim got back to the company dugout there were some letters and parcels for him on the table. His mother's parcel contained a big fruit cake, four jars of chicken and ham paste, and two pairs of socks she had knitted for him. In Mona's—beautifully packed by Fortnum & Mason—there was a small gammon ham and two white china pots of Gentleman's Relish. This stuff would come in handy as they were short of luxuries. The officers always shared their parcels.

Mona's letters were like all her letters. They said nothing, just that she missed him and hoped he was well. She thanked him for his field service postcards and hoped he would write soon. When was he coming home on leave? He'd only been out a month—what did she think the war was? A bloody picnic?

Then he opened his mother's letter, read a paragraph, got up and poured himself a drink. "Good God!"

"Something up?" Morland said. "Bad news from home?"

"Bloody queer news. My mother's getting married again. That's what happens if you leave them alone for five minutes."

"Well, she's quite young, I suppose," Morland said.

"I suppose she is, but I'd never thought of it that way. She must be about thirty-nine. I think she said I was born when she was nineteen."

Morland laughed. "Well, I suppose it is a bit of a shock if you didn't see it coming."

"See it coming? Of course I didn't. I knew she knew the old chap. Went out to lunch with him. Theatre and so on. Never met him, though. Kept him dark, as it were. But he's an old man—sixty. Cavalry dugout. Was in the Greys—a bloody major-general. Lots of money, she says. So she'll be able to help me if I want to stay on in the army. A general. Imagine having a divisional general for a stepfather!"

"Sixty is not so old. And there's many a good tune played on an old fiddle, or so they say."

"Well, it's bloody funny all the same, coming in from a patrol and finding your mother's sleeping with a bloody general. You'd be surprised if your mother did, wouldn't you?"

"I certainly would. My old man's very much alive and my mother is fifty and quite fat. I bet your mother's pretty."

"I suppose so. Here, take a dekko." Jim pulled a little leather folding frame out of his pocket.

"My God, she's lovely! She looks about twenty-five or thirty. Blonde, too. Can't say I blame the old boy."

"I still think it's odd. I mean it's quite a shock. He'll have to live with us. Fancy having a general in the house, a bloody stranger. But there's one thing: I can't send them much of a present, can I?"

"You could send a pair of Zeiss glasses someone took off a German. Or a *Pickelhaube*."

"Shut up, Morland," Jim said. "I want to read it carefully."

DEAR JIMMIE,

This letter has been very difficult to write. In fact it is my third effort! ! ! And I expect my news is going to surprise you. I am going to marry Major-General Sir John St. John Gore Blakeney, Bart. KCB, CMG, DSO. He is sixty and was in the Greys. He is very well off and I suppose in a way this influenced me, because now I shall be able to help you if you want to stay on in the army—you always wanted to be a soldier. But I am

111

very fond of him—the General, I mean—and have known him for more than a year. He is very handsome in a military way, if you know what I mean. Stooped cavalry back, gray hair and a moustache. Six foot one, thirteen stone. Size ten shoes. I hope you get the picture. He has rooms in Albany that look like Rowland Ward, full of heads, skins, guns and spears and things. Tigers, leopards, lions, bears. I'm sure you'll love it, and I hope you like him. Please try for my sake. I do hope you are taking care of yourself.

How on earth did she think you took care of yourself in war? Here he was, reading her letter with his face still black with the burnt cork he'd put on to go out into no-man's-land. Damn it, an hour ago he'd been lying in the Boche wire listening to them talk and wishing he knew German.

"You'd better get that stuff off your face, Jim," Morland said. "And when you've had another drink you'll feel better about it. After all, you're grown up. You wouldn't want to be tied to your mother's apron strings for ever. You'll get married. If you aren't killed, that is. You know, I often think about getting married. Having a nice girl to sleep with whenever I feel like it."

"You'll never get a nice girl to sleep with you, Jack."

"There'll be so bloody few of us left at the end of this that we'll have the pick."

"If you aren't killed too, old boy."

"There's something in that, as the monkey said when he put his hand in the pisspot."

They both laughed and raised their glasses.

"What's the wire like, Jim?"

"Perfect. Not a gap that I could find. Makes you wonder what the gunners are using, doesn't it? We crawled a long way along the line."

"Who went with you?"

"Goodby and Sergeant Mulholland. He wasn't supposed to go. Not a senior sergeant. We can't spare 'em. But he acts as if I was a bloody kid. His kid. As bad as Hargreaves."

17 : Routine

It seemed as if in war everything settled down into a routine—the line, rest, reserve, support and back into the line again. But things were pretty quiet even in the line. Half a dozen wounded in a tour and one killed. That was about the average. When there was a shout for stretcher bearers, Jim ran up to help them. He got used to it; to blood, to pain. You evidently got used to anything. Hardened. Curiously, the worst wound he saw so far as pain was concerned was Private Burton, who got a piece of shrapnel through the palm of his hand. The sinews were cut and the hand pulled up, contracted into a claw. "Christ all fucking mighty, Christ . . . Christ . . ." Burton looked up and saw him. "Sorry, sir." Jim squeezed his neck. He was holding his wounded left hand with his right. There was very little blood.

"Get him back to the dressing station," Jim said. "He needs morphia."

The most blood he saw came from a man nicked in the lobe of the ear. He bled like a stuck pig.

The dead. The dead, wrapped in a blanket, went back on the limbers that brought up the rations. Queer thing that, when you came to think of it—food coming up and bodies going down.

Imperceptibly June had come. June, and warmth. An early summer. With a periscope you could see the flowers in no-man's-land. Bloody marvelous. Red clover, ox-eye daisies, mauve scabious. Flowers. It was hard to believe. The guns on both sides seemed to do nothing except shell the roads at night to knock out the transport. When they were resting Jim always borrowed Ellen and rode into Poperinghe for a good meal and to see people again. Soldiers weren't people—civilians, old men, women, all of whom seemed to live like parasites on the

113

British Army. There were flashy-looking girls in the *esta-minets* who offered themselves for cash on the line, but Jim wasn't having any. Riddled with VD most of them. But he had no problem. He kidded them in French, he pinched their rounded bottoms, he bought them champagne, felt them and stroked their tits, but that was all. These public women were not his cup of tea, so he satisfied his needs by masturbating, and laughed at them as he thought of the old story about the two tramps—the one who fucked anything and the other who said he did the other thing because he got a better class of woman that way. In his fantasies he had Mona, he had Kathleen, he had film stars. Christ, that way you could have anyone you wanted. What bloody balls it was to talk about purity to young men. You got a stand, didn't you? What the hell were you supposed to do with it? It had to be a woman, your own hand or another man.

In Poperinghe he bought his mother a wedding present. A very nice German helmet, as Morland had suggested. A *Pickel-haube* with a golden spike, a gold eagle with outstretched wings over the black patent-leather front and a golden chain chinstrap. Something for the General's safari room. "A trophy. Sent to us by Irene's son at the front." Rather funny, really. He bought a dozen sentimental French postcards. Shiny photos of high, stiff-collared young men leaning over young ladies, offering them bunches of flowers, the whole thing surrounded by paper lace. He bought himself a ring made of aluminium with a little hole in it. When you held it up to your eye and looked through it you saw a tiny picture of a naked girl. How the hell did they get it in there? It was supposed to be made of a German shell fuse; he doubted it but bought two. One for himself and one for Mona. It would make her laugh. She'd show it to her friends. He felt no jealousy of the other men who slept with her. They must be all right, being introduced by one another. A club, as poor Maurice had always said. And he was grateful to her; she had made a man of him. Brought it out of him and put it into her. By God, that was rather clever! She wrote regularly once a week. Her letters were gossipy: about London, about shows, about the clothes she had bought. "I've got another red frock. Do you remember my red frock—you liked it. This is nicer still." That was the dress Maurice had made love to her in.

In a shop that specialized in such things he had bought her a pair of red *crêpe-de-chine* knickers and a very short chemise to match. "They'll match the frock. Save them for me, darling," he wrote. That had amused her. "Of course I'll save them for you . . . Hurry back and help me take them off. I'll bet you're sleeping with every French girl you come across." Just as if she was leading a pure and virginal life herself.

He answered her: "No girls; just you in my mind and then I toss myself off." A good thing officers censored their own letters. She answered that one with a moral letter about the dangers of masturbation and ended by saying she was glad there were no girls because she loved him. "I really do, Jimmie. I know you know about my friends, but I have to live and you're different. You're my baby."

Christ, he was sick of being everybody's baby. Sergeant Hargreaves, Mulholland. His own servant, King. They all nursed him, fussed over him. Even his men, like some kind of bloody mascot. But by God he was lucky! With Dashwood as company commander, Hargreaves and Mulholland his sergeants, old King his batman, and a fine lot of chaps in his platoon.

Sergeant Hargreaves came into the dugout, saluted and said, "I'd like to talk to you about one of the men, sir. Private Goodby."

"What's wrong with him?"

"That's what I want to know, sir. 'E's despondent, sir. A good soldier, but despondent."

"All right. Send for him, sergeant."

"I've got him here. He's with the signalers. Goodby!" he shouted. "Come in 'ere; the officer wants to see you."

The officer—that's me, Jim thought. He knew Goodby well. When they had been out on patrol together he had noticed that he seemed down.

Goodby came in and stamped his feet to attention. He saluted. "You want to see me, sir?"

"Sergeant Hargreaves says you are despondent. What's the trouble?"

The man stood still, silent; his eyes dark and unblinking in the candlelight. He was a big, powerful man, about thirty years of age. The three of them were still, frozen in a kind of frieze, a situation that had no name, their shadows black on the earth walls of the dugout.

"Have you anything to say?" Jim asked. "Any complaints?"

"No, sir."

"Then . . ."

Goodby looked at the sergeant. "Could I speak to you alone, sir?"

"It's against regulations," Hargreaves said, "but it might be a good thing, sir. 'E won't speak to me or his mates."

"All right, sergeant. You'd better leave us."

Sergeant Hargreaves saluted, turned about and joined the signalers on the steps.

"Now," Jim said, "take that damn tin hat off and sit down." He pointed to a packing case. He pushed a tin of Goldflake toward him and poured out a tot of whisky. "Drink that and tell me your troubles."

It was an extraordinary situation. Here was a married man ten years older than he but, as a platoon commander, he was supposed to be able to sort out his troubles. Goodby lit a cigarette from the candle with a trembling hand. He gulped his whisky, breathed hard through his nose and then it came out. "It's my wife, sir. She's left me for another chap. Couldn't stand the loneliness, she says. But they were always after her. She's a beautiful woman, sir, a lovely dancer. Like a pot of gold, the rainbow's end." Then he began to cry, his head on his arms on the table, his big body torn by racking sobs. The table shook under him. The man was being broken on the rack of his emotions; his mind, his heart, broken like a body lashed to a wheel by the actions of this woman, safe in England a couple of hundred miles away. And what the hell could he do about it?

116

"Do you want compassionate leave, Goodby? The CO will call Brigade. We should be able to get you away in a couple of days." That did it. That rang some kind of bell. Goodby sprang to his feet, put on his helmet and said, "No, thank you, sir. If I saw him I'd kill him." He looked down at his big hands. He was flexing them in front of him. "I might kill her, too—before she does any more harm. There were men before me, sir. They said one of them had killed himself because of her but of course I wouldn't believe it, not then. I'm the second one she's killed, sir. The man in me. There's nothing left of me, sir." He was standing very erect now, at attention, a statue in muddy khaki. "And sir," he said, "thank you for listening to me. It's done me good to talk. The worst is over now, sir. But would you be good enough not to mention my troubles? Not even to the sar'nt?"

"I'll not say a word." Jim got up and held out his hand. They shook hands. And another of those curious, close yet tenuous bonds that exist between men in wartime had been established.

Goodby saluted with a stamp of his heel, turned about and marched off—erect, stiff as a poker. But something in him had changed, as if he had come to some resolution.

Sergeant Hargreaves came in. "Sit down, Hargreaves," Jim said. He pushed the tin of Goldflake and the bottle of Haig & Haig toward him over the rough brown army blanket that covered the table.

"Well, sir?"

"I promised not to talk about his troubles."

"Home trouble?"

"That's it, but no details."

"I guessed it, sir. That's what breaks the best of 'em."

"What can we do, Hargreaves? He's a good man, isn't he?"

"First class, sir. But I've got an idea."

"What is it?"

"Give him his stripes. Lance-corporal, and full corporal next week. He'll take them now, sir, I think. He wouldn't before. Keep him busy, sir. Take his mind off things."

"I'll ask Captain Dashwood to put his name in orders tonight."

Goodby kept *the* letter as he called it, in his pocket, folded in his paybook. The edges were gray, the folds beginning to fragment. He knew it by heart but continued to read it.

DEAR ARTHUR,

I have some bad news for you. I have fallen in love with Jack Bradshaw [he had been the runner-up of the competition they had won, a wonderful dancer]. I simply could not stand the loneliness, Arthur, I have never been alone. I suppose I am not a good girl but it's so difficult to be good if a girl is pretty. And I am—you always said so. And he was always there and you know what dancing is. [Yes, he knew what dancing was all right. So why should he be surprised? There had been men before him. She was not a good girl, and she was not a bad one. She just wanted admiration, and thought that being made love to was love. Christ, but she was beautiful!] You'll get married again, Arthur, to some nice girl who'll want children. I never did, you know. And you should have them; you'd be a wonderful father.

Bugger the children, it was her he wanted, bad as she was. Only she wasn't bad; just vain and weak. Once a man had his hand on her, she gave in. No fight in her. She came at once. By God, he ought to know, oughtn't he? She'd taken his life. He was a dead man now, an empty shell. Sucked dry. He thought of his letters to her. She'd probably shown them to Bradshaw out of vanity. Just to show what she could do to a man with her body. Her sex. Her endless, insatiable heat. He thought of the way she danced, her pelvis pushed into his, with nothing between him and the mat of her belly but a thickness of silk.

There was a build-up going on for a big push in the south, or so the rumor went. Perhaps they'd move the division down there. That was what he wanted, a big show would take his mind off things. Things. There was only Enid. His Enid in bed with that man. With that man's eyes upon her, his hands . . .

Mona was at Fortnum's again sending off parcels to her soldier friends. It was early summer. The laburnums in the parks were dripping their fingers of gold. She walked up Piccadilly to the

Circus and bought a small bunch of tulips from an old woman who had a basketful.

"Pretty tulips, lady. Pretty tulips for a pretty young lady wot's making some lucky man 'appy, I'll bet. Make the most of it, dearie, 'cause it don't last for ever." What didn't last? Tulips? Girls? Looks? Life?

They knew a lot, these old flower women did. Been young and pretty in their time, some of them. Men had told her that a lot of them had once been whores. She shivered.

She knew about the build-up on the Somme. Everyone knew about it. She wondered where Jimmie was. My Jimmie. Mountains of shells, they said. Duckboards, war material. Preparations. Everyone knew about it. They shouldn't. It made her uneasy.

Piccadilly was full of soldiers, officers mostly, this being the West End. Officers with girls. She was almost embarrassed at being alone. A pretty girl like her, what would people think?

In Albany Lady Blakeney looked at her husband. He had given himself twenty-four hours' leave. There was no doubt now that she was in love with him. How ridiculous it was! A middle-aged woman behaving like a girl. But he stirred something in her, this handsome, gentle, almost animal man. He reminded her of a St. Bernard. He had no ideas in his head that went beyond soldiering, hunting, shooting and making love. He was as simple as a child. Simpler than Jimmie had ever been. She said, "I've bought some new clothes, John."

"Buy anything you like, darling. I want you to look pretty—not that you don't look pretty in nothing at all."

Irene felt herself blush. Like a girl. But she knew she stripped well—she was using his own words in her mind. Like a horse. He spoke of her like a horse. He patted her bottom like a horse's quarters. He was, in fact, more used to horses than women. She was glad of it. No poodle-faker. She smiled at him benevolently. She really felt quite maternal about him sometimes. Her John, with his *Vie Parisienne* mind. He liked the line drawings of pretty girls in their undies. Kirschner.

119

"Any news of the boy?" the General asked. He always called Jimmie "the boy." She wondered how they would get on. When she wrote to Jimmie she always sent best wishes from the General. When he wrote, he always said, "Regards to the General." It was all rather abstract—formal—as if neither of them really believed in the other.

She got up and took an OHMS envelope from the drawer of the writing desk and gave it to her husband.

"Seems all right," he said. "He says things are pretty quiet but he'd say that in any case. Doesn't want to worry you. A good lad, I'd say."

"He's a good lad," she echoed. She really was beginning to talk like the General. Clipped, short sentences. Think like him too, in a way. He had a trick of getting down to the essentials of any situation.

"Do you know what I'd like, Irene?"

"No, what would you like?"

"A boy of my own I'd never see him grow up, of course. But I'd like a son. You're not too old, my dear. Rising forty, just in your prime, and it's not as if you'd never bred before."

She began to laugh. To a man of sixty she was in her prime. Just a girl. And not as if she'd never bred before—like a mare. She loved this man. He amused her.

"We're doing our best, aren't we, John?"

"You mean . . ."

"Of course," she said. She'd known what was in his mind for some time, though he had never mentioned it. He'd been brooding about Jimmie. He wanted a son of his own to go into the Greys like his father and grandfather before him. An heir.

He came over to her. She rose to meet him. Her husband, her lover. The General. How safe she felt in his arms! She hoped she'd bear him a son. In the ten years of her widowhood she had had two lovers. Ephemeral affairs with charming men, while Jimmie had been at school. But then of course she had taken precautions. She broke away from his arms.

"It might be a girl, John. It might be nothing at all. It's twenty years since I had a baby. I may have dried up inside. Atrophied." But she knew she hadn't.

120

"All right, if you want to be obstinate. Have a filly if you'd like that better. It's just that I don't want to go and leave nothing behind me. And I'd like to see you with a kid in your arms. Make you really mine. A madonna."

To her surprise there were tears in his eyes when he kissed her.

But that wasn't the only thing in his mind. This offensive was not going to be a surprise. Everyone knew all about it. A lot of men were going to be killed. If anything happened to her boy, he wanted her to have another baby on the way. It must be terrible to be the mother of a son at a time like this.

Part Two

ARMAGEDDON

18 : Preview

THE BATTALION was leaving the Salient and marching down to the Somme, into some cushy place where they would be ready for the battle that was shaping up, or so the latrine rumor went, and the rumors were often right. News was picked up from divisional signalers, who got it from Corps, who passed it on to Brigade, and so on down the line. A word here and a word there, a two-and-two that seldom made exactly four but invariably added up to something.

This meant real war: the over-the-top kind. Not just defending trenches that were a quagmire, enfiladed by German guns on both flanks.

The rumor proved true and soon they were marching through Belgian roads into France behind the fifes and drums of the band, with the transport bringing up the rear. The limbers, the cookers, the water cart, the Maltese mess cart, the doctor's cart; the mounted officers riding in front of their companies. The men carrying nothing, for a change, except their packs and rifles. No sandbags, picks, shovels, flares or wire. No Lewis gun ammunition or the guns themselves. At night they piled arms and bivouacked by the roadside. At dawn they marched on. They marched for fifty minutes and rested for ten, with an hour off in the middle of the day for a hot meal from the cookers.

As they marched through Bailleul, very smart at attention, rifles at trail behind the band, the children ran after them, shouting, "Bullee! Bisquee!" hopping first on one leg and then on the other.

"Christ," Johnson said, "they like the bloody stuff. But it's good to see the little bastards, ain't it?" Little boys in black calico pinafores, little girls with their long hair flowing behind them as they ran.

"Pity they aren't a few years older," Bert Caslet said. "Wonderful wot a few years does to a girl kid. Rounds her off, like. Puts on the twiddly bits."

Jim, who was marching just ahead of them, thought: child, girl, woman. Like fruit ripening till it was ready to be plucked. Bloody annoying, the way women kept coming into your mind, creeping into every crevice of it once you stopped being exhausted, hungry and frightened. Even little girls, like the fair-haired child skipping along beside him. A bloody little Alice-in-Wonderland kid. Kathleen must have looked like that at her age. He wondered what this one would look like in eight or ten years; who'd have her and when and where and under what circumstances. He thought of Mona and wondered what she had been like as a child. Attractive to men, teasing, coquettish, flirtatious. That was curious, too. Some were and some weren't. But what was the good of thinking about them? Of aching for it? Still, you had to think of something and it was better than thinking about the war. Food, books, pens, paper, rifles, bombs, women. He thought of all the things a man touched and held in his hands! The soft nose of a horse, the soft thighs of a girl. He thought of Mona's thighs. Hands and fingers had a kind of life of their own. The hard, cold feel of a Mills bomb; its weight. The weight of Mona's breasts when he came up behind her and held them. The hard, smooth feel of a rifle butt, and the cold of its barrel. The softness of a woman's belly, the wiry harshness of her pubic hair. The messages the hands flashed back to the brain; the return messages from the brain to the body, every man his own bloody signal corps. And all this to the rhythm of the marching boots behind him. He knew the men had the same thoughts. Food, women, sleep, baths, clean clothes, no bloody lice. Each man with women of his own: mothers, wives, girls, sisters, cousins. Three or four to each man, three or four thousand to a battalion, all thinking of their men, writing to them, sending them parcels, knitting socks and mufflers for them, waiting for their letters, being faithful to them, unfaithful to them, praying for them and remembering them, trying to forget them. And this must have happened in every war. Nothing was new. Of course men had never faced such shellfire before, but fear, terror had, as it were, a point which could not be passed. A maximum threshold; when this was reached it could not be increased.

Some GS wagons, loaded with forage, went by. Troops—a battalion of Staffords—passed them going in the opposite direction. A despatch rider on a Douglas motorcycle, a string of limbers, a battery of 18-pounders. All directed by the military police on point duty. Red-caps.

The civilians on the pavement hardly looked at the military traffic. Just the children, with their shouts of "Tommee . . . Bisquee . . . Bullee. . . ." The women all in black. Only one of them looked at him, a young, good-looking woman with a baby sucking her bare rounded breast. Stared half in bitter mockery, half in invitation. Sorry for him, wanting him or any personable young man, and ashamed of her desire. That was what war did—gave a full-blooded girl a baby and then left her high and dry, in the flood of it. A widow, perhaps, who would become a whore, or the mistress of some base wallah with a cushy job in the town; a pen-pusher. God damn those bastards. Good food, girls in warm beds, safety. Clean uniforms, shining boots, rattling spurs. Bastards. He could not get the dark girl out of his mind. He saw her naked, voluptuous, her big breasts full of milk, her dark eyes burning. He knew he would remember her for days, that in this instant of passing there had been a sexual encounter; a challenge, a gift, an acceptance. All that, and in the twinkling of an eye they had made love on some inexplicable psychic plane. The trouble was you were too keyed up; all of them were randy as hell.

Now they turned east into the morning sun, into the line, leaving the town behind them. They were halted. They were told to rest. They would go no farther till dark. The cooks dished out food from the cookers. The men ate and then lay down beside their piled arms.

After dark they fell in and marched off. They were still a long

127

way back. Permission to smoke was given. Hundreds of matches flared like fireflies all along the line of marching men, pinpricks of light that could be seen three miles away. But they were farther back than that, still marching two deep, with an interval of thirty paces between platoons. But they were no longer a segmented insect creeping back to rest, a dog returning to lick its wounds, exhausted, bloody, after a tour of duty. They were a battalion of light infantry from a regiment that had fought with Sir John Moore in the Peninsula, with Marlborough at Minden three hundred years ago and had never died. Men could die but not a regiment; it had a spirit, a soul. Its battle honors and its dead marched with it. They must never be disgraced. That was the reason for lectures on regimental history, the basis of *esprit de corps*. They were well rested, reinforced with new drafts marching to war in a new place—France instead of Belgium. But even in a good tour some men were killed and wounded. How long would they be in this time? What would the trenches be like? In what sort of condition? Fire steps, dugouts, Lewis gun posts? And the front? How far away were the Germans? How good was the field of fire? What was no-man's-land like? Domestic questions, as if one was moving into a new apartment. And they were, in a way. The new line would be their home, the place where they lived till they were relieved, died or were wounded.

Some French infantry passed them, going down the line. Not marching in column but drifting, the mud-stained horizon blue paler than khaki in the night; flotsam in twos, threes or dozens, going toward some fixed *rendezous* in the rear. They could do this. They were in some ways more adult, more individualistic than the British soldiers, more able to *débrouiller* themselves.

They came, they passed in the moonlight—white-faced, unshaven, tired. Even groups of them did not march in step, but they moved fast. They waved, shouted "Anglais" and disappeared. Night, with its dark blanket, covered them. Any shells that hit the road would be blind, fired at a calculated venture, hoping to hit some moving troops, or transport coming up with the rations, limbers with food and rum and water, sandbags, bombs, ammunition, mail—the letters that linked the BEF with home, the trenches with parlor and drawing room, with good food and clean beds; with kitchens where mothers and wives baked cakes to send to John and Jack, filling them with the currants and raisins of love. A tenuous line, stampless in one direction, they were all the same. Just one letter written in a hundred thousand hands, going both ways. "I miss you. I love you." The men saying, "I am well, in the pink, hoping this finds you as it leaves me." Poor girl, how surprised she would be to find herself standing knee-deep in muddy water with shells passing over her head and lice in her drawers.

Food, women and thoughts of their children preoccupied the men. The officers too. But since they censored their own letters, Jim only knew his own. To his mother, to Mona and Kathleen. He continued to write to Kathleen though she never answered. There must be men in her life, she was eighteen. He thought of the other men with her, of their hands on her smooth white body. You couldn't help thinking of things like that. And Mona. The dark and the fair, Christ, what was the good of thinking of it when you were stuck here till you were hit or killed? A blighty, a nice blighty. A wound bad enough to take you home but not serious enough to leave you incapacitated for good. But suppose you were hit in the balls? Castrated. That had always been man's fear. A castration complex that had existed long before Freud gave it a name. But a real danger in war. That was why you bent forward in a fight and tried to cover them. The guts of a man. The man of him. He thought of the whorehouse at Rouen and the girls there. Mares served by hundreds of young randy stallions. Thousands in their lives. A dozen or more in a night. Lying on frowsy beds. Females rather than women, receptacles for sperm. And all these men, the long marching line of them, had known women, been born of them; babies born of women that had become men; their father's seed. What was this strange urgency of the loins, of the eyes and the hands? What had this to do with the summer days of Kathleen and the wild, hot smell of gorse when he had been a boy less than two years ago?

129

The battalion took over from a battalion of Irish Rifles. "A bloody good place to be, me bhoy," they said as they went out. "You leaves them alone and they leaves you alone. Quiet, with the peace of God."

Jim wondered what had become of his friend Jack Campbell, the rifleman with whom he had visited the Cathedral and the brothel at Rouen. He was not in this battalion.

No one thought of tomorrow, because only free men who could make their own plans could think of the future. Their future was arranged for them by generals. By fate, by God. Their thoughts of death were abstract. Each man was convinced he would not die. But each looked at his companions with a certain compassion. Poor bastards.

If individual soldiers really thought they were going to be killed, there would be no more wars. They did think of being wounded, crippled, but even this was more of a hypothesis than an actual thought. Nor did their dead comrades really seem to be dead. They had merely gone for ever. In each man was the fear of himself rather than for himself; fear that he would give into fear and break. Those who had been out a long time knew courage was expendable—that some men had more of it than others—but the end of it always came. Sooner or later the cup was drained.

19 : The Raid

IT WAS the Australians with their talent for the unconventional who had made the first daylight raid. The night before the raid they had crept out and cut the German wire. Then at about one pip emma, figuring the Boche would all be half asleep after eating, they had gone over the top and into the German trench, catching them completely unprepared. Once they were in they sent up a rocket and the Germans had been boxed in with a barrage. That was the trick. All simple as pie.

So now Brigadier-General Brandstone wanted to do the same. Wake the line up a bit. He had a name as a fighting general and he wanted to keep it. He wanted a division and this was the way to get it. Activity. Of course they'd have casualties, but it was war, wasn't it? He decided that the 10th Wilts should do the job.

"Send for Robinson," he said.

When the colonel came back from Brigade he called the company commanders to his headquarters.

"Gentlemen," he said, "we've got to do a daylight raid."

"Good God!" Dashwood said. "Like the Aussies."

"Exactly. That's what gave old Brandywine the idea. You can't imagine him getting an idea on his own, can you? Anyway, we're to have the honor of carrying out this assignment. A company raid."

"But what company?"

He produced a pack of cards. "Suppose we cut for it. Aces high. And the lowest gets the job. Do you agree?"

"Seems fair enough."

Johnson of A Company cut first. A king of hearts. Fenwick, B Company, a ten of diamonds. Berwin, commanding C Company, a seven of hearts, the lowest so far. It was Dashwood's turn. Three of spades.

"So it's us," he said.

They had a drink and went back to inform their companies of the operation.

Dashwood sent for the officers and sergeants of D Company: four officers, five sergeants, two lance-sergeants, company sergeant-major. Hargreaves.

"Well, gentlemen," he said, "we're for the high jump. The Brigadier wants a daylight raid. Tomorrow. One pip emma. No artillery preparation. A company is going to cut the wire tonight. The Leicesters are going to demonstrate while they do it. They'll make a lot of noise and simulate an attack. The guns are going to support them. The noise is supposed to prevent A

Company being heard working on the wire, and with luck it will. Now—about us. What's our strength tonight, sergeant-major?"

"One hundred and seventy-five other ranks, sir."

"Very well. Two men out of three with bombs and clubs. Pick your best shots for riflemen. We'll go over as quickly as possible, through the cut wire and into the German trench. Every officer will carry a rocket and so will you, sergeant-major. Once we're in we send 'em up. When the gunners see them they'll box us in on three sides with a barrage. We kill as many as we can and return with the prisoners in fifteen minutes exactly. Have you got that? In fifteen minutes we must be out with the prisoners and our wounded. Leave the dead. Is that clear? We'll synchronize watches when we assemble."

Clear. It was clear enough. But if anything went wrong, such as the wire not being properly cut, what a muck-up there'd be.

"You're coming with us, sir?" Hargreaves asked.

"I'll be there, Hargreaves, but I can't say I like the job. The idea, of course, is to catch the Boche after his lunch when he's resting in the shade of his dugout. Nice and cool down there. But when we go we must go fast. It's only a hundred yards to their line."

"And our own wire?" the sergeant-major said.

"We're going out through the sap. B Company are clearing the wire from it. We creep out slowly and lie in the long grass till we attack."

"We'll be bunched up, sir," Hargreaves said.

"Yes, we will, but we can't help it. The gaps in the German wire will be taped. Now tell the men and don't put the wind up them. Say, 'What the Australians did the Wilshire Light Infantry can do better.' " Everyone laughed.

Dashwood put a bottle of whisky on the table. When the glasses ran out they used enamel cups. A fine lot of officers and NCO's. He only hoped he did not lose too many of them.

It seemed a very long time to Jim from predawn stand-to to the assembly. Bomb-carrying belts, a kind of canvas waistcoat with pockets to fit the bombs—two rows of five each—were dished out. They had been sent up by Brigade. Bludgeons, clubs and trench knives checked. Water bottles filled.

Brigadier-General Brandstone had been nicknamed Brandywine in the South African war because of his taste for that drink. A heavy brandy drinker, a bottle a day man, they said. Red-faced, loud-mouthed, bellicose as a fighting cock, and proud of his reputation. The men liked him because he was often in the line himself, cursing, swearing, laughing and full of the devil. A nice peaceful sector was something he could not stand—would not stand. Aggressive. Best defense, attack. Only good German a dead one. No one ever complained about his courage. If anything he had too much. His brains were his trouble, and his wild Irish blood that was incapable of calculating risks. This raid, for instance, could serve no real purpose. But the brigadier could not stand inactivity.

In the sap the men crowded together, the bombers looking pregnant in their bomb-filled waistcoats. They moved up slowly. As the men climbed out into the long grass of summer the larks sang in the sunshine. Hundreds of larks, or so it seemed.

It was strange to lie in this unmown hay, speckled with wild flowers—marguerites, buttercups, poppies and clover—looking at your watch, at the second hand ticking away, pecking at time like a bird. Whether you lived or died those seconds had gone for ever. Zero approaching in little circles on your wrist—as if each time the hand went around it had taken a step. The men had been warned to be silent as they ran forward, not to cheer. Not a shout till they got among them. Germans. Huns. Boches. Fritzes. Jerries. Men who, they hoped, full-bellied from their midday meal, were sleeping, resting, writing letters, hunting lice in their shirts.

Five more seconds. Four. Three. Two. One.

Jim got up. All around his men were up. He saw Dashwood on his right. They ran forward. There were plenty of gaps in the wire. A Company had done a good job. They ran through them and jumped into the trench. Not a shot had been fired. The bombers were throwing bombs. Two rockets soared, hissing into the sky among the singing larks. The gunners must have been standing by with their lanyards in their hands, because before the rockets turned to fall earthward the barrage was screaming over them. In front of them and on both sides there was an inferno of exploding shells. Jim saw a German trying to mount a light machine gun to enfilade the trench and shot him. The men were shouting now, encouraging each other and themselves, whistling in the daylight dark of fear. The action became blurred. More shouts, shots, curses, bombs. Jim looked at his watch again. How extraordinary to be looking at your watch at a time like this. You looked at your watch to see if you were on time for an appointment with the dentist, to meet Mona, to catch a train. The watch his mother had given him, how extraordinary. Three more minutes. He blew his whistle, hoping someone would hear him. Hargreaves and two riflemen were herding some prisoners toward him. Two other men were carrying a wounded corporal. He could not see his face, only the two chevrons on his dangling arm.

"Come on," Jim shouted, climbing on to the parapet so that they could see him—one of their own chaps.

They came out in twos and threes. More prisoners. A couple of walking wounded. The barrage continued. But the Germans had opened up on the British front line.

Got to get through that, Jim thought, wondering who else would be hit. Two more men were wounded and one killed. They were dragged into the sap. There the company and their prisoners squatted like dogs in a ditch. Grim, dirty and bloodstained, but happy. What the Aussies could do they could do better. Good old Wilts L.I.

Jim found Hargreaves.

"Good show," he said. "What are our casualties?"

"I don't know exactly, sir. We left four dead. We've got two badly hit men, a dozen with light wounds, about twenty prisoners. I don't know if anyone is missing. Can't tell till we call the roll."

As usual the gunfire had excited the larks to a frenzy of song. In any lull they heard them.

Jim looked at his watch. One-thirty pip emma. Only half an hour since it had begun.

But this was no longer a peaceful sector. Old Brandywine had stirred things up. Like an infection, the gunfire had spread along the line on both flanks. How bloody silly it all was. Jim suddenly felt very tired. He wanted to sleep. He didn't give a damn for Mona, Kathleen or any woman.

There was a curious sequence of desires in men's minds. First sleep, when they were tired. Then food. And only then a woman—when they had been rested and fed. That was something the bloody civilians never knew. The sequence. Because they had never been really tired or hungry. My God, when a man was hungry the most beautiful girl in the world would be safe if he was offered a steak as an alternative. He wondered if any girl would believe him if he told her of his big discovery. He began to laugh. He laughed till the tears rolled down his cheeks. The soldier squatting beside him put a lighted cigarette into his mouth—a Woodbine. The shelling slowed up. They began to shuffle back, bent double, into their front line.

Fitzherbert always tried to entertain his general. "My general" he called him. That was part of his duty as an ADC. Keep the old boy ticking over and in a good humor. He had to think up subjects that would start him off. Campaigns he'd been in. Horses he'd owned.

Tonight he said, "Did you know Sir John French well, sir?"

"Of course I did, Fitz. Never liked the chap though. Pass me a cigar."

Fitzherbert passed the box, lit it when the General had pierced it with a gold piercer, and sat watching him. He was dreaming about South Africa no doubt. Well, when he'd finished he'd come to and talk. Anything to get him off the war and the way things were going.

Yes, by God, he'd known French and Haig as well. Served under them when he had commanded the 3rd Cavalry Brigade.

Brigadier-General Sir John St. John Gore Blakeney. He'd quarreled with them both. How the hell could you catch Boers if your men were cluttered up with so much stuff—spare shoes, heel ropes, fodder nets, rifle, sabre, ammunition? He'd had a plan to use pack horses for the extra gear. No wagons. He'd had another row about the horse losses. Fancy bringing horses from Europe and America in the winter and expecting them to go into action in the African summer—a hundred in the shade in Kimberley—or vice versa, from English summer into winter on the high veld. They should have had three months' rest after the voyage to get used to the climate.

Sir John Ponsonby French, a poor rider for an Irishman and a dragoon. Drank a bit and liked the women—nothing wrong in that if he'd taken care of his horses. As for Haig—a poodle-faker. Good looking. He'd married a lady-in-waiting to Queen Alexandra. ADC to the King. And now in command of the British Expeditionary Force. That was the way to get on. Some people said he'd even failed the Staff College exam, but had been pushed in. Influence, that was what counted. Know the right people, sleep with the right women.

When he'd been to see French at the War Office just before war was declared, he'd turned him down. No room for him in the BEF. Too old. "But I'll see you get a division, John. Home training." And that was what he'd got. Training men for other men to mishandle and send to their deaths. Send to hang like scarecrows on uncut German wire. Dugouts, that's what they called them, the old soldiers like himself who'd retired. French with his champagne and his women and his escort of lancers. Of course he had lancers, too, but that was different. Infantry, too. Being told to stay at home training infantry. By God, he'd practically had to go back to school again to learn about foot soldiers. Good boys, though. The best. Old Gore Blimey of the Greys. What a regiment, what a history! *Nulli secundus,* like the Coldstream. Regimental badge the eagle they had taken from Napoleon at Waterloo. He thought of Mother Ross fighting with them as a trooper under Marlborough. What a history the regiment had.

136

"That boy" had seen the regiment in France washing their gray horses down with permanganate. Written to his mother about it. Told her to tell the General. He'd taken the marriage pretty well, the boy had. A blow, of course. Hard for a boy to realize his mother was a woman who wanted her greens too. Irene was a hot little thing under all that well-bred calm and poise. Just right for him, but she made him wish he was younger. Not the man he had been by a long chalk. Have to get her up here again soon, or slip off to London. Give himself a couple of days' leave. Not many men of his age were in love with their wives. Been married to 'em for too long, and the women were too long in the tooth. Irene was not quite forty, just a girl. He thought of her in her lace and pink silk dressing gown, her long pale gold hair down her back, her feet in high-heeled mules. Funny what high heels did to a woman's leg. High heels, silk stockings, frillies, petticoats that rustled, scent. The whole apparatus of it was an aphrodisiac. And didn't they know it.

His cigar had gone out.

"Give me another cigar, Fitz. I never relight one."

What a fine old chap he was, Fitz thought. Marriage had certainly improved him a lot. He might try it himself one day.

"Think I should get married, sir?"

"I do, Fitz. Better to marry than to burn, my lad."

They both laughed.

20 : The Doctor's Daughters

LILIAN GOWAN had always dressed her daughter young. In short frocks, white socks and shoes till they looked ridiculous. Two years ago Kathleen had been as slim as a boy, showing no sign of development. Mrs. Gowan used to hope people would think she was thirteen. Fourteen at the most. She couldn't bear the idea of having an adolescent daughter. She knew what people thought when they said, "And how old are your children?" Then they took the age of the eldest, added twenty to it and they were generally right, or nearly so. She was thirty-eight, nearly forty. It had been bad enough when Kathleen had been six, a beautiful golden child. They'd made a pretty pair—young mother and her daughter. Sweet. She was a pretty woman, with an oval face, blue eyes and golden hair. Chocolate-boxy to an artist, but the top of a chocolate box was her idea of beauty— fair, blue-eyed, pert, with a small, soft, characterless rosebud mouth. But the mouth had hardened over the years and there was ice in the eyes where there had been only blankness. That was what came of being married to Dr. Nils Gowan. She should have done much better for herself but she'd wanted to get away from home. She wondered how many girls married because they wanted to get away from home. Nils had been twenty-nine, with very blond, almost silver hair. He had just bought a share in a practice in Bayswater.

She was still regretting Laurent Plage.

If they had to go to the Continent, why hadn't they gone to Deauville or Trouville? Somewhere gay. But he'd had to have quiet to finish his book. He was always reading, writing, out on calls or in his surgery. No regular hours.

She had not approved of Kathleen running wild with that boy. He was seventeen, almost a man, but Nils just laughed at her. "Let them run about and play in the sun. What better way could there be for them to find out?"

"Find out? You don't mean you approve?"

"Of course I do. They've got to learn about each other's bodies, how God put them together."

"Your own daughter!"

"Well, have you told her anything?"

"Of course not!"

"Then how do you want her to find out? From servants? From other girls? Half-truths? Dirt? This is the best way, Lilian."

"I am surprised at you, Nils, a professional man, a doctor."

"Perhaps that's why. I've seen the effects of ignorance too often. So don't stop her. This is the time. She's almost but not quite a woman. It's love play, not serious."

But everyone knew what Swedes were. Loose from the word go. Love play! How disgusting! There had been something wrong about the whole place. Not at all like England. That woman, the boy's mother. Living openly with her brother-in-law. Anyone could see she was that kind by the trouble she took with her appearance. Pretty too, and her own age. Just about. She wondered if Irene Hilton was really a widow, more probably divorced. Silk stockings and high heels in the country. And she changed several times a day; one only did that if one was interested in a man.

She thought of Mrs. Hilton in a fresh white dress and a big, floppy hat picking sweetpeas, snipping them off with scissors, smelling them as she put them in her basket.

She had said, "Do come over and pick all the sweetpeas you want, Mrs. Gowan. They have to be picked, you know, or they run to seed and stop flowering."

She'd said, "Thank you, Mrs. Hilton, I will." But she hadn't, and wouldn't. She did not care for flowers. And the nightingales everyone raved about had kept her awake.

If only she knew about those two. What had they done when they went off into the woods together? Did Kathleen let him touch her? She was sure she didn't. She had been so well brought up. She was such a quiet girl. And her husband actually saying he hoped such things were taking place.

Explorations. Discoveries. In natural conditions under a summer sky. Like Adam and Eve discovering their nakedness. Oh no! Not my Kathleen! Just a child still. When she grows up she'll be married and have a baby. That will make me a grandmother, she thought. The idea took some getting used to. But it might be better than having a grown-up daughter underfoot.

Mrs. Gowan tore up another field postcard from That Boy, as she called him. She certainly wasn't going to send it on to Kathleen at school. Why did he go on writing if there had been nothing between them? He'd started it all. Kathleen had not

139

been the same since they came back from France. Of course there was the war. Everyone blamed everything on the war—especially the mothers of girls. How often she lay awake wondering how far they had gone.

Kathleen had stopped being a sweet, nice, obedient little girl almost as soon as they reached England. Boy mad. That was why she had sent her to boarding school. But there were still the holidays. Girls had certainly changed since her time. Flappers. Lipstick. Sitting with crossed legs. She was sure Kathleen smoked. The sooner they could get her married the better. God knows she was pretty enough. Too pretty by half. A regular little honey pot. Boys—even men old enough to be her father—she attracted them all. And her father was such an old fool. He had tried to explain it scientifically. "The girl's nubile," he said. "Old enough to breed." His own daughter. Imagine him saying things like that about his own flesh and blood. Disgusting . . . "All you've got to do, Lilian, is to explain things to her so that she does not let anyone go too far. . . ." How far was "too far"? Knees, thighs, breasts? And how far had they been? How far did a nice girl let a boy go, today? If there were any nice girls left, that is. And he expected her to explain things like that to Kathleen . . . The act . . . Contraceptives. He'd said, "She's eighteen and she'll have to know soon, won't she? Nature takes its course. Nature knows best. Forewarned, forearmed . . ."

She sometimes thought her husband had gone mad. And who was this man Freud he was always talking about? A German Jew. And the things Nils spoke to her about. Things no one had ever even discussed before. Sexuality in babies, masturbation being natural—it did not send children mad. Boys in love with their own mothers—incest—hating their fathers. Fancy telling her things like that! Even if they were true, which she doubted, she did not want to know them.

She felt Kathleen was a rival. Eighteen to her forty, just coming on as she was going off. She did not like having her about. Because, in a good light—that was to say a bad light—she really did not look much over thirty.

At Castlerock School for Girls, Kathleen sulked. She did well in her work because she was clever and could not help it, but games bored her, she felt she was too old for school and ready for life, for men. She wondered about Jimmie. "Keeps your mind off things," Miss Carman said—she meant boys of course. Miss Carman was the games mistress, and looked like it—legs like a piano. Besides, she liked to think about boys. Fancy Jimmie in the army! She'd seen him a few times. On leave from camp. He'd taken her to the pictures. But she had not let him do much. Only that once. That one afternoon at the flat. She was sorry now she had stopped him. And her mother must have guessed something, packing her off to this damn school. Why hadn't he written? There were other boys, of course. He had been special; but she hadn't been smart enough to know it when she'd had him. She'd never forget those few days in France— the hot sands of the dunes, the rabbit-cropped grass, the smell of the hot gorse, the sun on her thighs.

He had said, "You'll write, won't you?"

"If you will I will." She had been coy, coquettish, sure of her conquest, and anyway, she had felt he wouldn't matter much once she was home.

There were other boys. It had just been because he was the only one in France and fun. Fun to see what he would do next. When she got back to London she knew Jim would scarcely be a memory. Just part of those few days she'd spent in France. "We were there when war broke out you know," she'd say. That would make her important. Of course she'd given him her address—Clanricarde Gardens, Bayswater Road. For her it had scarcely been an interlude.

That was what she enjoyed—her teasing power. She knew her parents had no idea of it, nor had anyone else but a few boys. She liked to feel their rising urgency and her own response.

Play, she called it. Fun. Those had been a good few days. She had sent him wild. But what a fool she had been not to have done more. Not to have let him see the whole of her, all of her beauty. And she would have before the summer ended. Bathing,

141

perhaps. Some way, if she hadn't gone home. She had laughed as she pushed him off her body. She thought of her mother saying what a modest, quiet girl she was. "Keeps herself to herself too much." Well, her mother didn't think that now. If only she hadn't lost touch with him. Why had he stopped writing? It was all her mother's fault. She hated her mother. Dad understood her. He said she was going through a phase. He said all girls went through it.

She supposed Jimmie must be at the war by now. My Jimmie. If only he'd write. She did not know his address so she could not write to him. Now she had to change for those bloody games. "Keep their minds off boys." Cricket. Cricket for girls. Good God, how stupid could people be, and it was such a lovely summer! Summer brides. You saw their pictures in the paper, some no older than she, with officers, going under arches of swords and things like that. Cutting a cake with their husband's sword. Summer was the time for love. It had been summer in France. Not think about boys? What the hell did those silly mistresses think the girls talked about?

She had told several of her friends about Jimmie.

"You're in love with him, Kathy?"

"I think so. I'll know if I ever see him again. If he's not dead by now."

"And what'll you do, darling?"

"I'll make him marry me. I'll make him make love to me and get me pregnant and then my mother will agree. That'll be the only way to bring her round."

Dr. Gowan knew his wife very well, her prurient mind, her respectability, her fear of sex, of the body and its reproductive functions. What a disappointment his marriage had been. The pretty, flighty, gay little creature he had courted had soon changed. She didn't like any of that. It had all been an act. Her duty, of course; his marital rights; but to expect her to like it—! There was no love in her, for him, even for Kathleen, for anyone. Perhaps she had loved Kathleen when she was a little girl—so pretty. But that had been as a possession. Like a living

142

doll. "My little daughter." Lilian liked *things*—her furniture, her carpets, her carriage; jewels, pictures, clothes, furs, objects. Luxuries which he fortunately could afford. What she liked to do was to impress people. But she was not a happy woman. He had reached the conclusion that happiness was a talent. Some people were born with a capacity for it, others weren't.

He had liked the Hiltons. George, Mrs. Hilton—smart, self-possessed, pretty. The boy Jimmie, well, good luck to him.

He returned to his manuscript, a study of *Tuberculosis in the Upper Class.*

21 : Armageddon

IN ALBANY the General was raging at the way the war was going.

"It's no good your being angry with me," Irene said.

"I'm not angry with you," he snapped. "But good God! There's going to be a big show and not a chance of surprise. Building up dumps the size of villages. Mountains of stuff behind the line." He was walking up and down the sitting room, his spurs clinking. "Too old," they say. "Just because I retired after the war. Dugout. I'm no older than Haig, and he's a fool. Always was."

My God, Irene thought. Jimmie. A mass attack. And what a good boy he was, writing so much. Well, not exactly writing, but sending field postcards with everything except "I am well" and "Thank you for the parcel" crossed out, and letters a couple of times a month. No news in them. Just that they were in the line or had just come out of the line. It was fine; it was wet. And he'd been riding the doctor's horse—a chestnut. Her name was Ellen. A fascinating piece of information for a worried mother.

Mona got field service postcards from Jimmie too, every week or so.

"I am well." "Thank you for the parcel." Her Jimmie. Her baby. She missed him. And something was up—all the chaps said so—a big show of some kind; and since everybody at home knew about it, so must the Germans. She did not read the papers much except for the casualty lists, looking for the names of her friends. Wounded, killed, missing. Those she would never see again. The wounded she often saw. If they were in hospital nearby and let her know, she visited them.

She had missed Jimmie's promotion. She never looked at the *Gazette*. She just sent parcels and wrote letters in a round, unformed, girlish hand to her friends. Tart? How dare any of those little gold-digging bitches call her a tart? She just had lots of friends. Real friends who helped her, that was all. And she made a home for them when they came back.

When the General had gone, Lady St. John Gore Blakeney burst into tears. Nothing like a good cry. That was June 30th. The next day the papers were full of it. A massive attack had been launched on the Somme to relieve pressure on the French at Verdun.

By July 2nd the news was out. Sixty thousand men dead, wounded or prisoner in the first days' fighting, and it was still going on. One division in two hours of fighting lost 280 out of 300 officers, and 5,274 other ranks out of the 8,500 who had gone over the top. A few days later came Haig's despatch: "To sum up the results of the fighting of these five days on a front of over six miles . . . our troops swept over the whole of the enemy's first and strongest system of defense. They drove him back over a distance of more than a mile and carried four elaborately fortified villages. . . ." It went on and on. Official. A cold statement of fact. But it had cost England 100,000 of her finest troops, of her finest men, the very flower of the kingdom.

How man women's beds would be for ever empty now? How many wombs? And what effect would it have on the

144

future, with the cream of England's stock skimmed off from the breed it had taken a thousand years to make?

How many women were crying, mourning their dead and those about to die, because the battle was still going on, and on and on. How many dead? And how young they died! Oh God.

She looked at the war map of the Western Front on the wall. They had moved a tiger's skin to hang it. The front line was marked with little flags on pins. Whenever the General got home for a day or two he checked them. Now he could move them again. Half an inch, perhaps, on a six-mile front. It would hardly show even on a big-scale map. And a hundred thousand gone to gain it. She went to look at the map again. She recognized the names mentioned in the paper: Montauban, Fricourt, La Boiselle, Ovilliers, Thiepval, Beaumont Hamel . . . Well, let the General move his bloody flags. War was a man's madness. It had nothing to do with women. She poured herself out two fingers of whisky. Bloody flags, indeed. She laughed, on the verge of hysteria. She had never sworn before she married the General. All those dead and no word from Jimmie. Every ring of the doorbell frightened her. Even if it wasn't this one, the next one might be a "Regret to inform you that Lt. James Hilton is . . ." Is what?

Her eye caught the German helmet Jim had sent them as a wedding present. They'd had to move a lion's head to put it up. How pleased the General had been with this kind of soldier-to-soldier present. All it did for her was to make the war more real.

Every morning when Mona got up she fetched the milk and the paper from outside her front door, washed, combed her hair, made up her face and put the kettle on for tea. When it was made she took it into the bedroom on a tray with the newspaper and woke her friend of the night.

"A nice cup of tea?" she'd say, looking very pretty in a lacy dressing gown, her hair over her shoulders and her feet in high-heeled mules. Pretty, delectable, ready for it. If he wanted it again. Sometimes they did and sometimes they didn't. Aubrey

Wentwood always did; left her a tenner, and even sent flowers. Roses, carnations, lilies, "With love from Aubrey" on a card in a little envelope. He was a rich man. How Jimmie's ring with a girl in it had made him laugh. It made everybody laugh.

They seldom wanted to look at the paper. She took the *Telegraph,* but never looked at it herself till they were gone and she was alone. If they had time she gave them breakfast and ran a bath for them like a wife or a valet. She wanted them to feel at home—"A Home from Home" was her motto.

Austin Philips had left at teatime yesterday, after a final whisky and soda. He was in the Royal Scots and wore Tartan trews that always amused her and annoyed him because they were the First Regiment of Foot—a very old regiment. Famous. Well, famous or not, tartan should be made into a kilt and not trousers. She liked kilts. She had several Highlander friends. Like lightning they were, with so little to take off, and the sporrans were pretty too. Jock McLeod used to make her wear his sporran when she had nothing on.

"Makes you look decent, my lass," he'd say. White fur, eighteen inches long, hanging between her legs. White angora goat fur, with black tassels. "A bloody fine figleaf it makes, covers your nakedness and natural-looking in a way."

If she was alone she bathed, had breakfast and then opened the paper. She had to be made up, dressed and have breakfast before she could face the casualty lists. The columns of names in small print. Cavalry, Foot Guards, Regiments of the Line, Artillery, Engineers, Army Service Corps—all under headings. Dead, wounded, missing. Missing, believed killed. She skipped the regiments in which she had no friends.

But today it did not work out like that. Giles Berwick was out of bed as soon as he heard the paper boy drop the paper at the door. A moment later she heard him swearing. "Christ all bloody mighty! Christ! Christ! Mona, just look at that!" He plunked the open paper on the bed. The casualties took up pages, column after column of them. With a trembling forefinger he pointed to his regiment. "Look at 'em! Jesus, just look at 'em. The bloody lot have gone west. The buggers have done

146

it again—sent us over against uncut wire. I've seen it, Mona," he sobbed. "I've been in it. Men hung up, skewered on the wire, trying to get through, the machine guns mowing them down like scythes cutting corn. The staff," he said. "They should send some of those bastards over with us, just to see what it's like running up and down under fire, looking for a gap that isn't there."

Mona pulled him down to her bare breasts. She put a nipple into his mouth, succor . . . All a woman could give a man was her body. A woman's body had held him for nine months in its womb, had fed him with its milk and then let him back into it twenty years later. This was her instinct—to hold him. To get him to take her if she could. If he could. And he could. "Yes," she said. "Yes, Giles!"

"Yes, yes!" he said. Brutal now. "And I'm going to fuck you, and then I'm off." He drove into her savagely, left her and began to dress. No bath, no shave, no nothing. He emptied his pocketbook on to the bedside table beside the pink lamp with the bead fringe.

Mona was crying now. No one had ever spoken to her like this before. All her friends were gentlemen. Gentlemen friends. "I don't want it," she said. "And your leave? You only got back yesterday."

"It's no bloody good to me, girl. I'm off."

"Off where?"

"Off back to the bloody war," he said. "And that's the last one before I'm killed. The last bloody fuck, the last bloody woman." He went out, banging the door behind him.

Mona went on crying quietly. She did not dare look at the paper. Not at all those pages of dead, of wounded. Men—how could you understand them? You'd have thought he'd have been glad to be out of it. And that language . . . "last bloody woman." She never thought of that before. For how many of her friends had she been "the last bloody woman"?

22 : The Roll of Honor

THE CASUALTY lists of the Somme battle ran into pages in the papers. The roll of honor.

The Germans had been ready for them, waiting for them when they came. And why not, when in every public house in England people had been discussing the big push for months? Why not, when immense stacks of war matériel had been building up behind the British lines since spring? A bombardment such as the world had never seen preceded the attack. But much of it had failed to cut the wire. Wire could not be cut by shrapnel, and the gunners had been short of high explosives. The shelling also failed to kill the Germans in their deep dugouts and out they popped as soon as the barrage lifted.

They knew all about this in England days before the troops who fought the battle, but the civvies read the news differently. The papers described it as the first phase of a victorious battle. But the troops knew bloody well better. Another effing muckup. You couldn't fool the men. Not for long.

The 10th Wilts L.I. spent a month in the trenches near Bailleul. After the raid the action had been stepped up—patrols, night raids—the whole division was being hardened up. Out of the line there were long marches with full packs and training attacks from dummy assault trenches. They'd be for it soon.

Then the rumors of disaster became a fact. By now more than a hundred thousand men had been chucked away. The story of the Serre attack came out.

Jim thought about the other platoon commanders in the company. Morland had been a rubber planter in Malaya. Telfer, articled clerk to a solicitor. Bolton, an older man, a stockbroker. Jim got on well with them all. Not that they saw much of one another, with one on duty and the other three sleeping, reading, writing letters or censoring them. Turn and turn about, four hours on, eight off. They had meals together in the company dugout: tinned soup, steak and potatoes, and vegetables if any were sent up from the transport lines; stew—bully beef cooked in various ways but still remaining bully; Maconochie, prunes and custard, tinned peaches with Ideal Cream; tea, coffee; marmalade, the eternal plum and apple jam ration; whisky and port. They drew army rations like the men and supplemented them with mess purchases, the cost divided among them all. And there were the parcels they got from home. Morland was a great reader; his wife was always sending him books—Nelson sevenpennies, bound in blue and red—that he passed on when he had done with them. Telfer stuck to poetry; he seemed to derive great comfort from it. He always carried a little leather-bound copy of Palgrave's *Golden Treasury*. They received newspapers, too. That was how they got the war news—a lot of bloody lies—about how well things were going, the splendid courage and morale of the troops, and so on. Balls.

Jim lived in curious and impersonal intimacy with these men. They seldom spoke of their lives, their homes or their ambitions. All these things were in abeyance for the duration. They had hardly even spoken of their war experiences. They were over and buried, and they did not want to dig them up again. Their thoughts they kept to themselves, but there was a curious bond between them—a close, yet abstracted kind of love. As if they knew they must soon face a terrible ordeal together. They talked about the men, about rations, about rum issues, about foot inspections, lice. They laughed easily at themselves and one another. They told dirty stories, the do-you-know-this-one kind. Bolton said most stories were invented on the stock exchange; a lot of good brains—very bright chaps—hanging about with bugger all to do. Limericks. "There was a young plumber from Lee, who was plumbing a girl by the sea" . . . "A fucking machine, concave or convex, to suit either sex . . ." Dozens, hundreds of them. They were safe. No memories in them, no hopes, no nothing. Just words. Words, because men were social animals and had to talk. No one was stand-offish, but no one was ready to give much of himself in case it got lost. If you gave a lot of yourself to a chap and he went west, you'd lost something.

When Telfer was killed, for instance—shot through the forehead by a sniper—only Dashwood went to look at the body lying on a stretcher with an army blanket over it, and he only went to get his watch and the things in his pocket to send to his mother. Another parcel marked deceased officer's effects. Then he wrote another of those I-am-sorry-to-tell-you letters . . . "I can assure you he did not suffer, being killed instantaneously. He was a very gallant young officer of whom you have every reason to be proud. Yours sincerely, L. Dashwood, Captain, 10th W.L.I."

The I-am-sorry letters, Jim called them. Always the same formula. For officers and men. Could they be any comfort to the recipient? Even if they had died in agony, they always said "no pain . . . instantaneous." Formula words. Always words.

But in spite of these contacts with others one still lived isolated, insulated. Of course in a sense you were always alone though you did not realize it when you were a kid, tied by an unseen prolongation of the umbilical cord to your mother's womb. But his mother's remarriage had fixed that one. Her letters seemed very happy.

What at first had seemed a marriage of convenience—that of a widow to a husband who would mitigate her loneliness—had turned into a love match. Good God! It was a strange thought that your mother could want to be slept with—screwed. There was something indecent about the idea. But that was absurd. Of course she had been lonely, and she wasn't old. Not really old.

Still, those thoughts about his mother worried him. He felt they were wrong but she had really brought them about herself by descending from her pedestal. The Madonna separated from ordinary life by the chasm of filial respect had become a woman

150

of flesh and blood whose impulses and desires resembled his own. In some ways this would make things easier between them. Not that their relationship had ever been strained, but in some obscure way this had put them on the same adult level. He also saw what a lot she had given up for him.

He supposed everyone was lonely unless they were married, or sleeping with a girl they knew well, like Mona. He was not lonely with her. Was sleeping with a girl the only answer? That did not seem to be enough. Certainly the chaps who went to a brothel were still alone when they came out. All they had done was to take the edge off themselves, reduce the manhood that was bothering them. But it came back. To protect yourself, you had to have an intimate association. A Mona. A Kathleen. What a fool he was to go on writing to her when he never got an answer.

There was one thing about the line here—cut into the chalk, it was dry. But the top soil was shallow and the shells burst on percussion, instead of going deep into the wet clay before exploding, as they had on the Salient, which made the shelling much more dangerous. The company dugout, sunk into a quarry, was comfortable and relatively safe. The men were able to carve themselves little niches—seven-foot kennels in the chalk of the parapet. The communication trenches were deep and in good condition. The shelling was only moderate, both sides having sent most of their guns to the battle that was raging to the south. They could hear them. The noise of the conflict never stopped; day and night the guns rumbled on.

That was their destination. It was in the back of all their minds. The trench routine continued. Stand-to at dawn and dusk, patrols, carrying parties. Mail. Rum issues. Foot inspection after route marches. A short-arm inspection, embarrassing to all concerned. Jim wondered how the hell he was supposed to diagnose venereal disease from this curiously indecent exposure. Circumcised, uncircumcised; large, small; tools, cocks, pricks . . . held by roughened hands, like pale sausages sticking out of the men's flies. What were you supposed to say? You just wondered at their diversity and thought of where they had been used. What women? Pretty women. Ugly women. Any bloody woman.

Then the orders came. The division was to march south. Colonel Robinson read out a message from the Brigadier—another kind of "England expects . . ." job, as if Brandywine was Nelson—and two days later they were off again.

The military road, built by Napoleon, ran straight as a bullet between lines of poplars with grass verges, dusty with chalk but untouched by the war, the poplars like twin lines of men, converging and getting smaller, minuscule, almost touching in the distance, as if they came together in fear, for company, as they approached Armageddon, the greatest battle the world had ever seen. Then they marched into a wounded land, turmoiled; its green grass-and-crop skin plowed and pitted, poxed, still littered with half-buried dead and festooned with rusty wire. The land that the war had passed over leaving its backwash of debris.

Soon the fresh new shell holes would begin. In another hour or so. Big holes. That was how it was. Peacetime roads leading to war, as the peacetime days had all unsuspecting led up to it. Then more shell holes and the battalion began to march in single file, trudging along the torn-up verges with the road between them, the khaki almost invisible, the single fat snake of a column of fours split down the middle into two long, thin worms, weighted with the impedimenta of action: sandbags, shovels, rockets, bombs, extra bandoliers of ammunition, even baskets of carrier pigeons, all having been dished out to them from a roadside dump—the paraphernalia of modern war.

The packs grew heavier with the heat each hour as time contracted. Each halt brought them nearer to the false safety of communication trenches—avenues, facetiously named, that led twisting like bowels to the support and front lines. This was the worst part, marching in the open within easy range of the German guns, the fear of being caught in the open, not yet hidden like rats in a ditch protected by walls of earth; this was the cumulative moment when all the various fears that had been building up became one—this last hour between the relative but

152

diminishing safety of behind the line, and the relative but understood danger and discomfort of the line itself. It was like saying goodbye: one wanted to get it over. Like being with a strange woman in that curious interval of time in which social exchanges turned into sexual action. Jim still felt it even with Mona, in spite of the number of times he had had her.

The dark had fallen. There was no sound of marching boots, just the creak of equipment, the rattle of side arms and entrenching tools. The sharp sound of a shouldered rifle hitting the edge of a steel helmet, and the smell of sweat—fresh sweat that was not only due to exercise. And old sweat. And dirt. There was very little talking. An occasional curse as a man stumbled. And then suddenly they came to a shuffling halt. They must be meeting the guides. In a few minutes they would be in the communication trench. When they stopped the guns seemed louder. They had been hearing them for hours but were so used to the noise that they hardly paid attention to it while they were moving.

Jim ducked as a heavy shell went over his head. The whole front was a pale salmon rose along the horizon, like a sunset. The rest period was behind him, behind them all; the fattening-up period. Soon, in a couple more hours of marching along the duckboards in the communication trench, they would be there, taking over from the battalion they were relieving, with nothing but wire and a few hundred yards of ground—if they were lucky—to separate them from the enemy. The Germans.

But this was different from anything he had ever experienced or imagined. The communication trench ended suddenly and they were out in the open, led by guides over duckboards set every which way between the edges of shell craters. They passed field guns standing almost wheel to wheel. There was an overpowering smell of the unburied dead—German, British, of dead horses and mules. He had smelled death before in the Salient, but these had only been dead a month or so. They appeared to be going through what had been a wood. Against the red glow of the sky, the trees looked like thick, snapped-off pencils, their stumps fragmented into spikes white as bone. The shell holes were full of mud and water. If you stepped off a duckboard you went into mud up to your knees or your neck. You could be drowned in it.

At last they got into a trench again; they had crossed a number of duckboard bridges to get here. This must be the front line. An officer said, "You the Tenth Wilts L.I.?"

"That's us," Jim said.

"Well, file along to the left. You're going over with us tomorrow. We're the Sixth North Kents. This is the assembly trench." So it was not the front line; that was two hundred yards ahead. Where the flares were going up—German magnesium flares and British Very lights—making it almost as light as day. This was what they had seen from farther back, like the light reflected in the clouds over a town. But they had been in dead grounds then, the actual line invisible.

Dashwood came round a traverse. "Get your men down, Jim. They'd better eat the unexpended portion of yesterday's rations and get some rest. We're going over with the North Kents before dawn, zero four-fifty, barrage at four-thirty. It will pound the German front for ten minutes and then lift and go on to their support line. Get your men into no-man's-land as soon as the barrage starts; get them on to the tapes. The RE have laid them out. The Boche will drop everything he's got on this trench when we start—if not before."

"The wire," Jim said, "is it cut?"

"They say so, but we'll soon find out, won't we? My God, they didn't give us much of a rest after the march, did they?" Dashwood went on to make contact with the next company.

Jim supposed the same thing was in every soldier's mind. The wire: was it cut or wasn't it? The Germans had very thick iron wire, ungalvanized, with long spikes. To attack over the top you took your chance, but to get there and find yourself held up by the wire, running along it under machine-gun fire, trying to find a gap, that was something no one ever forgot, if they lived to remember. He thought of Dashwood's description at Loos. It all looked so simple on the map: red line, blue line, green line; first wave, second wave, mop-up operations. Just words on paper that bore no relation to the reality.

But he could not get the wire out of his mind. Loos. The disaster at Serre only last month. He found Hargreaves talking to Lance-Sergeants Goodby and Mulholland. "Well, sir," Hargreaves said, "looks like the high jump. I've issued a rum ration and I'll dish out another one when the barrage starts. Puts heart into 'em, poor buggers." Goodby laughed. Hargreaves said, "Excuse the language, sir."

"You only expressed my own feelings, sergeant-major." Jim felt that none of the four of them were really there. "Men resting?" he asked. He did not want to feel his way along the line which was packed with troops squatting on the fire step, some even asleep on the duckboards.

Hargreaves said, "Some is sleeping like babies; some is praying, some cursing, some smoking. It takes all sorts, sir."

"It does indeed." What a ridiculous conversation. He looked at the luminous black-faced dial of his watch. Eleven pip emma—almost five hours to go.

"There's one thing," Hargreaves said. "We're going over in light fighting order and carrying nothing but our weapons. They've learnt that, them brass 'ats 'ave. We're dumping all the stuff we brought up. When the barrage lifts, sir, I've told the men to run like hell; we want to get in before the Jerries come up out of their 'oles. Then we'll drop a couple of Mills bombs, dumpity-dump 'opping down the steps, and push on to the right till we meet the North Kents. Do you agree with that, sir?"

"My God," Jim said, "I always agree with what you say. You're the old soldier here." Hargreaves took Jim's forearm and squeezed it. "You'll be all right, sir. I seen you in action when you was still wet behind the ears, as one might say."

"Thanks, Hargreaves. But I've got the wind up. This is a big show, and last time we were in it before we knew what was up. No time to think. We didn't know so much then."

"Don't worry, sir. You've got a good platoon."

Private King, at his elbow, shoved a flask into his hand. "Have a mouthful, sir. I pinched it from the mess."

Hargreaves said, "I've detailed Philips and his mate as your runners. They know you well, sir, them being the leading file and marching behind you. They're good men. I've detailed two bombers and two bayonet men to stay with you, sir. All good, the best we've got. Because if there's a German communication trench you'd better lead your party up it. I'll see to the line itself. Me and Goodby."

God damn it, they were still looking after him like a bloody kid. Just because he was only nineteen. The best bayonet men, the best bombers. Runners. His servant an old soldier. Tears came to Jim's eyes. He loved these men. He was much closer to them than to his brother officers. They were like children themselves. Simple soldiers, as the French called them.

Four hours, three hours, two hours, one hour. Forty minutes. The men were standing by, their bayonets fixed. Bolts were being opened and closed as they loaded. He heard Hargreaves say, "Put on that bloody safety, lad, and don't forget to take it off when you're over."

Jim had just lit another cigarette when the barrage started. The whole German front was aflame with bursting shells. The field guns were blasting the wire with high explosives. Over them, rumbling like trains, the heavy shells fell in the German support line. The whole earth shook and trembled.

Five minutes. Four. Three. Two. One. Zero.

"Come on!" he shouted. No one could have heard him but those nearest to him saw him climb the assault ladder out of the trench. A moment later they were all out, keeping a good alignment, almost a man to a yard. They plowed on till they came to the white tape in no-man's-land the engineers had pegged down. Here they lay while a sheet of flying metal passed over their heads. They were only just in time because the Germans were bracketing on the trench they had left.

Jim looked at his watch. In three minutes the barrage would lift. He watched the second hand go round and round. Seconds. Time. How valuable time was!

The barrage lifted; it was almost quiet. They must get to the German trench before the machine guns opened. "Charge!" he shouted, and ran forward. He fell and King pulled him to his feet. They were in the wire. It was cut. Shredded. The bombers pulled the pins out of their bombs, lobbed them into the trench, waited for them to explode and then jumped down. They had just been in time. The Germans were pouring out of the dugouts. King fired and charged in, his bayonet driving a German back; then, standing at the mouth of the dugout, he poured rapid fire into its deep, steep throat. "Give 'em a bomb, Jack!" he shouted. One of the bombers rolled a bomb down the steps, underhand. "Bumpity-bump, oppity-op," Jim found himself saying, as he led the way on.

They came to a communication trench. "Come on, chaps!" He led the way up it, a bayonet man just in front of him, going around each bend with the utmost caution while the bombers lobbed their bombs over their heads. More dugouts were dealt with and then they were blocked. The Germans had set up a light machine gun in the communication trench itself.

Suddenly Jim saw Goodby on the top out in the open. He knocked out the machine gun, dropping a bomb in the trench almost at his feet. He flung himself down till he heard it explode, then he led the men who had followed him on. When Jim reached the gun the crew was all dead and the gun smashed.

Some Leicesters under a subaltern came up from the rear carrying wire and a Lewis gun. "I'm going to set up a post here," the subaltern said. "We're the second wave. I'll hold it. You'd better get back and support us."

Again, as in the Salient battle, there was no shelling. The shells from both sides were going over them, as they always did in a confused position, neither side being sure what had been gained or lost, while counter attacks were being mounted.

Sergeant Goodby's men were following him like dogs. He was the man with a charmed life—wildly, recklessly exposing himself. First in everything and never a scratch. Bullet holes in his tunic, his tin hat blown off his head once. But never a wound.

The reports of what had happened were coming in. After Lance-Sergeant Goodby had knocked out the machine gun he had gone in with a bayonet, followed by his party. There had been no one left to kill so he had led his men up a communication trench, again over the top, lobbing his bombs down the dugouts as they passed them. When they had used up all their bombs, Goodby brought them back, in the rear of his party this time.

"This should get him an MM, Hargreaves," Jim said.

"Try for a DCM, sir."

"All right. He deserves it."

"Do you know something, sir?"

"Know what?"

"It's a queer thing, sir. Them as wants to get themselves killed can't do it. And that's what he's been trying to do ever since the day I brought him in to see you, sir. But he's not despondent no more, sir. He's right cheerful, sir. He's happy because he's found a way out, he does not mean to go back to Blighty. He's a killer. And murderous, now. And such a quiet chap he was. Wot I mean is, sir, I'd not send him back with a batch of prisoners today. I don't think they'd get there alive. He goes out alone at night and lies out there quite near their wire, hoping to get one. And he has, according to his chaps. But he never reports anything. By God, what a woman can do to a man, sir! Turn him into a savage beast. Though he's gentle enough with his boys."

All this going on in his platoon and he had known nothing about it.

A runner came up with an order to consolidate the German trench and hold it.

23 : Aftermath

THERE WAS one good thing about a German trench. The dugouts were deep. Sixty foot and more. Since they always held the high ground they were dry, and generally well furnished with looted stuff—beds, chairs, chests of drawers, pictures, even tapestries and carpets. Cozy. Snug as bugs in a rug. Officers, and men too, with their rows of beds, safe even from a direct hit from a heavy. Of course they all faced the wrong way and so were open to the German shells. The parapets had to be reversed, a firestep dug in the parados which, by the trench's capture, now faced the enemy. But the trenches were good, from eight to ten feet deep; narrow, with plenty of traverses.

It had taken a little time to haul out the Germans who had been killed by the bombs they had dropped down the dugouts' narrow throats. To some death had come fairly tidily, but others had been blown apart into bits and pieces that had to be shoveled into sandbags. Jim's new home still smelled of blood and explosive, but it certainly gave you a sense of security; of otherworldliness. A mole world of earthy silence. The construction was beautiful, the sides of the dugout were riveted with heavy balks and divided by bulkheads. Clothing hung on pegs. In the HQ dugout there was even a green-tasseled cloth on the table and a vase of roses, brought from a back area, that had not been upset. There they had stood in the cut glass, beautiful, fragrant, right through the battle. It was this kind of paradox that gave war its terrible poignancy with their memories of peace. Roses, the singing larks.

But there were rats here too. Enormous, bloated, fearless. They sat up and cleaned their whiskers within a couple of yards of you. Some of them were blotched pink with a kind of mange in big hairless patches. They lived on the army refuse and the dead. Some must weigh a pound or more. There was a vermin control section at division that put down poison—a bloody lot of good that did. He supposed the Germans had one too. But they bred up again to full strength and more in a couple of months. He'd seen figures somewhere—two rats could produce 100,000 in a year, or something equally fantastic. Nothing seemed to bother them. Shells. Gas. Enough always survived to breed up again. Meat-eaters. Dead men—English, German, mules, they didn't care. They bit the men, too, when they were asleep. He'd been bitten himself. One must have been walking on a beam of a dugout when it was shaken off by the vibration of a near hit. It had landed on his face and he'd snatched at it in his sleep; woke up pretty sharp, though, when it bit him in the hand. The stretcher bearer had put iodine on it.

"No telling what it's been eating, is there, sir?" No telling indeed, but a bloody good guess. Strange to think if you got scuppered out there in no-man's-land that that would be the end of you: unconsumed portion of the rats' rations. Loathsome, gray, furry, with long scaly tails. A war was just the thing for them. Their cup of tea. Rats, lice, crabs. Vermin. Camp followers in every war. They'd probably bitten Roman legionaries in their time. By God, that was one of the worst things about it: trying to keep clean. The officers were much better off than the other ranks, but they still got lousy. The other thing he hated was going to the latrines. They were always set at the end of a short T-trench. Piss-buckets and a deep ditch with a pole over it on which you sat with your pants down. Bumph, Bronco in your pocket, if you didn't run out and have to use newspaper. The stink of fecal matter—shit, in other words—and chloride of lime. "All fecal matter to be covered with chloride of lime. . . . Steel helmets not to be used for culinary or other purposes." How many of the men knew what "culinary" was? Other purposes? Don't cook or pee in your tin hats. He sometimes wondered who wrote the orders. "Our allies, the Portuguese, are not to be referred to as 'the bloody Portuguese.'" The Portuguese had sent a token force to the Western Front, but most of it was said to be in hospital with venereal disease.

By God, having a crap in war was a frightening affair. Suppose you were hit and fell into it? Your bowels were always loose with fear. It was in the Bible. Bowels turning to water. Three thousand or so years ago, that was. Men hadn't changed much, had they? But the sooner you finished and got your pants on again, the better. And it wasn't easy to balance on a pole, like a monkey on a bloody stick, with shells going over your head like bloody express trains. No place to sit and read the jokes in the *Pink 'Un*. Up, Guards, and at 'em! That was Wellington at Waterloo. Up pants, and out of this bloody place, Jim boy! Hurry up, my lad! These were things people at home didn't think about. How could they visualize any of it? Even Dante would have made a poor job of describing the front line in the Great War that was to end all wars.

He met Goodby when he got back into the trench.

"Glad to see you back, sir. I always worry when you've gone in there."

"So do I, by God!" They both laughed. Some things were funny when they were over.

Sometimes when he was there he thought of Mona's pink-tiled bathroom with a pink toilet-seat, pink paper and a woolly pink mat at his feet. Natural functions. But even a latrine was better than going in the open in a battle. That really put the wind up you.

It took them about twenty-four hours to finish the consolidation of the German trench: digging a firestep; setting out wire; making repairs with sandbags that a carrying party had brought up the line—"and I heard the relief had come." About time too. A battalion of Northumberland Fusiliers, the Fighting Fifth, had taken over the line.

Some ground had been gained. The battalion that had gone over the top six hundred strong had suffered two hundred and fifty casualties, seventy-five of them killed. Out of twenty officers, only ten remained. Dashwood had taken over as second in command. Hardy had been badly hit and Jim was the only officer left in D Company. Telfer had been the first one to go in Bailleul. Now the others had gone too. Planter, stockbroker, tinker, tailor, soldier, sailor, rich man, poor man. Colonel Robinson gave Jim command of the company and put him down for a temporary captaincy. He had also recommended him for a regular commission.

But the action, it turned out, had only been a demonstration. There had been no intention of driving any farther into the German line. They had demonstrated to take the pressure off a bigger push on their right, a push that had failed.

But the final big drive before the winter set in was still to come. They were going back to rest and fatten up again. Get a

161

new draft and wait for the real thing. As if seventy-five dead were not real enough.

The march back in daylight was a nightmare. Dead men, British and German, lay scattered. Putrescent, swollen, covered with a black fur of flies that rose when disturbed and landed on their faces. Delville Wood, smashed to matchwood, was filled with dead South Africans and the Germans who had failed to dislodge them. Bodies floated bottom upwards in the mud of big shell holes. Trones Wood was splintered. How absurd it was to call them woods. Equipment—tin hats, rifles, bandages, scraps of paper. The smell of rotting dead, of gas, of lyddite, of chloride of lime, of excreting dirty men. The smell of war and the noise of it.

Jim's mind went back to the action. Once you were in the German trench it was all right. You had no time to think, it was just bomb your way along and hand-to-hand scuffles in passages cut through the chalk. Kill or be killed. Something helped you then. Age-old inherited animal courage. You stopped being a man, a human being. You pushed on. You shouted—not that your voice could be heard in the inferno of bursting shells, bombs, rifle and MG fire. You left your wounded when they fell. You walked on the dead. You consolidated, set up Lewis gun posts, reversed the trenches, digging out new firesteps; blocked your flanks with wire. Only then did the reaction set in. You thought of your own men. How many were hit? How badly? How many dead? How many prisoners and walking wounded to be sent back? There were ammunition and bombs to be checked. Rations. Water. It was always the same. You wondered how often you'd come through something like this. You prayed to Mr. Luck. How many officers were left, how many NCO's? You went among the men. "Good chaps! Well done, boys!" They were cleaning their rifles, reloading; wiping the blood off their bayonet tips. Arranging their bombs neatly, like black fruit on the parapet, ready to fling. And it took them all differently. Grim; laughing; hysterical with excitement; in tears at the loss of a mate. Paranormal, the bloody lot of them, drunk with the smell of powder, of cordite, of lyddite, of blood;

162

turning out the dead Jerries' pockets for souvenirs. He'd seen a dead German officer with his ring finger cut off. Not one of his chaps, he hoped—at least no one knew anything about it. A gold wedding ring, put on who knew how long ago, and now in some British soldier's pocket; Mauser pistols that could be fitted with a wooden stock and fired from the shoulder; Zeiss field glasses; wristwatches; pornographic pictures—naked girls and men copulating in front of a camera, a funny thing to be found dead with; photographs of women, girls, children, houses, horses, dogs, cats; letters in sharp, spiky German script—how he wished he could read them . . . maps. All scattered with broken equipment, rifles, potato-masher bombs, bloody bandages. What a bloody mess there always was! The dead pushed over the parados out of the way—their own and the Germans. Brothers in death.

That was battle: hundreds of dead and wounded to capture a few hundred yards of useless ground. A village that was no longer a village, just a map reference. But they'd call it a victory in the papers, and the "business as usual" bastards at home would move their little war-map flags. Proud of their soldier boys. The bastards. And then back to it again. Would the wire be cut next time?

Jim began to think of his mother. His mind kept going back to her. He was sure she had had a couple of affairs while he was at school. She'd been very careful in the holidays but she had introduced him to men who had called her Irene. She'd looked different and dressed differently. And there had been things in the house he had never seen before and which he was sure she would never have bought for herself: a gramophone with a great big horn, a silver cigarette box, bottles of scent on her dressing table. But he'd had to grow up himself, had to know Mona to find out how much women wanted love; needed it. But he had not really thought of his mother as a woman till she had married again. From this distance in time and space he could even see that she was a very pretty woman, with a girl's figure, pretty legs. The little gray in her fair hair only turned it ash

163

blonde. He could imagine a man wanting to touch her. She had a kind of Dresden china beauty. Touch her, and go to bed with her. Well, good luck to her. He wondered if he'd ever tell her about Mona. He doubted it. She'd guessed there was someone, of course. She'd told him to be careful. He knew what she meant. Not to get some shop girl in the family way, or pick up a dose of clap. They didn't have to cross their t's and dot their i's. He supposed there was a certain indecency in his thoughts. Wondering what she was like naked, what she was like in bed. Vaguely incestuous, but funny in a way. Especially under these conditions. Still, just fancy his mother sleeping with a divisional general . . . Whenever he saw a general—which was not often —he thought of it, and wondered what would happen if he asked him if he knew his stepfather, General Sir John St. John Gore Blakeney of the Greys. He probably would. So many of them were cavalrymen. The old peacetime army had been a pretty closely knit affair, especially among the crack cavalry regiments. It was an amusing thought to play with. Mother and the General. Mona. Kathleen. The woman with hot eyes and a baby at Bailleul . . . Goodby came into his mind. He was a full sergeant now. He wondered if he'd got over his wife running off with another chap. Hargreaves didn't seem to think so. She seemed to have been something special, a competition dancer— pretty, vain, weak. Slight, no doubt, slim. Thistledown on the dance floor. Poor bastard. Perhaps a man was better off with a run-of-the-mill girl. Nice-looking, no more than that. Mona, for instance; if she hadn't been so pretty she would probably be leading a respectable life working in an office or a shop. And Kathleen. How his thoughts kept coming back to her, God damn her!

He wondered how many other men's wives, besides Goodby's, were being unfaithful to them. They got home so seldom. Their separation allowances were so small. What temptations there were for a pretty young woman who missed her husband. Money, companionship, sex.

But there was one thing about a war—you certainly grew up

quickly. There was no bloody nonsense about war. It stripped men down to their essentials. He marched on.

They had been out of the trench for some time now and in the open on duckboards that twisted, crooked as a dog's hind leg, between the shell holes and the dead, who lay grotesque as broken dolls. This was another wood they had come through in the night on the way up, but like the others, the wood had disappeared. It was impossible to believe that these shattered stumps had been trees so recently, trees bowing before the wind, leaning toward one another in leafy conversation, their leaves turned upward, rustling before rain, drooping in summer heat, changing color and falling, driven by the autumn winds. Courting couples had walked hand in hand beneath their shade, made love on the cushioned leaves where the dead now lay.

He felt no respect for the dead, not even his dead friends, for they were gone. What was left was carrion, to rot, to be buried later neatly in the ordered rows behind the lines or powdered with shoveled chloride of lime if there was not enough left to be sent back. A body was an *it,* a thing. The he-ness, the maleness, the spirit had gone out of it. It, they, were things to be cleaned up, got rid of. He was convinced dead Germans smelled different, that one could even recognize them in the dark, the way a dead horse smelled different from a dead mule. A matter of diet, he supposed, though horses and mules drew the same rations.

He picked his way along the duckboards that led through the matchstick trees. They wound about like an idiotic snake, avoiding the biggest shell holes, bridging the smaller, and behind him came the men, stumbling and cursing.

As long as one was at war the future had no real existence. Even tomorrow was in doubt. Even this evening: tonight. There was only boredom and immediacy. And fear. But once in action there was no fear, only a kind of terror that turned a quiet man into a maddened killer. But cold, ice cold, if he wanted to live. Oh, a man must walk delicately in battle, with eyes at the back of his head. He must not think of himself, only what the enemy was doing or likely to do. He must put himself in his skin, become, as it were, his own enemy, to save himself. Besides, to lead troops a man must cease to exist as a person. He had to be a brain, a maker of decisions on which the lives of his men might depend. And all the while inside himself he knew he was not dependable, that it was all an act, a question of balancing responsibility against fear, of doing a kind of arithmetic while one wondered if the sum would turn out right. But you seldom got a second chance. It was all by guess and by God, with the laws of luck playing their haphazard parts.

A hand stuck up out of the ground, the fist clenched in pain or anger. A hand that had fought, caressed, loved; that had written letters, cut up food, played with toys in childhood, with the hair of women. But now the hand and forearm were isolated, a kind of symbol. As if in the end this man had refused to disappear in his entirety. Sunk, drowning in the earth, but refusing to go. Of all the dead Jim had seen, this hand struck him the most; differently, because the others had been whole men or shattered men. This was different. Dry, sun-cured, gnawed by rats. Also it was anonymous. It had no sleeve. It wore no uniform. It was neither German nor British—unidentifiable—just the arm of a dead man sticking up out of the ground, the earth, as if in protest at burial. No earth to earth for him. A clenched hand challenging the sky, stiff as a stick. Stiff as a prick. A man, neither friend nor foe; a stranger waving out of the earth as a man might wave out of a railway carriage—goodbye, Godspeed. Or drowning out of the sea. A final gesture of defiance.

24 : The Pleasures of Love

THERE WERE pleasures out of the line when the battalion was resting. Getting really clean, getting better food in the mess, having meals at *estaminets:* omelettes, ragouts—*civet de lapin* in which he was sure a cat sometimes replaced the rabbit—

steak and chipped potatoes. He still kept away from the women —afraid of disease, and unable to stomach their coarseness. Great country girls, who offered themselves for sale, their little brothers often pimping for them: "My sister . . . jig-a-jig. Very good . . . young . . . very cheap." They smelled of bad scent and stale sweat. He had been spoiled by Mona for anything like these black-cotton-stockinged parodies of sexual attraction. They were merely temporary vehicles, to be used, to serve a certain purpose. But he liked eating and drinking in the company of other divisional officers at a café. There was generally someone who could vamp the popular tunes, and they'd all sing. It was very gay. Fifty or sixty young men in the prime of their valor, men already shaped by the millstone of war, trying to forget it by the classic means of food, wine, women and song. And succeeding, too. Still effervescent with the optimism of youth; each invincible, always sure that some other—not he—would be killed. And, by God, it was true too. Even when they were hit they could not believe it. Not me. Men dying, calling on God, saying "Mother, Mother," cursing, crying; dying grim and silent, or fighting to the end like lions brought to bay. What a variety of ends he had seen, each man different. Guts, cowardice—all wrapped in the same parcel. Another bottle—*vin rouge* . . . *vin blanc* . . . Whisky . . . Here's luck! Cheerio! Down the hatch! *Prosit!* Wine that gave you hope and courage and was metamorphosed into piss.

Then there were the transport lines. He spent a lot of time with the horses and mules. Sixty-four animals to an infantry battalion—draft animals and chargers—from all over the world: the United States, Australia, the Argentine, England. Millbank, the transport officer, had been a rancher in the Argentine, a valuable asset because some of the mules were Spanish-speaking and only he could handle them till he had taught the drivers a few words of Spanish, and the animals learned some English. Bloody funny that was, in a way, when you came to think of it. Millbank told him about the pampas, about gauchos; of how they had more than a hundred color names for the horses—a bay with a star, a roan with a black mane and tail, a chestnut with an off-white sock—all different. Millbank had been born there, an Anglo-Argentinian. He was always delighted to talk horse with Jim.

The CO sometimes let him borrow Rajah, a bright bay waler, almost clean bred and very excitable—unmanageable to anyone with bad hands—but a beautiful ride. On Sundays, when the divisional band played in the Grande Place or at some cross-road, Jim liked to listen on Rajah's back. The horse danced—sidestepped, crabbed, bucketed—to the music, shaking his head from side to side reaching for his bit. Alive, from the tips of his pricked ears to the nails in his shoes. Beautiful, sentient—a kind of equine poem.

Then sometimes, in open country, he rode down partridges. If you put up a covey and galloped after them, keeping your eye on them, you flushed them again. They never made more than three flights, but they were easy to miss as they cowered in the grass. It was fun to gallop with the wind roaring in your ears, to feel the horse stretching himself between your knees; fine to be on cultivated land again—fields of grass, clover and corn stubble; on land undesecrated by shellfire, unblemished; to see trees that were still trees, with leaves and branches; to trot past peasants working in the fields. But even this back country had been fought over in other wars, and earlier in this one when the action had still been fluid. Horses . . . men . . . war . . . women . . . fire . . . blood . . . death . . . loot . . . rapine. That was all history was, but they never taught you about it at school. A town was taken and sacked—that was what the men had fought for. Given the license, the troops would do the same today. Men had not changed much in the last few hundred or even a thousand years. Here they were, two Christian nations at war with each other. And yet they did not really want to fight. Look at the fraternization that had taken place at Christmas in 1915 in some parts of the line. Tommy and Jerry exchanging rations, smokes. But they had soon put a stop to that—they, the brass hats. The generals who sat safe in their châteaux with their maps.

168

Jim was filled with hatred for the men who manipulated the troops. He realized that this was one of the things that came between him and his mother's new husband, though he might like him as a man when he met him. They lay so bloody clean and cozy; they lived so well. Present arms. General salute. Lancer escorts with little red and white flags on their lances. Pennons. Shined-up bandoliers, all spit and polish. All spurs and jingle. Looked down from their tall horses on the Poor Bloody Infantry that did the fighting for them. Some of them must be all right, he supposed. He'd heard of brigadiers going over the top with their brigades, and parsons too. But he had never seen one do it. Only the RC's with the French. Religion. C of E. RC. Other denominations. If you were other denominations, you got off church parade. Words, all words. "Onward Christian soldiers, marching as to war." Of course they were. *Gott mit uns. Gott mit* everyone. God was everywhere, even on a battlefield. He wondered what God made of it all. God was love. What kind of love? Not his kind with Mona, oh no! You needed a bit of paper for it. A license. A license to own a dog or screw a girl.

He patted Rajah's arching silken neck, slacked his reins and tightened his knees and they were off, the ground unreeling beneath the pounding hooves, the wind in his ears, the birds in the air. This was the last day of it. Tomorrow they'd be back into it again. Make the most of it. A wide ditch opened in front of him. The horse rose to it, beautifully.

It had been wonderful to get out of it for a few hours. You could forget it on the back of a good horse—or the belly of a girl. He was sure he'd forget it all when he got back to Mona.

The battalion moved off at a run. The ground they covered had been fought over since the first of July. Tons of metal had plowed it so that the shell holes lay lip to lip, round gaping mouths of liquid mud in which the old dead lay drowned, and the living, who slipped off the duckboards, held on to them for support. The duckboards, insecure, slippery, greasy with mud, wound their way over this strange pitted sea, a crawling wooden

169

serpent along which the troops, loaded with equipment, staggered like a line of harvester ants.

Shells landed on the already wounded ground, sending up great spouts of mud as they burst beneath the surface. Geysers that shot straight up into the air grew into black trees that disintegrated as the fragments, losing impetus, began to fall. But the shells did little damage. These once fertile fields were beyond hurt now. They had no hard surface skin; it was all one great scrofulous, pockmarked wound—miles of it, as far as the eye could see or the imagination reach. The Germans might as well have been shelling water!

And the ants went on through the shelling in single file, a distance of five paces between each laden man. Each isolated, their slow forward movement the crawl of a multisegmented insect, a khaki caterpillar moving over a brown carpet of mud into the wood. At least what was marked as a wood on the map.

It was a place of horror. Like all the others the trees sheared off, smashed, their scarred trunks splintered into giant toothbrushes, or knocked down, flung sideways, their roots extended —dark fingers to the summer sky. The place stank of the gas that hung in the shell holes as, vaporized by the heat, it rose to join the reek of the unburied dead.

And the shells were still coming over; woolly bears—high-explosive shrapnel—that burst into the long, black, fat worms tinged with the green and yellow of lyddite fumes that gave them their name. But worst of all were the almost inaudible thud and pop of gas shells that cracked open on contact to liberate death, to set it free on the soft summer breeze. All more terrible, more terrifying, when seen through the fogged-up goggles of a gas mask. Each man alone, his companions unrecognizable; hooded, helmeted men from Mars. Each with a tube like a jointed bowel, like the covered spring of a child's jack-in-the-box, leading from his covered mouth to the filter on his breast. Strangers to whom one could not speak or give an order. Ciphers in khaki, hooded like hawks, half drowning in their own spit. Men no longer in their anonymity; bloody great

170

ants, inexorable, slow, in the glutinous mud, only alive till death did them part from it. From life as if it was a possession. That was an idea. It was not just a woman a man was married to, but to his own body as well, to the life of it. To the blood and sperm in it. So there were two marriages in man's life, and the first was to himself.

A single magpie, long-tailed, white, bronze and black, flew past to perch unperturbed on a broken stump. Birds flew above the gas that was heavy, only rising to the height of a man.

Men's primary weapons had always been sexual: daggers, swords, spears, bayonets. All instruments of penetration, to make men and kill them. To force something that was part of you into something that was not part of you, and thus make it yours. Your woman, your corpse. That was why Jim had been so frightened till Mona had taught him. The first woman, the first man you killed.

The magpie rose and flew on with its long-tailed, dipping flight. One magpie was unlucky. Unlucky for whom? It might be him this time. Two were lucky. He wished the goggles on his helmet were not so fogged up; perhaps there were two magpies. And how the hell were you supposed to see where you were going? That, of course, was the idea of gas. Bewilderment, fear, panic. And it was getting dark.

This ground had also been fought over two years ago. The crumps were turning up French bodies in long blue coats and red trousers. You got glimpses of them in the shell bursts; you trod on them. There was a lot of old half-cut wire about. A piece caught Jim's foot and he fell. My God, onto a dead man. He'd put his hand right through his rotting guts. He pulled himself up and wiped his hand on the back of his trousers. Smelled his hand—he couldn't help doing it—then retched and threw up. He rinsed his hand in a shell hole full of water with shells going off all around him with big spouts of earth. He got the worst off but it was still there under his nails and around them in the cuticle. Tears of rage and frustration came into his eyes as he ran to catch up with his men. Thank God they were out of the gassed area.

"All right, sir?"

"I'm all right."

"Afraid you was hit, but we was told not to stop to assist the wounded. I wanted to but the corporal said 'no,' so I went on."

"The corporal was right. Jenkins, isn't it?"

"Yes, sir. Private Jenkins. Glad to see you, sir. It's hard not to stop, ain't it?"

How curious this was, conversing as they moved forward. The shelling had slowed up and you could hear yourself speak again. He smelled his hand once more. Christ, how long would it be before he got it out? Soap and hot water. Jeyes Fluid. He wondered if he had a cut from the wire on his hand, if he'd get blood poisoning. What a way to die! Blood poisoning. Killed by a Frenchman who'd been dead for years himself.

He picked up a bayoneted rifle from beside a man who had been killed in the first wave, opened the bolt, ejected the round in the barrel, watched another rise from the magazine as he closed it, and went on. He never carried a rifle now, he just picked one up. But it felt good, with his right hand on the small of the butt and his left hand over the barrel. He was raging with fury. The bastards, the bloody bastards.

Back again through Trones Wood, Bernafay, Delville, still full of dead South Africans—six hundred left alive out of three thousand. Villages. Montauban, Carnoy, Fricourt. All were blurred in Jim's mind. March, countermarch. Exhausted, rest and back again for more of it. Officers, NCO's and men were killed, wounded and out of it before you even learned their names. No time for regret-to-inform-you letters. Just field service postcards to his mother and Mona saying he was well, knowing he might be dead before they got them, postdated ten days and more ahead and left at the transport lines.

"Send one each day, Quarter."

"I'll do that, Jim."

Hargreaves, Mulholland and Goodby were still all right, though Goodby should have been killed a dozen times. The

172

three of them. Brothers. Very close. Contracted, tied into a tight bundle by the other casualties. Musical chairs with the guns for music. Drums. What the French called drumfire with their quick-firing 75's. They shook hands when they met, he and Goodby, Mulholland and old Hargreaves. Bugger discipline. They were survivors, wishing each other luck. Out of the line they saluted, of course. But they smiled as if they knew something special. "Nothing with your name on it today, sir."

"No, not today." But such luck could not last. The law of averages could only be defied for just so long.

King was all right too, and so was Philips. The men stayed close to him as if he was some kind of bloody mascot. Sixteen was supposed to be a lucky platoon what with him and Mulholland and Goodby. But it put the wind up you. Too much luck was dangerous. Anyway, they should be all right for a week or two, they were going into the training area again.

For the life of him Jim could not have described the last weeks in detail. They had been too confused. He was too shaken by what he had gone through. Attacks. Over the top. German counterattacks. Night marches. Day marches. Barrages. Dead and wounded men. The noise, the stink, the exhaustion that had to be conquered by will power. Legs that must be made to march.

They were going to Carnoy and then to some camp. All he had to do was to keep going.

25 : The Secret Weapon

ON SEPTEMBER 15th the rest was over. They had been fattened up again and were going back. This was going to be it. What they had been waiting for. Victory, this time. All ranks felt it. Something special. There was a rumor that a secret weapon that would end the war was going to be used. This time they were going to break through: Bapaume and Combles were just the first objectives.

Again as they went up Jim felt the curious rhythm of marching. Once a march began it gained momentum like the flywheel of a machine. The boots of it, the 1,200 odd boots gripping the road like cogs. The battalion, a long mechanical snake, winding; a giant toy articulated, wound up, by the key of its orders, without a will of its own.

Since July the war had lost its purpose. Marching, countermarching. Up and back again. Fighting, losing men and picking up strangers. New faces, new names, all men with their own lives, professions, jobs. But each isolated from the others, cut off. Replacements of broken parts neatly fitted into this war machine. The battalion, part of a regiment that had a history, a long life detailed in the battle honors of the colors that hung in the chapel of the depot. Old flags scarred with wounds, torn, that had once gone to war like the Eagles of the Roman Legions which had also, in their time, marched these same roads. But now they had a new purpose. A new resolve, or the old one revived. They were going to get their revenge. This time they'd show the bastards.

Columns of cavalry, infantry and guns marched through villages where women, holding their children, watched these strange men file past. Left, right, left. The men sang "It's a long way to Tipperary . . . Farewell, Leicester Square . . ." Six hundred-odd men singing as they marched to war. They sang "Little grey home in the West" and "Oh, oh, you beautiful doll." Jim thought of the time he had played it over and over on Mona's Decca, waiting for Maurice to finish making love to her so that he could begin. It was strange how a man could share a woman who was not his wife. It must be because they all kept her and she was not the exclusive property of one. A select kind of club whose playing field was a bed.

As they marched through Carnoy an astonishing sight presented itself. Thousands and thousands of horses stood in saddled rows with slackened girths, the troopers standing or sitting beside them. The sunlight glistened on the steel points of the lances, the groomed horses, shining, metallic. Probably there had never been so many beautiful horses assembled in one place before. The cavalry was waiting for the breakthrough the infantry was going to make.

So the rumors had been right. They must be going to use some new secret weapon that would smash all resistance. Break through. The cavalry would flow like water into the gap and fan out to cut all communications. The end of the war was in sight. September 16th, 1916, was a day that would never be forgotten.

The fighting here had been over long ago. The shell holes were grown over with grass, the roads repaired. They passed immense tarpaulin-covered dumps of ammunition, of food— advance casualty clearing stations in marquees. They were signposted. More dumps. GS wagons. Limbers, guns, all on the move. Troops everywhere. All moving forward, up the line.

The sound of war, and the smell of it, and the shouting of the captains were like some strange aphrodisiac. Even the sight and stink of the dead. The half-sweet putrescence of their broken, ridiculous bodies. Even the torn and ravished earth was symbolic of some hidden cult. Furrowed by shellfire instead of plows, manured with dark human blood. A fertility rite, each soldier a possible sacrifice. Each counting on his luck, some charm, a medal given to him by a girl, a fetish found somewhere and carried with the feeling "as long as I have this on me I'll be all right." Me, not anyone else. Only me. Because battle drew each man into a terrible isolation of self-consciousness; and yet not even that, for even the *me* was unreal, not really there, yet part of the whole. A cipher in a great chess game where whole regiments were pawns.

But war, like love, clarified the mind, releasing it from the body. Setting it free to wonder, to watch its own exertions and sufferings with the objectivity of God. In battle, when the guns opened up, there was a kind of exultation. The deafening noise, the bursting shells, the smell of high explosive. The power of it, as if man had said, "Christ, now we'll show God what we can do."

175

They marched on. The neat buildings and farms were behind them. There were signs of recent shellfire everywhere: holes, sagging roofs, gaping glassless windows like the eye sockets of skulls; trees blasted, the earth torn up. The murmurs of gunfire had turned into an intermittent roar. Before long they should come to the emplacements of the heavies.

Jim was overcome by a curious tenderness for this vast concourse marching to death, to victory. This time there was no question about it. But what was this new weapon? Well, they'd find out in God's good time. Tonight they were to be in Bapaume. They were to hold it while the next wave of the attack leapfrogged them and the cavalry poured through.

The roads leading up to the line merged with the battlefield, they melted into the mud and were littered with the debris of war: smashed limbers, dead horses and men. Dead men on stretchers. A screaming horse standing on its forelegs, its back broken. They passed staggering wounded feeling their way to the rear. Over it all a canopy of shells going in both directions.

They entered a communication trench called Skittle Alley, an alimentary canal that carried the food and wastage of war. A throat and a gut. Flowers—red poppies, red as blood, and marguerites with he-loves-me, he-loves-me-not white petals—leaned over the trench.

Zero hour was 10 A.M. Then they'd go over under the umbrella of a barrage. Ten minutes to get into the German front line with the barrage bursting fifty yards ahead of them. The shelling increased as the trench wound its way through another splintered wood of toothbrush, toothpick trees. They crossed an old German lined filled with troops. There was a smell of death, of the unburied dead. More bits of equipment and a broken stretcher lay on the top of the trench. There seemed to be hours of monotonous marching over duckboards between chalky walls before they reached the line where the Leicesters moved to the right to make room for them. The men were very thick in the assembly trench, almost shoulder to shoulder.

Nine-thirty, nine-forty, nine-forty-five. The rifles were loaded. Jim gave the order to fix bayonets. As it was passed down he could hear the steel being ripped out of the scabbards. Nine-fifty—ten minutes to zero. The British guns opened with a frightful scream, a horizontal curtain of noise that passed over them. Field guns firing shrapnel that burst in the air above the German trench, heavies sending up great spouts of earth, French 75's that had been lent to the British cutting the wire, firing so fast that the whole German front seemed to be going up in one continuous explosion.

Jim lit another cigarette. How many had he smoked since they had reached the line? Nine-fifty, nine-fifty-five. Five minutes to go. His eyes never seemed to leave his left wrist. Nine-fifty-eight, nine-fifty-nine. Ten. Jim jumped on to the firestep, put his feet onto the pegs that had been driven into the trench wall, was up and out in the open. Nothing in front of him now but Germans. He felt rather than saw the men beside him. They walked on under the barrage, walked quite slowly toward the exploding inferno in front of them, their rifles at the high port, their bayonets bright in the sun. As soon as the barrage lifted on-to the German support line, they'd charge. German shells were bursting in no-man's-land and above it. Crumps, 5.9's, woolly bears. No one was to stop for the wounded. On. On. And then he heard them.

What the hell was that, a noise he had never heard before? Great wedge-shaped iron monsters on caterpillar tracks were among them. The secret weapons.

The men were closing on them like chicks around a mother hen. And they were drawing fire. He saw one get a direct hit and burst into flames, but the others went on. They were about a hundred yards apart. The barrage lifted. He blew his whistle, no one heard it, and he began to run. The wire had not been well cut. The men bunched, ran toward the iron monsters that would flatten any wire. They did. But two of them stuck, straddling the trench, their caterpillar treads revolving, unable to get a grip.

But they were through. Jim jumped down into the German trench, his men behind him. They were into the first objective; running along it they bombed the dugouts and took prisoners. There was no resistance. The line had been lightly held. But when they used their assault ladders to get out of the deep German trenches, they were swept back by fire from the pill boxes of a strong point to the left. Jim saw two tanks swing toward it. Both were knocked out. There were not enough of them. If they'd had a thousand . . .

What they had to do now was reverse the trench and wait for dark. There were no orders; the line the signalers had laid was cut twice, repaired and cut again. The second wave that should have leapfrogged them had not come. He sent out two runners but got no reply. The stretcher bearers had patched up the wounded. He'd evacuate them when night fell. The prisoners he'd driven out, much against their will, into what had been no-man's-land to find their way back to the barbed-wire prisoner's cages behind the British line.

"Got the list yet, sergeant?" Sergeant Mulholland looked beat. There was mud and blood on his face. Not shaved, of course. No one was shaved, but he was a dark man and it showed more. Dirty too, all of them. Mud, blood, torn uniforms, the lot.

"The list?" There he was getting his bloody little book out of his pocket. The bloody list. Bloody was right. That was what it was. Dead, wounded, missing. The missing dead too, blown apart, most likely. Not much left of a man with a direct hit.

The sergeant held out the little black book with its carbon paper showing. Jim could hardly bring himself to look at it. In one way he was used to it. For every show they'd lost men—twenty-five percent, thirty, fifty. How the hell could you help it? You got used to it in a way. Besides, he didn't know many of them. Strangers. New drafts. New to it, poor bastards, except for a few who'd had blighties and been sent back. Old soldiers. Old soldiers at eighteen and twenty.

Bloody veterans, like me, he thought and almost laughed. If he laughed he'd break down. So they'd failed again. The secret weapon was a secret no longer. And it would have done the trick if there had been enough of them. A rotten fuck-up. The cavalry could not get through today. Not today or ever. And this was not the last battle.

26 : The Little Black Book

"NOT TOO good, is it?" Jim said, still not looking at the names, only the pencil-written pages in the book Mulholland had given him.

"No, sir, best part of one hundred and twenty in the company and you're the last officer."

"Captain Dashwood?" he said. In command of the battalion since the colonel had been killed. Major Hardy was hit. Captain Fenwick had been killed. Johnson was missing. Christ! He had no idea it had been so bad.

"We've lost some good ones today, sir. Some of the best."

"Any of our chaps?"

Mulholland knew what he meant. Men who'd come through the other attacks the way they had.

"Two, sir. Smith and McDonald."

Good ones. Christ! The best. Smith was only seventeen. A baby, a bloody brave little baby who threw bombs like cricket balls. Public school boy. Ought never to have been allowed to enlist. Westminster. Last summer he'd been playing cricket, in the First Eleven. "Well played, Smith." McDonald was thirty, married, with two kids and expecting a third. He knew that from the letters he'd censored. Write to her, he thought. And Smith's mother. Next of kin. How many more would he have to write when he had time?

Mulholland's list would go to battalion headquarters with his report. Brigade, Division, Corps. There'd be telegrams, hundreds of regret-to-inform telegrams from the War Office. Telegraph boys all over England ringing bells while loving letters from home were still on their way to the dead.

He began thinking about the wounded. "We can't get the wounded away, can we, Mulholland?"

"Too many, sir. We can't spare the carriers even if we had the stretchers."

"How many are there? In round figures." It was easier to ask than to count them, going down the page with his finger. He didn't want to see the names. Names were people . . . men . . . figures were abstract.

"Forty hit bad; eighty walking wounded. We'll try to get them as can walk to the dressing station if things gets slacked off a bit."

"None missing?"

"No, sir, not in our lot."

It was not going to be easy with all the company officers gone.

"I saw Mr. French killed, shot in the throat," King said.

There were men grouped around them, listening and fiddling with their rifles.

"Sentries posted?" Jim asked.

"Yes, sir."

"Then we'll have a look at the wounded and go down the line. Are the flanks in touch with us?"

"The right flank, sir."

"I'll take a couple of men and see what's going on on the left, then."

"We're pretty thin, sir, with only twelve men left."

"Fourteen with us."

"That's about it."

"And our company front is a hundred yards?"

"More, sir. We don't know how far away anyone is on the left."

"Can you spare two men to go with me, sergeant?"

"You can't go alone."

"My runner was hit, you know. Philips."

"I've got him." The sergeant tapped his little black book.

"I'll take King, and who's a good bomb-thrower?"

"Davis, now that Smith's gone."

"All right, Davis. We'll pick him up as we go along the line. Close the trench behind me with some wire and set up a Lewis gun in case there are some Jerries in with us."

"How'll you get back?"

"I'll shout."

The men stood like exhausted horses with bent knees. "Come on," the sergeant said. "Spread out—six-yard intervals—and lie down on the firestep. Get some rest before the bastards come back. No dugouts." He knew if they went to ground they'd stay there.

One of them drove his bayonet into a sandbag, pulled it out and looked at the point. "That's better," he said. "I 'ates blood on me things." The other two laughed. "God all effing mighty, 'e 'ates blood."

"Well, you've come to the right place for it, chum. Blood and mud and shit and piss. Right bloody picnic." They all laughed.

"It's me own blood I 'ates," the first man said.

They were tired, exhausted, nearly hysterical with fighting and killing, at being survivors, saved somehow. Showed they were special, that did. Select. No effing bullet or shell with their names on it. Not today. Not yet, anyway.

"Get a bloody move on," the sergeant said. "Spread out a bit—six-pace intervals, I said." He turned to Jim. "Come on, sir. I'll show you the wounded and we'll pick up Davis and some bombs."

They went down the trench, the sergeant, Jim, and King who had never left his side. Like all German trenches it was deep, the dugouts good, but the British heavies had done their work well, with some direct hits right in the trench. In other places both the parapet and parados were blown in. The sentries had cut notches to stand in. "We'll reverse the firestep tonight," the sergeant said, "and get some wire out in front of us if any comes up."

Rations, wire, ammunition, bombs, rum. That was what the men needed now—a rum ration. "Get some tea brewing, sergeant." A bit of char—tea—bully, biscuits, that would see them through.

"I've got a man going through the Germans' stuff, sir. Maps, letters, orders, food too. Black bread, tinned meat. One chap even had some bananas in his pack. It's a hell of a time since we saw a banana. I got one saved for you, sir."

"Eat it yourself, sergeant."

"Come on, get that bloody bugger out of the road!" They came round a traverse to find two men standing on the firestep struggling with a German body. They had got him up, a big gray doll with a sagging shaven head, and were rolling him into what only this morning had been no-man's-land. "Be a hell of a stink here in a day or two, sir," the sergeant said. "If we had more men I'd like to bury them while they're still fresh."

"Don't worry about reversing the firestep, Mulholland."

"Why, sir?"

"Because as soon as its dark we'll get out and lie in the open, fifty yards or so forward. Once they know they've lost this trench they'll plaster it and counterattack. They'll have the range to a yard."

"By God, that's an idea, sir. And when they come we can give it to 'em."

"Glad you agree with me, sergeant."

Jim had a great respect for Sergeant Mulholland. Like Hargreaves, he was an old sweat with both Boer War medals, an MM and twenty years of service behind him. One of the Old Contemptibles. If he hadn't had a taste for the bottle he'd have been a sergeant-major.

They passed more German dead who had been dragged off the duckboards and leaned sagging against the walls of the trench.

"Here you are, sir. Sick bay."

Some were sitting up. Others—the badly wounded—were lying on German stretchers covered with German blankets. " 'Ullo, sir. Blighty. That's wot we got. Anyone at 'ome you want us to give your love to?"

Blighties. A lot of them would never reach the dressing station. Simpson, the only stretcher bearer who had not been hit, was with them, giving them water and putting lighted cigarettes into their mouths. "No stomach wounds, Simpson?"

"No, sir. Chest, back, arms, legs. Lucky, ain't they? Going

182

'ome too." He winked. Keep the truth away from them. Let them be happy while it lasted. Some of them wouldn't last till dark.

"Well, we got 'ere, sir," Hawkins said. "But the buggers could fight." He had his arm in a sling.

"Saxon Guards," Jim said.

"Buggers!" It was a man he didn't know, one of the new draft. They were taking it well. But the worst was yet to come for them. Their flesh was bruised by the impact of their wounds, the nerves numb. Later it would be different.

"Going to get us away, sergeant?" Hawkins asked. "I'm sick of this bloody war. Want to go 'ome to the missus and be a bloody 'ero. Wounded 'eroes, that's wot we are, chums. Bloody wounded 'eroes." There were three bays of wounded.

Jim raised his hand in greeting, in goodbye. Well, living or dead, they were out of it now. When the carrying party came up with the rations they'd take them down. When they came. If they came . . . The Germans were shelling heavily behind them.

"The dead?" he asked.

"In the next two bays."

There they lay. In neat rows side by side, on either side of the trench.

They went on and found Davis. He was with Clarke—Nobby—one of the old lot. "You all right Nobby?" Jim said, taking his hand.

"Fine, sir. And what about you?"

"Fine, thank you . . ."

"Well, done it again, sir. But there's not many of us left now. You and Sergeant Mulholland and me, and Humber. That's not many, is it sir?"

"Not many, Nobby," Jim said, and they went on to get the bombs. There were two sandbags full a bit farther along.

"This is our last sentry," the sergeant said.

"How far along the trench did you go, sergeant?"

"A hundred yards or so. Then I thought I'd better get back and tell you."

"Bring a couple of men and some sandbags. Block the trench here while I'm away and set up a gun and have plenty of bombs ready."

Jim was thinking about the wounded.

"Get the walking wounded away as soon as you can, Mulholland. And the badly hit into a dugout. Mark it in some way and leave a man with them."

"How many men shall I leave here, sir?"

"A couple. Now we'll go on."

"Good luck, sir. And take care." Just like his mother. Like Mona. Take care of yourself, Jimmie.

Take care. How the hell did you take care?

27 : A Dirty Picture

THIS KIND of thing put the wind up you. The three of them were quite alone. What was there in front of them? What kind of a Jack would pop up out of the box?

There were a lot more dead here—Germans and British, chaps who had been killed fighting hand to hand. No one had cleaned the trench up. It was as the battle had left it. A wounded German killed as he bandaged himself. Others lying in every direction, in every position, with bloody bandages unwound on broken duckboards and the mud. Broken weapons. Papers. Photographs. German newspapers. How the hell did all this stuff come adrift?

King went first, his bayoneted rifle shortened as he peered around each traverse. Behind him came Jim, pistol in hand. Behind him Davis with two bombs ready. Nothing. Nothing but the dead. No wounded. The German wounded must have got away.

They came across a dead officer. Jim searched his pockets.

Letters, papers, a trench map. They'd wanted stuff like this at Brigade. Second Saxon Guards. The man's name was Captain Wilhelm von Alven. He looked about thirty. He had good teeth, very good teeth, big teeth like a horse. He looked back and saw Davis taking a signet ring and a watch from his wrist. Loot. No looting. But what was the good of leaving things on the dead? He pretended not to see. They must have gone four hundred yards before they heard a challenge.

"Halt! Who are you?"

"Tenth King's Own Wiltshire Light Infantry."

"Advance, King's. But no bloody nonsense."

Some Germans talked good English. Been waiters. Been teachers. You never knew. He was quite right to be suspicious.

"Wait," Jim said to King. "Cover me. I'll go alone." The voice might be a trick, too. But it wasn't. It was the Rifle Brigade. He had made contact. "Take me to an officer," Jim said. "Sit down and rest," he said to the men.

"How far away are you, sir?" the soldier asked.

"Four or five hundred yards."

"Christ! Then our flanks are open."

As they walked down the trench, Jim said, "You're thin on the ground, too."

"We fair copped it," the rifleman said.

"How many have you got left?"

"A couple of hundred, they say." They passed more riflemen.

"The officer's farther down," Jim's guide said.

"What's his name?"

"I don't know, sir. He's a new bloke. Ours copped it."

They found him twenty yards away—a lieutenant. "Well," he said, "this is nice. Dr. Livingstone, I presume." He was a tall, slim young man who had come through the battle but still looked neat.

"I'm Hilton," Jim said. "Tenth King's Own Wiltshire Light Infantry. We're on your right, four to five hundred yards away."

"I'm Hartley, Sixtieth," the young man said. "Five hundred yards? That's a nice gap, but it doesn't really matter. We're covering a mile with two hundred men." He had been looking at

185

a photograph when Jim came on him. He showed it to him. "What do you think of that for a bit of fluff?" It was the photograph of a naked girl. Slim, beautiful, with long fair hair. It was signed: *"Deine Liebe Trudi."*

"Where did you find it?"

"In the German colonel's pocket. Too good for Intelligence, don't you think, Hilton? But I did send them most of the dirty pictures. He had a lot of them in another pocket. Sacred and profane. The right-hand pocket not knowing what's in the left sort of thing. But you know, I don't think Trudi need worry, do you?"

"Not with that shape."

"I didn't send all the pictures," Hartley said. "I kept a couple. Two lesbians making love. Soixante-neufing. Pretty, aren't they?" He gave Jim the photograph. They were blondes in the position he described. Slim young girls reversed on each other.

"And this one." The rifleman gave him a print, postcard size, of a dark handsome woman, nude but for high-button boots that reached to her thighs. She had a dog-whip in her hand.

"Takes all sorts to make a world, doesn't it, Hilton? But things like this are interesting when found on a dead man in a battle."

"Little girl lesbians. Flagellation by a dark woman. A beauty too, in her way. And then I suppose, when he was all worked up, the adorable Trudi." Jim laughed.

"I wonder what my mama will say if I'm killed with these in my pocket and they're sent home with my stuff. But they wouldn't do it. Too bloody tactful. And they'd want them for themselves. But it would do her good. Mama, I mean. An abominable woman who murdered my father with her Victorian chastity. Interesting thought, isn't it?"

Jim said, "I think I'm going to lie in the open tonight. In front of my trench."

"Not a bad idea."

"Well, now we've made contact I'll get back to my chaps."

"Good luck, old boy."

"Same to you, and love to Trudi."

Coming back along the line, it looked different. The bodies looked different, lying at different angles the way scenery does returning down a strange road. And they were the scenery, about all that differentiated one fire bay from another. Bent, twisted, crumpled men. No, not men, bodies in field gray and khaki, decorated with medals of blood and mud. The real war medals that decorate the brave. And the less brave, men who are there only because they have to be.

Jim passed the dead Saxon Guards officer with the beautiful white teeth again. Funny the way one looked at the teeth in a body. Like a bloody dentist, he thought, as he stepped over him. Of course, the mouth was generally partly open. Even the most determined jaw sagged in death. And teeth had a certain fascination. They remained the same. They were indestructible. The same in death as in life. A human skull did not look very human, but the teeth were just as they had always been. Exposed in a grin of death.

If he took his men out into no-man's-land and the Germans attacked, he'd surprise them. If he put two Lewis guns on his left flank he could enfilade them as they poured through the gap. They'd do that. It was the line of least resistance—of no resistance.

"Hi, there!" he shouted as he reached the trench block. "Hilton patrol coming in."

"Come in, sir." Mulholland was waiting for him. "You found them, sir?"

"Yes. The Sixtieth Rifles, five hundred yards away. What's your news?"

"Bad, sir. Captain Dashwood's been killed. Direct hit. While you were away."

"Then who's commanding the battalion?"

"You are, sir."

"No. Not again. It couldn't happen again."

"And the battalion's down to two hundred men."

"Good God!" It was not possible. Four hundred-odd casualties and all the officers. "Rations?" he said.

"Some have come up. And water." Jesus, that filthy water in five-gallon tins, never properly washed out, that still tasted of petrol and chloride of lime.

"Any rum?"

"Yes, sir. I issued it and poured the rest away, except for a water bottle full. I kept that for you."

"Thanks."

The battalion . . . My God! Try and form a strongpoint, a square of linked shell holes. Because if they came he'd have to fire in all directions. Stand like a rock in a flood.

"Ammunition?" he asked.

"Yes, and bombs and a little wire."

"Thank God for that."

"And I got the walking wounded away, sir, and others into a dugout."

"The dead?"

"They're buried."

"How did you manage it?"

"I didn't. A shell blew in the trench on top of them. Salvo of five-nines. Direct hit. You were right, sir. They've got us taped."

"Then we'll get out as soon as it's dark. How are we off for NCO's?"

"Fair, sir. Two sergeants, four lance-sergeants, eleven corporals, two lance-corporals."

"Hargreaves?" he said.

"Dead, sir."

So they had got one of them. Their run of luck was ended, more of them would go now.

"But Goodby is all right, he was asking for you."

He hadn't been able to ask about Hargreaves at first. It had been an effort. He had been afraid to ask.

With Hargreaves gone west life had changed. As Company sergeant-major he had seen more of him than ever since they shared the company headquarters. Hargreaves had, in a way, become a kind of father to him. It was his company but Hargreaves had always been there in the background. In addition, he was the first of them to go. The run of good fortune was

188

broken. They were no more immune than anyone else. Mr. Luck was getting sick of them.

Who would be next? Himself? Goodby? Mulholland? King? Carter? Pulling himself together he said, "We'll have to dig in the open, Mulholland."

Dig in the dark, tie some shell holes into a little knot with trenches three or four feet deep. String what wire they could. Set up the Lewis guns. Bomb posts. He saw it all as a picture in his mind, with Trudi—her long fair hair, her breasts, her navel—as a backdrop. An artist's model, perhaps, or a show girl, because she was shaved.

Well, this was it. Death or glory. You couldn't have both and might have neither. He had no feeling about it. He was very objective. By tomorrow or the day after it would be over. They'd be dead, relieved, wounded or prisoners. He had no worry about the men. They'd fight. What he proposed was something like the old-fashioned British square that had stood up against the might of Napoleon at Waterloo. It would be all right in the dark. But if no reinforcements came up during the night to close the gap they'd be blown to hell in the daylight. He sat on the German firestep to write a dispatch to Brigade.

10th Bn KO Wilts L.I. reduced to one officer and two hundred effective other ranks. Proceeding after dark to advance one hundred yards and dig in. Gap five hundred yards to 60th on left, four hundred to Leicesters on right. Please inform artillery. Map reference A/7–3/6 approx. Will endeavor to form strongpoint and wire in.

J. HILTON, CAPT.

18 hrs 16.9.16   Comdg. 10th KOWLI

He tore off the sheet, checked the carbon copy and gave it to Mulholland to send back to Brigade by runner. He felt tired but well. Strong. With so many dead he felt no regrets. One could only be sorry for a few people. A man, five men—not hundreds. Besides, he had not seen them hit. In action one didn't notice it. Even Philips, his runner. He'd seen him shot in the chest and go down but it had not registered. He couldn't understand it, nor understand himself. A queer elation that had come over him at the thought of action, of being in command, if only for a few hours, of a battalion of the King's Own Wilts L.I. This was a real test.

He wondered who would be sleeping with Trudi tonight. With Mona? Would there be a letter from his mother if the post came up the line? Would he be alive to get it? A pull of rum had put fresh life into him and the desire to get it over with. Win or lose. Live or die. He went down the trench to talk to the men, to find Nobby Clarke and ask him to be his runner.

It was all a question of time. He was happy because he had survived. He had read a line somewhere—"The old men know when an old man dies." The old men felt superior, as if they had some extra quality. Well, in war, everyone was old. In a day of battle more took place than in a lifetime of peace. A friend killed an hour ago was separated by such a vast sequence of events, by so much action, fear, emotion, so much tension, so much adrenalin released into the blood that a man's actual constitution might be changed; his whole temperament. The first time under shellfire, the first attack, the first man you saw wounded, the first blood other than a cut finger; the first man you killed, the first friend you lost. The first time you were wounded. That had still to come. But this luck could not hold for ever. So many firsts. An hour ago was years ago. He was nineteen, and an old man. The men knew he was an old man, survivor who had the necessary experience to help them to survive. Two things only. Kill and survive. That summed up war. But the balance had to be exact. If you took too much care of yourself, you were a coward. If you took too many chances, were reckless in your killing, you died. It was all very simple, really. Absurdly simple. The only death he'd really felt was Maurice's. Because he'd been at home then, where death was still abnormal. Maurice and the others he'd served with for a year, the bloody lot of them almost, officers, men, NCO's. And now Dashwood had joined them, cut to pieces. He'd cried then, because he was so much younger. The war months that were to be like years were still in front of him. He had still wondered about himself. Still afraid of being afraid. Of course he was afraid at this moment, and always, but so was everyone else. He had not known then that you could ride fear like a horse and master it.

"Be your runner, sir? Yes, sir," Nobby said. "Be glad to. The two of us. We know wot's wot, we does. Old sweats."

Old sweats. He was young enough to be Nobby's son.

Hargreaves's son. Daddy Hargreaves was dead.

Who was fucking Trudi in Berlin tonight?

She was as real to him as Mona. As real as if he had touched her smooth hairless belly and had her. Carter brought him back.

"Seen 'em come and seen 'em go, sir, that's us."

Jim turned, worked his way to the middle of the battalion with Nobby Clarke behind him. Curious. They'd go into battle together now, he and Nobby; and King, his servant. Together till death or a wound parted them, like marriage. In an hour it would be dark and they could get out. Christ, how tired he was! Suddenly. Sleepy. And the men too. Change sentries every hour. But there'd be no sleep for him or Mulholland and the other NCO's. They'd have to dig in first. Like a lot of bloody moles. Trudi. *Deine Liebe Trudi* came to his mind again. It would be evening in Germany too. She'd be getting ready to go out with some officer. Like Mona. Like Kathleen. Kathleen grown up. Grown up for a girl was younger than for a man. It was the age of consent. It was when they could be legally served. Be under a man and breed him a brat. Why didn't she answer his letters? He took the little green oiled-silk-wrapped package from his right breast pocket and looked at it. Her handkerchief. His talisman. He wondered if it had saved him? Surely a girl's nose-wipe was as good as a bloody rabbit's foot. He saw it all clearly now. None of these things were any good in themselves. It was just a question of Mr. Luck liking them. He thought of the captain in the 60th. Trudi's picture and the other two in his pocket. If he was killed they might be sent home with his effects—to his mother, his wife. Unless the man who went through his things kept them for himself. He had seemed certain that they would not be sent home. Do his mother good, he'd said, if they were.

But the idea of it was interesting. Like French letters and things like that. A whole lot of things that were kept from mothers and sisters and nice girls.

He was sure they knew about them, but vaguely. To know there was such a thing as a contraceptive was one thing, but to find a kid brother blowing it up into a balloon was another. He was sure his mother knew about Mona. Not who she was, but that she existed in the flesh.

That was good. In the flesh. Like Trudi.

28 : The Strongpoint

SINCE THEY were moving to what had been the rear of their German trench there was no wire and not too many shell holes. The men crept out quietly, tentatively.

The stars were bright in the moonless sky. Pinpricks. The Great Bear, Orion's Belt, the Milky Way. Cold, distant pinpricks, little leaks of light in the curtain of the firmament. God was up there. If there was a God. War and danger were supposed to make you believe in him. But it hadn't worked that way for Jim. And how could you pray to be saved, ask God for a special favor? It was better, more honorable, to do it on your own and just take a chance.

King and Nobby were with him. When they had gone a hundred yards, Jim said, "Tell them to lie down. Pass the word, King. I'm going forward."

"Not alone you won't. Nobby and me'll go with you," King said.

How far should he go? How far away was the German support line? He had his pistol out. King held his bayoneted rifle at the ready. Clarke had left his rifle and had a bomb in either hand. They moved carefully, and then, about thirty yards beyond the waiting men, he found what he wanted. A big shell hole. The water in the bottom of it, six feet from its edge, reflected the stars. Pretty, that's what it was, like a girl's black velvet dress spangled with stars. Mona had an evening dress like that. Long, soft, trailing, draped to her figure. Why did he have to think of girls all the time?

There were some smaller shell holes around it. They would link them up.

"Go back to Mulholland, Nobby. Tell him to bring the men up."

"Shall I leave you the bombs, sir?"

"Thanks." Jim holstered his pistol and took the two bombs. They felt nice in his hand, hard ovals, heavy, warm from Nobby's hands, moist with sweat.

The men came up in single file. A black ribbon in the black night, blacker, deeper. Jim led them around the perimeter, set up the Lewis gun posts and told them to dig in. It was very quiet, not a gun on their front was firing. As usual, the gunners did not know where their own men were. The silence was palpable, menacing. Another calm before another storm, Jim thought. A cliché, but clichés were true. There generally was a calm before a storm. Situations tended to repeat themselves. The only sound was that of men digging, and their whispered curses.

Mulholland came up to him. "I'm taking a carrying party back for the wire and rations."

"All right," said Jim. "If you see anyone tell them about the wounded in the dugout." Then he went out beyond the digging men to the Lewis guns that were covering them. He wasn't so tired now. You were only tired when you stopped. He took a biscuit from his pocket—hardtack, like a dog biscuit.

If this quiet lasted till they got finished digging they'd be safe till daylight and the German sausage balloons went up, or a plane came over. The hell of it was he could not see what he was doing. He did not know where the Germans were, or what his field of fire was. All they could do was dig in and hold fast.

When he got back Mulholland had got the wire out. A dozen strands hung on screw pickets. Just a token defense, but nice to have. All according to field regulations. Entrench the position . . . Wire . . . He nearly laughed. A handful of men with six strands of wire to keep off a German army corps. He wondered how the 60th were getting on. He thought of the dead German's lovely teeth again. He'd bet some girl had said, "You have lovely teeth." Some Trudi when he'd smiled at her like a wolf. He sat on the edge of the big shell hole, his headquarters, and looked down at the mirrored stars in the black water. The men were cutting a shelf around it and shoveling the earth into the water. It made the stars dance. Twinkle, twinkle, little star. Well, he had done all he could. He dozed off with Clarke and King sleeping beside him.

He woke, as he had known he would, in an hour. It was a trick he had learned. A war trick. Besides, the cold before dawn always woke him. He left King and Clarke sleeping. Let the poor buggers sleep. They lay like dead men, exhausted. He went around the line, stepping over sleeping men, talking softly to the sentries. He went out to the Lewis gunners.

They had put ground sheets over their guns and were lying beside them with just a sentry awake. He would not know if he'd placed them right till dawn. He had six guns. He had placed two facing the Germans and two on either flank. It got colder. The gray in the east became pink. He could see the men, white-faced but cheerful when he spoke to them. If only they could brew up some tea. But they couldn't make fires. Still, as soon as it was light they'd be able to smoke, with no striking matches to give them away. He told Sergeant Mulholland to issue rum. Another jar had come up with the wire and rations. The nondrinkers gave their ration to their friends. The sergeant measured it out in the little after-dinner coffee cup he carried for the purpose. He moved one of the guns. The field of fire was all right. He searched the ground with his glasses and made out the German support line three hundred yards away. They'd kill a lot of them before they got up to him. But he'd hold his fire till they came within a hundred yards. He went around to tell the NCO's.

"Wait till they're a hundred yards away." The whites of their eyes. That had been Waterloo or the Peninsula. Wait till you can see the whites of their eyes. Battles won on the playing fields of Eton . . . Balls, all balls. But they were well dug in. They had worked hard. He went around again, waking the men and inspecting their rifles. Then he told them to sleep again. Only the sentries stayed awake. He spoke to Sergeant Nolan, the platoon sergeant of No. 1 Platoon, A Company. He did not know him, but he seemed all right.

Jim did not stand the men to in the dawn. Let them rest. There would be no attack, no one knew they were there. No attack. No hot food either. Not much water. But they were all right for ammunition and bombs. Mulholland's party had seen to that, even stripping bandoliers from the dead in the trench behind them. It was just a matter of waiting for something to happen. A German counterattack, reinforcements to come up, something. The men's rifles were clean. They had bombs. They were in position. He had sent Clarke to Brigade but he had not come back. He might have been hit and never got there. Or they might have kept him as a guide.

The men were waking up slowly, chewing the rag, munching biscuits, smoking issue cigarettes—Woodbine, Hussars. Most of them had their helmets off. It was no good chasing them, the fewer orders the better now. They knew what they were doing and what they were up against. Like him, they were waiting.

A redheaded private he did not know had taken off his shirt and was going down the seams for lice. A pastime. A hopeless task. The most you could do was to keep them down. Next time they went down the line with luck they'd get baths and be deloused. It was a month since they'd had a bath. The officers got a sort of bath in their green canvas saucers, but the men could only get the worst off, washing in buckets of cold water.

The sun was well up now—a lovely day. It was going to be hot. He'd have to be careful with the water. If anyone was wounded how the hell was he going to get them out? He saw

195

them already in his mind—bloody, bandaged, moaning in the shadeless heat. He'd never got used to having men wounded.

The German balloons were going up, sausages climbing into the sky, floating there, unnatural as turds. That was the beginning. Observers with telescopes pinpricking the front, calling down map references. There was a dead man, German, floating in the bottom of the shell hole. Bloated. He hadn't noticed him before. Perhaps he'd just come to the surface. He stank.

Still nothing, only distant gunfire.

Then it came. He looked at his watch. 11 A.M. With a scream, shells of every caliber passed overhead and fell in one endless exploding curtain on the German front line they had left.

"Christ, we wouldn't 'alf 'ave copped it if we'd stayed there." It was Nobby. He'd got back. He handed over a message: "Hold on. Reinforcements on the way. Routledge GSO. 1. 65 Brigade." Well, now they know where we are. He patted Nobby's shoulder. "I was worried about you, Nobby."

The men were all up. Their tin hats on, their rifles in their hands. Each with their bombs—like little black heaps of manure behind a stabled horse—beside them. There could be no orders. There was too much noise.

The old trench was going up, exploding into earthen trees, hedges. The air smelled of lyddite. He watched the men half open and close the bolts of their rifles, peeping into the breech to reassure themselves that a fresh cartridge was lying neat and snug in the chamber. Carefully, shyly, as if they were lifting a girl's skirts to peep. There was nothing more to do. Just wait. How much waiting there was in war! Boredom, fear. Waiting, marching, exhaustion. He watched the German support line with his glasses. They were coming. "Here they come, chaps!"

The men had seen them. You didn't need glasses. All the glasses did was to bring them nearer, to give them faces. Toy field-gray soldiers, advancing massed. "Bloody bastards . . . Buggers . . ." They came on. British shells began to explode over them. Shrapnel in white cottonwool bursts. Some went down but they did not falter.

We'll have some men hit, he thought. Our chaps aren't sure where we are. It was always worse when your own artillery pounded you. How long it took for them to come! Hours. Minutes that were hours. Then they were there. His Lewis guns began to chatter. That surprised them.

Stoppages. If only they had no stoppages. They had lost most of the gunners. These chaps could use the guns but would be slow fixing a stoppage.

Jim picked up his rifle and got into the line. The men were firing steadily, but fast. Ejected shell cases were flicking out, bright as gold sovereigns in the sun, as they opened and closed their bolts. They were holding them. Jim took careful aim at an officer and brought him down. Then he went into rapid fire. They were so close it was impossible to miss. Thirty yards, twenty, fifteen. Some of the men had put down their rifles on the parapet and were throwing bombs. We're holding the bastards, Jim thought. "Hold them, the buggers!" He hardly recognised his own voice. Both the Lewis guns on the flanks were firing now. Enfilading them. His gunners had done what he knew they would do, pushed forward fast where there was no resistance and outflanked them.

The Germans were shouting guttural commands. Their guns were quiet again. Only shouts, rifle and machine-gun fire. A German NCO was leading a charge. They were going to try to overrun them. The sun glittered on their bayonets. A Lewis gun that had ceased firing began again. A stoppage or a new drum. It caught the German NCO and cut him almost in two, and traversed on, bowling the Germans over like ninepins, but they came on—six men . . . then four . . . then two. One man got to the wire and threw a stick bomb. It looked like a potato-masher turning in the air. Someone shot him before it exploded but he'd made a good throw. The bastard. The next moment there was a shout of "Stretcher bearer!" A man hit. God damn it! They'd been so lucky till now.

There was no second line of Germans coming. The British guns had dropped a barrage on their support line. The German dead and wounded were lying every which way around them.

The right and left had held, too. They'd tried to get through the gap but they'd been held. When the reinforcements come, they'll pull us out, he thought. What's left of us to regroup, rest, bathe and delouse. Christ, what luck they'd had! He went to look at the wounded man. There were two wounded men. The stretcher bearer had just finished bandaging them. Two wounded and one dead, his head blown off by the potato-masher. But how lucky they had been. Only one dead and two hit. If they had stayed in the captured German trench they'd have been dead, the bloody lot of them.

The dead man was a stranger. One of a new draft. His brains had spattered on the wall of the trench. His blood had poured out in a great pool, staining the chalk.

Jim told Mulholland to get his pay book and papers and clean up the mess. "I'll take his identity disc too, sir. It won't stay on without his head."

Mulholland was right. As a rule they left the discs on the body for the burial parties who eventually came up to deal with the dead, so that their graves could be registered and marked. But what could you do with a headless man?

As he turned away he heard Mulholland supervising the men he detailed to clean up. Upsetting, all that blood. Puddles and splotches of it. On the ground and the wall that was white as whitewash.

The earlier casualties that had decimated the battalion seemed long ago now. Yesterday was long ago. He began to cry. Quite softly, gently, the tears rolling down his dirty cheeks, furrowing them with clean white lines. Relief, exhaustion, sorrow, reaction. Mulholland patted his shoulder. "It's all right, sir. We did a good job. We held the bastards. It's over now." Somebody was always patting him. Like a bloody horse. Comforting him.

But it wasn't over. Now by a long shot. The German sausage balloons had spotted them and the gunners were bracketing on their position. At the third salvo they found them and there was nothing they could do but sit down to it. Huddle against the walls of the trench they had built linking the shell holes and take what the Germans were dishing out. It was impossible to move till they stopped, but they were having casualties. Several direct hits, screams, shouts for stretcher bearers. At last it stopped and Jim shouted, "Stand to!"

If they were going to come they'd come now. But they didn't. Not worth the trouble, no doubt, after that pasting. Christ, and he'd thought they'd been lucky. He fought his way down the trench, dead and wounded everywhere.

And this had been the great battle that was going to end the war.

29 : Walking Wounded

THE STRONGPOINT, which wasn't so strong after all, had been held. There were no more attacks on the second night. What was left of the battalion was relieved. Jim had succeeded in getting away his wounded. Rations of a sort had come up. Water in five-gallon petrol tins, the battalion mail. He'd sent Sergeant Nolan around with it and he'd had to bring most of it back. They went into support and over the top again two days later, and lost more men. There was going to be no real rest. Support and attack again. The High Command was trying to gain as much ground as it could before the rains and cold of winter.

Then at last they were pulled out, having handed their line over to the Canadians. A long march back to Montauban where the cookers were waiting for them—a hot meal at last. Bread instead of biscuits. The men had hardly finished eating when a runner came from Brigade on a motorcycle with a message for the OC 10th Wilts L.I., Colonel Lynch, who had only been with them a week. He called Jim.

"Hilton," he said, "we've got to go back."

"Go back, sir?"

"Yes. The Canadians have lost the trench we took."

"My God!" Jim said. "We're all beat."

"We've got to go. Fetch the other company officers. As soon as your men have finished eating, issue ammunition. Two bandoliers, bombs. You know the bloody drill."

Jim called Mulholland—Acting Company Sergeant-Major now, with Hargreaves gone—and gave him the news. "Fall the men in. SAA, bombs, flares. We're to send up flares when we've got the trench back."

The return march was hell. It had taken them six hours to get out of the line. They had to get back in four in order to attack before dawn. Men slept as they marched, and fell down. A Lewis gunner was drowned in a shell hole under the weight of his gun. Lost in the mud.

They attacked in the gray light of dawn, supported by the Canadians who had reassembled in the support line. The trench was carried—what was left of it after being plastered by both British and German guns. They should have come out now but instead they had to join in the attack that was taking place the next day on the Le Transloi position.

Jim had been over the top six times in a month and had not had a scratch. Only a handful of men and NCO's that he'd marched down with were left, and no officers. All strangers, the bloody lot of them. Except for Mulholland, Goodby, Clarke and King. It was too good to last.

Each time, each move, with each casualty replacement, a new little society was formed. Faces, voices, joined the group or disappeared from it. They gave each other nothing. There were smiles, the illusion of permanence, with words, companionship, the bond of danger, hardship, suffering and fear. There was the chain of command, an obscure feeling of family relationship within the battalion, the company and platoon: the colonel, a father; the company commanders uncles; the other officers brothers; the men, even older men, children to be led, taken care of. A family affair, jealously guarded, bound with the twin cords of discipline and regimental history. A colonel was killed, wounded or promoted but the father had not gone; he was at once replaced. How many there had been since the regiment was first formed! How curiously they grew, like boys, into uncles and fathers! A colonel, the father of a thousand men on paper strength, though rarely that in war. But always, whatever the casualties, a nucleus was left that grew and grew. Grew new men as lizards grow new tails. The King is dead, long live the King. But it was not just the King, unless every man was a king, for as one died he was at once replaced. Millions of kings in khaki; kings to their mothers, their wives, their girls. To them they were irreplaceable. Gone for ever.

They went over in single file. The third wave over ground that was being replowed with shellfire. Shells were bursting all around them, sending up great spouts of earth that grew more groves of brown trees. To cross this bare space over the open seemed an impossibility, but they were doing it. Marching back up the line ten days ago had seemed an impossibility, a counter-attack with exhausted men impossible, but they had done that too.

Jim knew where Le Transloi was because the shells that burst there were red with the brick dust of the demolished village. This time he was sure he was for it. Mr. Luck had done all that could be expected of him. He was sitting back on his arse, that's what Mr. Luck was doing. Sick of him.

They crossed a deep German trench on duckboard bridges and advanced in line—the ground was not so cut up here—and then something hit him. It felt like a blow from a wooden mallet. It spun him around and he sat down. Christ, he was hit! In the shoulder. He spat up some blood. The lung, he thought. King knelt beside him.

"You're hit, sir," he said.

"Yes, I'm hit." What a bloody silly conversation. His left arm was no good. King was getting the field dressing out of the front of his tunic where it was sewn. He stripped off the jacket, pushed him back, broke the ampoule of iodine and poured it into the wound.

"A nice one, sir. A real blighty." He put on the pad and

201

wound the bandage about his chest and arm. "Smashed your shoulderblade, sir. But you'll be all right."

"Put on my jacket again," Jim said, "and make a sling with my nose-wipe."

"And now, sir, shall I come back with you?"

"No, I'll find my own way. I'm walking wounded. Leave me and join the other chaps."

Jim watched Private King go forward toward the line of men silhouetted on the rise. King—batman, friend. He wondered about Mulholland, Goodby and the others. Who were left? Would they get through this show too? How many men had they lost? He had never felt so alone before as on this deserted battlefield with only the dead and badly wounded for company. In the distance he saw stretcher bearers, giving first aid and carrying men away. They had impressed some German prisoners to help them.

It was an extraordinary sensation. He felt nothing as he wandered over the debris of war toward the guns. He was not even in pain. He was not bleeding much. He remembered Hargreaves saying when they pissed on their handkerchiefs that it was like blood. First it ran hot, then cold. He had been right. That was what it was like. But the curious thing was that he was not here; he was somewhere else. On a high place, like Jesus when he was tempted, looking down at this solitary figure picking its way between the shell holes. He thought: that's young Captain Jim Hilton, that little figure. I wonder if he'll make it. It would be a pity if a shell got him now that he's out of it with a blighty. There were shells bursting here and there; it was all completely objective. He was an observer, not a participant. It was always like that in war though he had not realized it before. You were never you. The I part of you was somewhere else. You acted on a series of reflexes. You went forward, you fought, you marched. But still it wasn't you.

The dead tanks, stalled monsters, were surrounded by dead and dying men. Attracted, like iron filings to a magnet, they collected there. Clustered. Trying to shelter beside something solid in a sea of mud, but the Germans went on firing at them, dead or not, slamming shells into them that burst on the iron with a shattering clang.

They lay like dead elephants, great diamond-shaped things, their caterpillar bowels spread about them when they had been stripped off. Those that got through the wire had gone too fast for the infantry and the Germans had closed the gaps with machine guns. The tanks had made gaps their own width through the German wire that the infantry could not find. They should have left markers. There should have been more tanks. They should have operated close together in one gigantic drive.

He passed newly killed men whom the stretcher bearers had marked by driving their bayoneted rifles into the ground and sticking a tin hat on the butt. A smashed horse-ambulance, one wheel in the air. Dead horses and mules. Equipment. Later on the salvage people would come and save what they could—rifles, equipment, tin hats. Someone would take the dead men's pay books, and possibly bury the corpses if there was time and there weren't too many of them.

Now he was among the older dead. Some—killed earlier—were dry as mummies in the summer sun. Others, green-blue, bloated, covered with that awful fur of flies. Maggots, crows, rats would all do their scavenging work. Here and there over the battlefield were other wounded making their way back. He jumped out of his skin as a field gun fired from a hidden emplacement. He went toward it. An officer said, "Hullo! Been hit?"

"Yes. But it's not bad."

"Have a drink." The officer pulled a silver flask from his pocket.

The whisky burned his throat and put new life into him.

"Go straight on back—" the officer pointed to the rear—"and you'll see a notice board WALKING WOUNDED. The CCS is not far."

Jim said, "Thanks," and moved on. Casualty Clearing Station. He saw the notice board. The CCS was cut into a sunken road. Old German dugouts. The side of the road was lined with men on stretchers, awaiting their turn. He sat down and got out his cigarette case and extracted a cigarette. How the hell did you light it with one hand? A soldier, hit in the arm, said, " 'Ere, sir, you 'old the box and I'll strike, sir."

When his cigarette was going, Jim said, "Have one and I'll hold for you."

"Thank you, sir. Not bad, are you, sir?"

"Through the shoulder."

"I got 'it in the arm, sir. Missed the artery. Reckon we're lucky, sir. Couple of blighties."

Two ammunition limbers came galloping up the road. A shell burst near them and the horses swerved away over some of the stretchers, smashing them to bloody pulp, and went on swinging and swaying up the road.

"Christ!" the soldier said, as they ran toward the crushed men. There was nothing they could do. The hooves of twelve horses and eight wheels of loaded limbers had flattened them out, burst them like grapes, spreading their brains and entrails on the white chalk of the road. An RAMC sergeant rushed up with some prisoners to clean up the mess. The men had not even had time to scream, it had been over so quickly. No one's fault. It was war. A terrible sight. Jim was surprised he had felt so little. But then he wasn't there, not Jim Hilton. No, he was miles away on his high place. An RAMC corporal came up, undid his tunic and shoved a needle as thick as a nail into his right breast. It was astonishing how thick his skin was. The corporal had to push quite hard to get it in. Then he tied a label on a button. "Antitetanus," he said, and went on to the next man.

Jim and the match-striking private joined a queue that was forming in front of the dugout. Head wounds roughly bandaged, arm wounds, wounds in the upper part of the body. Walking wounded, in fact. Men who could walk. Stretchers were being carried in past them. From another entrance, men who had been dealt with were coming out, walking or being carried, labeled like parcels, to await the ambulances that would take them to the hospital trains awaiting them at Doullens.

It was evening by the time Jim's turn came. He raised the blanket gas curtain, went into the dugout and was dazzled by

204

the glare of the acetylene lanterns hanging from the beams of the ceiling. The dugout stank of ether. Four surgeons, in white aprons stained like butchers with blood, were working on tables under the lights. In a corner there was a pile of severed arms and legs, piled up like joints of meat. What in God's name did they do with them? Beyond shock, beyond feeling, still an objective observer, Jim waited, in line with the other walking wounded on the left of the big dugout. The bloody theatre was on the right. He supposed they threw away those severed limbs. Buried them. Did a parson pray over them? They were dead, weren't they? He almost laughed.

His line shuffled forward toward a doctor and two medical orderlies. They were bloodstained too, but more smeared than dripping like the surgeons. He got a closer look at one of them as he wiped the sweat from his face with a bloody rubber glove. God, they were working fast! A rough job of patching up and chopping off. He heard a saw grate on bone. The earth floor was festooned with discarded bloody, muddy field dressings and bandages, the first aid done in the field by the wounded soldiers themselves, their comrades and stretcher bearers. This was second aid. He smiled at his invention of the term. This would get them to the hospital train. With luck. With the help of Mr. Luck.

His turn had come. An orderly took off his jacket and shirt. "Lie down."

He lay down. Another orderly took off the field dressing King had put on and threw it on the floor with the others. He wiped the wound with alcohol. The surgeon said, "Lift him up." He was raised.

"The bullet went through you," the surgeon said. So it had been a rifle bullet. He had not thought about it before, but there had been no shrapnel burst so it had to be a bullet. How stupid not to have thought of it for himself. Some bastard shot me, he thought. That anoyed him. To have been aimed at and hit by some damn sniper. The bugger.

"Clean wound," the doctor said. "Smashed your shoulder-blade though, going through. No pain, is there?"

"I don't feel anything."

"You will, boy. You're bruised now. Bullet going two thousand miles an hour when it hit you. I'm going to plug it; this may hurt. Tape!" he said. The orderly gave him some tape from a bottle, holding it with bright forceps. He held the tip over the bullet hole. "Probe!" The second orderly handed him a thing that looked like a knitting needle, and he began feeding in the tape, stuffing it down.

Christ, it did hurt! Jim clenched his jaw. He could hear his teeth grinding. But it was still objective. The man that was being hurt wasn't really he. It was that young Hilton who had got a blighty.

"Right. Next!"

Another orderly bandaged him, helped him on with his shirt and jacket and said, "That way out." It was marked Exit. It was dark outside, faintly lit by a stable lantern. The walking wounded were sitting or standing about; the others, doped with morphia, lay corpse-still on their stretchers. By God, he could have done with a cup of char with some rum in it, but there was nothing. Just water, tasting of chloride of lime and gas.

"The ambulances will be back for another load before long, chum," the man next to him said. So that was it. Just wait for the ambulances that were shuttling between the railhead and the CCS.

30 : England, Home and Beauty

THE AMBULANCES came—khaki, canvas-topped, with red crosses painted in a white circle on either side. Fords. They took four stretchers in two tiers, and four walking wounded sitting down. As soon as they were loaded the convoy bumped off over the wornout road to the siding where the white hospital trains, also marked with red crosses, waited. Here they were

checked off and lists made. Name, rank, regimental number.
The usual rigmarole that reduced men to figures. Numbers to be
measured against space, hospital beds, rations. Types of
wounds. Names to be sent to the War Office for listing to
appear among the casualties in the press.

An orderly helped Jim to undress and get into a real bed,
with sheets, on a train going home. Out of it. He, all of the
chaps in the train. The war and its horror was behind them. He
slept, exhausted, through the fields of France. They had been
given tea, and stew in a bowl. They were content. At Rouen
they transferred to ambulances again and were driven to the
hospital to await shipment. Wards, with regular army nurses in
gray with red-lined capes, some of them had medal ribbons.
They were not young. They were hard. He supposed they had to
be. Iron women, inured to suffering and death.

The man in the next bed to Jim's was badly hit. An Australian. ANZAC. He was fully conscious, alert, sharp with fever.
"I've had it, mate," he said. "Never see down under again,
cobber. Never ride another bloody horse or have a woman. I'm
off to never-never land. Plenty of pals there," he said. "Gallipoli." Then he said "Gallipoli" again. "Poor bastards running
up the bloody beach. You should have seen it, mate. Right
dinkum."

Then the trolley came along, white enamel, with basins,
bottles and dressings. Shining scissors, forceps, probes. The
metal clinked as the trolley ran on rubber wheels down the ward.
A red-faced nurse was standing beside Jim. She undid his
bandage, got hold of the tip of the plug of tape with a pair of
forceps and pulled it out. A red streamer. Christ, it hurt. The
doctor had been right— "It'll hurt later when the bruise wears
off." She dropped the tape into a slop pail on the lower shelf of
the trolley. It was filled with mucky dressings; bloody, greenish-
yellow pus on pads. "I'm going to put another in," she said, and
in it went. Clean, sterile, rammed in with a probe. Sweat broke
out on Jim's forehead, but he hadn't said anything. Not a
bloody word. Proud of him, he was. Because he was away
again, watching them dress young Hilton's wound. He was given

207

tea and food. He slept. He woke once at night, wondering where the hell he was. He saw the night nurse sitting at a little table at the end of the ward, reading a book. Except for the light at her table, it was dark. All around him men were sleeping, groaning, snoring. The Australian was breathing with great gasps. There was a red screen around him when Jim woke—it was light.

Piss-bottles like flasks, bedpans, temperatures, a wipe over with a wet cloth. The orderlies did the bottle and bedpan business, but the red-faced nurse washed him. Impersonal, like changing a baby. A woman washing his privates. No one had done that since he was three years old. It didn't embarrass him because she wasn't a woman. Not in that sense. Not nubile. And it wasn't true about nobody since he was three. He'd had a bath at Mona's flat and she had washed him once. Soaped him all over, just for a lark. My baby.

Mona. Kathleen. Women. The woman at the Empire. Gwen was the first woman he'd seen naked, but he'd not been able to do anything. Impotent. Not a man. And that was why he had gone with her to prove he was a man. Quite old, thirty. He should have taken a young one. There had been lots of pretty ones, eighteen or nineteen. Frightened of them. They might laugh at him not knowing. But he knew now. Mona had taught him. Gwen had tried but he was no good with her. But she had been nice to him. Given him a good breakfast. Bacon and two eggs. Toast, coffee. He dozed.

When he woke, someone was talking to the Australian. The screen had been moved a little and he could not see what was going on.

"I think you should see a minister." The matron had his card in her hand. "C of E, I see." She threw back her short, gray, red-lined cape. She was a regular army nurse, bemedaled from other wars: South Africa, Egypt, North-West Frontier. An expert on death. She knew the sound of his wings. A big, rawboned woman, stayed with steel, girdled, her milkless breasts flat with efficiency; no mother's milk had ever swelled them, no milk of human kindness. Dry, flat dugs. The big bitch. She bullied the nurses. He could see they hated her, but copied her stiff, starched, rustling efficiency. Professional. Jim had heard her talking to a young nurse still tender from her vicarage home. "You feel things too much, nurse. You mustn't let it affect you. They are patients, bed numbers. Not people, not men."

"But, matron . . ."

"Don't 'but' me. Thirty-five years I've been at it. India, Africa, England, here. Men," she said, "don't think of them as men. Forget you're a woman till you take off your uniform. That's when you're a woman."

The Australian was a Captain Cook. Tough, hard. A real Aussie.

"I don't want a bloody parson," he said.

"It's not what you want, it's what I order."

"Going to peg out, eh?" he said. "Kick the bloody bucket."

"I didn't say so. I merely think a minister could help you." She looked smug, her mouth closed like a gin-trap, one of those things with teeth in it that the Society for Prevention of Cruelty to Animals was trying to get declared illegal.

With an effort, Cook turned his back on her.

But he came, an hour later. The sky-pilot, the devil-dodger, the soldier-burier. In khaki with black buttons. Captain the Reverend somebody, C of E, who ministered to the sick of heart and spirit in the base hospital. He stood between Jim and the dying man. He had a fat bottom.

"Captain Cook?" he said.

"That's me, mate. Packing in my chips, eh? Never see down under again, never see the bloody sun again. Never sweat again, never another drop of booze. Never another woman. Think you can comfort me, padre? Christ Almighty," he said. "What do you know? Never been drunk, never killed a man, backed a horse or fucked a woman." He laughed. It was a terrible kind of laugh.

"Your Maker," the parson said. "You should prepare to make your peace."

"My Maker? My Maker was my dad, a drunken old bugger who'd ride any buck-jumper till one killed him. Savaged him, padre, chopped him. Died like a man. Like me. That's the way I'm going to die."

"You mustn't say that, Captain Cook, God loves you. Jesus . . ."

"So that's why he blew my guts out? God and Jesus? Listen, padre, I'm not the first and I'll not be the last. I've lived without God and I'll die without Him. Die like a bloody man even if it's in bed with my boots off. More's the bloody pity. But I killed a lot of the fucking bastards before they got me. They lay around me, padre, I stuck 'em like pigs. I shot 'em, I clubbed 'em. I've no complaints, reverend. I've lived hard, like a man, and I'll die like one. Now bugger off and let me die like I want—alone, like a man, like a dog in a ditch."

The parson was a peaceful man. Cook had frightened him. When he turned away he had tears in his eyes. Jim was fascinated. This was the way to do it. With guts, with style.

"Gave him what-for, chum," Cook said. "Bloody bastards. Black crows." Then an orderly came and fixed the bright red screen so he couldn't see the Aussie any more.

The Australian died. When Jim woke next day the red screen had gone and there was a new chap there. Dead men's shoes, dead men's beds. Must have fetched him in the night, carried him away on a stretcher. Changed his sheets and brought the other chap in.

More dressings, bedpans, bottles, sponge baths. By God, he hated the sound of that bloody trolley, lying there waiting his turn. Some men screamed when they ripped off dressings that had stuck with dry pus.

Then they fetched him. "You're for Blighty," the orderly said. "Got ter make room for bad cases."

Jim was carried onto the hospital ship on a stretcher protesting that he could walk quite easily. The channel crossing. Destroyer escort. Folkestone—London—Victoria Station. Everyone laid out on the platform. Another train. Reading. All in a kind of dream. The reaction had set in, one thing merged into another. Nurses, doctors, orderlies. Why the hell did they wake you so early?

And then suddenly he was sitting up and taking notice. Talking to the other chaps—some on crutches, some in wheelchairs, some walking about in dressing gowns. All from the Somme battle. Hundreds in every hospital in England, and thousands dead over there. They told each other their names and regiments. McBey, Black Watch. Fettle, Surreys. Simpson, Sussex. They all had stories. But their stories were all the same, each was a tale of the great fuck-up.

But he was one of them. They had all shared this thing. In a way it was like being at school, only here they were all new boys, and very old boys at the same time. Chaps who knew what it was all about. They talked about war, about women, about what they were going to do when they got out.

He decided to write to Mona.

DEAR MONA,

Here I am in hospital in Reading. It's the workhouse that has been taken over. Come and see me if you can. Say you are my sister, Miss Hilton. Not that you couldn't see me anyway, lots of visitors come, but it might be fun to pretend. I am not badly hit. Left shoulder, so I can't use my left hand and it's a bit hard to hold the paper. Much love. Your Jimmie.

P.S. We'll have to do it the other way, with you on top.

Then he wrote to his mother. It was still difficult to think of her as Lady Gore Blakeney. Bloody silly name. He gave the letters to an orderly to post. He was glad he could write himself. Civilian women came into the wards to write letters for chaps who couldn't write. He wondered what one of them would have made of his letter to Mona. That was the kind of letter the other chaps wanted to write too, but they'd have to wait till they could do it themselves.

So it had come at last. The telegram every mother, every soldier's wife in England had been waiting for. Fearing. Expecting.

Lady Gore Blakeney stood, afraid to open it. The sun was

211

pouring in at the window. Surely it should not shine on a day like this? She opened the telegram quickly, tearing at it.

"Regret to inform you Captain James Hilton 10th KOWLI has been wounded in action."

Not killed. Thank God. She sat down, her knees suddenly weak. Wounded. How badly wounded? Where was the wound? Head, body, legs? Where was he? Still in France? Had he been evacuated? Was he in England within a few miles of her? England was so small. John would be able to find out. Pull strings. What a good thing at a time like this to have a husband who was a general. He knew everyone. She picked up the telephone. It took her half an hour to get through.

"Divisional Headquarters."

"Is the General in?"

"Who is speaking?"

"His wife, Lady St. John Gore Blakeney. It's urgent."

"Hold the line, madam." A pause, another voice. "This is Fitzherbert, Lady Blakeney."

Freddie Fitzherbert, John's ADC, she liked him. "Can I speak to the General, Captain Fitzherbert?"

"He's out, I'm afraid. Can I take a message?"

"Yes. My son has been wounded. Will you ask the General to find out where he is? I mean if he is in England?"

"Of course I will. And I'm sorry, Lady Gore Blakeney, but don't worry. Most wounds aren't too bad. Didn't say seriously, did it?"

"No. Just wounded in action."

"I'll tell the General. Try not to worry." What a bloody silly thing to say. Not worry. He rang off.

She sat back. Now it was in the hands of God and the General. John would do everything it was possible to do.

How curious it was to be in love for the first time at forty. Mervyn had married her out of the schoolroom at eighteen. Jim had been born when she was nineteen. She had been happy with Mervyn and her little boy, but it had not been anything like this. A young girl was not sexually mature. Mervyn had been a good husband, but not a good lover. Never what the French called a

212

moderately sensual man. Not with her, anyway. She wondered how much truth there was in George Hilton's stories about other women. She had been sorry when he had been killed in a railway accident. She had mourned him and retired into widowhood to raise his son. Her baby. It was still difficult to believe he had been hurt despite the casualty lists, despite the death of her friends' husbands and sons. Despite the fact that she had been waiting for the telegram. Trembling every time the door bell rang.

By the time the General got to Albany at eight next morning, he'd found out everything, pulled strings. His news was good. He'd come down on the night train. They'd go and see the boy and he'd go back tonight. He'd never met the lad, but this wouldn't be a bad way to do it. Soldier to soldier. He put his key into the door.

Irene was still in bed. "You lazy little creature," he said. It must be all right or he would not speak to her like that, or have that look in his eyes. "I'm glad you're still in bed."

"Oh, John, tell me."

"It's all right, my dear. He's at Reading. Hit in the shoulder. We'll get there for lunch. I've ordered the car. I'm going to have a bath now. And don't get up, darling." He had gone clinking out of the bedroom but he'd soon be back. She brushed her hair and made up her face. Like a girl, she thought; like a bride. What would she have done without John at times like this?

Jim was surprised when he saw his mother and the General come into the ward. The officers who were sitting reading stood up. "Sit down," the General said. Of course his mother had said she'd married a general but he had not seemed real and here he was as large as life, all medals, red tabs and spurs. And in his life. Somehow you never expected to have generals in your life. You saw them in the distance with their staff, with an escort of lancers. Sometimes a brigadier or staff officer came up the line. That was all. And here was this chap standing by his bed. Very tall, slim and soldierly-looking, with a cavalry stoop. He looked

213

at him curiously. So this was the chap who was sleeping with his mother. Well, she looked very fit on it. Prettier than ever and beautifully turned out. Of course she had plenty of money now. Money and a general. There were tears in her eyes as she bent over to kiss him. "Are you all right, Jimmie?" she said. A bloody silly remark really, because if he'd been all right he'd not have been here.

"I'm all right," he said. "I'll be up in a day or two."

His mother looked from him to the General. She was smiling. My two men, she thought. My soldiers. And he was safe, not even badly hurt. But fancy someone shooting her Jimmie. Safe for a while anyway. "Jimmie," she said, "this is General Sir John St. John Gore Blakeney, your stepfather."

She seemed proud of him, Jim thought. Well, why not? He was a fine-looking general as generals went. No belly. He'd seen plenty of action from his medals. "How do you do, sir," he said.

"Glad you're not badly hurt, my boy. I'll leave you with your mother now. And Jim," he went on. "when you get out, you come to Albany. Spare room. Latchkey. No questions. Hotel," he said. "Wounded hero." He smiled. "Young once myself." Inarticulate. Soldier. Embarrassing situation, meeting a young chap like that when you've just slept with his mother. Not four hours ago. All square and above board and all that, but still . . . Leave them together. He turned to his wife. "There are some cavalry men in the hospital, I hear. Have a word with them." He turned away from the bed and went out. The officers who were sitting stood up again. He said "Sit down," again, and he was gone.

"You'll like him, Jimmie," his mother said.

"If you do, I will."

"I do." And he could see that she did. His mother was happy. He was glad. He would not have to worry about her anymore. That was the General's job now. The General and his mother. Me and Mona, he thought. But how different . . . Still, he supposed an old boy of that age still could. He must, from the look of his mother. He couldn't help wondering. When and how

214

often? Christ, he wanted Mona. His mother kissed him again. There was not much to say really. "I must go, Jimmie. The General's got to get back tonight. I'm glad you like him."

Funny, her always calling him "the General." When she had gone Fernley, the one in the next bed, said, "Well, I'm damned. A bloody general for a father."

"Never saw him before," Jim said. "Stepfather. That's what happens if you leave your mother alone for a few minutes."

"She's a pretty woman," Fernley said.

"I think so too. Young-looking. Sometimes people think she's my sister."

When the General had gone back to his headquarters, Irene went to look at the spare room. It was a nice room, a bachelor's room, but comfortable. Nice bed. Chest of drawers, walnut with brass fittings, made in two parts, old army style, a hundred or so years old, John had told her. Two Persian carpets, an engraving of the Scots Greys charging in the Crimea, two oil paintings of horses. A pair of crossed scimitars. A soldier's room where John used to put up his friends. A vase of flowers would make a difference, she thought. Early chrysanthemums—late roses. She had the greatest confidence in flowers.

She wandered through the flat. Their bedroom—she'd managed to make that a bit feminine without changing too much. Just moving the furniture a little, and putting her cut glass and silver things on the dressing table. And flowers, naturally. There was a small dining room. Sheraton table and chairs, red Turkey carpet; lithographs of cavalry officers showing them mounted in full dress. In the whole place there was hardly a picture that didn't have a horse in it. A horse standing in a loose-box, or a mounted charger. She'd taken them out of the bedroom and put in her own pictures. A mezzotint of the Hon. Mrs. Graham, two Flint water colors, a charming French nude in black and white. She had changed the carpet too—put in a blue Chinese carpet and heavy silk curtains to match. The hall was just a hall—small and rather dark. The sitting room was a fine room—very large—a kind of museum that made her want to shudder or to laugh, according to her mood. Crossed lances, long inlaid Arab guns, swords, a snarling tigerskin on the floor. Leopard heads hung on the walls. Heads and horns. Buffalo. Sambur. Oryx. Kudu . . . He enjoyed telling her about them all. There was a large bookcase filled with books about the army, about war, about shooting. And of course horses. There were two more tigerskins. Their heads were flat, not mounted, with the Persian rugs on the floor, and a leopardskin draped over the back of the leather-covered sofa. Two big leather armchairs, a desk, some other chairs, a glass-fronted gun cabinet filled with shotguns and rifles. And there you had it. The room of a soldier sportsman, with plenty of money. But it was part of him and she didn't believe in trying to change men. She supposed she'd get used to it, used to being glared at by those damn tigers and the leopard. After the war they'd move. Get a bigger flat with a drawing room, and a boudoir to herself. And he'd still be able to have his museum all complete the way it was now. "You see, darling," he'd said one day, seeing her look around it, "it's my life. My memories. I'll chuck them all out if you want me to, but I think I'd lose something."

She'd laughed at him. "Leave it, John. I expect I'll get used to the tigers." And she had, in a way. They were part of the General. Better than women, anyway.

She picked up the War Office telegram. How lucky she was! How many thousand telegrams had been sent: "Regret to inform you Captain X has been killed in action. Lieutenant something else has been seriously wounded. Missing in action. Missing, believed prisoner. Missing, believed killed." How many variations of this awful theme? How many women had opened them with trembling fingers?

Jim Hilton was getting a reaction now. He had not meant to let his mother know where he was, not for a few days, but with a bloody divisional general for a husband she had been able to find out. All right? Of course he was all right. A blighty. He was home. He'd be out of bed before long; out of hospital in a month. But that wasn't it. It was the gap between himself and

216

the people at home. The people who hadn't seen it, heard it, smelled it. Smelled the dead rotting by the hundred in the mud, seen their friends killed, their men shot to pieces. People who didn't know what it was to survive time after time in attack after attack, till at the end you were alone among strangers. Nineteen, and an old soldier. Blood, mud, explosions. The whole bloody world exploding in your face. It was all right here in hospital with the other chaps, but when you went out into the world again you'd be like a ghost among men, or a man among ghosts. And the nights were terrible—dreams, nightmares. One chap would start the others off. They'd shout for ammunition, for bombs, for stretchers, they'd cry like babies in their sleep. Suppose it happened when he stayed with his mother and the General? How ashamed he would be if he screamed in the night!

He was separate now; another umbilical cord had been cut. Separate not only from his mother, but from all civilians. He could only bear to be with chaps who had known it. He wondered if they all felt the same. It wasn't something you could ask, like about being afraid when you went up the line for the first time. Suppose some kid asked him now, what would he say? Afraid? Christ, it was such fear that it went beyond fear, a full circle back into courage.

When you caught a chap's eye, he smiled at you because you were brothers in experience, he knew the fear that you had beaten down like a dog at your throat. We all know it, us chaps, he thought. But if you saw them when they weren't looking at you, they just stared at nothing. Their eyes didn't even blink. The same thing was going on in all their heads. Going around and around and around.

Mona would help. Only Mona, only a woman. A man could escape into a woman. The little piece of him that was more than the whole. Back into the warm security of the womb. But that belonged to the General now. He began to laugh hysterically. Fancy thinking of his mother's private parts and a major-general's tool.

217

Fernley staggered out of bed and hit him. "Shut up, you bastard," he said, "or you'll have us all off."

He came to. He became himself again. He said, "Thanks, Fernley." They shook hands like children saying goodbye at a party. Very polite.

The first news Mona got of Jim Hilton's wound was seeing his name in the casualty list as she went over it. Under King's Own Wiltshire Light Infantry. First *Killed,* then *Wounded,* and there was his name. Hilton, J. E., Captain. Her Jimmie. How badly was he wounded? Where was he—still in hospital in France, or home? His mother must know. She would have got the War Office telegram and would have found out. She remembered Jimmie telling her she had married again. She did not even know her name. And if I did, what could I say to her? I am not engaged to him. I'm just his friend. She'd see through me. Ask what I did, how I lived. A kept woman, and not even by him. Not even by one man. To be kept by one man suddenly seemed very respectable—practically like being married. Mona burst into tears. All she could do was wait. He'd write. Yes, Jimmie would write if he could. If he wasn't too bad to write.

Part Three

LONDON LOVES

31 : The Station Hotel

THE STATION Hotel was a solid bit of Victorian redbrick architecture. Foursquare, uninviting, it was used by commercial travelers and businessmen who had to spend a night in the town.

The hotel had none of the atmosphere of larger hotels in larger places. There had been few dramas here. Few lovers' meetings and partings. Few women running away from their husbands, few suicides, or the murders that occasionally occur in the great caravanserais of any metropolis. Few girls had sobbed themselves to sleep in the bedrooms. Few drunks had passed out. People who wanted to do such things went to London. If the walls of the bedroom could have talked they would have had few stories to tell.

Mona arrived there after dinner one night, registered as Miss Hilton and went to bed. The night clerk thought her a pleasant change from the usual run of visitors and wished he had a job where he saw more pretty girls.

In the morning, after a good breakfast, Mona went to the desk and said she hoped her room would be tidied by ten.

"Of course, miss. It's probably done by now," the reception clerk said.

Mona, very neatly dressed in black, wearing no make-up, dabbed at her eyes with her handkerchief and said, "I'm expecting my brother, Captain Hilton. He's in hospital here—wounded—to come and see me at ten. I've got things to discuss with him. About my fiancé. He was killed last month." She used her handkerchief more vigorously. "And I can't do it in the public lounge. I want to take him to my room."

"Of course. I quite understand, Miss Hilton."

"Then we'll have lunch and I'll go home—back to Manchester. My brother is all I have now. My fiancé and I were going to be married on his next leave. If only we'd been married before he left! I might be going to have a baby, something of his. He was going to buy a little house." The handkerchief again.

By this time Mona had fallen into the part. The dead fiancé, the little house, the baby, the pram, dog, cat, canary and garden of her dreams all seemed quite real to her. She shed some genuine tears at her loss. And in the last months she had lost, if not a fiancé, at least several intimate friends.

"A terrible thing, this war," the clerk said. "Terrible." He was a man of fifty with grown-up children: two sons in the army. But he could not help thinking what this chap had missed by being killed. Even in mourning and crying, she was lovely.

Mona sat down by a large potted palm to wait for Jim. Then she decided not to wait. If they went upstairs together he might pat her bottom or something. So she went to the desk again and said, "I'll go to my room. I think I am going to cry. When he comes, send him up. Captain James Hilton."

"I will, miss."

Mona went upstairs slowly, a tragic little figure bowed with sorrow.

When Jim arrived, his arm in a black sling, he said, "I am Captain Hilton. Has my sister come?"

"She's waiting for you, sir. Room twenty-six. Very sad, is it not?"

"It's terrible," Jim said. "Poor girl. They were going to be married on his next leave."

"Tragic," the receptionist said, wondering if the dead man had had her first, and if that would make it better or worse.

Jim knocked on the door.

Mona said, "Come in!"

As soon as he was in the room, she locked the door. "Oh, Jimmie!" she said. "What a long time it's been! How thin you are!"

He put his cap on a chintz-covered chair.

Mona took off his belt and helped him with his tunic. Then she slipped off her dress, black like her hat, coat, gloves and shoes, and stood in front of him in the red *crêpe-de-chine* chemise he had sent her from Poperinghe.

He took her in his right arm. The left in its sling was pressed against her belly. They merged together in a long kiss. As he pushed her backward, she said, "No, Jim. Not the bed. Remember you're my brother." So it wasn't the bed.

At eleven they went downstairs and had tea and buttered toast. Then they went for a short walk and came back to lunch: watery soup, fish that tasted of nothing, boiled leg of mutton, potatoes and cabbage, roly-poly pudding and coffee that Mona sweetened with saccharine. Only the army got sugar.

Mona gave him her news. Nothing about the war or her friends who had been wounded or killed. She talked about plays she had seen, about food shortages, about the price of food, about war profiteers, about the new curtains she had made herself that she had put up in the flat.

Jim did not mention the war either. He talked of his mother's marriage and the General. He showed her his mother's photograph.

Mona said, "She's very pretty. I hope I am as good-looking at her age." It was impossible to think of Mona being his mother's age. "And fancy him being a general and a Sir," Mona said.

"Yes, just fancy!" Jim said.

Mona was thinking about her beautiful boy, her Jimmie. How thin he was, and how changed. His face was much leaner. His eyes had a different look. He had grown a small, rather thin moustache.

"You've got a moustache," she said.

"Yes, it's growing. Against the King's regulations to shave the upper lip. But I'm going to. I want it to grow stiffer."

They both laughed.

The reception clerk who happened to be passing through the dining room was glad to see her happier. Her brother seemed to be a nice young chap. He had cheered her up, anyway.

Jim said, "I wish we could go upstairs again." He could still smell the carpet and see the design of coffee-colored roses on a beige ground.

"Well, we can't," Mona said. "Not if you want me to come again."

"Of course I do."

"And besides, once is enough. You're not well yet. But I'll try to come every week till you get out."

"I should be out in a month," Jim said.

"Oh Jimmie, I'm so glad to have you back." Tears came into her eyes. Jimmie was the dead fiancé miraculously come back to life. What a lot of dead fiancés she had!

"Don't cry, you silly little thing."

"I'm so happy," she said.

They went to the desk together.

"I'll pay my sister's bill," Jim said. "She may be back next week."

"We shall be very pleased to see her, sir. You seem to have cheered her up."

They crossed the road to the station and he put her in the 2:35 for London.

"Goodbye, Mona." Jim kissed her.

"Goodbye, Jimmie. See you next week." She waved her handkerchief out of the window as her train pulled out. Jim saluted.

There were two officers in the first-class carriage. Mona crossed her legs to show them off. One of the officers, a major in the Staffords, offered her a cigarette out of a gold case. She thanked him with lowered lashes and a half-smile. What a lot of regimental badges she knew!

"I've been to see my brother in hospital," she said. Then, innocent as a child, she said, "My fiancé was killed in July."

"On the Somme?"

"Yes, on the Somme." And so they had been. Several of them. She dabbed her eyes with her handkerchief.

With luck he'd take her to dinner and a show. She had recently discovered that men liked nothing better than to comfort

224

a pretty woman in distress. There was no better way to make new friends.

As Jim walked back to the hospital he laughed. What a trick they had played, what fun it had been! "My sister, Mona." How pretty she had looked in her red underclothes! How wonderful it had been to have her again! Once a week and then all he wanted in London. While he was with her there was no war, no nothing, not even any Mona. The dead and wounded disappeared. The blood, the noise, the rats, the chloride of lime—everything was gone, washed out by a girl's white belly. It was astonishing, the relief overwhelming. And at ten o'clock in the morning, too. How clever Mona was to have thought of it! It never seemed to occur to people you could make love at any time of day. Not to civilians, anyway, who had all the time in the world. Their whole lives spread out like a carpet in front of them. Carpet. He laughed. It had been like making love outside. Like Kathleen— only they hadn't.

What surprised the General was the fact that no one had realized that the function of tanks was that of heavy cavalry—of Life Guards, Horse Guards, Dragoon Guards—to employ their weight and mass against infantry. Big men on big horses. The bloody fools had thought of tanks as land battleships. Haig as a cavalryman should have seen it at once. Using a few widely spread when he should have had a thousand operating in tight formation. Could one imagine Napoleon telling Murat, the cavalry genius, to send a troop of cuirassiers against an enemy position? At Waterloo they had come in their thousands, regiment after regiment. A thousand tanks, even if half of them had been knocked out, would have made the gap the infantry required.

And what were the actual facts? Fifty-nine tanks had reached France; forty-nine got as far as the battlefield; thirty-five reached the jumping-off point; thirty-one had crossed the German trenches. But only nine had surmounted all difficulties. One of them near Flers, seeing the infantry held up by wire and machine-gun fire, had crossed the trench and, traveling behind it, had forced three hundred Germans to surrender. Just the sight of a tank had been enough to do the job. Seeing it, the Germans had fled or surrendered.

Here was an example of one of the greatest surprises in the annals of war being thrown away.

The Germans had done the same thing when they used gas for the first time at Ypres. They had been too astounded at their own success to exploit it.

Even that little Welsh lawyer, Lloyd George, had been against the premature employment of tanks. Churchill, an ex-cavalry officer with a vision of their true use, had protested to Mr. Asquith, but without effect. General Swinton, who organized the tank corps, said large numbers of tanks should spearhead the attack, followed by strong infantry masses and cavalry. Instead, the tanks had been dispersed in pairs and even sent singly against specific strongpoints.

He spat all this out at Irene who sat, her hands folded in her lap, hardly taking it in. He was always giving her military lectures. A captive audience on whom he tried out the tactical talks he gave to the officers of his division.

He went on to talk about the casualties. By midnight on the first day of the Somme fighting, July 2, 60,000 men were listed: missing 20,000; dead or died of wounds 10,000; permanently disabled 10,000; 20,000 lightly wounded. The waste of it all maddened him.

When the news of the battle had been published, Irene had thought only of her son. Had he been there? Was he safe? Hundreds of thousands of women must be having the same selfish thoughts, but she could not feel ashamed. Thousands meant nothing to her. For women there were no thousands. Only individuals.

The General went on. He evidently meant to end his talk on a lighter note because the next thing she heard him say was, "I wonder if when they sent them over they sent them in mated pairs? A male and a female. The male tank carries a four-pounder Hotchkiss as well as his machine guns, Irene. The female only has machine guns. Rather curious to bring sex into it, don't you think? A Hotchkiss sticking like a cock out of its steel flies. Of course I shan't put it in that way. But they'll tumble to it. Fine chaps . . ."

Men. She wondered if any woman would ever understand a man. This savage, brutal side of them that could find a kind of ironic humor even in battle.

She thought of the Bairnsfather cartoons, of Old Bill looking at a shell hole through a house and saying, "Mice." Men. Soldiers. My God, when would it end? When would men become people again and would they ever be the same? What effect would these experiences have on the young men who had fought? On Jimmie? She hadn't got near him in hospital. He had been a stranger.

Back at his headquarters Major-General Gore Blakeney thought over what the boy had told him about the failure of the tanks in September. That was the second chance there had been of finishing the war. One in September '14, two years ago, the cavalry, if properly employed, could have smashed von Kluck, and now this in '16. And the field marshals—cavalry generals at that—had not seen it. First French, then Haig. Bloody fools. He'd bet it was the Treasury—too expensive to build so many tanks. Men were cheaper. Men—volunteers—didn't cost anything. His blood boiled, his face became red as a turkey cock's.

"Chucked away another chance—bloody fools!" he shouted, banging his desk.

"Yes, sir," Fitzherbert said. "Who are?"

"None of your bloody business."

"No, sir."

"And let me finish. . . ."

"Yes, sir." Old boy in a real tizzy about something, but his bark was much worse than his bite. Showed he was in good form, though.

"All of them, Fitz. War Office, Treasury, Haig. From the little I've heard, if Churchill had had his way we'd have had thousands of 'em, and the war'd have been over by Christmas." And the boy would be safe and Irene'd stop worrying and be able to pay him some attention. "Now they've got to wait for the Americans to come in, if they come in. And if they do they'll say they won the war."

"Thousands of what, sir?"

"Tanks, you fool."

"Yes, sir."

"In September 'fourteen if French had been willing to push out his horsemen he'd have cut off von Kluck's supplies—his whole corps would have been finished—but he was afraid to risk it. It's the old story of cavalry officers hesitating to commit their horses."

But the war could have been won then instead of settling down to this stalemate. And the horses were too big and too good. He'd learned that from the Boers. The *arme blanche,* the sabre and lance, were finished. Mounted infantry were the thing. Tough ponies that would get a man to where he could use his rifle. Revolutionary, radical. Me, old Gore Blimey of the Second Royal Scots Dragoons. Radical. The Greys. Good God! you had to move with the times. You had to learn from experience, but they didn't, and they'd had the audacity to call him a dugout.

Tanks. And now the fools had let the cat out of the bag. The Germans would soon build their own. He thought of the Kaiser saying, "The sword has been forced into our hands. We shall, with God's help, so wield the sword as to restore it to its sheath again with honor. I commend you to God. Remember, the German people are God's elect. On me, the Kaiser, has God's spirit descended. I am his sword, his armor, his instrument." Wilhelm II, with his moustache and crippled arm. Good God! But the German army was the finest military instrument in the world. "By God, sir, the bastards can fight!" the boy had said. British Guards and Prussian, bayonet to bayonet, the dead propping up each other. That had been in the papers. But what a lot wasn't in the papers.

A scrap of paper. How often would that phrase be used in the future? A contract not worth the paper it was written on.

K of K with his "Your King and Country needs you!" Never liked Kitchener. No one liked him. Not like Bobs, Lord Roberts. The BEF. Six infantry divisions and one of cavalry, but all of them long-service soldiers who could shoot. It was a Jew called Weizmann who had invented acetone, the basis of cordite, out of maize. Clever chaps, Jews.

Only two machine guns per battalion—imagine it. The stupidity of it.

If he got a chance he could teach the boy a lot. Teach him as much in a month as he'd learn in six at Camberley. Principles of war. Basic, no change. Alexander the Great, Julius Caesar, Napoleon. Forrest, the American Civil War general, with his "Get there the firstest with the mostest." Simple. Common sense. Rarest sense of all. Men—how he loved them! Marching, singing, riding, squadron by squadron. Englishmen. Scots, Irish, Welsh. Soldiers of the Queen—King now. George V. But it was the old Queen's commission he had held, then Edward VII's— Teddy, the playboy-diplomat. He hoped he could get nearer to Jim. Too old, too much rank, too many medals. North-West Frontier, Afghanistan, Egypt, Matabele Rebellion, Boer War, Queen's and King's. Always managed to see the fighting, got himself seconded from the regiment—Omdurman with the 17th. Met Churchill there, a Hussar. Important man now. But he'd remember him, Winston would. He'd lent him a horse once in Egypt—a black Arab mare—what the hell was her name?

Williams came in with a pair of top boots, polished, boned, till you could see your face in them. In the Greys too, been everywhere with him. But he was getting on. Had to dye his hair to get in this time. He'd pulled some strings to get him back.

"Williams," he said, "what was the black mare's name we lent Churchill in Egypt?"

"Black Arab, sir?"

"Yes. How many black mares have I had?"

"Three, sir. If we include India. 'Er name, the Gippy one, was 'Ouri."

That was it! "Thanks, Williams." Houri. He'd sold her to a chap on Kitchener's staff. A mistake. He should have brought her home and bred from her. "We should have brought her home, Williams, and bred from her."

"That's wot I said at the time, sir. But you was always pig-headed. Never listen ter me. But I don't care no more. It's 'er ladyship's funeral now—God bless 'er. I've 'anded over, sir."

32 : The Captain's Wife

IT WAS an impulse that led Jim when he got out of hospital to Elmhurst, No. 56 Mayland Road, Golders Green. Quite by accident he'd come across the squared sheet of paper Captain Legget had torn from his notebook in the train in April. Seven months ago. Seven years, seven lifetimes. He was going to see Mona, but this first. Duty first. Why duty? It was all an accident. If he hadn't found the bit of paper . . . But he had found it and he went. Took the Underground and walked. He knew it would be close to the station. Legget had to get to the office every day.

It was a nice house. Bastard Tudor, white stucco with imitation beams, but not small. Comfortable-looking and a biggish garden surrounded by a golden privet hedge. "Elmhurst" on the dark oak gate in polished brass letters. He pushed it open and went up the flagged path. Standard roses on both sides—leafless now, of course. Why hadn't he telephoned? Why? Because he had come on an impulse. Just like that. Seen the address on the bit of paper and said, "I'll go." Tell her I saw her husband in April. Why, he might have been home on leave since then, though it wasn't likely. Might have been wounded and be back, like me. Might anything. Silly of him to have come. He didn't even know Legget. Just a couple of days on a train, that was all. He rang the bell.

A smart-looking parlormaid in cap and apron opened the door.

"Mrs. Legget?" he said.

"Mrs. Legget," she repeated.

"My name is Hilton. Captain Hilton."

"This way, sir." He followed her through the hall. She opened a door and said, "Captain Hilton to see you, madam."

A slim, fair woman of twenty-seven or so rose from a chair. She looked as if she had been crying. "Captain Hilton?" she said in inquiry.

"Your husband gave me the address. He said, 'Look us up if you're in London.' "

"When did you see him last?" she asked.

"In April. I have no news of him. Just that I saw him; we went up the line together."

"April. When he went out," she said. "We went to *Chu Chin Chow* the night before and had supper at the Savoy afterward."

"I remember his saying that, Mrs. Legget." He wondered why he had come. How silly of him to come to tell a woman he had seen her husband seven months ago in Belgium. He thought of the parlormaid, the provocative way she had swung her hips. Or was it just his imagination? He looked at Mrs. Legget more carefully. She was beautiful. Slim as a reed, graceful, with immense brown eyes. Very striking in a blonde woman. Her face was pale and there were dark rings under her eyes that made them look even bigger.

She came toward him and extended her hand. Till now she had just stood looking at him, white-faced, tragic. Her hand was cold. Boneless. Lifeless, in his. "How extraordinary!" she said. Her voice was very soft.

"Extraordinary?" he said.

"Yes, Captain Hilton. You see, he's dead." When she went past him to the mantelpiece he got a whiff of her perfume—Lily-of-the-Valley, he thought it was. She turned back with a telegram in her hand.

He took it from her. ". . . regret to inform you Captain John Legget has been killed in action. . . ."

"Good God!" he said. "I'd better go. I must apologize for the intrusion. I had no idea."

"You had no idea when you came, Captain Hilton. And at the time when you decided to come I had no idea either. The telegram only came half an hour ago. I was just sitting here

231

thinking and remembering when Ethel showed you in." She smiled. How brave she was. "I think I'd like a cup of tea. Will you join me?" Seeing him hesitate, she said, "It would be kind of you. I don't want to be alone." She rang the bell. "Bring some tea and scones, Ethel."

They made conversation. He told her he had just got out of hospital. She said the children were with her parents for a week. They were waiting for the girl to come back with the tray. When she had put it down, Mrs. Legget said, "You can go, Ethel. Take the afternoon off." When she had left the room, Mrs. Legget said, "I couldn't have stood her in the house. I want to be alone."

Jim got up. "I can understand that."

"Milk and sugar, Captain Hilton? I don't mean you. You are a link. You are a coincidence."

"Yes," he said. "Milk and sugar—I mean saccharine." He laughed and took a scone.

Mrs. Legget sat back and crossed her legs. She had beautiful ankles. There was something about her; her perfume, a femininity. Her eyes had changed. They had lost their tragic look. They had gone flat, blank. She said, "It was a shock, Captain Hilton."

"Of course it was." He went over to her and took her hand. It was warm now, almost feverish.

She looked up at him. "Would you take me out to lunch?"

"I'd be delighted."

"I'll have to change, of course." She rose with one fluid movement. "You'll excuse me, won't you? Please smoke." She pointed to a silver cigarette box.

He watched her go out of the drawing room. A few minutes later she called him. "Captain Hilton!" He followed the sound of her voice. A passage, a door ajar. He knocked.

"Come in."

Mrs. Legget was standing in the middle of a bedroom that looked like a film set. She had on a chemise, stockings and shoes. Her long fair hair was down. "Close the door. You needn't worry. We are quite alone."

"But . . ."

She came up to him and put her arms around him. "My coincidence," she said. "My God-sent coincidence."

"Legget," he said. "Your husband . . ."

"He never loved me. Not after the first year. He used me, took me for granted, and I was faithful to him. Do you know why? Because I didn't want to be divorced. I wanted all this." Her eyes swept the room. She undid his belt buckle.

He pulled her to him. "My God, you're lovely!" he said.

"Lovely?" she said. "And you're lovely, too, for today!" She was laughing as she unbuttoned his tunic.

When it was over she lay on the pillows looking up at him. "I deserve a good lunch, don't I, Captain Hilton? Can you understand a man not enjoying me? Oh," she said, "I know he blamed the children. Said I'd changed. But it was him." She jumped up, naked but for her garter belt, stockings and shoes, slim as a girl of eighteen. "Pity to waste it all for six years, wasn't it?" She ran her hands over her hips. "Just Saturday nights, regular as clockwork. Can you imagine it? Sit there and watch me dress. He never watched me dress. I think a woman should keep her stockings and shoes on. I always wanted it that way. Or dressed; quickly, like a rape. Something is lost by too much preparation, Captain Hilton."

"My name is Jim."

"I like Captain Hilton. Captain Coincidence Hilton. You see, I don't really know you." She took a black coat and skirt out of a cupboard. "Black always looks well on a blonde. And of course now it's most suitable." She smiled at him adorably, sweetly. A madonna. Butter would never melt in her mouth. She put on a neat black hat of fur and velvet. She put on black kid gloves, working them over her fingers. She took a sealskin coat off a hanger and held it up for him to help her into. She said, "What about the Savoy? And *Chu Chin Chow?* There's a matinee today. That's what we did that last night. It will round it off very neatly."

"You must have hated him."

"I did. But I stuck the course. He was such a good man, Captain Hilton. I was not made for a good man."

They went down the flagged path. The gate closed behind

233

them. They picked up a taxi near the station. "The Savoy," Jim said.

The lunch was very gay. If she didn't care about Legget, why should he? She was pretty enough to turn heads as she led the way into the grill.

"You looked so tragic when I came in," Jim said. "What were you thinking of?"

"The wasted years, Captain Hilton."

When they came out of the theatre Frances Legget said, "Goodbye. No, don't take me home. I'll get a taxi from here."

"But, Frances . . . ," he said.

"It is goodbye, Captain Hilton. It is over. You were very kind. You got me over a difficult hour. You broke the ice, as it were. The ice that had been forming for six years. If you were a bit older, I'd marry you. But a rich wife would ruin you. So it's goodbye, and thank you."

He'd helped her into a taxi, saluted and watched it get lost in the evening traffic.

In the taxi Frances Legget was smiling a secret, cat-swallowed-the-canary smile. How right she had been! He'd broken the ice. And she'd look out for another husband. She wasn't going to go off the rails. A very respectable, beautiful and wealthy war widow. That's me, she thought. She laughed when she thought of Ethel. She'd come back and see the rumpled bed. She knew a thing or two, did Ethel. She'd see the picture. But she'd be too clever to say anything.

When she got home the bedroom would be tidy. Tomorrow Ethel would ask if madam could spare her red evening dress; madam had had it a long time. Next day she'd ask for an advance on her wages. "Could you advance me a fiver, madam?" If she refused there would be hints about the Captain. Would madam mind if she wrote to the Captain? Oh yes, she knew his address but she would not want to do anything without telling madam first. How furious she would be when she found out he was dead.

She was not going to tell anyone anything for a while. She

234

had picked up the telegram before she left the house. Her husband's parents were dead, so who was there to tell? She'd just let it go. When it came out in the casualty list everyone would say how brave she'd been. I didn't want to bother anyone. I didn't want sympathy. It was my sorrow, mine alone. She'd smile sadly.

She thought of the boy again, her Captain Coincidence Hilton. What luck to have a randy boy turn up like that! Very nice, but there must be no more of it. You could get into the habit.

Poor Ethel. She was a hot little bitch and she'd think she was on to a good thing. She'd have some fun with her for a day or two. "You'll never leave me, Ethel, will you?" "Never, madam." Who was going to leave a goose that laid golden eggs?

Her mind went back to her husband. It was curious that he had fallen in love with her and then become ashamed of love, of his own desires. He was just too good, too respectable, and she had embarrassed him. Not at first. At first he had liked it. Then he had changed and blamed her. Anyway, it was all over now.

33 : The Love Nest

MONA HAD picked up some knowledge of military customs from her friends. Captain George Lloyd of the Welch Fusiliers had explained the bunch of five black ribbons, in memory of the queue, sewn onto the collar of his tunic. She learned that the Coldstreams could keep their caps on in mess because George III, somewhat sozzled as a guest of the regiment, had kept his on and had extended the custom to cover all officers.

These were titbits that amused and interested her, conversational gambits for officers of other regiments. She learned some regimental numbers too, and referred to the Royal Scots as the First Regiment of Foot, and the Black Watch as the 92nd Highlanders. Nicknames, too. The Buffs, the Green Howards, the Fighting Fifth, the Death or Glory Boys. Cherry Bottoms. Titbits, verbal *apéritifs* that made the boys feel at home. Not many girls knew these things and they didn't take the trouble to remember them if they were told. Regimental badges, mottoes, were all filed away in her brain, ready for appropriate use. She had an Army List in the flat and looked up all her friends. She collected cap badges.

That was one reason men liked her. One more reason. She seemed to understand what they meant when they talked about their regimental history and battle honors. Mascots—the Wolf-hound of the Irish Guards, the Goat of the Welsh Fusiliers, the Antelope of the Leicesters. Bits and pieces that made her an ideal companion to soldiers. She kept a tin of Globe brass polish and a button stick, and used to shine up their buttons herself. A little soldier-servant and housewife all in one, that's me, she thought.

She looked around the apartment.

A love nest, that's what it was. She was glad it was winter and got dark early. Everything looked so much more cozy lit up. Pink, like the inside of a shell. The rose-shaded lights, the dark red carpet. The chairs and big sofa upholstered in pink. Pink made a girl look prettier. Peaches, strawberries, cherries. All pink and red fruits, succulent, delicious.

There was a bunch of pink chrysanthemums in a vase on the table. Chrysanthemums lasted well. She smiled around at the sitting room as if it was a person. Good taste. Nothing tarty about it. Just feminine.

Everything was ready. The tea tray laid, the kettle on the stove, the muffins buttered, just waiting to be popped into the oven. Even aspirins on the tray, a small bottle. He might want an aspirin. Jimmie Hilton, her baby soldier. He'd be here by five. She had lots of time. She thought of her shock when she'd seen his name in the casualty list. Wounded. They never said how badly and there was no way of finding out. Then his letter had come, badly written because he couldn't hold the paper down. Left shoulder. "I can't use my left arm." And she'd gone up to Reading to see him. Thin, pale, his arm in a black silk sling. When they had made love in her room at the hotel, it had hurt him. But he'd just laughed.

She ran in her bath. Lots of bath salts, violet-scented. She could soak for a quarter of an hour, a lovely feeling, the hot water on her belly and her breasts. Lovely. She had beautiful skin, smooth and very white. Not olive like some dark girls. She raised one foot out of the water and looked at her toes. Perfect. No corns, no blemishes. She wondered if he'd kiss them. He did sometimes. She kept them for him. Ten toes, all his. She'd not let another man touch them, even when they wanted to. She soaped herself with violet-scented soap and rinsed it off with an enormous sponge someone had given her. She'd seen it in the window of a chemist's shop in Piccadilly. A whole stack of sponges between those lovely big jars full of colored stuff, one pink and one green. Water, probably. The man hadn't wanted to sell it. "It's just for show," he said. "It stops people. You don't often see a sponge like that. They come from Greece, you know." She hadn't known, but her friend had bought it for her.

She dried carefully. She powdered her body with violet talcum powder. She put dabs of scent on herself in special places. She'd learned that long ago from an older girl. Gracie, her name was. But she didn't like to think of that time. She hadn't been a lady then. She put on her underwear. Black *crêpe-de-chine*. A chemise, short, wide-legged, lace-edged knickers, black silk stockings with black ruched satin garters on her thighs. She smiled. Dressing for a man was such a waste of time, and yet it wasn't. The prettier the clothes the more they wanted to take them off. She did her hair, twisting it into a knot on the back of her head and pinning it. Then she took it down again. Jimmie liked to see it down. It reached almost to her waist. She tied it with a wide piece of black moiré ribbon. She looked like a schoolgirl. From the wardrobe she took a black cashmere coat-dress with gold buttons all the way down the front. Twenty buttons. She had counted them. She kicked off her mules and put on patent leather court slippers with very high heels. There was still her face to do, not that it needed much. A touch of rouge, powder and lipstick. She licked her finger and smoothed her eyebrows. She was ready. There was still fifteen minutes to go.

She went into the sitting room and turned the gas fire up. The little white composition skulls glowed brighter, turned scarlet. She sat on the sofa, her feet together, her shoes shining like the hooves of a deer, and her hands in her lap. This was a time she enjoyed. The anticipation, the waiting, ready. A mixture of expectation and memory. She looked at the photos of the men on the mantelpiece. At Jim's picture. How the war had changed her baby! She had no other engagements. There had been one but she had canceled it. The little flat looked lovely. Warm in the rosy light of the pink-shaded lamps and the glow of the gas fire. She looked her best, too. She had been to the hairdresser to have her hair washed and water-waved. The black dress with gold buttons was new. It was cut quite low. She was *chic,* neat, perfumed. A little fast-looking, but in the house that was all to the good. She went over everything in her mind: the vase of flowers on the table, the tea, the muffins ready to pop into the oven. Everything.

She sat quite still on the sofa, her ankles crossed, waiting for his double ring. When it came she got up and went quite slowly to the door. She wanted to enjoy it, to savor it. This was so different from the others. She smoothed her dress down. Not that it needed smoothing. Not cashmere. But to savor the moment, the instant, like chocolate on her tongue.

She went to the door. How often had she gone to the door to let a man in! Into her. Because the flat was part of her. The rosy pink beginning of her, as it were. To come into the flat was already a kind of lovemaking. An entry.

She didn't see him clearly in the passage as she opened the door. Just the shape and his arm in the sling. "Darling!" she said. He pushed past her into the room. She closed the door and followed him. He turned, put his arm around her, pressing her

238

to him, bending her backwards as he kissed her, forcing her face back with his arm. He had been drinking. He had not shaved. He went on forcing her back silently, without a word. His body against hers, step by step, till the backs of her knees were against the sofa and she fell. A moment later he was on her, ripping her knickers off, smashing the elastic. He took her. The buttons of his tunic and belt buckle hurt her, pressing into her breasts and belly. He seemed enormous, terrifying, a complete stranger who was raping her. His left arm, folded under him on her body, felt like a bar of iron. She tried to push him off, her hands as ineffectual as butterflies. Then, as suddenly as it had begun, it was over and he was crying, sobbing, and saying, "Christ, oh Christ!" He had rolled off her and was lying, his face hidden against the cushion of the sofa, his body racked with sobs that shook it. Her baby. My baby, she thought. Oh my baby, what have they done to you? She pulled his head on-to her breast and held him. The sobs ceased, he was crying softly. But wetly, as if all the tears that had been dammed up for years were suddenly let free. How awful it must be to be a man and unable to cry! Afraid to cry. Holding it in. Holding it in till something broke. She stroked his hair. Her baby. Then she slipped her dress off one shoulder and raised her chemise and put her nipple into his mouth, holding the breast for him. His arm was around her. He sucked her, nuzzling like a child, an infant, a baby. If only she'd had milk to give him, something more than this dry softness. The sucking ceased, the arm around her shoulders relaxed. He was asleep. Propping him up with cushions, she got clear of him.

What an experience! What he must have gone through to change like this . . . The laughter—and they had laughed at Reading—had gone out of him. She went to the kitchen and put on the kettle. A cup of tea and an aspirin was what she needed. And she'd got them out for him. What an experience! Primitive, that's what it was. Being raped by a man and suckling a baby all in fifteen minutes. She was excited, sexually excited, profoundly moved by something she didn't understand. Some deep thing in her bowels, in her womb. Her instinct.

She looked at the drinks she had got ready: whisky, brandy, sherry. A siphon of soda. She'd put a spot of Johnnie Walker in her tea, lace it. When she went to take the kettle off, her knees were trembling. Warm the pot, take the pot to the kettle, not the kettle to the pot. One spoonful per person and one for the pot. All the rules for making tea.

She made it. Three spoons in case he woke up. She poured a cup. Milk, sugar. Her friends brought her sugar. She got the whisky bottle, her hand still shaking. She shook out an aspirin, swallowed it with a mouthful of tea, and went back to sit beside Jimmie. Somehow he seemed more than ever hers. She'd been the first one and now he'd taken her like that without a word or a by-your-leave. A woman who belonged to him, something he needed desperately and had to use. No one had ever needed her before. And she had taken him to her breast, quite without thought. Like a mother. She had only done that once before. She supposed some girls would think it disgusting. But why was it? It was beautiful but strange, a man in the dual role of stallion and infant. Incredible. She was calmer, the whisky and aspirin were doing their job.

The next thing was to undress him and get him to bed. She went to the bedroom to turn down the bed. She looked at herself in the long glass. What a state she was in! Five buttons were gone from her frock, but she'd find them easily enough and it wasn't torn. The pretty lace knickers were, though. Ruined, but she'd keep them. Girls did keep things. Dance programs, letters, nightdresses in which they'd made love, wedding veils.

She looked as if she had been raped. And so I have, she thought. But she looked well on it, her eyes bright, her lips full, the color high in her cheeks that were generally on the pale side.

She went back into the sitting room to take off Jim's shoes. She took off his belt. She got the right arm out of his tunic. She undid the knot of his sling and let the arm hang down. He had no use in it, some nerve or something. Then she pulled the jacket off. She slipped his suspenders over his shoulders, and taking his trousers by the cuffs—there was no need to undo any buttons—she pulled them down. She got his shirt over his head and down over the hanging arm. She put his arm in the sling again and tied it. He had hardly moved, just vaguely tried to help her as he felt her hands and her tugs. His underpants, his socks. Now he was naked except for the black silk sling. She put her arm around him, her right arm, the hand under the right armpit that was moist with sweat. "Stand up!" she said. "Stand up! Try, Jimmie, it's only a few yards, and hold on to me." He made the effort, his eyes still closed, staggering. But she got him there. He sat on the edge of the bed and fell back. She put her hands under his knees and lifted his legs up. Then she shoved him over toward the center so that he would not fall out. He wasn't drunk, she knew that. He had just been drinking a bit and it had hit him. He was breathing heavily, almost panting, with his mouth open. She bent to kiss his forehead and found it moist with perspiration. She fetched her washcloth from the bathroom, wet it with cold water and wiped him. She wiped under his arms, his loins, and dried him. A baby, helpless. There was something in women that made them like men being help-less. A kind of revenge for the way they dominated them. Lords and masters, or babies. The whole thing was a revelation to her. And she'd thought she knew so much about men. This was another side to them. When a man was used up he reverted to childhood. A young man exhausted, an old man worn out with his years, senile in second childhood.

Let him sleep. She had some sausages in the little meat safe in the window. She sat down on a chair in the kitchen and began to peel potatoes. She put a saucepan of water on to boil. Sausage and mash. The spuds wouldn't take long if she cut them up. She was hungry. She made a fresh pot of tea and went to the door for the evening paper that was lying on the mat. But she couldn't read it. It was all war news. She didn't want to hear any more about it, not today. She went back to thinking about Jim.

He'd called from the Regent Palace Hotel. He'd left hospital yesterday—leave—and then he was going somewhere for treatments. Something electrical for his arm, she'd gathered.

241

But he hadn't said much, not really. He'd said, "I'll tell you everything when I see you." Like hell he had. Not a word, not a peep; just "Christ, oh Christ!" Action, not words. But they spoke too—the savagery of it, and the letdown. Breakdown, really.

She decided to have another bath—very hot—and go to bed. He hadn't moved but was breathing more quietly. More bath salts. This time she soaked for half an hour. More talcum powder, more perfume. She didn't put on a nightdress—enough had been torn for one day.

She switched out the light and pulled him to her. She made love to him till he responded—gently, sleepily. But she made him. She believed in love. It was therapeutic. She had read that somewhere. It meant "good for you."

And then suddenly he burst into tears, lying there on top of her. Great sobs racked him again. She felt his tears on her neck and breast. She struggled out from under him and held his head to her bosom. Her lover, her baby. What had they done to him? What had the war done? A few minutes later he was asleep with her arms around him.

In the middle of the night he woke shouting for bombs—"Bring some more bloody bombs!"—and his hands were at her throat as if he was going to choke her. Then he woke. He was sweating, the sheets were wet with it. She was wet where she had held him to her.

"I had a nightmare," he said. "Did I scream?"

"Yes, you did. You wanted more bombs and you tried to choke me." She switched on the light. He was relaxed now, lying back on the pillow, more like himself. Her boy. "I'll make some tea." She jumped up. It was three in the morning.

"You're lovely like that," he said. "I've often thought of you like that, naked, in a dugout at night, after a parcel came from you as if you'd sent part of yourself in it. And then I'd make love to you. Masturbate. But it was you, Mona, always you. I could feel you, smell you."

She put on a dressing gown. He'd made her feel naked.

"I'm sorry," he said. "I don't know what's the matter with

242

me," and began to cry again, softly, like a child who has lost something. But he wasn't a child. He was a man. She pulled him to her and they made love again. Quite slowly, as if he wasn't there, only the man part of him seeking release. What he needed was to get that terrible man-stuff out of him, the killing-stuff. The love-stuff. Perhaps they were part of the same thing.

Then he slept, breathing easily, while she lay beside him thinking of what had happened. Of the brutality of it; his attack; the way he had forced her thighs open with his knee and torn off her clothes; his nightmare; and then afterwards as gentle as a kitten. All the same man. The same boy. Her great big baby at her breast. All that in a few hours. Such changes. Other men had had nightmares in her bed, but never like this. Perhaps it was because he was so young. Perhaps it was the great battle he had been through, the Somme battle that had been going on for months till the autumn rain had stopped it. The casualties. So many of her friends dead. And almost all of his. He'd told her that when they met in Reading. Several times he'd been the only officer left in his battalion. And he was only just nineteen. The dead, the stink. What should she do? Keep him here and nurse him? Let him wear himself out with love? They'd see in the morning when he was rested and had had breakfast. She'd make him a good breakfast. She'd act natural, as if nothing had happened, and leave it to him.

What should she do? Keep him here, put everyone else off and nurse him with love? Exhaust him, use it all up, all the reserves of it he'd built up that were posioning him, turning sour in him? She was sure, with some kind of woman's knowledge, that this happened if men did not make love. They were like starved dogs. He was on sick leave. A month, he'd said. And then what? "Go back," he said. "I must go back. I can't leave them there." They were so short of officers now. Officers with battle experience. That was extraordinary, too. This boy a veteran. When he woke they'd make love again. Men were always better afterwards; quieter, more relaxed. It took the edge and the temper out of them. She'd had plenty of friends back from the war, but not lately, not from the front. The ones who were there stayed; alive or dead. There was no leave from this battle, no respite. The only way out of it was to be wounded. Most of her friends were new friends. Only two or three of the old photos remained on the mantelpiece. The dead she had put away, buried in a dress box from Harrod's.

When Jim woke he seemed much better. She did not mention the night or the way he had raped her. If he had forgotten so much the better. She gave him a cup of tea, made breakfast and teased him into making love again because she wanted it. She ran his bath for him. She washed his back and saw the wound, a big red scar where the bullet had smashed through his shoulder blade, and a tiny hole in the front of his chest. She had tears in her eyes as she dabbed at it with a washcloth. She'd never seen a fresh red wound close up before. She dried him and helped him to dress.

"Where are you going?" she asked.

"The Regent Palace. Plenty of life there. People. Women. Girls, men I know. It's wonderful to see women again, Mona. To smell scent and furs and listen to the orchestra." Then he had kissed her goodbye, picked up his cap and gone.

But something was wrong. He hadn't looked quite right. He'd forgotten his stick and his gloves. He hadn't shaved or said when he'd be back.

34 : The Ambulance

WHEN HE left Mona, Jim had no idea where he was going. None of his memories were very clear. He'd left the hospital, come up to London and gone to the Regent Palace Hotel; taken a room and left his bag there. He'd called Mona and met some chaps. They'd been in some of the same places. They'd had a few drinks and talked about the war and girls. The Regent Palace

Rotunda was a good place to pick up girls. They came in pairs generally. They sat about in the Palm Court, showing their legs. "Get a dose from them, too," one chap said. "Amateurs who don't know how to take care of themselves. Sooner have a real tart any time than one of those flappers."

The nightmare was the clearest part in his mind, clearer than Mona. He'd asked her, "Did I scream?" God, the horror of it—to run out of bombs or ammunition . . . Girls. Bombs. A dose of clap. Why did they call gonorrhea clap? And he'd been to Golders Green. What the hell had he gone there for?

He was walking fast, marching heel and toe, a short, light infantry step, a good four miles an hour. Very soldierly, a gold wound stripe on his wounded arm, his shoulders back. He knew where he was going, and he didn't know. Leave it to his legs. They'd get him there. They were in charge. Men's legs, strong and hairy. Girls' legs—long, sleek, soft, white above their black silk stockings. Asking for it with their short tight skirts.

Two soldiers saluted him. He took no notice. He passed a general officer—red tabs, gold hat, medals, boots, spurs. He paid him no compliment. "It's not the man you salute, it's the uniform." Bugger the uniform. He was busy, he was going somewhere. If legs could talk they'd tell me where I'm going. Legs! Where are you bloody bastards taking me at such a bat? They acted as if they knew the way. Of course they knew the way. Everyone knew it. Up the Bayswater Road toward Notting Hill Gate, with the railings of the park on the left.

He hadn't given them any orders. His bloody legs were acting automatically, running away with him like a horse. He was going to find out why Kathleen hadn't answered his letters. Kathleen, his golden girl. He laughed. Funny, thinking I made that up. Lots of men must have golden girls. Lots. Lots. Mona was dark, ivory-skinned, with a black triangle drawn neat as a ruler across the bottom of her belly, and little twisty black tassels in her armpits. Why had he done that to her when she was so good to him? Like a sister, like a mother. In. Out. Point, withdraw . . . Hah! Christ! Like a bloody bayonet, as if he was trying to kill her. He saw the swinging straw-stuffed sacks, the sergeant shouting, "In . . . Out . . . In . . . Out . . . The butt . . . Shout, you bastards, when you stick it in their guts!" Her guts between those soft, lovely thighs. How had he done it? But he knew why. He hated her. He hated all women for their soft power, for the moist magnet that drew men's iron into them. For the weakness that was strength. He had hated Mona because she wasn't Kathleen, because she was dark. Ebony, when he wanted the gold he had never seen because it wasn't there then. Because she was too young. Just pigeon fluff. But it would be there now—a yellow bush, a golden fleece. It was fear that made men angry. That made them go back. You went back to a woman because you were afraid of her and you had to prove you weren't. Like a battle. That was why he'd go back to the war, had to go back. He must show he wasn't afraid, conquer his fear or he'd be finished.

Then they turned, the legs did, and marched him right across the road and into a block of flats. Clanricarde Mansions. Kathleen. That's where they were taking him—to see Kathleen. How clever of them! Legs with brains. His golden girl. He didn't take the lift; he walked up the two flights and rang the bell.

A maid he'd never seen before came to the door. Irish, her eyes smudged in. Dark, with blue eyes. Mona had brown eyes. But she looked hot, as if she'd take it. Little white cap and frilly apron. Nice legs.

"Miss Gowan?" he said. That was her name. Kathleen's. Funny, you thought of a person with one name and asked for someone else, and they were the same.

"She's away, sir."

"Where is she?"

"An' why may you be askin'?" She had dropped the "sir." She didn't like Englishmen or uniforms—and why should she? She didn't like England—only the money she made here. Irish still, remembering Cromwell, and God bless the Hun.

"None of your bloody business," he said and pushed past her. "I'll see Mrs. Gowan."

"Who's that, Moira?" He heard her voice.

"A man, madam. A sodjer. Drunk, I think."

"It's me, Mrs. Gowan. Jim Hilton."

"Come in, come in!" She rustled toward him. He knew what she was thinking. She supposed he'd come for tea. She led the way into the drawing room. "Do sit down," she said.

He sat down. How well he remembered it! They'd sat on that chair, the big one with a cretonne cover of red and pink flowers, and made love on it—kids' love—kissing and exploring. Mrs. Gowan had been out, Dr. Gowan was at the surgery and it was the maid's day off. "We're all alone," she'd said. They hadn't been alone for months, not since the woods and dunes in France. He sat in the chair and she sat on the arm. He pulled her over onto his lap, laughing, her long slim legs in the air.

"I've missed you," he had said.

"Me, too."

This was what they had missed, the kissing, feeling and hand-loving. That was before Mona. Between Gwen and Mona. Between failure and success.

Mrs. Gowan was staring at him. He looked funny. Wild-eyed and unshaved. It showed when the light caught his face. "What did you want to see me about, Jim?"

"Kathleen," he said. "Where's Kathleen?"

"She's at school. I felt she needed boarding school. A little discipline. Girls at that age—" she made a vague gesture with her hands— "difficult," she said. "The verge of womanhood . . ."

He knew what she was thinking: what was the good of trying to explain such things to a boy? But he knew better than she did how near Kathleen was to being a woman.

"My letters?" he said, standing up. "What about my letters? She stopped answering them."

"I made her, Jim. She's too young for that kind of thing. It's a phase all girls go through, thinking you're in love."

"You couldn't," he said. "You couldn't have stopped her."

"Then why didn't she write to you?"

"Because you stole my letters. Christ Almighty!" he shouted. "I was fighting and you stole my bloody letters!"

"She was too young."

"Then you did!"

"Yes, I did." She was exasperated. She wished her husband was here.

"What could she have thought of me?" Jim asked.

"That you were grown up now, a soldier, and didn't want to be bothered with a little girl. That's what I told her."

"God damn you!" he said. "God damn you!"

"How dare you!"

"Dare? You silly old woman. Have you any idea of what it takes to frighten us now? Us kids, us boys, us puppy lovers? Jesus," he said, "don't you read the papers?" The room was beginning to go around and around, the floor rising and falling like the deck of a ship. He felt himself reel. He recovered, reeled again and fell, as the maid came in with a letter on a silver tray.

"Mother of God," she said. "He's drunk. I said he was."

"Why don't you lie down?" Mrs. Gowan said. She took his arm and helped him up. "I'll take you to Kathleen's room."

It was a nice room. A girl's room, with mirrors and teddy bears and muslin frills on everything—the dressing table, the bed. It seemed to smell of her. He lay down on the bed.

"I'll take off your shoes and bring you a cup of tea."

Why the hell did everyone want to take off his shoes and give him tea?

Mrs. Gowan went to the telephone and called her doctor.

"Is that Dr. Burns?"

"Yes. Who is it?"

"Mrs. Gowan."

"Anything wrong?"

"I've got a boy here, a friend, a young officer. He fell on the floor in a kind of faint. He behaved in a very queer way, then he staggered and fell. What shall I do?"

"Take off his shoes, put a pillow under his head and a blanket over him. I'll be there in ten minutes. I'll come as soon as I've called an ambulance."

That was the first thing Jim saw when he came to—the doctor bending over him, pulling back his eyelids, and that

248

bloody woman, and the Irish bitch of a maid looking at him as if she hoped he'd die.

"Shell shock, Mrs. Gowan," the doctor said. "A delayed reaction. The ambulance should be here in a minute."

That was the last thing Jim remembered, the doctor, a middle-aged man in a frock coat, bending over him and saying, "Drink this, my boy, and you'll feel better." The doctor and Mrs. Gowan blurred together. He heard the doctor say, "The ambulance will be here in half an hour, Mrs. Gowan."

Ambulance? Jim struggled to get up. "I don't want a fucking ambulance," he said. "I'm walking wounded."

35 : The Doctor

THE GIRL who came into Jim's room was blonde, as fair as Kathleen. Gray-eyed, her white-gold hair piled up under her little cap. Her uniform was the pale blue of a hot, washed-out summer sky. Her crisp white apron was belted with a band like a man's white stiff collar. She was tall. Slim, with a willowy, tree-in-the-wind-like carriage.

"I'm Moran," she said. "Nurse Moran."

Jim stared at her from his bed. He had never seen anything like her. The girl of his dreams. Kathleen grown up. He couldn't take his eyes off her face.

"You're Captain Hilton, aren't you?" she said, as if she had to say something.

"Yes," he said. "Hilton. Jim Hilton. King's Own Wilts Light Infantry."

The pause was not awkward. The girl stood in the door, the boy lay in bed, both held by some enchantment. As if the whole war had been for this, to bring them together in this ward. That was what it seemed to him, as if the war had been a cause and this was its effect.

"I've come to take your temperature," the girl said. Only then did he notice a potted-meat bottle in her hand with half a dozen thermometers standing in some liquid. Mona had often sent him chicken and ham paste in pots like that. It struck him as extraordinary.

She came over to the bed, starched and rustling. He noticed her white cuffs. Stiff too, like the belt. She bent over him and put the thermometer into his mouth. For an instant her fingers touched his lips. For an instant her eyes were very close to his—deep gray pools with black irises, blank with official function. But under all that white starch and blue linen was a girl, white-skinned, tipped with gold. Like Mona, only gold instead of ebony. Gold like Kathleen.

She was looking down at her watch, silver on a black leather strap. She took the thermometer out of his mouth, read it and flicked the mercury down, her cuff clicking. Then she entered it in his chart.

"No temperature, have I, nurse?"

She smiled. "I'm not allowed to tell you," she said, and went out of the room.

Dr. Charles Davis was interested in his new patient. James Hilton, Captain, KOWLI. Shell shock after having been wounded in the left shoulder on the Somme. GSW. Gunshot wound. But it was healed. And then suddenly his arm had become useless. This was obviously psychosomatic, a defense mechanism to keep him at home, something of which his conscious mind was completely unaware.

Dr. Davis's main interest before the war had been masochism in women. As a Freudian, he attributed this to an escape mechanism too, a way of avoiding responsibility, a kind of security such as was found among some prostitutes who, having sunk to the bottom, could fall no farther. No more effort was required. There was in a way a certain parallel between these women and soldiers in the line; between a man rescued by a wound from hell and a woman reconciled to a way of life because there was no way out.

The principles that governed human behavior were constant. A pain-pleasure syndrome irrespective of sex or age. The shell shock of this boy, like so many others, had probably been produced by his confrontation with civilian reality, with life after a nightmare. He was also again faced with the possibility of making choices. Of alternatives. For months he had lived without option; only able to go in one direction. To run away and avoid danger—a natural inclination—would have precipitated danger—the danger of being disgraced and shot for cowardice. For months his every act had been dominated by subconscious fears. They had been removed by his wound and revived by its cure. He would have been, until his arm became paralyzed, fit for service in a month. A month's sick leave and then he would have gone back. Dr. Davis was convinced that if the war ended tomorrow, young Hilton would regain the use of his arm immediately. However, since the war was not likely to end tomorrow, they would have to count on time and women who, with a young man, could be considered as a form of time. Sex. Women for men. Men for women. They were the adjusters, the regulators which, with luck, brought the ship back on to an even keel. Or wrecked it.

He had given the boy a pretty nurse. Sick officers were not supposed to have anything to do with nurses. Against regulations for them to go out together even when they were well enough to do so. A stupid regulation. A pretty VAD who came into his ward to take his temperature, to help him eat up his food, could change the focus of his mind, lead it away from horror, lead it forward into life, because women were life.

Shelagh was an attractive girl. Pretty, with a nice figure. Nubile. She had been engaged to a man who had been killed on July 1st, with the other thousands. The beginning of that endless engagement in which this boy had also been involved. The girls of her generation were going to be hard put to find husbands. These losses were having an immediate effect on morals and later would affect the nation genetically. The very

251

best, the cream of England, had gone west. A curious phrase, he wondered at its origin. If death was west, was birth east, the rising sun its symbol? And what would be the effect of the war on the survivors? What traumas? What loneliness for the few who, in the end, survived their generation? Men in their twenties whose friends were all dead.

Jim, lying in bed, found he had very little recollection of the last few days. There was something about the captain's wife, about Kathleen's mother, but they were all confused in his mind. He remembered being out in the streets. The people, the buses, the taxis, and the next thing was waking up here with his left arm useless. Though it had still been in a sling, he had been able to use it for essentials when he got out of hospital. Cut food, dress, and so on.

The door of his room opened and his mother came in.

"How are you, Jimmie?" She had flowers in her hand. Flowers for the sick, for the dead. No flowers for the dead in France. Too many of them. Not enough flowers in the whole bloody world. How bloody cheerful she was! And why shouldn't she be cheerful? Married to a bloody general, sleeping with a murderer, an assassin. That's what generals were, the bastards. Murderers. Throwing men onto uncut wire, wave after wave of them.

She looked younger. She had on a nigger-brown tweed suit, a black fox scarf, a black hat, gloves and shoes. A bloody picture. It was hard to believe she was forty and his mother. It wasn't like it had been. There was a man between them, a general at that. Once he had been her whole life, now he wasn't. Just part of it. He said, "I'm doing pretty well. Just this arm. But they say I'll get the use of it back. Nothing organic. They can't understand it."

"I don't care about your arm, Jimmie. You're safe. The General says he thinks he can wangle a staff job for you. ADC."

Not to save his life would he take anything the General got him. Not his life on a platter, like John the Baptist's head. And why the hell did she always call him "the General"? Why not "John"? When she moved, she rustled. She must have on a taffeta petticoat. Like Mona's. Like the nurse, Moran. Everybody seemed to rustle. Taffeta . . . starch . . . his mother . . . Mona . . . Moran. Girls, women. Of course he had never thought of his mother as a woman before. Most chaps didn't. Incest. He had always wondered how such a thing was possible. He didn't now. It was obvious his mother was in love. A woman in love had a kind of aura. It showed. Mona. Why hadn't he gone to see her? Or had he? That was the bugger about all this. After leaving Reading on sick leave he didn't know what the hell he'd done.

His mother had sat down and crossed her legs. Her ankles were beautiful. He wasn't surprised at the General wanting her. Or any man. Even a young man. That was pretty bloody extraordinary.

"I had my hair done before I came," she said. "I wanted to look pretty for you."

"You are pretty. Getting married has done you good."

Irene felt herself blushing, as if she knew what was in her son's mind—that he saw her as a woman. And she saw him as a young man, not a boy anymore. A young man who had had women, girls. She wondered about them. How strange it was that her little boy should do that, get into bed with some girl she'd never seen, and fondle her. Feel her. Fuck her. Good God, who would ever have imagined she'd use a word like that, even unspoken, in her mind? But she'd been up to the General's headquarters quite a lot. She'd heard the troops talk when they didn't know she was there. She'd spoken to the General about it. "Their language, John . . ."

"It doesn't mean anything, darling. Just adjectives to qualify the noun. 'Pass the bloody butter, Bill,' and 'Where's that effing tea?' " He'd laughed. "Soldiers," he said. "The only soldiers who never swore were Cromwell's mealy-mouthed psalm-singing bastards."

So she'd got used to the idea but she never thought she'd stored the words in the dictionary of her mind. But why not? What other word was as good? Old Saxon, John said. Sleep with, lie with, have carnal knowledge of. Euphemisms, all of them.

And one day he'd find the right girl and marry her. My baby. And have babies of his own, and she'd be a grandmother.

"How are you off for books, Jim?"

"They've got a good library."

"And food? Is the food good?"

"First-class, Mother."

He knew she was just talking, her mind elsewhere. She was a mother visiting a soldier son in hospital. It was a kind of set piece. "Yes, I go to see him every day, poor boy."

"Oh," she said, "the flowers! We mustn't let them die, must we? Chrysanthemums."

Where had he seen pink chrysanthemums before? "I'll ring my buzzer," Jim said, and pressed the button.

A pretty girl in a pale blue VAD uniform came in. Starched, crisp. But under all that she was a girl, a woman. Lady Blakeney wondered if a man had ever found her—the woman under the uniform, under the skirt. If her son ever would . . . If . . .

"Oh, nurse," she said, "I'm Jim's mother, Lady Blakeney." She rose, holding out her hand. They shook hands. "I was wondering if you could find a vase. Flowers make such a difference, don't they?"

"They do indeed, Lady Blakeney." She took the flowers and went out.

"What a pretty girl, Jim!" Wounded hero, pretty nurse. "I'll tell the General; it'll make him quite envious."

God damn the General! "She is pretty, isn't she? And she's nice, too. Takes my temperature and cuts up my food."

His mother laughed. She had a pretty, rather girlish laugh.

The nurse came back with the flowers in a vase. "They look lovely, don't they? Such nice long stems."

"I love chrysanthemums," his mother said, "except that they come so late in the year. Practically the last flowers before winter, aren't they?"

"I feel that too," the girl said. "It's the spring I love. Daffodils, pheasant's-eye, fruit blossom."

Bloody women. Spring meant summer. Summer meant more offensives. Too wet for war now. There'd been rain ever since he'd left. He'd had a couple of letters. Cold, mud, rain, sleet, snow. He thought of the snow in April when he'd been at Ypres. He wished to Christ they'd go and leave him alone. He had a lot to sort out in his mind.

The nurse did go. She said, "Goodbye, Lady Blakeney."

"Goodbye, my dear. Take good care of him."

The girl turned at the door with a rustle of starch, smiled and said, "I will. I will, indeed."

And she would, too. There was something about the boy that touched her. The way he had looked at her the first time he had seen her. Stared. Just stared at her. Wounded in the Battle of the Somme where her Francis had been killed. They should have got married. She'd never forgive herself.

"I'll go now, Jim." His mother bent over to kiss him. He smelled her perfume—lilac. He smelled a kind of feral, animal smell from her fox scarf. He smelled the woman in her. It was embarrassing because she was his mother. She said, "Oh! I nearly forgot. I brought you some cigarettes. Abdullahs." She took a box out of her bag and put it on the bedside table beside the flowers.

He only smoked stinkers. Player's Navy Cut, Goldflake. Not Egyptian cigarettes. How the hell would you get them in the line? They were for generals.

"Goodbye, darling. I'll be back tomorrow. Is there anything you want?"

"Goodbye, Mother. No, thank you, I've got everything."

She went out.

That bloody girl. The spitting image of Kathleen—his little golden love—but older, of course. She was what Kathleen would be like by now. Grown up. He had stared at her when he had first seen her, confused between the two. Trying to turn her into Kathleen.

Mona. He'd write Mona a letter. Tell her where he was and she'd come to see him. What the hell was her address? An hour later it came back to him.

When Dr. Davis heard that a young lady was asking if she could see Captain Hilton, he sent a nurse to ask if she would be good enough to come into his office.

"This way, please. Doctor, Miss Moon."

Dr. Davis rose, came forward and took her gloved hand. "I am so glad you came," he said. "I want to talk to you about Captain Hilton. Please sit down." He pointed to a chair.

Mona took off her gloves. She always made a thing of it, a ritual, as if she were undressing. He offered her a cigarette. A very pretty young woman, dressed entirely in black as if she was in mourning.

"Now, Miss Moon," he said, going back to his desk, "do you know Captain Hilton well?"

"Yes, Doctor."

"Intimately?"

She crossed her slim legs and looked at him. "What do you mean by that?"

"Have you ever slept with him?"

"Oh, yes."

"And are you fond of him?"

"Yes." Fond, she thought. I love him. He's my baby soldier.

She was almost beautiful, almost a lady, and extremely attractive sexually. She must have lots of friends.

"Have you slept with him since he came back from the front?"

"Yes. At the Station Hotel at Reading when I took a room as Miss Hilton, saying I was his sister. He was allowed out, doctor, so we had lunch together and made love."

"And he was normal?"

"He was sweet." Her eyes grew tender at the memory.

"And the next time?"

"Last week at my flat. I was expecting him; he had been given a month's leave, but his arm was still in a sling."

"And what happened?"

"I had everything prepared," she said. "Kettle full, muffins ready to pop into the oven. Fresh flowers . . ." She saw it all in her mind.

"And what happened, Miss Moon?"

She sprang up. "Jimmie raped me! As soon as the door was closed, he caught me, pushed me down on the sofa, tore off my clothes and had me." She moistened her lips with her tongue. There was no anger in her voice. After all, if she had been angry she wouldn't be here to see him. She said, "I don't mind now. He had to do it. He was like a bent spring. Seeing me there, all pretty and waiting for him in the flat where we'd been so happy, was too much for him. He went off pop, sort of off his head." Looking back on it now, she was glad he had. That she'd had the power to send him crazy. And it had been exciting. This was the first time she'd really known the full savage strength of a man. She'd abandoned herself to him. She'd never given herself like that before. It had brought her closer to him. She was his woman. If he wanted to rape her, let him. She was dreaming, her eyes distant.

"And what happened then, Miss Moon?"

"He burst into tears and said he was sorry. That he'd been drinking. And then he passed out and I undressed him and got him to bed. Then he came round and we made love, doctor. I believe in love for men," she said. "It's therapeutic."

"Who told you that?"

"I don't know. I'm not even sure what it means. I think it means good for them if they are in a state."

"Oddly enough, that is my own theory, Miss Moon."

Then Mona went on, "In the middle of the night he had a nightmare. He shouted for more bombs and tried to kill me. He had his hands around my throat. I pulled his hair to wake him and he started to cry again. I nursed him, doctor, like a baby, I mean. I put my nipple in his mouth and he sucked it and went to sleep in my arms. Do you think that was an awful thing to do, doctor? I mean immoral, disgusting?"

"No, dear. I think it was a wonderful thing to do." He was getting to like this girl. "Very therapeutic."

"Well," she went on, "he slept and slept. He woke about

257

lunchtime and I gave him bacon and eggs and tea. I'd hidden the clock. He didn't know how late it was—thought it was breakfast time. But he was very sweet and quiet, and then he got up and had a bath, dressed and went out. But he wasn't right, doctor. He didn't shave and he forgot his gloves and little stick. I'll bring them around next time I come. Can I go and see Jimmie now?"

"Just one more thing. When you made love at the Station Hotel he had his arm in a sling?"

"Oh, yes. I had to help him undress and dress. We laughed about it."

"And when he came to your flat it was still in a sling?"

"Yes, it was."

"Then how did he push you down and rape you, and then later on try to throttle you? You said he had his hands on your throat. Both hands?"

"Well, he did. I can't tell you how, doctor. But he was very strong."

"And when he left your flat?"

"He had put on his sling again. You know, I've never thought about it before, but it's funny, isn't it?"

"No, Miss Moon, it's not funny. It's sad. And because you are his friend and can, in the long run, do more for him than I, I am going to give you what I think is the explanation. You will keep it to yourself, please; don't mention it to him or to his mother, Lady Gore Blakeney, if you meet her in visiting hours."

"I didn't know his father was a Sir."

Dr. Davis smiled. Just as he had thought—almost a lady. What a lot she had learned, but not everything. "It's his step-father, my dear," he said.

"So that's why he stayed at the Regent Palace?"

"Perhaps. But now I'll tell you what is wrong with him, why he has no power in his arm. It doesn't react to electric shocks or needle pricks."

"You have been hurting him!" Mona was on her feet, her eyes blazing.

"No, dear. That's just it. He doesn't feel anything."

"Then why?"

"As long as his arm is useless, Miss Moon, they won't send him back to France."

"But he wants to go back—he told me so—to his battalion."

"That, my dear, is one part of him—the duty part, King and Country, and so on. That's his conscious mind. But his unconscious mind, which is nature, has taken over. The law of self-preservation. And it has paralyzed his arm to save his life."

"He's not a coward," Mona said.

"Of course he's not, my dear. But he's had all he can take. Time, with your help, will cure him. Now go up and start the treatment." He took her bare hands in his. It was very warm and soft. Vital. "Come and see me any time," he said. "We'll work on your Jimmie together."

"Me work?" she said. "Me help to send him back?" Men were all mad; doctors, the bloody lot of them. "But thank you all the same, doctor." She went out of the room. He watched her small neat round croup swinging as she walked to the door. For a moment he was envious of Captain Jim Hilton.

But Dr. Davis was worried by Hilton. Under his rational, calm exterior there was a latent violence that was hardly surprising considering his recent experiences in battle and responsibilities that were enormous for a boy of his age. What Miss Moon had told him only confirmed what he had felt. A company commander at nineteen and for a short time in command of the remnants of his battalion as the only officer left in the field. He was evidently highly sexed, but this might only be nature's remedy for violence. This was his theory: only women could soften men, or conversely, that without women men became savages. When he had enough data he was going to write something on the subject. There was a psychic balance between the sexes that had to be maintained if there was to be no breakdown. The wires were so easily crossed, and that after all was his job—to get them functioning again. A kind of human electrician, fixing circuits, replacing blown fuses. Fundamentally, a young man was a warrior—civilization muted this instinct, war encouraged it. But a young man today had to be what amounted to both a savage and a modern civilized man at one and the same time.

259

It was a fascinating problem for an observer, but for a boy like James Hilton it was a tragedy of which he was himself completely unaware. A hidden conflict that, despite his apparently normal behavior, was tearing him apart. He was convinced that time would heal the boy; time, and an association with women in civilian life. Just seeing them about in the streets. Women and children, for whom he had been starved. Just seeing them—the effect of their presence within the range of his eyes. And, of course, intimate involvement with one or more of them.

Jim spent Christmas in hospital, but he had lunch at Albany with his mother. He kissed Shelagh for the first time and was regaining the use of his left arm. He made love to Mona at her flat. In January he was transferred to a convalescent home in the country.

36 : The Convalescent Home

LADY WINMORRIS had turned Dortall Hall into a home for convalescent officers. It was a beautiful house, part Tudor, part Georgian, the parts separated by a walled rose garden. The Georgian part, built in a grand yet restrained manner with the wealth of the Indies, dwarfed the Tudor part, reducing it to almost cottage size by comparison. But since it was much more comfortable than the more modern building, Dorothea Winmorris had moved into it and left the big house to the recuperating officers.

Lady Dorothea, as the officers called her, was a big tweedy woman with no nonsense about her. She had a tweedy secretary, Miss Teasdale, an old butler and a staff of maids all forty or over. No nonsense at the Hall. If the men, being men, wanted that kind of thing they could go to Luton. Lots of girls there.

Not that she approved of it, but it was something you couldn't stop in either peace or war, men and girls being what they were.

Jim liked her. She met him when he arrived from the station in a two-horse brake. "So you're Captain Hilton?"

"Yes, Lady Winmorris. Wiltshire L.I."

"Young, aren't you, for a captain?"

"It's only temporary. And quite fortuitous."

"How fortuitous?"

"Accidental. Through the accident of survival, madam."

"Don't 'madam' me, young man."

Jim laughed.

"And don't laugh."

Jim said, "I thought it was funny. Accidental survival rather than accidental death."

"Sit down, boy, and have some tea." She rang the bell. Disturbed. Aftereffects of wounds. Nice-looking boy. If he married a nice girl they'd breed some good children. Very short of men like him now. Pity they couldn't bring in temporary polygamy. And why not? Because it was too logical.

"Too logical," she said aloud.

"What is?"

"Polygamy."

Queer old girl, Jim thought. He said, "What about the expense, Lady Winmorris? More than one wife, I mean."

"Subsidies, my boy. Government subsidizes everything nowadays. I'm a farmer," she said. "Always have been. Compost. Indore process. And imagine letting all the sewage run into the sea! But I'm fighting it. Now we've got the vote—women, that is—we may be able to do something. Sewage farms. I dream about them. No waste. You interested in farming, Captain Hilton?"

Captain Hilton one minute, boy the next. A character. Jim thought he'd have a shot in the dark. "Do you by any chance know my stepfather, Major-General Gore Blakeney, Lady Winmorris?"

"Gore Blimey of the Greys? Of course I know him. Every-

261

body knows him. Tried to seduce me once." She laughed. "Pretty gal then, looked very well on a horse. Hunting. The Quorn . . . Pytchley . . . Then I married Win. Killed in the war. Kimberley. That's when I took to farming, took my mind off things." She stopped talking and gave Jim another look. "Your mother a pretty woman?"

"I think so."

"Must be, or he wouldn't have married her. Good eye for a woman or a horse. Must be sixty, if he's a day. Toast? Muffins? Crumpets? Eat, boy. That's what you're here for. Country air, country food. Grind my own corn, compost-grown, no fertilizer. My own butter. Jerseys. Best herd in England."

Jim ate his tea.

"I've got a nice lot of men here, Captain Hilton. You'll like them, I'm sure." When he had finished, she said, "I'll take you over to the big house now and introduce you." At the door she paused and swung around. "No nonsense here, my boy. Nor in my village. Plenty of girls at Luton. Factory town. Used to make staw hats." She led the way out through the hall and across the rose garden.

When Jim had been at the Hall a month he asked for three days' leave. London. Mona. His mother. Shelagh.

He had no difficulty. After all, his mother lived there and she was married to old Gore Blimey. So once a month he went to London to see Mona, Shelagh and his mother. A few shows, some meals at restaurants, some time at the club seeing if there was anyone there he knew and getting the latest news from the front—the stuff the papers didn't print—because there were really two wars going on: the one the soldiers were fighting and the one the papers—so patriotically and unobjectively— reported. For them, the slightest German setback was a fore-runner of defeat—the writing on the wall—and every British raid a sign of the splendid aggressive spirit shown by our boys. But no one in one part of the line knew what was going on even fifty miles away till they read the lies about it in the papers. The war in Mesopotamia with the Turks, in East Africa, or German

West had never seemed very real to anyone on the Western Front. The area for each of them was a few hundred yards wide—a battalion or brigade front, a divisional area. That was all that concerned them. The French at Verdun only took the pressure off them, just as for the French the British were only there to relieve pressure on them. Still, at the club, at the Empire Bar and the Savoy, you got snippets of news—soldiers' snippets that each man fitted together to make a kind of overall pattern. That was another thing about going to London—to keep in touch. But Shelagh and Mona were the first objectives —first and second line, as it were. Mona was the key because she had to be free. He'd write to her, suggesting some dates. She'd wire back, "Expect you 17th or 19th," or whatever it was, and sign it "Mother." Then he'd show the telegram to Lady Winmorris and she'd say, "Of course, my boy. Give my love to Gore Blimey, if you see him, and I do hope I meet your mother one day."

Then he'd tell Shelagh when he was coming. Propose dinners and theatres so that she could arrange to get leave from hospital.

He was in love with Shelagh and he slept with Mona. The two things were quite apart. Of course he'd sooner have slept with Shelagh, but Mona was good fun and Shelagh didn't know about her. Though she must have guessed he did something like that when he was in London. She knew enough about men to guess. She liked to be kissed, made a fuss of, but no more. So he went from her to Mona; from love without making love, to making love without love. A curious system that seemed to work, provisionally at any rate. One day the values would change. As Shelagh gave him more, he would want less from Mona. The dark and the fair. The good and the bad—only it wasn't as simple as that. Mona wasn't all bad, nor probably was Shelagh as good as all that. He wasn't even sure she was a virgin. So he shuttled from one to the other, with a mixture of hopes, fears and satisfactions. A young man caught in the pincers of his age and the time.

He was getting used to his mother's marriage, accepting the

General in a vague way—the way he used to accept the existence of God. An all-powerful being in red tabs who, descending like Zeus from Olympus, had taken possession of his mother, a Sabine happy in Roman arms. Simile after simile occurred to him. One afternoon at tea she caught him smiling at her in a queer way.

"What are you smiling at, Jimmie?"

"You and the General, Mother. I'm getting used to it but I still think it's funny."

Irene lost her temper. "God damn it, Jimmie," she said, "I've got a right to my own life. I'm a woman. You're grown up now and sleeping with any bit of fluff you can pick up, so why shouldn't I get married again?"

Was this little, perfectly turned out woman, standing up in front of him and swearing at him like a trooper, really his mother? He burst out laughing, put one arm under her knees, picked her up and kissed her. "I adore you, Mother. You're so pretty! So angry! So changed! The General has certainly done you good."

"Put me down! It's not respectful, not even respectable, to carry your mother about."

"You feel nice in my arms." He put her down. "But you're right, Mother. You are a woman—all woman—and I'm glad you're so happy."

Irene burst into tears.

There was no understanding women, any woman except Mona. There were no problems about Mona, that must be why men liked her.

The General, John, had told Irene to buy some more corsets—fancy ones, satin and lace—more frillies, underclothes, more silk stockings. More petticoats that rustled. He liked those things. Feminine. I'll bet these damn suffragettes don't wear 'em, Irene. Don't want a vote, do you? My God, short hair, flat heels, no make-up. Votes for women that aren't women, and not men either." Red rag to the General, that's what suffragettes were. That terrible business with the King's horse at the Derby.

Chaining themselves to lampposts, going on hunger strikes. Saying they would revolutionize the world when they got the vote. Irene thought they were silly. Women had enough power. She could make John do anything she wanted, within reason; even some things that weren't reasonable. It wasn't votes that gave women power. She knew how they'd vote—with a man, if they loved him, against him if they didn't. And if they were in doubt, for the most attractive candidate. They'd get more her way. Frillies, lace and satin stays, silk stockings, high-heeled shoes, rustling petticoats. Scent.

Jimmie had lent her some books that doctor of his had told him to get. Freud . . . Havelock Ellis. A book called *Sex and Character* by Otto Weininger. Extraordinary books for a boy to read, but he said they helped him to understand himself. Know thyself—wasn't that in the Bible? But she'd discovered some surprising things. That John, a British major-general, was a fetishist, for instance. How she had laughed when she read about it! So that was why there was all this fuss about her underclothes. High heels, corsets. About textures—taffeta, silk, satin. That was why he liked to watch her dress and undress. Brush out her hair. Bend to do up her suspenders at the back. All these things excited him. Visual aphrodisiacs. All decent, respectable. Not like the dirty pictures she'd heard about. And what fools women were not to take advantage of such things, of their half-revealed charms. Of perfume. Sounds—like the rustle of silk, the quick tap of high heels on a parquet floor. She supposed these were the artifices used by kept women and tarts. Well, there was no reason to give them a monopoly. If more respectable married women used some of their tricks, more men would remain faithful to them. If they seduced their own husbands, if they made them make love to them, they'd be faithful. After all, you couldn't get blood out of a stone.

How she'd changed! Jimmie was right. The General, John, had changed her. Freed something in her, enabled her to think clearly about things that had been only vague feelings—submerged before—in what those books called her unconscious.

37 : The Runaway

LILIAN GOWAN had been very pleased when young Mr. Oates telephoned to ask if he could take Kathleen to a dance one of his mother's friends was giving. Kathleen was quite a problem in the holidays. And Freddy Oates seemed such a nice young man. Such good manners. He was twenty-five years of age, a lieutenant in the Middlesex Regiment. He was going to be a solicitor and join his father's firm in Lewes.

They had met him at a dinner party given by Dr. Marsden's wife. The Marsdens were old friends. And Frederick—Freddy—Oates was spending a few days with them. Dr. Marsden and his father had been at school together.

It was wonderful the amount of information Mrs. Gowan could collect in a half-hour's conversation, particularly if it was about a young man. Young men were in her mind almost as much as they were in Kathleen's. Anything to get her over that Hilton boy. A child in uniform. How irritating girls were. Still at school but wanting to be a VAD. Nursing men. Seeing them naked. Exposed to all kinds of things. Orgies. She had no idea what an orgy was. Goings-on. Her mind balked like a frightened horse at her own thoughts.

"That nice Mr. Oates called me and asked if he could take you to a dance. So polite. I said yes. You could wear your powder blue to match your eyes. You like him, don't you?"

"Oh yes, Mother. I thought he was very nice." And she had. He had made what her mother would have described as improper advances to her. Right there in front of them all, and no one had suspected anything. She hadn't moved a muscle when he put his hand on her knee under the tablecloth. Then he had worked the dress up with his fingers till his hand was on her silk stocking.

She laughed and said, "Oh yes, he's very nice. I expect he dances well." They had dancing lessons at school. Not the tango, bunny hug or anything like that. But the girls taught them to each other surreptitiously, a stolen step at a time. The powder-blue voile would be nice, though she was tired of Mother saying things matched her eyes. Because her eyes changed. If she wore green they turned quite green, like a cat's.

He wanted her and he was a man, and not a boy. He wasn't going to get her but it would be fun. As she dressed she wondered how much she would permit. If only it had been Jimmie! But she had lost him in the shuffle of war. He might even be dead. Why had he never written? Why hadn't he answered her letters? Perhaps she should have written more, but she had been too proud. Especially a letter like that last one.

The dance had been a great success. The other girls had all been jealous because Freddy was in uniform. The only man there. The others had all been boys. He had been very charming, said nice things about her dress, her hair, her eyes, her face, her figure. He had said she was beautiful. He had been surprised she was still at school. He found out when she was going back and said he would write.

"We aren't allowed to get letters from men."

"Not even from your Auntie Maud?"

"Auntie Maud?"

"That's me." How they had laughed.

He said, "And you can write to me at home. They will forward it. Mrs. Frederick Oates. Don't make the *s* too clear and it will be forwarded to me. 'Dearest Auntie, My thanks for your letter, etc., etc.' What a rag! Under their noses."

Everything was better, more fun, if it was done under their noses. Grown-up people thwarted you at every turn. Her mother, the mistresses at school. A lot of dried-up old maids. Daddy was all right. He understood her. She could wind him around her little finger. Men were all right.

She had champagne to drink. Two glasses. Horrible stuff that prickled her mouth, but it made her feel gay—made her want to dance, to sing. . . . She came into Freddy's arms. He held her close. He was very strong. He waltzed beautifully and reversed as soon as she began to feel dizzy.

In the taxi on the way home he kissed her properly, his tongue in her mouth. He touched her breasts. His hand slid up her stocking under her dress.

"I want you, Kathleen. Let's go somewhere."

She supposed he meant a hotel or something. And this was Mother's nice, polite young man.

"No, Freddy, no."

"I'm going to make love to you one day. You want me to, I know. I can feel you do."

Of course he could. She could feel herself melting in his arms. It was the music, the champagne, the dancing. It was because she was a girl and he was a man. But the answer was still NO. NO. She pushed him away from her.

"Well, I'm going to. I'm going to see you in London. I'm going to make up to your mother. I'm going to see you at school."

"You can't."

"I can. And I shall." He lit a cigarette. She took it out of his mouth. He laughed and lit another.

Next day a big bunch of yellow roses arrived for her mother and a small bunch of lilies-of-the-valley for her.

Frederick Oates had also sent flowers to his hostess and a nice "thank-you" note for "a wonderful evening." But he was in a temper. That bloody girl had done something to him. He was going to see her. Again—and again. He was going into hospital in ten days for an operation. There would be sick leave after it. He'd go down to her school and see her. If he had had her he would have forgotten her by now. But she wasn't a shop girl. Obstacles always excited him. If she hadn't been a virgin. But she was. He was sure of it, or she'd have let him. She had wanted to. She was as ripe as a plum.

During the next week Freddy Oates took Kathleen to the zoo, to the pictures twice, and called at the flat in Clanricarde Gardens where he set out to charm Mrs. Gowan, who was delighted. He seemed serious about Kathleen. He was just the kind of son-in-law she would have chosen. Frederick Oates knew what was in her mind and played up to her, flattered her. He had done all this before with other girls but he wasn't married yet. To get a girl you had to court her mother. He had even made love to one of them once, a very pretty woman of thirty-eight. He had persuaded her to let him court her daughter to deceive her husband. He had told the girl he had to make a fuss of her mother to get permission to take her out.

Kathleen watched him with interest. An idea was forming in her mind, something one of the girls had talked about at school. He was crazy about her. She'd keep him that way. She'd not draw back but he'd get no further with her. Not yet. Not till just before she went back to school.

Each time they went out together he became more urgent. At last, working him up to fever pitch, she said, "Where could we go?"

"I know," he said.

He tapped on the glass and gave the taxi driver an address in Bayswater. Not a mile from home.

It was a small hotel. He did not book or anything. He just took her upstairs and opened the door of a bedroom with a key he had in his pocket. He must have had everything arranged. She wondered if he had brought other girls here.

"You expected to bring me here, Freddy?"

"Yes, darling. I was sure you loved me." He took her in his arms and began to undress her.

It hurt her but in a way she enjoyed it. It ought to have been Jimmie, but this would teach them. This was what they had been afraid of—Mother, the bloody lot of them. It would be something to talk about at school. There were three other girls who had gone the whole way too, or so they said. They were always talking about it and she was sick of it. Freddy was going into hospital next day and she was going back to school.

"You'll write, won't you, Freddy?" Darling Auntie Maud.

And he had written a couple of letters, but not love letters. Not anything she could show to the other girls. But he gave his address. He said, "You remember that young man Freddy Oates, in the Middlesex, that your mother liked so much? He had an operation and is now back with the 18th Battalion at Hounslow. The cat has had kittens. One very pretty one, gray and white, that I think I shall keep. Much love, Auntie Maud."

It was two full months since she had seen him. His remark about the cat and the kittens amused her. Because he would have kittens too when he got her letter. "Dearest Freddy," she wrote, "I am afraid this letter is going to upset you. I am going to have a baby. It's over two months since that afternoon. . . ."

Frederick Oates was upset. Christ Almighty! He'd taken every precaution. But even if you did such things could happen. Perhaps he hadn't been as careful as he thought.

Kathleen had gone on, "I am desperate and shall have to tell the headmistress before long. She'll tell my mother and she'll tell your father."

Tell Dad. Good God! There'd been trouble about girls before. And this wasn't the kind of girl who could be bought off for a couple of hundred pounds. A doctor's daughter. There was only one way out. He'd have to marry her. But she wasn't twenty-one. How would he get her parents' permission and how would he explain the hurry?

He wrote her another Auntie Maud letter. "I shall be coming down tomorrow and staying at the Clarence. I hope you can manage to get away for an afternoon."

She did manage to get away. They met in a big lounge full of palms and caged love birds. It seemed symbolic in some way.

"What are we going to do, Freddy?"

"You're not going back, Kathleen. We're going to run away for a couple of days. Go back to the hotel. They know me there. And then go to your people. Once they know we've been living together they'll give their permission and we'll get married at a registry office."

So it had worked. Everything had worked.

"Oh, Freddy," she said, "you're making an honest woman of me."

"Not much else I can do, is there?" Good God, his father would cut him off with the proverbial shilling if he did any less and he'd not get into the firm. There was no option and she was a lovely little thing.

Two days later they went to the Gowans's apartment. Mrs. Gowan ran forward like a mechanical toy. "Kathleen, we've been crazy with worry about you. Wires, telephone calls. Where on earth have you been?"

"In London, Mother. Freddy will explain everything."

"Explain?" Mrs. Gowan turned on him like a toy on a turntable. "Mr. Oates?"

The best plan was to take the bull by the horns. Take the wind out of her sails, bring her up short.

"It is very simple, Mrs. Gowan. I have seduced your daughter. She is pregnant and we need your permission to get married, since though she is over the age of consent she is also a minor and under the age to get married without her parents' leave."

Mrs. Gowan sat down.

Freddy offered her a cigarette. He knew she did not smoke.

She said, "I don't smoke, Mr. Oates."

He passed the case to Kathleen, who took one. He lit a match for her.

"Smoking!" her mother said.

"Yes, Mother. I've been smoking for a long time."

"Perhaps you would like a drink?" Freddy said.

"I don't drink in the daytime, Mr. Oates."

"Well, I do," Freddy said. He poured out two drinks—one for himself and one for Kathleen.

Kathleen—drinking and smoking in front of her like this! Mrs. Gowan was breathing hard.

"Now, I think," Freddy said, "if you will write a note to say you and Dr. Gowan agree to Kathleen marrying me—we shall get on with it at once. You see, with Kathleen pregnant every day is important. She's two months gone."

My God, Mrs. Gowan thought. That this should happen to us! He had seemed such a nice young man. It was the war, of course, and that boy. He'd started it all. She blamed Jim Hilton more than she did Freddy Oates. Anyway, she'd wanted him to marry her, but not like this. She went to her writing desk.

As if he knew she did not know what to say, Oates said, "We, Dr. and Mrs. Gowan, agree to our daughter Kathleen's marriage to Lieutenant Oates."

"What about her father's signature?" Mrs. Gowan said.

"Sign his name too, Mrs. Gowan. Forge it. He's not going to argue the point."

He told Kathleen to call the maid.

Moira came in.

"Just witness this," he said.

She signed her name at the bottom of the page of notepaper.

"I'll get another witness," Freddy said. "Or forge it too." He laughed. "What's in a name anyway?"

Kathleen laughed too. How she'd foxed the bloody lot of them. Pregnant. Pregnant my foot! As regular as clockwork. He'd find out, of course. A false alarm, she'd say. Eighteen, and she'd taken them all for a ride because she had been a virgin, and pretty, and blonde. Life was really very simple.

Kathleen pregnant, laughing, smoking and drinking a whisky and soda in front of her like that. Her own mother. What was the world coming to? How would she tell Nils? Forging his name too. He'd blame her, of course.

"Well, goodbye, Mrs. Gowan," Frederick Oates said.

"Goodbye, Mother." Kathleen had turned on her heel with a flounce. No kiss, no apology, no nothing. Brazen, wearing an engagement ring and a wedding ring—and pregnant.

Now she had missed the engagement party, notices in the papers, the wedding. The dress, the trousseau, the fittings, the invitations, the presents. All the things a mother with a beautiful only daughter looked forward to. How lovely she would have looked in white with a veil and orange blossoms! The wedding march. But it was a nice diamond—two carats at least. Oh dear, such a nice young man doing a thing like that. She must have led him on. My daughter. How was she going to tell Nils? Drinking and smoking in front of her. Couldn't be good for the baby. Oh dear!

When Dr. Gowan came home he found his wife in tears.

"What on earth's the matter, Lilian?"

"It's Kathleen. She's been here."

"Just what I told you. Nothing to worry about. You should never have sent her away. She hated school. It's what I said. She just ran away. Can't say I blame her."

"I suppose you wouldn't blame her for coming here bold as brass and saying she's pregnant?"

Dr. Gowan began to laugh. "Girls," he said. "I told you she was nubile. Ready for it."

How disgusting he was. His own daughter, too.

"Came with her young man, I expect, didn't she? The *fait accompli*. Wanted your blessing?" He sat down and lit his pipe.

"You never did understand the facts of life, Lilian. Nature. Kathleen's a woman, not a schoolgirl. She needs a man."

"She's two months gone, Nils."

"She'd want to be certain, wouldn't she? Missing twice?"

Mrs. Gowan gave up. What could you do with a man like that? He had not even asked the seducer's name or what he did.

"He's a solicitor," she said. "You met him. He came here to dinner. Frederick Oates. You remember him, don't you, Nils?"

"Oh yes. He seemed all right. You thought so, didn't you? You let him take her out."

"So it's my fault!"

"No, my love. It's God's. It's nature's. And I can't say I'm sorry. It will be good for her. She was getting very nervous and irritable."

"You talk as if she was just anything—just something female —a cat or dog."

"A bitch is the word, Lilian. A pretty little bitch in season." He was really very tired of Lilian's mealy-mouthed approach to everything. He poured himself out another whisky, raised his glass. "To the young couple. And I hope they are enjoying themselves."

38 : The Reserve Battalion

THE RESERVE battalion of the Wiltshire Light Infantry was in hutments near Lempton on the border of Salisbury Plain. The depot was at Woolton Basset, only twenty miles away. All open country and windswept, but good for training. The battalion consisted of young officers and recruits being broken in by a permanent staff of officers and NCO's, disabled or unfit as far as active service was concerned, but good enough for home duty. All the usual stuff was going on: infantry training, close order drill, route marches, musketry, bayonet fighting, bomb-throwing, trench-digging, field days. The routine of an army in training for active service. When they had passed out they went off, the regimental band enlivening their march to the station and glory.

The rest of the establishment consisted of wounded officers and other ranks, on light duty or passed fit, waiting their turn to rejoin the expeditionary force.

When Jim reported for duty he found a number of men he knew—officers and other ranks. He got the latest news and gossip of the 10th Battalion from them. Some of them had been wounded after he left France. One piece of bad news upset him. Corporal Newhouse, a man he knew well as a first-class soldier, had been court-martialed and shot for cowardice. Newhouse had been in Frence two years. He had come through the Somme operations without a scratch. And then in December he had been picked up by the police in Doullens, miles behind the line, where the French girl he was living with was hiding him. My God, what a travesty of justice! No account had been taken of his previous service, of his Military Medal, and his exemplary behavior in action.

Jim knew what had happened. He could take no more. The thought of Christmas had probably done it. He wrote to the colonel: "If I had been there I could have testified in his favor. Why was I not informed? I could have written my evidence. Newhouse was a brave man. I have been with him in action, out on patrol with him. I could not ask for a finer comrade."

The colonel had replied:

DEAR HILTON,

Many thanks for your letter. I agree with all you say and we did all we could—the Brigadier and I, other officers in Bn, the RSM—but to no avail. It came down from Corps. They wanted an example. There had been a few desertions. Some men have not been found yet. We tried to get the sentence commuted but nothing came of it. A terrible affair. We all know that courage is expendable, that even a brave man has only so much of it. He uses it up. And Newhouse had only one leave in two years. He was used up. When the police picked him up he was wandering about like a lost child. He had escaped from the girl who was hiding him in a cellar. She has been charged with aiding a deserter. He had helped her to nurse her old mother and she was sorry for him. An additional factor was bad news from home. The usual story of an unfaithful wife. It was all too much and it broke him. However, and this is almost the worst part, before the execution he regained his mind and, refusing to be blindfolded, died as a Wiltshire Light Infantryman should—at attention, facing the firing squad with open eyes.

What more can I say? It has aged me, hurt me deeply. He was one of ours and one of the best. It is something that could happen to any of us.

I am glad you are better. Heard, too, that your MC has gone through and I assume you will be invested before long. I hope when you are fit we shall get you back. We have lost more of the old lot, but Mulholland and Goodby are well, and when they heard I was writing to you asked to be remembered to you.

By the way, I have quite recovered from my wound.

Yours sincerely,
HENRY ROBINSON,
Lt.-Col., 10th KOWLI.

It was good to know Robinson was back with the battalion—the first report had been that he had been killed.

A scene was precipitated when, in the anteroom, Geoffrey Short, a lieutenant Jim had known in France, now a captain, referred to Newhouse's cowardice in front of a group of young, newly gazetted officers, in Jim's hearing. Jim turned on him and said, "Newhouse was a splendid soldier. He was in my company and I knew him well. And talking of cowardice in the field, I'd like you to recall September sixteenth when you walked out of the battle with a nick in your ear that wouldn't have checked a boy of twelve. You were bleeding like a pig because an ear does bleed. And it got you home. But do you know why, Mr. Short? It was because we didn't want you. It was a way of saving your face and ours. So let's hear no more about Corporal Newhouse."

Captain Short stepped up to him, his fists clenched. "How dare you?" he said. "Lies. Lies. I was badly wounded."

"Don't," Jim said, as Short came closer. "A scuffle between officers in the anteroom would get to Brigade. There would be an inquiry and it would all come out, wouldn't it? And you wouldn't like that. And besides, I'd bloody near kill you."

Jim turned his back on the group and told a mess waiter to bring him a dry sherry.

Light duty meant doing very little. An occasional lecture to the men about trench warfare, some orderly-room work, and that was about all. He managed to get in a bit of hunting with Bierly when they met reasonably near. He did a bit of beagling. And he bought himself an Indian motorcycle. A lovely red and nickel-plated monster on which he ran up to London to see the girls—Mona and Shelagh and his mother.

The news of his investiture came in a white envelope with the royal coat of arms in red on the flap. A royal command. His Majesty, etc. . . . . at Buckingham Palace at 11 A.M., etc., etc.

He wired his mother he would stay with her at Albany. She wired back, "The General is coming with us." The General. He'd look very impressive. He'd probably take them to lunch afterward.

Irene Blakeney didn't remember ever being more excited. Dear Jimmie, going to be invested with a Military Cross at Buckingham Palace by the King on the 20th. He was coming to stay on the 18th. She wired prepaid to the General. He must be there. The answer came: "Congratulations. Arriving 18th. Love John."

And Shelagh. They were as good as engaged. At least she hoped so. She must get leave. She'd speak to the matron herself.

She picked up the telephone. "I want the matron, please. Lady Blakeney speaking. Lady St. John Gore Blakeney."

There were voices at the other end of the line, a pause, and then someone said, "This is the matron speaking."

"This is Lady Blakeney."

"Yes. What can I do for you?"

"A special favor. My son is being presented with a Military Cross, an investiture, on the twentieth at eleven A.M. I was wondering if you could give Nurse Moran the morning off. They are more or less engaged. My husband, the General, is coming down from the North."

The matron laughed. "I think it can be managed. She's a good girl, as girls go these days. Does she know?"

"No, not yet."

"Then I'll tell her."

"Thank you so much."

So there would be three of them with him. Of course he was wearing the ribbon—white with a purple center. But the cross was silver. He would have a miniature to wear with his other medals, because there would be war medals at the end of it, in evening dress. Of course he had no tails. He had been too young to have them at the beginning of the war. Only a dinner jacket. And he'd have grown out of that by now. It was all so extraordinary.

That evening Shelagh called her.

"Lady Blakeney?"

"Yes."

"This is Shelagh. The matron has given me the whole day off

on Friday the twentieth. Isn't it wonderful? I mean, we shall see the King and everything."

"You'd better come early, dear, say nine-thirty. The General is coming. You haven't met my husband, have you?"

"Not yet. But I'm sure I'll like him."

"He'll like you. He likes pretty girls."

Shelagh laughed. "I must run now. Goodbye till the twentieth."

Jim rode up on his red Indian, left it in a garage and walked up Piccadilly to Albany. The commissionaire, who knew him, saluted. He opened the door with his latchkey.

The General was there, shining, bright, larger than life. Jim saluted.

"Good afternoon, sir." They shook hands. "Glad you could come, sir."

"Wouldn't miss it. Irene's boy. Practically a son. And I didn't come alone. I brought Williams. Shine you up, my boy. Get into some plain clothes and give your stuff to him. Belt, shoes, cap, badge, buttons. Shine like mirrors. Like gold. Williams!" he shouted.

Williams came in.

"This is our lad, Williams."

Jim shook his hand. "I hear you're going to tidy me up."

"Yes, sir. And from the look of it you need it, sir. Oh dear, just look at that belt and those shoes."

"I'll change and give them to you."

"Thank you, sir."

His mother had brought some of his suits over in case he ever wanted to wear one. He got into one of them and came into the sitting room laughing.

"Look!" he said. "Just look at the way I've grown." He couldn't button his jacket. His sleeves ended well above his wrists. The trousers were two inches too short.

"That's the army," the General said. "Develops men."

"Men?" Irene said. "He was just a boy." Tears came into her eyes as she thought of how young he still was.

The bell rang, and a moment later Williams, Jim's uniform

still over his arm, his boots in his hand, opened the door and said, "Young lady to see you, sir."

It was Shelagh.

"I was so excited I had to come and see if he was here. Oh!" She went into peals of laughter. "How you have grown, Jimmie!"

He went over to her and kissed her cheek. Brotherly—almost brotherly.

The General said, "You've got a good eye for a girl—horses, too, I'll lay six to four. Got to get you into the regiment when this is over. Greys," he said to Shelagh.

"This is Miss Shelagh Moran," Irene said. "She nursed Jimmie."

"Saved my life. Most devoted." Jimmie smiled into her eyes. How nice it was for them all to be here together. He could see Shelagh and the General would get on.

Williams put his head into the room. "I've got the kettle on," he said. "We can all do with a nice cup of tea and a bit of buttered toast."

"God damn it, Williams!" the General roared. "Who told you to take over? I brought you here to clean Captain Hilton's kit."

"Yes, sir. But if I don't, 'oo does? All 'er ladyship 'as is a char in the morning—an' 'er ladyship won't slave over a 'ot cook stove while I'm around."

"You see?" General Blakeney said. "Can't call my soul my own now, what with him at headquarters and Irene down here. And now the pair of them together."

By God, he liked the look of the blonde filly. She'd strip well. She stood nicely, with her hocks under her. Moved well, too. A good judge of a woman for so young a chap.

For dinner they had a mixed grill that Lady Blakeney and Williams cooked together. "Will your ladyship do this, do that—while I do the other things?" No friction. Quite the opposite. The General was vastly amused. She knew how to handle Williams. More than he had learned in all the years he'd had him.

Williams laid the table, opened the wine. Then he ordered

Lady Blakeney out of the kitchen. "I can manage now, thank you, your ladyship. I'll 'ave it ready by the time your ladyship 'as tidied 'er hair."

The General stifled a guffaw. "That's the stuff. Tell her to go and clean up. My God!"

"I'll come with you." Shelagh followed Irene into the bedroom.

The men could hear them laughing. "Seem to get on," the General said. "Glad of it. Never can tell with women. But they're the same type. Your mother must have looked like her as a girl, before she matured."

So that was the way he looked at it. His mother had not got older. Just matured.

It was a gay little dinner. Cups of Bovril, the mixed grill—kidneys, chops, bacon and fried eggs—and a big dish of fried potatoes. A custard for pudding. Coffee. With Williams talking almost as much as anyone else.

"Ought to choke you off, Williams," the General said.

"We're not in the army now, sir. We're 'ome. And please remember, sir, I've looked after you man an' boy, serving the colors wherever the Queen sent us, always at your side. Aye, sir, charging stirrup to stirrup."

"Only once you did that. At Omdurman."

"Once was enough, sir. Saved your life, I did. An' I dyed me 'air an' come back as soon as I 'eard you 'ad joined up again. Didn't I, sir?"

With that he had left them.

"Fine chap," the General said to Irene. "Make the boy shine like a new shilling."

At ten Jim took Shelagh home. In the taxi she said, "Oh Jimmie, I am proud of you and I do like your mother and the General."

"I'm glad," he said. "I'm beginning to like him myself. A fine old boy." He kissed her.

"Don't muss me, Jimmie. I've got to look decent when I go in."

"Is that the only reason, Shelagh?"

"I think so," she said, laughing.

They all left Albany at ten to be in plenty of time. Williams had done a wonderful job. "Up arf the night, sir. Never seen stuff in such shape. Like to 'ave a word with the chap wot calls 'imself your batman."

There were almost a hundred other officers and men in the Buckingham Palace yard, standing grouped with their wives and relations. There were some children, holding their fathers' hands. After some milling around they were lined up. One VC, then the DSO's, MC's and for the other ranks DCM's and MM's. Some women in black—wives or mothers of dead men—getting their decorations. Posthumously was the word. A medal to fill a blank space in a woman's life.

The King came with his ADC's, equerries and staff. He walked slowly down the line, pinning on the medals that were handed to him and saying a few words to each man. Then it was over and they drifted off to lunch at the Berkeley Grill. A kind of engagement party though no one had mentioned it.

When it was over the General and Irene went back to Albany. Jim and Shelagh went for a walk in Green Park. If he'd had somewhere to take her Jim was sure he could have made love to her. But somehow there was no urgency about it. The time would come.

39 : The Silver Cigar

SHELAGH AND Jim were having dinner at the Elysée when the guns in Green Park opened up. Another air raid.

"I'm going out," Jim said. "I've never seen a zep."

"Think it's safe?"

"It may be safer than in here."

They went up the stairs together. It was a bright, moonlight night. The zeppelin looked like a silver cigar caught in the crossbeams of two searchlights. It hardly seemed to move. It was heavy, majestic, enormous. The ack-ack couldn't reach it. Some fragments of shell fell fizzling through the air into Piccadilly within a few yards of them. Jim put his arm around Shelagh's waist. She pressed herself against him. He left her to pick up a piece of shell casing, jagged, hot. He put it into her hand.

"Souvenir, Shelagh," he said.

The street was empty of people. They had all scuttled to shelter. Except for a policeman who said, "You'd better take care, sir."

Jim laughed. "I don't think they've got one with our name on it, constable."

The only other person in sight was a hansom cab driver, standing by his horse's head trying to soothe it, stroking its neck and saying, "It's all right, my girl. It's all right." All the other traffic seemed to have disappeared. The policeman went up to the cabby.

"Can't drive her with them bloody guns popping off. She's a hot one. Nervous, like. I got to stand by her."

The zeppelin moved on, still illuminated by the searchlights that drew their white ribbons through the sky. The guns continued to fire. At least they could make it hold its altitude, keep it high if not away. It was evident that London was not the target tonight.

Well, that was that. Not very exciting but something to have seen if you hadn't seen one before. Jim took Shelagh's elbow and led her back down the stairs. The shared experience seemed to have brought them even closer. He ordered more coffee and brandy in big balloon glasses.

"The bastards," Jim said. "Gas first and now this. Killing civilians, women and kids. I saw it at Ypres. Dead children in the streets, little girls. Christ," he said. "Forgive me, Shelagh. I didn't mean to speak of it but it upsets me. Shooting hostages. Flamethrowers."

His face changed as he spoke. Shelagh saw his war face, suddenly hard, much older, all in a flash. Then it was gone and he raised his glass. "Here's to us," he said.

Shelagh raised hers, her gray eyes looking at him over the top. She was getting very close to this boy. He did something to her. She found herself thinking about him when she was alone. Wondering about the other women in his life. There must be women. A woman, anyway. Because young soldiers were like that. She wondered if it would ever be her. She supposed all girls must think of the men they were out with like that. But it was something she had never talked about. With Merton, for instance, the girl she shared a room with in hospital; she was sure Merton let them go a long way. All the way, perhaps.

So far Jim had done nothing but hold her hand and kiss her in a taxi. When he had tried to do more, to put his hand on her knee or into her blouse, she had just taken it away and held it in hers. He had offered no resistance, but one day he'd want more. Or less. One day he mightn't even be there anymore, and the other girl would have all of him. She didn't think she could bear that. Not to see him again or to give him up to some other girl. She looked into his eyes as if she could read his story in them. The air raid had excited her. The hand he had put around her had held her breast. She had felt it swell and harden under his touch. He had been aware of it, of course. He was more possessive since they had come back to their table.

Jim was thinking how beautiful she looked tonight. Her gray eyes enormous, her mouth moist, her fair hair catching the rose-shaded light of the small table lamp. She was wearing a gray silk evening dress that was cut quite low. She had a necklace of small pearls around her neck and no other jewelry.

"Is that a new dress?" he asked.

"Yes," she said, wondering why she had put it on just to dine with him. It was a party dress. It was the first time she had worn it but she had wanted to look her best. How divided she was! She wanted to look pretty for him. But she didn't want the effect her prettiness would bring about. Or did she? Were there two parts to her? Two girls in her? One drawing back and the other going forward into adventure.

There was one party of six at a table—four older people and a young couple. An engagement party, perhaps. All the other tables were occupied by couples. She wondered how many of them were sleeping together.

"Jim," she said, "tell me about your friends. Your other women friends."

He laughed. "I haven't got any. Only you, Shelagh."

"I don't think I'm enough, Jim." She knew she was leading him on but could not stop.

"You will be one day," he said. That was both an admission and a promise. She wished she was more experienced, and then she was glad she wasn't. The same ambivalence. The good girl and the bad. But he certainly attracted her. He began to talk about his mother and about a fair girl called Kathleen he'd known in France before the war.

"She was very like you, Shelagh. Of course I was just a kid then. But we had a lovely time that summer, running about in the woods and the dunes, bathing, playing."

"Did you kiss her?"

"I kissed her. But never properly. We were both just kids. I saw her in London for a while and then I lost touch with her. You could have been sisters," he said. "Where were you that summer?"

"On a houseboat on the Norfolk Broads. I was staying with Francis's people."

That was when Francis had proposed. A moonlight night like tonight. He had kissed her and she'd let him touch her. But what a lot of time they had wasted. She'd had on a white piqué dress. She still had it. They should have got married but he had said he didn't think it was right in a war. And she hadn't thought making love was right without marriage, not at least till it had been almost too late. Before he left for the station they had cried in each other's arms at all the time they had wasted. "I should have married you, Shelagh." "Oh, Francis, I should have let you make love to me sooner."

"That was when I got engaged, Jimmie," she said. "On the Broads in the moonlight. A great big full moon reflected in the water making a path of light across it."

He leaned over the table and squeezed her hand. "And then he was killed on the Somme," he said. "And now I've come along."

She smiled back into his eyes.

Now they both knew it was just a question of time, place and circumstance. They were committed to each other.

In her little evening bag Shelagh had the piece of shell he had given her. A souvenir. The war had come close to her tonight. The fragment. The change in Jim's face when the curtain had gone up for a second. She'd seen the man then, the young captain concealed in the laughing soldier-lover. Which was the real Jimmie? Which was the mask?

While they courted, making half-love on his leave, London— the Hub of Empire—hummed like a zither with a million other individual vibrations, lives interlocking and apart, joining for business, to drink, to eat, to make love; singly, in pairs, in groups, bound by ties close or tenuous, but all with one thing in common—the great war being waged only a few miles away, with the Navy patrolling the Channel. Britannia still ruling the waves, pursuing the submarine wolfpacks that sought to bring her to her knees.

The West End pavements were alive, seething with uniformed men and girls at their seductive best. Officers and men of the allied nations. Khaki, horizon blue, all polished, sharpened with the abrasives of war. The women of the night, sad sidewalk flowers, offering themselves for cash, competing with flappers who offered themselves for nothing. Everyone except the prostitutes, who stood still, moved with high-clicking heels, rattling spurs and the ring of iron-shod ammunition boots. Over it all was the rumble of traffic, of turning wheels: double-decker buses, taxis, four-wheeler cabs, smart hansoms, brewers' drays drawn by immense Clydesdales and Shires; vans; butchers' pony traps, the butcher boys smart in blue with straw hats; carriages and pairs; private cars. An endless parade of people and vehicles: soldiers exercising horses in the Row; the Palace Guards in khaki. And behind the façade of houses old men were dying and children being born in bed as others were created. An antheap driven to fury by lust, by money, by fear, by patriotism. A ferment of ordinary people, of crooks, of whores, of war profiteers, of conscientious objectors, of good wives and un-faithful women; of wounded men, men just back from the war or returning to it; of civilians.

The war had not changed human nature; it had simply altered values. Chances were taken that had never been taken before. Women who had only considered adultery now committed it. Girls who had hitherto restrained the hands of men now gave them their way. The speed of everything was accelerated. The dull gray sky of England was the limit. The all-lady orchestra at the Café Royal fiddled with verve, conducted by a redhead. The double service doors swung, the waiters going in on the left through SER and the door with VICE standing closed till it, too, moved as dishes were brought in. It seemed somehow symbolic. Upstairs the small private dining rooms, each with a sofa as well as a table and chairs, were all occupied and dis-creetly served by white-aproned waiters.

In Kensington Gardens the children played with dolls in little prams, with hoops, with wheeled toys on strings as pet dogs gamboled on the grass and the nurses gossiped. But war or no war, the flowering shrubs blossomed and the great planes and sycamores brought forth their leaves and lost them.

At night the searchlights swept the skies.

When Jim put Shelagh into the taxi and got in beside her, she said, "Where are we going, Jim?"

"I don't know."

"What do you mean, you don't know? We must be going somewhere."

"I gave him a couple of Bradburys and told him to drive anywhere he liked."

Shelagh began to laugh. "You're crazy, Jim."

"No, I'm not. I just want to be alone with you."

He took her in his arms.

"People will see us!" Cars and cabs were passing them.

"They won't know who we are. They're busy with their own affairs." His hand was on her knee. She let it find her thigh and then stopped him.

"Not yet, Jim."

Shelagh was laughing softly. Then she dabbed at her eyes with a handkerchief. She was crying.

"What's up, darling? Don't cry."

"It's so funny, Jim. And so sad. A taxicab because we've got nowhere else to go."

When she got back to the hospital, Muriel Merton, with whom she shared a room, said, "Well, what have you been doing, Moran? You've been up to something."

"Yes, dear. I've been riding around in a taxicab." She burst into tears. The poor boy. Poor Jimmie—nowhere to take her. Perhaps she should not have stopped him. In her mind she still felt his hand heavy on the soft flesh of her thigh. One day I won't. One day I'll let him, she thought. She thought of Francis, of their six hours of wild love just before he sailed. The terrible waste of it. If she had been going to do it why hadn't she done it before? For a couple of weeks she'd hoped she was pregnant. She thought of other men. How alike they all were! All wanting to touch, to stroke, to feel. Alike and different. She didn't know if she was sad or happy, only that though nothing had been said, everything had changed. That her life had taken a new course. She cried again, softly like a child, and slept.

That was the way Merton found her when she came off night duty. Asleep, with a single tear on her long lashes and tear marks on her face. Taking it hard, Merton thought, wondering if she had been seduced. She smiled at the sleeping girl, bent over and kissed her. "You'll get used to it, dear. We all do. It's just the first time that shakes us up." She wondered who the man was, if she knew him. She supposed she'd find out in God's good time. They weren't really friends; they just shared a room. All they had in common was being girls, VAD's in their early

287

twenties. The other girls thought Merton a bit fast. Well, perhaps I am, she thought, but this is no time to go slow and play by the old rules. Besides, she liked men. She hung up her uniform, put on her pajamas and went to the bathroom.

40 : The Interview

MAJOR-GENERAL Sir John Gore Blakeney was resplendent as he stood in his sitting room, his back to the mantelpiece, his feet on the skin of a lion he had shot in Kenya in 1908. Black-maned. One shot. Resplendent. Khaki, scarlet tabs, shining boots, belt, spurs, medal ribbons, the bloody lot. Fine figure of a man. Pukka soldier, typical cavalryman. The Greys and all that.

The General looked at Jim standing in front of him. A tall, slim, good-looking boy with an MC ribbon and a wound stripe on his left sleeve. "I came down specially to see you, Jim," he said.

Like hell he had. He'd come down to see his mother. But something was up, something in the wind. Bloody generals.

"Yes," the General went on, "I've been thinking."

A general who could think—a bloody miracle that was. "Yes, sir?" Jim said.

"Well," the General went on, "let's not beat about the bush. You've been out. You're a regular now. You've been wounded and I want you for my ADC. Been to the war house and got it all fixed up."

"My mother, I suppose?" Jim said. "I mean, she's at the back of it?"

God damn this boy. "Well, if I hadn't married your mother I'd never have met you, would I?"

"I suppose not, sir."

"Well, what's the answer?"

"The answer is no, sir. I can't do it."

"And why not, may I ask? Because I happen to be your stepfather and I'm offering you a cushy job at home?"

"That's partly it, sir. But that's not the whole thing." Jim's mind was working fast. He'd tried to put off thinking about it but the General had forced a decision.

"Have a cigarette," the General said, offering a gold case.

Everything gold, everything glittering, everything rich. "I'll smoke a stinker, sir, if I may. Easier to get than those gyppies over there." He lit the General's cigarette and then his own.

"Well?" the General said.

"Well, sir, the thing is this: I've got to go back."

"Why?"

"Because I don't want to, because I'm afraid. I feel like I did the first time I went out. Wondering if I'd be afraid, being afraid of being afraid. I am still afraid, sir, and it won't do. I can't let it master me. Fear, I mean. It's like a horse, sir, if you know what I mean." Jim felt himself getting confused. "Fear, sir, if you let it master you, could become a habit. Never be able to ride it again." He had reverted to his horse simile.

Gore Blakeney came over and put his hand on Jim's shoulder. "All right, Jim. I think I understand. But I don't know how the hell we're going to explain it to your mother."

"Nor do I, sir."

"God damn it, she'll cry. Never could stand a woman crying."

"They can't understand, can they, sir?" The General had said "we." There was suddenly a kind of soldier-bond between them. "It's just something we know we've got to do."

"Yes, that's it. Now let's have a glass of sherry." A good lad, a very good lad indeed. A well-bred 'un. Irene's. "Jim," he said, as they sipped their sherry, "when all this is over, how about transferring to the cavalry? The Greys? I'll be able to arrange it. And don't worry about money—horses and uniforms and things. I've got no children and I don't like my nephews. Young pups."

"I have some money of my own; about a thousand a year Aunt Julia left me. I expect Mother told you."

"Yes, she did. But I understand there's a girl in the offing. Is it Shelagh?"

"Yes, sir."

"Well, anyway, you're not to get hot under the collar about money, Jim. A wife, kids, chargers, polo ponies . . ."

Jim laughed. "A long way to go, sir."

"A few years seems a long time at your age. At mine they go in a flash. But I'm glad we had this little talk. Difficult thing to do. You see, I know I have come between you and your mother. But you're grown up. You'd soon have left her and she'd have been alone. I was alone, Jim. Very lucky to find each other."

"I expect you're right, sir. Just a bit of a shock, sir. I mean her marrying a major-general."

"You'll find I can be useful to you, Jim."

Irene came in then, looking very young and pretty in a pale green silk dress. "Well?" she said, standing framed in the door and looking from one to the other.

"He won't, Irene," the General said.

"Oh, Jimmie!"

"I've got to go back, Mother."

"Oh!" she said again, running out of the room and slamming the door.

"You see, Jim?"

"Yes, sir. Women. I think I'll go now. And thank you, sir."

"And leave me to it?"

Jim laughed. "Mother's your pigeon now, sir!"

His pigeon, his pretty crying pigeon.

That evening after dining at his club Jim went to the Empire. The lounge was full of pretty women. Decorous, well behaved and beautifully dressed. This was the Temple of Venus where men—almost all in uniform—mixed with girls who were ready to sleep with them for a price. A market of flesh, silk, satin, fur, lace and perfume. Red plush, gilt-decorated, as a temple should be. The girls were more than dressed—they were *en grande toilette*. Stage clothes, almost. Large hats, half veils. They rustled, they whispered, they laughed softly. Beautiful nocturnal birds, ready to perch on any finger.

The bar was crowded with officers from every service. Men met friends last seen at the war to discuss others, dead or wounded. Actions, events, zeppelin raids. The Dardanelles failure. The Somme, Jutland. Allenby's cavalry charges in the desert. Colonel Lawrence's exploits. Food—Scott's, the Savoy, the Troc. Women. The men moved about among the girls, looking for the one they would pick like a flower for their beds.

The Lounge led to the parade, a wide passage behind the stalls with a plush-padded rail on which one could lean to watch the show. Vaudeville. Variety. Dancers, trick cyclists. Harry Lauder. Marie Lloyd. Stars. Harry Tate, with his "How's your father" gag. Chorus girls in uniforms, drilling. Spangles, tights and music with emphasis on the brass. War songs: "Tipperary," "Little Grey Home in the West," "Oh, You Beautiful Doll." "Now, all of you, all together . . ." And the audience joined in. Marching songs they had sung going into battle. It was bright, gay, perfumed as nights in Araby, a dream of wine, women and song come true, a curious mixture of patriotism and what the bluenoses called commercial vice. The cream of England's manhood and the pick of England's whores. Mars and Venus, and Cupid with his arrows sheathed holding out his hand for cash. Crisp Bradburys, big, beautifully engraved fivers. Money the price of a night's happiness, of bellies soft as satin, pink-nippled breasts, round young buttocks, all for hire, like taxicabs. This was what they thought of in the trenches. When I get back . . . The old Empire . . .

Jim watched the pulsing throng. All in their best, all unthinking as animals in their courting plumage. He saw Gwen, who was still alone, and spoke to her. She remembered him.

"You've grown up," she said.

"How do you know?"

"Your eyes," she said. "We know a lot about men, we girls do." She laughed.

"I'm surprised you remember me."

"You shouldn't be. I don't have many failures."

Jim felt himself blush. She put a white-gloved hand on his wrist. "You're all right now, aren't you?" she said, as if he had been ill.

"Yes, thank you."

"You've got a girl of your own now, a young girl?"

He said, "Yes," again. Mona. Shelagh.

"That's the way it ought to be." She was not old—twenty-nine, thirty, thirty-two, something like that—but she knew the best of her was gone, the bloom of it. "I see someone I know, Jim," she said.

He took her hand. "Goodbye, Gwen." He watched her till he lost her in the crowd. Svelte, beautiful, but no longer in her first youth. Just someone else he had lost. Was life always like this, or was it just the war? What else did he know of life but war? You met, you went along together for a few hours—a night or a month—and then you parted. Something intervened—orders, illness, wounds, death. Fate, God, something. You never did what you wanted to.

There was a crash of music, a roll of drums, and the national anthem began. ". . . Send him victorious . . . happy and glorious . . ." The whole audience was frozen stiff at attention, the girls quiet as partridges beneath a circling hawk. "Long to reign over us . . ." Everyone was singing. The men—officers holding the King's commission; the girls holding love's. All as it were under orders. Victims of circumstance.

Then it ended. The orchestra played a march. The rocks that had stood so still became a tide flowing to the doors, to Leicester Square. The night. Couples paired off, two by two, coming out of the Empire Ark. Male and female. He was glad to see Gwen had a field officer with her. He had not expected to see her again. It seemed a good omen.

The General and Irene dined alone at home.

"So I've got high blood pressure," General Gore Blakeney said. "Of course I've got high blood pressure, Irene. First the mess-up in 'fourteen when the cavalry could have got through and French frittered them away, then a shortage of shells for the eighteen-pounders—three a day. My God! Then the misuse of tanks, the Somme battle—four hundred and fifty thousand casualties. And now Passchendaele with another four hundred thousand, not to mention Gallipoli . . . My God!" he said, tramping up and down the room, his spur chains and rowels jingling.

Irene loved him like this. His indignation, his fury. And his blood pressure was not serious. She'd seen his doctor—Sir James Laton, "my vet."

"Not at all serious, my dear Lady Gore Blakeney. Much better, in fact. Marriage has done him good; he owes a lot to you."

She liked Sir James. Pompous, Victorian, frock-coated. Wearing a stethoscope like a decoration. As much friend as doctor. "Do you mean making love is good for high blood pressure?" She asked demurely, looking at her gloved hands neatly clasped in her lap.

"You know what I mean, Irene, damn it! And don't tease me. I mean a regular life."

"That's what I said, James. A nice quiet wife instead of chasing little bits of fluff." That was the correct term, she believed. Chorus girls, and so on. She smiled at the thought of the General, of John, chasing some little long-legged blonde. And she loved teasing Sir James. She had got to know him very well. It always started with "Sir James" and "Lady Gore Blakeney" and ended with "Irene" and "James." He'd been John's doctor for years. They were of an age and sometimes shot together. It was curious that men like John showed friendship by asking someone to come and shoot pheasants or partridges or grouse with them. Come and kill something.

"I'll do my best," she said.

"Moderation, Irene. Remember he's not a young man."

"That's what he keeps saying. 'Not the man I was.' He's still quite a man but he gets very upset about the way the war is being run."

"And you're a very pretty woman, Irene."

"Yes, James," she said, getting up. "I'm lucky. I've worn

293

well. But I'm glad you've been able to reassure me about John. You see," she said, her hand in his as she said goodbye, "I love him."

On the way home in the taxi she thought how lucky she was. John well. Jimmie home and convalescent. She did not dare let herself think of what would happen when he was passed fit again. The war might be over. Anything. She thought of all the other women—mothers, wives, widows. Of men crippled for life, damaged beyond repair. The dead. She thought of the fair girl, Shelagh. He was writing to her, seeing a lot of her. It was the other one, the dark one, she was afraid of. Mona somebody. She could never remember her name. It took one girl to replace another. She thought Shelagh would do the trick; she hoped so.

The time at the reserve battalion passed neither fast nor slowly. It had a kind of rhythm. Medical Boards at Caxton Hall every three months. They seemed to be in no hurry to send him back. Davis must have told them he was shell-shocked. A bit of hunting and shooting at country houses in the vicinity, rides up to London on his Indian. A rhythm, a pattern. His mother. The General. He went up to his headquarters once and there was another attempt to get him to take the ADC job. Mona and Shelagh.

It was all very odd. He had told Mona about Shelagh. She hadn't minded. They still got on very well. She liked going for rides into the country on his motorbike with her arms around him. They knew each other so well now that their love had assumed a pattern. A series of moves and countermoves. Of phrases, of acts of love play, all with a curious innocence, so that the act seemed to be only a prolongation of the kisses they gave each other.

Shelagh did not know about Mona, but he knew she guessed from things she let drop. She allowed him to go much farther now, giving herself to his seeking hands. But a taxicab was not really a satisfactory place to make love.

He took her to Albany once when his mother was with the General. Things had gone farther and in greater comfort, but neither had wanted more at the time. It was as if they had a tacit understanding and were moving up a staircase step by step. One day they would reach the top.

This was a period of waiting. The interval between the acts. Act I, that had ended with his wound, was over. Act II was the present time. Act III would begin when the curtain went down on Act II.

At the moment he wasn't really living. He was passing through time as a goldfish passes through water in a glass bowl. All life was outside it. His adventures with Mona and Shelagh had ceased to be adventures. There was nothing new in them, nothing unexpected. No refusals, no surprises. Everything was soft and friendly. There were no scenes of passion, of recrimination. They were in the glass bowl too, going around and around in it with him.

Shelagh was in love with Jimmie now. She would do what he wanted when the right moment came, but he must choose it. She liked to kiss him, liked his hands on her body, looked forward to his lovemaking. She thought about him a great deal. She also thought about Francis. What she felt for Jimmie was quite different. Perhaps it was because she was no longer a virgin, was older, had met so many men.

On the whole, Mona was relieved about Jim's affair with Shelagh. She was making plans of her own. Somehow she must contrive to meet a man who would be really interested in her.

41 : Kathleen

JIM FOUND Mona was changing. She had lost the gaiety and sparkle that had made her such a good companion, in bed or out. He had taken her to lunch at the Café Royal but it had not been a great success. The place had as usual been full of officers and girls. She had looked at them disparagingly. "Look at them," she said, meaning the officers, not the girls. The girls had not changed. "Different, aren't they? Not what they used to be." What she meant was that these were middle-class men, even lower-middle-class. They weren't hard for her to recognize because that was her own social stratum, the one she had climbed out of. And the others? The others were dead or married, or both.

"Do you know, Jimmie," she said, "the other day one of them didn't leave me anything."

"Good God, what was he?"

"A captain in the Fusiliers. And Swan and Edgar's," Mona said. "Bombed. I used to do so much shopping there." The zeppelin raids had frightened her. Times were changing so fast; she felt much older.

When they went out Jim bought her a little bunch of violets, surrounded by their own leaves.

"You're so sweet, Jimmie," she said.

He took her hand. "I'll call you in a day or two."

"And then you're off? Back to France?"

"Back somewhere. This is my embarkation leave. I told you."

"Yes, you told me, but I can hardly believe it. You've been back so long."

"Yes, a sort of fixture. And I can't say I'm looking forward to going back." Looking forward . . . Christ Almighty! But he was a regular second lieutenant now. Temporary captain. The army was his career. But that did not affect the fear that lay waiting like a dog, ready to bite him.

They said goodbye. Jim put her into a taxi. When it drove off he wished he had gone with her. He felt very much alone. But she might have some other appointment. That was what she called them. "Not tomorrow, Jim, I've got an appointment. The day after I'll save for you." And she'd write his name in her little red diary.

Fancy that chap not leaving her anything. It was the first time she had ever mentioned another man like that, or referred to money. Of course she spoke of her other friends—gunners, Highlanders, infantry, cavalry, one guardsman. Friends. He might go home and see his mother, but Albany wasn't home. It wasn't Melbury Road, it was the General's place. Albany. His chambers. The General had created this pretty, fashionably dressed woman in the place of his mother. My God, he thought, if I passed her in the street I'd hardly know her now. Marriage and the General's money had done it. She'd grown younger as he'd grown older. The plus of the one and the minus of the other had changed things between them. Money, too. He had his own now, not just his pay. Not that he had ever liked Aunt Julia much. She had hairs on her face. He had hated kissing her as a child.

He walked on, going nowhere in particular. He might look in at the club, the Junior Naval and Military, in Piccadilly. Have a drink if there was someone there he knew. But there were fewer chaps he knew now; under the sod, so many of them. He supposed that never before had men of his age been so alone. School friends. Most of them were either gone or were out there. He agreed with Mona about the new type of officer; also the type of men. Conscripts, their hearts weren't in it. From what he heard they went sick at the drop of a hat. Put bullets through their feet. Swung the lead in every way they could. No pride in the regiment. Well, you could not have it both ways; if you killed the best only the second-rate were left.

A soldier saluted him. He saluted a major in the West Yorks, a field officer with a DSO.

Next day he ran into Kathleen. She was looking in Asprey's window. There was no mistaking her. He hadn't seen her for two years. She had grown but it was her all right. Taller, still slim. At first he had thought it was Shelagh. He went up and stood beside her. Their faces were reflected in the glass like ghosts, through which the things in the shop window— clocks, picture frames, silver flasks, Copenhagen china animals, gifts of every kind—showed clearly. He saw her give a start of recognition.

"Jim!" she said. "Jim!" her soft mouth open in surprise.

He took her arm. "We'll go into Stewart's and have a cup of coffee," he said. "Or chocolate. You always liked chocolate." They went toward Piccadilly slowly, hips brushing, alone on the crowded pavement. Quite isolated by time and memory.

Stewart's smelled of chocolate and cakes, of coffee, furs, perfume, women, leather and cigarette smoke. He held a chair for her. She sat down. He sat beside her. A waitress came for their order.

"Two chocolates. No, nothing to eat." The girl wrote "two chocolates" on her little pad.

"Now," he said, "why didn't you answer my letters? You did at first and then you stopped."

"You stopped writing," she said.

"No, I didn't."

"Then it was Mother. She must have taken them. She said I was too fond of you. That I was too young. That it was absurd, I hardly knew you. Just those days in France and then the few times I'd seen you in London. Puppy love. She said all girls went through it and she sent me to boarding school. It was horrible."

"Then you cared?" he said. His hand found hers on her knee. She pulled it to her.

"Yes," she said. "There were other boys but you'd spoiled them for me. And now . . ." Tears had come into her eyes.

"Now what?"

"I'm married, Jim. I ran away and got married."

"Who to?"

"Freddy Oates. He's in the Middlesex. I'm staying with his people in Sussex, near Lewes."

"That's near Brighton," he said, for something to say. His Kathleen married, his golden girl.

"I'm up for the day shopping and seeing my mother. My father died, you know. It was very sudden. They've got such a lovely garden—the Oateses, I mean. Near Lewes. But of course nothing is out now." She was going on almost hysterically, making conversation. Her knee found his leg and pressed

298

against it. I'm married, she thought. All those letters I never got. How could she? How could a girl's mother do that. . . .

"Are you happy, Kathleen?"

"I don't know. I thought I was in a way, being grown up and all that. Exciting. He was so good-looking, so—" she hesitated, looking for a word that would do— "so urgent." She was staring down at the cloth. "Other girls were doing it," she said. "It's the war. Everything goes so fast in a war. One grows up. There's no time. I wanted to wait for you but I had no news of you. I wrote to France but I don't suppose you ever got the letter. I wasn't even sure of the address."

"I got no letters, Kathleen. I couldn't understand it."

"Where are you staying?" she asked. "I want to be alone with you. We can't talk here."

"I got a week's leave and a friend lent me his place in Jermyn Street."

"Let's go there."

"Drink your chocolate, Kathleen, and we'll go." She needed something. She looked very white. He watched her drink. He'd always liked to watch her do things. Eat, drink, comb her hair . . . things. The play of her hands, her expression. When she put down the cup there was a little brown moustache on her lip. She wiped it off with a handkerchief.

"I've got a handkerchief of yours," he said. "I found it in your room."

"In France?"

"Yes, after you'd gone I went to see if I could find something you'd left. I carried it all through the war."

She smiled at him and pushed her chair back.

He paid at the desk and they went out into Piccadilly: Solomon's, the fruit and flower shop; the Ritz; the Berkeley; the Elysée restaurant downstairs; the Burlington Arcade; the Academy; the roar of the traffic; the women and girls, the men in khaki; red-capped, white-gloved and belted military police; the whole swirl and eddy of it; a current of humanity; buses, taxis, hansom cabs, horse-drawn delivery vans. This was the heart of the Empire; its greatest artery fed by sidestreet veins. All redolent of war, and love its byproduct.

The flat belonged to Harold Bligh. He was a rich man and he often lent it to brother officers if they were going up to London and he wasn't using it. The third floor with a little lift like a box. It consisted of a large sitting room, a little kitchen, a bedroom and bathroom. A bachelor establishment.

"Now," Jim said, as he closed the door, "let's look at you. By God," he said, "you're beautiful, Kathleen!"

She was wearing a small blue velvet hat and a navy coat and skirt. Simple. But it showed off her figure. The short skirt showed her long beautiful legs in black silk stockings. He watched her take off her black kid gloves and her hat. She shook out her hair.

"Satisfied?" she asked, and sat down crossing her legs.

He came up behind her, bent over and, taking her face in his hands, kissed her. Then his hand found her breasts through her blouse. She unbuttoned it. He had them in his hands. Heavy, hardening under his touch. "Christ!" he said, letting go of her, "and you're married."

She got up and faced him, her arms around his neck, kissing him, her body pressed arching into his. "Don't let that worry you, darling. It doesn't worry him. It never did. Not from the beginning."

He sat down and pulled her onto his lap. "Tell me," he said.
"All of it?"
"Yes."

She paused, considering. How much should she tell him? Then went on abruptly, as if she had made up her mind.

"Well, it's not a pretty story. I let him seduce me. You think nice girls don't do things like that, but they do. Why . . ." She stopped as if she was thinking why. "Because of the war, because I was angry at being sent to boarding school, because I was hurt at getting no letters from you, because I was bored. Because I was a girl and wanted it, I suppose, without knowing. And there I was in the family way."

It was hard to believe.

She went on. "When I told him he just laughed and said he'd marry me. Went to my people, bold as brass. You can imagine the row. He got my mother's permission in writing. She forged my father's name. Moira, the maid, witnessed it. My mother says it killed him."

But it wasn't that. It was her nagging, not understanding him. He just gave up.

"The baby?" Jim said.

"A miscarriage three months later," she lied. "But by that time he was after the other girls. Any girl. Bits of fluff, that's the word he used. Me, and any other girl he could get hold of."

The bastard. Fancy having her and going elsewhere. "Where is he now?"

"Aldershot," she said. "Going out any time. Expecting his last leave. And I know what it will be. Parties and bed. Drink and bed. You said, was I happy? I'm not happy but I can put up with it. He's not bad, really. But I want some fun too." Her big gray eyes darkened. "I'm going into the bedroom," she said, and left him. Five minutes later she called, "Come in, Jim!" And he saw her lying naked on the bed, smiling up at him.

"Do you remember the larks singing and the hot sun, and the warm, soft sand? And your hands on me? I was just a girl then, but I liked it. I wanted you to see me, not just to touch me."

There was the smooth skin, the soft white thighs his fingers had stroked. But the pigeon fluff that he'd felt was gone. This was the golden fleece. She lay back on the pillows with her hands behind her head. When he was ready she opened her arms.

"My darling," she said. "My darling."

An hour later they went out to lunch at the Trocadero with its orchestra and potted palms.

"I wish I'd been the first one for you, Jim! But that's too much to expect, isn't it?"

He laughed. "I'd like to have been the first one for you, too."

"But I'll tell you one thing: you were the first boy ever to touch me."

301

So his had been the first hands on her.

"And now," he said, "what shall we do now?"

"Have lunch." She laughed. "And then we'll make love again. After that, we'll see. He'll be going out soon and there'll be no one else. I promise that."

They had a light lunch—mutton broth, fried whiting holding their tails in their mouths, lamb chops and half a bottle of white Alsatian wine. Jim felt very much the man of the world ordering food and wine, lunching such a pretty girl. As pretty as any in the room. His love, his mistress. He didn't feel wicked, only elated and at the same time sad because this could only be a beautiful interlude. He also felt grateful to Mona who had taught him to make love. As he watched Kathleen eating he thought about her body under the clothes. Its white silken softness, the rosebud breasts, her navel, the soft parts of her thighs.

They had coffee. They smoked cigarettes—hers Abdullahs—and went back to the flat. This time he undressed her, slowly, lovingly. This time they knew their bodies and lay together afterward like children, like puppies, entwined. But at last it was time to go; the wonderful day was over. They did not say much as they dressed, each lost in the memories of the summer when they had been children, and the now when as man and woman they had come together again, young, still scarcely more than adolescent, but forced into maturity by the circumstances of war.

"I wish I could write to you," he said.

"You can, darling, but not a proper letter. Write as if you were a girl and sign it Betty or Muriel or something. I'll give you the address in Aldershot. I was very lucky to get a room there. He's in camp but gets away some nights."

"I don't want to think about it."

"No more do I. But there's nothing we can do, is there? What can we do, Jim? You're only twenty and you've got no money. You've got no job. You don't know what you'll do after the war."

It was extraordinary how practical women were. Even girls. Oates had money. His father was a lawyer and he was going into his firm. He was unfaithful but he'd settle down. Just wild oats. Oates sowing his wild oats. A joke. She'd made her bed and so on.

This was something she'd wanted to do because she loved him, because she wanted to pay her husband out with a sauce-for-the-goose-and-sauce-for-the-gander act and have the laugh on him, a nice sweet laugh with the memories of today. He didn't tell her he'd been left money or that he was a regular soldier now and going to stay on in the army. There seemed to be no point in it.

"We may manage to meet again," she said, as if she really hoped it.

"We may," he said, thinking how difficult it would be to arrange. Leave. He might get leave in six months if things were quiet, but there was the problem of her getting away at the same time, and there was Shelagh.

"Let's just hope," she said, as she put on her hat. "Let's just hope. And remember those lovely days when we were together in France and fell in love with each other, and today when we're able to do what we wanted to do then but were too young and too shy."

At the door of the flat they kissed. They walked down the stairs hand in hand. In the street Kathleen said, "I think I'll take a taxi. I'm a little tired." She took his hand again and said, "Thank you for a lovely lunch."

He stopped a cab, put her into it and watched it go, lost in the traffic, one cab among many. He knew it was the end. She was married; she belonged to another man. If she hadn't been, if she'd got his letters, they could have waited. Something would have turned up. There'd have been no Shelagh, the other golden girl. How extraordinarily alike they were, or seemed to be! When he had seen her in hospital for a moment he had been sure it was Kathleen. A little older, a little taller, with a more oval face. Kathleen's was heart-shaped. Those gray eyes were alike. And their manner. But he was in love with Shelagh now. Kathleen had disappeared into her, become merged with her in his mind. If Kathleen had not been married. If . . . If . . .

In the taxi Kathleen was crying quietly. It was all more than she could bear. This was the boy she wanted. She'd always felt it and now she knew. She didn't know how she would talk to her mother. She thought of the afternoon they'd spent alone in the flat, petting in the big armchair. He'd been there to look for her. He'd told her about it. About how her mother had sent for the doctor and they'd taken him away in an ambulance.

Her mother kissed her and said, "You look tired, darling. You'll feel better when you've had some tea. And how is dear Freddy?"

Dear Freddy who had seduced her and was supposed to have put her in the family way. She had quite forgotten how she had teased him and led him on. Or that she hadn't been pregnant. It was really impossible to understand Mother. Moira brought in the tea and they sat, cups in hand, with nothing in common between them. Her mother had never understood her. Suddenly she became angry with this complacent woman who knew nothing about life. Why, even she knew more, had seen more.

"Why did you never give me Jim's letters?" she asked.

"His letters?"

"Yes. He wrote and wrote. He sent them here and I never got them."

"Whatever gave you that idea, darling? How absurd!"

"He gave me the idea."

"You've seen him?"

"I had lunch with him."

"I hope you didn't do anything silly, darling."

"Like sleeping with him?"

"How can you be so vulgar?"

"Well, I did. I did twice, and I'm glad. Glad."

Her mother put her hand up to her breast. "I think I'm going to have a heart attack."

"I doubt it," Kathleen said.

"You'll kill me like you killed your father."

"I didn't kill my father. You did. He understood me and you drove me to it, sending me away to school and keeping my letters." Kathleen got up. "I'll go now and I don't think I'll ever

304

come back. I'm making the best of a bad job with that dear boy who sleeps with every tart he can find because he's made like that. But it's you I blame. It's you who ruined my life before it had begun."

Mona had been taking stock. Sorting things out in her mind. A woman could separate her memories. She had developed a technique for it. By putting away a photograph a situation was ended, the warm sun of a presence eclipsed by the closing of a drawer or the lid of a box. The youth in her still called to youth. The dead must bury their dead. God knows, there were enough of them.

At first, with the early ones, there had been tears, regrets that she might have disappointed them, have offered more. But she had discovered that there was a limit to sadness. The cup that was full could hold no more. It was not that she was getting hard. It was just that she was learning the wartime trick of living for the day, for each day, as if sufficient for it was the good thereof. Man had merged into man, a composite excitement in khaki that took her dining, dancing, to the theatre and to bed. It was no use thinking of yesterday, of any of the lovely yesterdays. No good thinking of tomorrow or the future except to put money aside for it. She still hoped she'd meet some man who'd marry her. She was normal. That was what she kept telling herself: I'm normal. I'm just like other girls, only I don't know how to type or take shorthand and I couldn't work in a shop. She knew when the war ended, and it would end, all this would be forgotten—a dream. Or wouldn't it? Was she tricking herself? How she longed for a man who would take her seriously.

Irene Gore Blakeney was worried about Mona Moon. She had met her visiting Jimmie. A shop girl type. Superior. What a word! Too obviously ladylike. Had called her "your ladyship." But pretty, smart, chic, and more than half in love with Jimmie. She supposed she had slept with him. And now with the money Julia had left him he was a free agent. He might even marry her.

She wondered if she was good in bed. If a woman was good in bed she had a hold over a man. The General had explained all this to her. Fancy reaching her age to discover the facts of life! That accounted for some extraordinary marriages that had seemed so inexplicable to her. For the things, even unfaithfulness, some men would put up with . . .

John had said, "You're good in bed, my dear." She felt herself blushing at the thought. And he was good. The General— John. Lots of practice, she supposed. "Got to settle down some time, Irene. Just a matter of meeting the right woman. Took a long time, that's all." She wondered if she'd give him a baby. She'd been to a gynecologist. Vet, John called him. "Get yourself vetted, my dear." And she had, and she was all right.

"I see no reason why you should not conceive, Lady Gore Blakeney. Of course you're not in your twenties anymore. . . ." Polite, wasn't he? She was not even in her thirties anymore. "But you've had one child, which increases your chances. Just keep trying." She'd almost laughed.

She was glad Jimmie had met a nice girl. Shelagh. She thought of the Moon girl again. She was clever. She'd learned a lot. But what did she do? How did she live? She'd asked her.

"And what do you do, Miss Moon?"

"Do? War work. Entertaining the troops and so on, your ladyship."

It sounded very vague and girls who entertained the troops did not get paid. She had a look of the theatre about her. Not flashy, but self-possessed; and her clothes, a bit too smart, a bit theatrical. Well, there was nothing she could do about it. She'd lost touch with Jimmie. He was grown up now and she had remarried. The General and Jimmie seemed to get on, superficially anyway, with a "Well, my boy, how are you today? Having a good time, I hope? Only young once," kind of thing on one side and a "Yes sir, no sir," on the other.

When he was at the war she had worried about him getting hurt; when he was at home she worried about women. Now he was going back she'd worry about the war again. Jump every time the doorbell rang for fear of another telegram. He was on his final leave now. Embarkation leave. He telephoned her. He popped in for a drink or tea or a meal. He'd taken her to lunch. He would unquestionably come and say goodbye to her. After that, just letters and field service cards. "Thank you for the parcel. I am very well. . . ."

Part Four

THE SECOND ROUND

42 : The Second Round

By the time Jim reached France in June 1918 the German breakthrough of March had been halted, the line stabilized and the British were preparing to attack once more. Since the arrival of the Americans there had been no question about victory. The exhausted Germans were in no position to stand up to the extra weight of America's millions: millions of men, millions of dollars, the immense resources of the United States that had been thrown into the balance against them.

There was a spirit of optimism everywhere. At last the end of the war was in sight. The men were singing, "Over there the Yanks are coming, you can hear them humming over there."

It was strange to be back in Boulogne. He thought about August '14 when he had stood with his Uncle George, talking to Colonel Black, watching the cavalry come ashore. Four years ago he had been a boy. Now he was a man.

The train took the landing troops to the infantry base at Etaples, where they would wait till they were drafted up the line. He wondered what battalion he would go to. With luck he might manage to wangle the 10th again.

Colonel Gordon, the camp commandant, turned out to be a Wilts L.I. man. He asked the adjutant if he could see him. He had no desire to spend a week in the Bull Ring bayonet fighting, bomb-throwing and doing the physical jerks with which the authorities occupied the waiting men. Time-fillers to keep them out of mischief.

"You wanted to see me, Captain Hilton?"

"Yes, sir."

"Well, what can I do for you?"

"I'd like three days' leave, sir. My uncle lives at Laurent Plage, twenty miles away. I haven't seen him since August 'fourteen."

"I don't see why you shouldn't go, Hilton."

"Thank you, sir. And there's one thing more."

"Yes?"

"Do you think you could get me back to the Tenth Battalion, sir?"

"I'll try. Put in an application in writing when you get your leave pass."

An hour later Jim was on his way, a pair of pajamas, his shaving kit and toothbrush in his haversack.

Leaving the town, the road went through the pines and the dunes, then into open country bounded by hedges, and finally the forest, through which it ran like a white ribbon. As Jim marched he had plenty to think about. Twenty miles would take five hours plus an hour of rest. Ten minutes in the hour—say, six. That was all distance was, miles divided by four, by five if you were in a hurry. He could do thirty miles in a day easily, if he had nothing to carry. Left, right, left.

He was in the forest that he loved so much, once a hunting ground of kings. He passed a remount depot carved out of the trees. Neufchâtel, the straight military road with grass verges. A blackbird was singing. There were butterflies everywhere. A red admiral unwound its long watch-spring tongue on a roadside flower and he stopped to watch it. Peacocks, tortoise-shells, sulphur yellows with their hind wings ending in points. The hum of insects, all so quiet, and war only a hundred miles away. He thought of women.

He was not the only one. All the others were the same—young men in fighting condition, well fed, hard marched, womanless. Their thoughts and talk turned to women—to girls—obsessed, randy. First, the woman herself, abstract. But the necessity of having one pressed against their flies in acute, embarrassing discomfort. This was something women didn't understand—mothers and aunts—when they talked about virtue, restraint, chastity. Girls could go without it, they weren't battered by it, it was not being continually brought to their attention. A picture, even a thought, was enough to trigger the whole mechanism. A man's limbs, his arms and legs, where he went, looked, even what he heard, were to a great extent controllable. But not his cock.

The war accelerated things. With so many dead, nature seemed to be trying to make up for them. The men randy, the girls in heat, as if the leak of dead men could be dammed with babies. Replacements, as it were. And the fear of it. That was why men were shy, diffident, afraid. Marriage might be a holy sacrament, but all intercourse was a mystery—the giving up of something more than sperm. War was a matter of essentials, like life, death, love, fear, boredom, exhaustion—all intense, more than normal. A watch no longer made sense as far as real time was concerned. You needed it to change sentries, to synchronize an attack, but it had nothing to do with time. Hours might take days, a seeming lifetime to pass, and days go in a flash on leave. The prewar yesterday didn't belong to you at all. The postwar tomorrow—and how far away it was—might never come. Not for you. Not for your friends. And the mind went on tramping the treadmill, the same steps, around and around.

Jim's mind was a whirlpool of memories. How well he knew this part of France. What a lot had happened since he had been here last. The war. Kathleen. Mona. Shelagh. His dead friends. His wound. A lifetime of experience compressed into four years. So many events which, in ordinary times, would not have happened or been separated by weeks, months, years, were squashed together into a solid block.

He marched fast, with a short light infantry step. His boots rang sharp on the macadam. There were roebuck and wild boar in the forest. Birds and butterflies of all kinds in the clearings where he and his mother had picked blackberries in the late summer, and wild daffodils and cherry blossoms in the spring. He and his mother. He had lost his mother now. Swapped her, as it were, for Mona and Shelagh, just as she had swapped him for the General. People's lives spun like tops, the young breaking away from the old, each seeking contemporary friendships.

313

He stopped to pick some meadowsweet from a ditch. Its sweet, sickly, almost acrid smell made him think of Kathleen again. It was somehow female, an aphrodisiac in the early summer heat. Like girl-sweat.

He laughed as he threw the flower away. A young soldier marching alone down a white dusty road, sniffing at the flower he held in his hand.

Out of the forest into the beginning of the village. A turn to the left and there was the big green gate of his uncle's châlet. He opened the postern. Everything looked the same but the garden was neglected. He whistled. Where was Tim, the Irish terrier? No dog. But a pretty dark girl appeared on the verandah.

"You are looking?" she said in French.

"For my uncle, Monsieur Hilton."

"Mon Dieu! I will tell him."

So his mother had been right about Uncle George, the *célibataire*.

A moment later his uncle appeared. "Jim," he said. He looked much the same but older, and neglected, like the garden. Jim wondered if his mother's visits had kept him up to the mark. He hadn't shaved. His shirt was not quite clean. The girl was standing just behind him. Twenty-five or so. Pretty in a rather flashy way. She had on a short white dress and white shoes.

"This is Marie," his uncle said.

"Bonjour, mademoiselle."

"What are you doing here, Jim?"

"I've just landed and got a couple of days' leave."

"How did you get here?"

"Walked over. It's only twenty miles."

"How's your mother?"

Jim almost laughed. It was like a Harry Tate show with his "How's your father?"

"Very well, thanks. She married a general, you know."

"Yes, I know."

"I suppose you can put me up?"

"Of course, my boy. Delighted to see you." But he didn't look delighted.

Jim supposed he was worried about Marie. Afraid he'd write to his mother about her. He wouldn't. None of his damn business. But he couldn't tell him so. Instead he said, "Where's Tim?"

"Dead, Jim. Run over."

"And Gipsy?"

"I sold her. No use for her now. Feed difficult. No labor. And she was getting old."

"Sold her? Why didn't you shoot her?"

"Never thought of it."

Marie was looking from one to the other of them, moving her head, her big black eyes curious, as if she was watching a tennis match.

"I thought she was supposed to be mine. Mother bought her."

"She was getting old," his uncle said again.

And that had to do for an answer. The bastard. Selling her to a horse-butcher. A pet. It all added up. You couldn't trust anyone. He relapsed into silence and stared at the girl.

They had lunch: vegetable soup, a ragoût, a soufflé and a bottle of Pommard. Coffee.

He saw he could have the girl if he wanted her. And he might, to pay his uncle out for Gipsy. The bastard. She kept looking at him under her lashes. When he lit her cigarette her finders touched his and for an instant she raised her eyes to stare into his, a half-smile on her moist lips.

43 : The Countess

THE VISIT was proving a disappointment. His old room seemed quite unreal. It belonged to his boyhood. Everything reminded him of Kathleen whom he had lost. His uncle had sold Gipsy and never mentioned it in a letter. Tim was dead, run over by an army truck. It was the mare and the dog he had come to see as much as his uncle. Well, they were gone. His uncle had betrayed him—the pony was supposed to be his.

Jim had no particular desire to visit the château, but he had nothing to do and it would pass the time. It really was a castle, with a filled-in moat, dungeons, crenellated towers, ivy-covered, with a big ilex and walnut trees in the courtyard that must have been used in medieval times for exercising troops. The British had taken it and sacked it once in the fourteenth or fifteenth century.

He greeted the lodgekeeper, old Laseur, in a green uniform that showed a lot of wear.

"Monsieur is back from the war? On permission?"

"A few days' leave. Is Madame the Countess home?"

"Madame the Countess will be glad to see Monsieur le capitaine. Since the Count was killed . . ." He shrugged his shoulders.

Jim walked up the drive. Edged with rough grass, it cut through an ancient wood of oaks and beeches. When he rang a jangling bell, a village slut opened the door.

"Madame the Countess?" he said.

"Come in, monsieur." Again a curious look, rather like that of old Laseur. Questioning, quizzical, bordering on a leer. She wasn't bad-looking either, especially from behind with her switching hips. If her hair hadn't been so greasy, if she had been clean . . . She flung open the door of the small salon.

"A monsieur, Madame la Comtesse."

The Countess rose. She came toward him. He could see she had no idea who he was. She was in widow's black. French mourning always seemed more profound, blacker and more funereal than any other. Her small face was very white, her lips bloodless, unpainted, her dark eyes enormous, her piled hair luxuriant. Thirty-five at least, but she moved quickly, gracefully as a girl. He had not remembered her as pretty, but why should he have? He had been a boy and the Countess a married woman almost old enough to be his mother—biologically old enough.

Then she recognized him. "Jim! *Mon Dieu!* Already a man in this short instant . . . a captain!" She held out both her hands.

He took them in his and raised her right hand to his mouth. It was perfumed, soft, boneless, cool.

"Sit down," she said, "and give me your news. You have been wounded, I see." She was looking at his wound stripe.

"On the Somme. Slightly," he said, making little of it.

"You heard about the Count, my husband?"

"Laseur told me at the lodge."

"A hero's death," she said. "Early on in the first months of the war, leading a charge of cuirassiers. Imagine it!"

He remembered now. His mother had told him about it, but he had forgotten. They had not been friends. Just grown-up people whom he knew.

He was looking at her legs. Something in him was stirring.

"You will stay to lunch, Jim?" She pronounced it Jeem.

"Thank you."

"When do you go back?"

"Tomorrow. To Etaples."

"How did you get here?"

"I walked."

"And your uncle?"

"He is well."

She ordered wine. They had lunch. The slut who brought it served them, managing to lean over him to show the curved beginning of her breasts, the dark cleft of their separation, her thigh against his each time she approached to bring or remove a plate. She smelled, not dirty, but ripe. Like a cheese that is *fait*. Of woman. She was all woman, like an animal.

They had coffee and talked of the progress of the war. Of the Somme battle and Verdun. She said, "I am poor now. Not only a widow, but poor. Only four servants. Just that little village tart and a cook, and outside old Laseur and a boy. I am selling my woods. Imagine it!" She got up with a rustle of silk. She had left him before lunch to change. "To do you honor, Jim. It is not every day I can entertain a young hero, one of our gallant allies."

The dress she now wore was black too, but silk. The petticoat was pleated around the bottom. She had on shoes with higher heels.

"Come," she said, "you will stay to tea and in the meantime we will gossip in my boudoir." She led the way down a passage and through a green baize door into a bedroom hung with tapestry, with an enormous four-poster on a dais, and on into a much smaller room, part of one of the towers, its wall curved, the mullioned windows set back five feet, showing the thickness of the defensive masonry.

The Countess sat on a sofa, half reclining. He looked out of the window at the lake and the forest in the distance. That was where he and Kathleen had played, chased butterflies, laughed and discovered each other. Kathleen . . .

"Come here, Jim."

He turned toward his hostess.

"Here!" she pointed to the chair beside her. "Do you know what I would like?"

"No." What could she want?

"I'd like you to kiss me."

He stood up, embarrassed, blushing.

"Come," she said. "I am lonely. I'd like a kiss, just one."

He leaned forward. Her hands were on his shoulders. She pulled him down, her knee rose gently to his groin. Her kiss enveloped him, her tongue found his, her fingers were on the buttons of his clothes, ravenous. . . .

When it was over she laughed and kissed his hand. "You are a sweet boy, Jim. Now I will tidy myself and ring for tea." Nearly three hours had passed.

She left him, her high heels clicking on the parquet between the rugs, her skirt rustling. He had made love to a countess. He realized that he had never made love to a woman before, only girls. Mona, for all her experience, was just a girl.

She returned, neat and composed, looking younger, happier. She had a silver-mounted comb in her hand. She said, "Sit still and I'll do your hair." They were both laughing, laughing at nothing, when the girl came in with the tea tray.

When she had gone the Countess said, "You must call me Louise." Then she spoke of her husband. "I was married to him when I was seventeen," she said. "A *mariage de convenance*. I never loved. He was nice enough but he bored me. I regret his death, but in a way it is good to be free to love. Oh yes, I have lovers—you will hear of it in the village if you stay. From your uncle, perhaps. And why not? I am still young, passable, and it is war. *C'est la guerre, mon petit, et à la guerre comme à la guerre.* Love," she said, *"l'amour.* What else is there in life for a woman?"

"I must go, Louise," he said.

She put out her hand, holding it rather high and drooping from the wrist. He kissed it. She laughed. "I like that, Jim. It was subtle. You will be a success with women. To kiss me would have been an anticlimax."

"Merci, madame," he said, bowing, and left.

The servant girl was waiting for him. "A little something, monsieur, for a poor girl? It is usual."

"So all visitors give you something?"

"But yes, monsieur. Silence, they say, is golden. I learned that at school, and should monsieur require any little service I am free after nine o'clock." She smiled up at him. She had undone two more buttons of her blouse. She had long breasts, like white cucumbers. Her teeth were good.

He gave her fifty francs and she dropped him a derisive curtsy. A hot, not unattractive little slut, if you weren't too fussy.

When Jim had gone Louise lit a cigarette and relaxed. It had been a very pleasant afternoon. He was a nice boy, good-looking. Fair, clean, his body almost hairless with youth. How stupid people were about sex! It was an appetite, like hunger. And it was better this way with no emotional entanglements. No heartbreaks. And, of course, equally, no ecstasy. But in the end they canceled themselves out, those two, the pain and pleasure evenly balanced on the scales of time. She liked Englishmen, less subtle than the French, less gallant, but with a certain doglike sincerity. They were predictable, controlled, without temperament. But that hand-kiss at the end had endeared Jim to her, rounded things off with panache, style, had given it a patina of beauty.

How extraordinary, how *drôle,* to think of him as he had

been four years ago! A child, a boy. And now what was he? Both boy and man, the two merging into each other. The man in him advanced, the boy pushed back by the circumstances of war. But to have slept with him . . . If she had become a mother at fifteen—and God knew that was not very original— he might have been her son. Still, she looked young, much younger since her husband's death. She took more trouble with herself, did exercises. And love kept one young. Or if not love, the act of love. There was no doubt about that, just look how young most loose women looked.

He would go back to war. Out of her life, probably for ever. How young they died, these boys! It was something to give them a little pleasure. A little life. She poured herself a whisky, the present of a staff colonel. What a chance war gave to women, their men away or dead, to alleviate in the name of patriotism the loneliness of strangers! What an excuse for lubricity, each bed spread with a flag! For *la patrie,* for England, for France— and no doubt for Germany. For all the combatant races. Desire —and who could deny a woman's desire, her curiosity, her interest in change—that now had free rein? As free as her courage and conditions permitted. As in men there was a hidden desire to kill, so in women there was a hidden desire for love. Both made guiltless, or at least excusable, by war. But she at least was without hyprocrisy. She liked handsome, well-made men, liked their hands on her knee, her thighs, her belly, her breasts; liked their kisses. Their smell of tobacco, hair tonic, whisky and fresh sweat. Liked her power to arouse them. What a shame to waste it, to hide it under the bushel of inhibited respectability, to drive it inward and allow it to destroy her, turning the sweet fruit sour, wrinkled, bitter! Her organs atrophying with disuse, her warm moisture drying up because it was unsought.

She had a great deal of time to read now and was learning, in understanding herself, to understand others. Culture, civilization, were really little more than a veneer, even in a woman like herself. The human psyche was cramped by custom, like a body in a corset, to a specific moral shape. But it never really changed; it was only confined by the steel and whalebone of convention. Nor were morals and customs of general application. In one place or time a woman could expose her breasts and must hide her face. In another, as in Europe, the face was bare and the body covered. It was all nonsense, there were no real rules.

Jim walked home slowly. He had had what was called an amorous adventure. Fortuitous, unexpected, out of context. He had gone to call on the Countess out of politeness and boredom. He had known his mother, when she heard he had been to Laurent Plage, would say, "Did you call on the Countess?" Now when he wrote he could say, "I called on the Countess." He had often called on her with his mother, gone there to tea with her. Sometimes to lunch, sometimes to pick up the walnuts that fell from the tree in the courtyard, to use their green outer husks to stain his skin brown when he played Indians with turkey feathers in his hair. A little boy with a homemade bow and arrows, and the Countess, a grown-up woman, married and in her twenties. And now he had caught up with her, that was what puzzled him. As a still smaller boy, he had sat in her lap. He remembered it. This afternoon her particular perfume had brought it back. Heavy, sweet, rich, sensuous. Sensual. How clever she had been not to undress or expect him to! He would have been overcome with shyness, with memories, as he was now, of being a little boy, almost a baby, in her lap. She had loved him, kissed him, cuddled him. His mother said it was because she had no children of her own. But was it? Was it not the woman playing with the little man, the boy, who would be what he had become today, as if she had been prescient? How cleverly she had seduced him—physically—knowing the nature of man and his reflexes! She had taken him quickly before he had had time to think. Only that he had to have her because he had to, because he was a man, because she had made him. That was the first time. But now he had possessed her, taken the initiative with her laughing up at him, giving in to him, it was different. It was like a dance. The first dance she had led him, but not in the second.

He was surprised that the village looked the same, the row of houses with a little stream in front of them, their big kitchen gardens hidden from the road. He even recognized some chickens and a white duck with a feather pompom on its head. Dogs; people—women, girls and children; no men. It was all the same as it had been. The elm trees and hedgerows. Only he had changed. He thought of the maid. Her hand out— "But yes, monsieur, they always give me something." Free after nine. Free for what? For anything, for a walk that would end in the long grass or the hay of a barn. This appeared to be the sum of life, the end everyone secretly sought. To couple, body to body. Soldiers, officers, women, girls. They all did it or played with the idea of it, warming themselves at its fire.

His uncle's house was nothing without Mother. She had always been the center of it, the nucleus. And Gipsy—every night after dinner during the holidays he had gone to the stable to say good night to her. To pat her, pull her ears and kiss her mousy nose. And no dog. Empty, the place was a shell, the garden neglected. He'd lost all feeling for his uncle. A god with feet of clay.

"So you went to see the Countess?" his uncle said at dinner.

"Yes. I had lunch and tea with her."

"What did you do, Jim?"

"We talked about the war, about people. She is an interesting woman. Very well informed."

There was no doubt his uncle guessed how he had spent the afternoon. "Very well preserved, my boy. You'd never think she was almost old enough to be your mother."

It had not been a satisfactory meal and he was glad when it was over. And tomorrow he'd be off—out of this dream world back into reality.

Jim thought of the way his uncle had bawled him out about Kathleen. "If I catch you kissing that girl again . . ." The old hypocrite. Being here brought Kathleen back into his mind. Not that she was ever far out of it. Just a layer down. Shelagh on top, then Kathleen—like layers in a cake. The place, the heat of summer, the smell of the meadowsweet that had reminded him of the smell of her body. Her navel. The sweet scent of soap, of sweat, of meadowsweet.

He thought of his uncle, the old bugger. With this kid, Marie. Old enough to be her father. He saw something else, too, that had escaped him because he had been too young to understand his uncle's character. He had wanted his mother, his dead brother's wife. He wasn't even clean. And once he had thought of him as a god. Big, bearded, omnipotent. Well, the war had cut him down to size.

He remembered the way his mother had always locked the door of her room. She never did at home. "It's because we are abroad, Jimmie," she'd said. Abroad, hell! It was because of Uncle George. But why had she come every year? A lot of reasons. For his French, for a nice quiet holiday. Because she liked Uncle George's admiration though she fended him off. Because she liked to get out of England for some months so as not to become too involved with other men. He recognized this now. And why not? Why shouldn't she have had a discreet affair or two? How grown up he had become! Understanding motives, seeing life as it really was. Dr. Davis had opened the door to the room of understanding. And what a difference there was between sex and love! Sex was Mona and Louise. Love was Kathleen and Shelagh. He thought of her in the flat in Jermyn Street, of Kathleen's body as she lay naked waiting for him. Of her interest at lunch when he had taken the little green oiled-silk packet from his pocket and unwrapped it. There had been flowers on the table. Pink carnations. Always pink. Rose, salmon. The pink horizon of war. Mona's pink-shaded lamps. The pink lamps at the Elysée in the air raid. Women's lips, bodies, blood, flags, everything was red or pink. *Couleur de rose*. The color of life and death.

"What's that, Jimmie?" she'd said, extending her hand with long, pink, polished nails.

"Something of yours, darling, that I found after you left Laurent. You forgot it. I've carried it ever since."

"Oh," she'd said, "an old dirty hanky." A little girl's hanky. Now she had pretty ones. Lawn, lace-edged. The hankies of a

323

married woman. A girl with a husband whom she didn't love who slept around. It was strange that because a girl slept with a man she should have lace-edged handkerchiefs. Tears had come into her big gray eyes.

"And you carried it all through the war?"

"All the time. I used to take it out and look at it. Most of the men carried something for luck. Medals, crosses, rabbits' feet, little dolls. Something for Mr. Luck."

"Oh," she said again.

They'd talked about themselves and about puppy love. How real it was; how pure; how ignorant.

"And we didn't know what to do—did we, Jimmie?"

It came back now. That awful ache of ignorance. The pain of a desire neither had understood, of touching, of looking, of feeling, of mystery; of how he had known even then that this, this love business, was going to be a big thing in his life; that he was on the edge of experience, with a pain in his belly and his genitals. It was like what you felt when you looked over the edge of a precipice. Perhaps that was why some people jumped off high buildings. Maurice and he had been the same that way about girls. Mona. Some chaps it didn't worry at all. Sexless as eunuchs. He wondered about Marie. Should he make love to her? Would she give him the opportunity? He knew that now, too. A man might make love but the girl planned it. Put herself in a position where it could happen. Marie reminded him of Mona. All dark girls did. Just as all fair girls reminded him of Kathleen and Shelagh, who were one in his mind, as if in the world there were only two girls—one dark and one fair. Versions of each other, like different editions of the same book.

Marie said she was a *steno-dactyle* and was helping his uncle with a book on wines, typing it for him. Was Uncle George really writing a book on wines? How many girls had helped him? He knew enough about wine to write a book. Wine and women. Pleasures that could become escape mechanisms. That was what women were in war. Getting into them was a way out of it. To touch them, warm and soft, after the hard things of war—rifle butts, Mills bombs, hard, cold. God damn it, he

324

wanted it! You could not keep it out of your mind. What nonsense to say it was wrong! Fornication—balls! If God had created men and women that way, and dogs and cats and cows and bulls, and stallions and mares, how the hell could it be wrong to exercise the instincts He had put into all living things? It really made God look rather stupid. This terrible God who had allowed this war to come about, who blew the men who prayed to Him to pieces. Well, those who wanted Him could have Him. He thought of the red screen again, the dying Aussie. "No more whisky. No more horses between my knees. No more sheilas." Curious that the Aussies should call a whore a sheila. The first to come to Australia must have been Irish girls. What a strange thing it was to come back and find a girl like Marie in his uncle's house! She probably hated George Hilton. It was impossible to think of her loving him. He guessed at the series of circumstances that had brought her to Laurent Plage. Need of money, of a holiday by the sea. He supposed his uncle interviewed girls at a typing agency in Paris until he got one that was willing to come and stay at the seaside. But even girls like that had their pride. If they could get revenge they would. To be made love to by a dirty old man like Uncle George was an insult. To put up with the indignities, the unbearable intimacies.

In her room Marie was smiling as she did her hair. It looked better this way but she wasn't going to bother for that grotesque old man with his ridiculous book. Who wanted to know all that about wine? Wine was either good or bad. For her part she didn't like it too dry. Barsac was her favorite. A white wine of Burgundy. When she told him he had laughed at her. Well, she had her money. She had been here two months and felt wonderful. It had really done her good and now she would make a cuckold of him, betray him with this *beau garçon*. She had given him what she called her look. He had understood it. She would see that George had plenty to drink tonight. He slept like a log. Like a pig. He *was* a pig.

At the agency in Paris she had known exactly what he wanted.

"You take shorthand?"

"But certainly, monsieur."

He had looked her up and down. She had pulled her skirt tight with both hands and stood with her heels together.

"You would not mind working at my property at Laurent Plage? It would make a nice holiday for you. A paid holiday. The air is very good."

"How much will you pay, monsieur?"

She had sat down, pulling her skirt up a little to show her knees, and said, "I do very good work, monsieur. I am very skilled."

He had understood and the salary he offered was sufficient. A free, well-paid holiday and a nice little sum with which to buy more government bonds. There would also be other things. Stockings, lingerie. Men were always willing to buy such things. In another year or two she would have a respectable *dot* and be able to marry a clerk or small government functionary. That was as far as her ambition took her. It was safer than being the mistress of a rich man.

She changed her stockings.

Life, when it was not disgusting, could be amusing. Very *drôle* indeed.

Jim was not surprised when Marie came to his room. Ten o'clock. They had turned in early. He had watched Marie plying Uncle George with wine, filling up his glass as soon as it was half empty, giving him three liqueur brandies with his coffee.

Marie lit a candle. There was no electric light at Laurent Plage. She looked charming in a lacy peignoir, her long hair over her shoulders.

"And him?" Jim said.

"He sleeps, snoring like a pig. He is drunk, *chéri,* and to be sure I put two sleeping tablets in his coffee." She laughed. "One would have said a dead man. *Un mort.*" She took off her peignoir and said, "Look at my *chemise de nuit*—is it not beautiful? White satin with lace insertions. One would say a wedding dress, would one not?" She laughed. "He gave it to me. That and much else—perquisities well merited, I can assure you." She sat on the bed and lit one of Jim's cigarettes. "I said

326

to him, *'Monsieur,* for a *lune de miel* there must be a trousseau.'
So he bought me everything." She pulled the nightdress over her
head. "It would be a pity to crush it, would it not, Jeem?"

An hour later she had gone. When he woke he thought about
it. It had been rather like a dream. The dark girl making love in
the soft candlelight, her lips, her hands on his body. Her
laughter.

"Ah, Jeem," she said, "now I shall find it less insupportable.
Let him do what he wants—I have made a fool of him."

He did not see her till lunch, when she was particularly atten-
tive to Uncle George.

"He has a headache, Jeem—imagine it! This morning I had
great difficulty in waking him. The poor man!"

It was time to go. He said goodbye.

"Afraid it was a bit dull for you, my boy," said Uncle
George, who was obviously glad to see him go. "But it was a
change. A bit of a rest. Better than the Bull Ring."

Rest? Christ! He said, "Yes, Uncle George. Don't worry. I
wasn't bored, and it was wonderful being back." It would have
been if the mare and Tim had been there. He kissed Marie's
hand.

Uncle George said, "Why don't you kiss her? You wouldn't
mind, would you, Marie? A soldier going back to war?"

"Not at all. Kiss me, Jeem."

He kissed her, waved at Uncle George and marched off. Now
for a truck going to Etaples. There should be plenty on the
national road. It wasn't long before he picked one up.

Jim had never hated his uncle; he had admired him. Now he
despised him because of his pony. How could a man sell his
nephew's pony when he was at war? But the situation had
changed. Since he had last seen his uncle he'd been in action,
slept with girls, and now he'd had a woman—not a kid but a
mature woman. "Old enough to be your mother," he'd said.
There had been a sting in that, but not for him. He was moving
into life as his uncle was moving out of it. Backing off the stage.

327

The war had changed everything, all values. But it would have been all right except for the pony. That had been a dirty trick. He'd not even needed the money. It was just that she was a nuisance. He was not using her. Oats had gone up, there was a shortage of labor. Things like that.

He thought of his mother. Was Louise a kind of mother-substitute? Had he, in making love to her, been making love to his mother? This was Freud's idea. Make love to the mother, hate the father as a rival. It was curious the way one read serious books, deep underground in a dugout, buried like a mole, with a war going on over your head. The immense boredom of war gave you time to think. The loneliness in a crowd. Even this loneliness was interesting: it existed because there was no certainty, no continuity. All friendships were provisional and so you were driven into yourself, into introspection.

He laughed. Marie had paid his uncle for Gipsy. Two women in one day. If it hadn't been for the mare he would have left Marie alone.

There was plenty to think about on the drive. Dr. Davis had said, "In the end everything boils down to sex." And how bloody right he was! He said, "What do people talk about? Money, sport, books, music, theatres, food. But money is made to spend on women, success in sport impresses them. Food is enjoyed in the company of women, a prelude to intercourse. The rest is just pretense, a cloak thrown over the first religion, the old fertility gods that we still serve."

War, women, church, sex. Death. Weren't they all mixed up? Church steeples, maypoles, Morris dances. "We're all part of some great life pattern," Dr. Davis said. "Instincts, emotions, the conditioned reflexes of training. A complex mechanism of springs, brakes and triggers. Of scar tissue from old wounds, of curiosity, of urgency. All different and all basically the same."

Shelagh said Dr. Davis had been very nice to her and asked about him. "Did I still see you? I said yes. But I didn't say how often."

When they went into action he'd leave postdated field postcards for his mother, Shelagh and Mona, as he had last time. But last time there had been no Shelagh.

44 : Plain Bloody Murder

THREE DAYS later Jim was back with the 10th in command of A
Company. Two letters from Shelagh had been waiting for him
when he got there. He had gone straight up the line and now,
sitting in the company dugout, was writing to her. ". . . I've
just been around the line. All quiet, and moonlight. One of the
men was sitting on the firestep reading the *Daily Mirror*. 'Just
the headlines, sir, and the pictures.'

"A nightingale was singing; another took up the song. At
moments like this it's hard to believe there's a war going on. In
a way it makes it worse. Whenever there's a full moon I think of
us and the zep raid. That's when we both really knew, wasn't it?
I wish we'd had some place to go to make love. I didn't want to
take you to some hotel bedroom or back to Jermyn Street. I
wanted a nice place. Romantic. Thatched. A Christmas-card
sort of place. Not the kind of place where other chaps had taken
girls they'd picked up in the streets. You'd have let me, wouldn't
you, darling? I think so. I could feel it when I held you. . . ."

He heard Colonel Finch's voice. He had taken over after
Colonel Robinson had been wounded again.

"Captain Hilton in?"

"Yes, sir."

The colonel pushed his way through the Vermorel-sprayed
blanket curtain. Jim sprang to his feet.

"You wanted to see me, sir?"

"Yes. I couldn't telephone. . . ."

"Is the line out? I'll send a linesman at once." But why
hadn't he sent a runner?

"It's not that, my boy. Give me a drink."

Jim poured out a whisky and squirted in soda. The colonel
sat down.

"You're a regular, aren't you?"

"Yes, sir."

"So am I. First Battalion."

"Yes, sir." What was this leading up to?

"Christ!" the colonel said, "I don't know how to tell you."

"Tell me what, sir?"

"We've got to send out a patrol, a fighting patrol. We've got to get a prisoner for identification."

"My God, it's as light as day!"

"I know. I called Brigade. It's not their pigeon. They tried to get the order canceled. It's Division Intelligence. Adamant, Jim." It was the first time he'd called him that.

"I'll take it, sir. I couldn't send anyone—not on a night like this."

"You won't. I can't spare you. I've not got enough officers with experience. They're all too young, too new."

That was good, that was, talking about officers being too young. But he knew what Finch meant. Too young in battle experience.

"And besides," the colonel went on, "you seem to forget you're not a subaltern any more. Company commanders don't go on raids unless they are at company strength. This bloody war! Division," he said, "sitting on their arses in their châteaux drinking port. Too bloody idle even to look out of the window. You've got to send Mulholland, Jim."

"No, sir. I'll go. He's my friend, he's had enough. Mons, the Aisne . . ."

"God damn it, boy, I know! And you won't go. I'll court-martial you if you move out of the trench. So get it organized. Mulholland and four or five men. The best plan is probably to try and take the listening post they've got out in front of your sector."

"It's wired in, sir."

"Of course it is. But they could bomb it, cut the wire and see if they can get out a wounded Boche. Even a dead one would do for identification."

"And what'll the Jerries be doing while we're doing that?"

"Counterattacking. Traversing with their MG's, so as soon as

330

the first bomb goes off start a demonstration yourself. Open up. Throw a few bombs, fire some Very lights well clear of your chaps." The colonel picked up his stick.

"I'll come out with you, sir," Jim said.

They climbed the steps of the dugout. Jesus, what a night! A bloody great round moon and not a cloud in sight.

"It's murder, sir," Jim said.

"Don't tell me what it is, Hilton. I'll tell you. It's orders from Division. Good luck, boy. Report to me later. I'll be waiting."

"Will you telephone to them again, sir? We could call it off at the last minute."

"What the hell do you think I'm going to do, Jim?"

Jim watched the colonel turn the bend of the communication trench. He called King.

"Yes, sir?"

"Find Mulholland."

"Yes, sir."

"You heard what the colonel said?"

"Most of it and I don't like it. Light as bloody day, that's what it is."

"Well, don't stand there talking about the weather. It's fine. It's bright. There's not a bloody cloud in the sky and we've got to capture a German. Go on, get Mulholland."

"Poor buggers," King muttered as he went up the trench. "Poor bloody sods. Not the chance of a bloody icicle in hell, they ain't."

Five minutes later Mulholland reported.

"Mulholland, sir."

"You've got to take out a patrol and get a Jerry. Division wants one for identification."

"It's a bit bright, isn't it, sir? The moon, I mean?"

"Bright? When I went around the line one of the men was reading the *Daily Mirror*. He said, 'Just the pictures and head-lines, sir.' Christ! . . . I said I'd go, Mulholland."

"And he wouldn't let you. The colonel . . ."

"No."

"Quite right. More sergeants than captains." He laughed. "I'll do my best, sir. How many men shall I take?"

331

"Is six enough? Seven with you."

"It should be. Less of a target, too."

They shook hands. "Good luck, Harry," Jim said.

"Thank you, sir." He went off to organize his patrol.

An hour later Jim saw them out of the trench. Seven black shadows creeping on their bellies over no-man's-land. He counted them again. There were eight. He went down the line to check the sentries. He had to do something. Goodby. Where the hell was Sergeant Goodby? Nobody knew.

Half an hour passed. An hour. The bloody watch ticking off seconds. The bloody moon shining on civvy lovers at home. Lighting up the bloody front line like an effing lantern. The bloody generals.

A German flare went up. A second and a third. Three in the air at once. Christ! Two machine guns opened up. Bombs. Mulholland was throwing bombs.

"Stand to," Jim shouted. But there was no need for orders. The men were at the parapet.

"They're coming back, sir," the man beside him said, as if he had to be told. It was as light as day with moonlight and the German flares.

"Give them covering fire, lads!"

The men began to shoot rapid fire. A Lewis gun chattered. Four men were coming back. Four out of eight. Fifty percent. No, five—one of them had someone on his shoulders. Fireman's lift. They were nearer. They'd make it. Then another man went down. The man near him stopped to look at him and came on. He must be dead. Four men now—three walking and one being carried. They were running, all except the man carrying the wounded man. He just walked on steadily. German bullets were spattering the parapet, throwing up little puffs of white dust as they hit the chalk. The German machine guns were still firing but they were high. The men were in a patch of dead ground. A minute later they were through the gap in the wire and back in the trench. The wounded man and the man carrying him were still plodding on.

The men were leaning against the parapet breathing hard. One of them was crying. "Oh Christ! Christ!" he said.

Jim slapped and shook him. He pulled himself together.

"Murder," he said. "That was bloody murder."

The man who was carrying the wounded man was out of sight. He was lying down. But near. Only twenty yards or so away. He shouted, "Give us a hand! I've got Mulholland."

"Who are you?" Jim cried.

"Goodby. I've got Mulholland. Help me get him in. I think he's had it."

Two men crept out and they all came in together, dragging Mulholland between them with Goodby in the rear.

Jim looked at him. He'd had it all right. Harry Mulholland had gone west.

"Too late, was I, sir?" Goodby said.

"Couldn't have saved him," said the stretcher bearer who'd come up.

Jim was raging. Bloody murder. "And what the hell were you doing out there, Goodby?"

"He was my friend, sir. Harry Mulholland was my friend. And with Hargreaves gone there's only you now, sir."

Christ, only me, Jim thought. Only me and Goodby.

"You ought to be court-martialed, but I'm going to put you in for a DCM."

This was the end, not only of Harry Mulholland but of God. The end of God. The falling sparrow that was always perceived. What about the men? The agony? If there was a God why didn't He stop it, and if He couldn't stop it what kind of a God was He?

There was too much time to think in war. On duty in the night with men sleeping all around you. Just the sentries awake, staring into the dark. The night bowl, blue-black, star-pierced, filled with menace and the scent of the rotting dead. A scuttling rat would bring a sentry's rifle butt to his cheek. A Very light, a manmade star, fired upward, fizzing till it sank slowly earthward, turning the immediate night not into day but a pattern of black and white, a kind of lino-cut—sharp enough but hard to define. And the Germans not so far away with *Gott mit uns* on their belt buckles, hundreds of thousands of belt buckles, as if they were brazen prayers, as if their reiteration could embarrass God into being on their side. Till tonight God had seemed

333

neutral, like Sweden, not really giving a damn. Perhaps the prayers of the opponents canceled each other out in some gigantic bookkeeping operation. Now he saw God as malevolent, a God of hate, not love.

So far Jim had not been impressed with death, only horrified by pain, revolted by corruption and shocked at the waste of it all. Dust to dust it might be, but the period in between—being a living man and becoming dust, earth to earth—was revolting, sickening, without dignity. The sagging jaw, the emptied bowels and slowly rotting flesh eaten by rats and maggots. The broken dolls of battle oozing red sawdust, smashed, mashed by high explosive. These were the heroes? Men born of women, lovers of women? To see them lying there it was impossible to believe that they had ever done these things or even walked.

And now Mulholland was dead. Murdered. A splendid life just thrown away because some bloody fool at Division had been too idle to look out of the window. Christ! Christ, damn it!

A signaler was standing beside him with a cup of tea. He had his hand on his shoulder. This bloody officer was all right. That was what the chaps wot knew him had said, and they was fucking well right. "I put some rum in it, sir," he said.

"Thank you, Smith. It is Smith, isn't it?"

"Yes, sir."

He gulped the tea. Now for Finch and battalion headquarters. He worked his way down the communication trench in a kind of dream. He pushed past the signalers and runners at the entrance of the dugout.

"Colonel," he said. "Colonel Finch, it's me—Jim Hilton."

"Well, Jim?"

"Tell Division Mulholland's dead, sir. And three others left in no-man's-land for the bloody rats. Sergeant Goodby brought him in, sir. Under fire. Will you put him in for a DCM, sir?" Jim sat down and began to cry. "Mulholland," he said, "Harry Mulholland. Murder, bloody fucking murder."

"Give him a drink," the colonel said. "Four fingers neat. We'll keep him here tonight."

334

Furse, the adjutant, poured it out. The doctor took off his jacket and gave him an injection.

"A pity it should happen his first time back in the line."

"They'd been through a lot together, he and Mulholland," the colonel said. "The Somme. Survivors. He's a good boy."

In a half-coma Jim's mind went back to the afternoon in Jermyn Street, to the second time he and Kathleen had made love after lunch. The first had been too furious, a kind of rape in which Kathleen had immolated herself, had helped, victim and participant in haste, in urgency. It had been like a sudden squall. The meeting. The quiet walking down the street and up in the little lift. And all the time it was boiling in them both. She'd told him to wait for her in the sitting room. Then she'd said, "Come in, Jim." And she'd been waiting for him on the bed, naked, her hands clasped behind her head, her yellow hair spread on the pillow. She had turned her head, smiling at him as he undressed. He had bent over her, kissing her eyelids, her mouth, her neck, her breasts, feeling them swell and harden under his lips. He had kissed the little twists of golden hair in her armpits that had smelled of sweat and scent. He had kissed her belly, the stiff golden bush of her pubic hair. He had said, "It wasn't like this in France. Just sparse little hairs like the yellow down on a young pigeon's breast."

She had laughed and said, "You never saw it!"

"I felt it!"

"I wanted you to see it, to see all of me. But we didn't have time. The war . . ."

"Yes, the war." The cavalry disembarking and him wanting to ride with them. Colonel Black who had said, "There'll be lots of time. Only the fools say it will be over by Christmas." He thought in pictures, one superimposing itself on another. He was using Kathleen to cover Harry Mulholland's death like a blanket.

He'd said, "Whenever I saw a pair of squabs at a poulterer's, I thought of you, Kathleen. I knew they were like that." How funny! He thought of the little dead pairs of pigeons—squabs—with their soft beaks lying in the poulterers' shops. How their

335

scattering of yellow fluff had made him think of Kathleen's belly which, as she said, he'd never seen—only felt—but knew as if his fingers had eyes. In Jermyn Street he had run his fingers through the triangle of it. Kathleen, gold; Mona, black. He had buried his face in the juncture of her thighs. Then he forced her legs open with his knee and got into her as she waited, moist and ready, her arms around his back, her belly raised to his thrusts. They had melted into each other. "I love you," she'd said. Mona had never been like this because Mona had never loved him. Then she had given a little cry and fallen back gasping, her breasts rising and falling as she fought for breath.

That was why he had fallen in love with Shelagh. That was what made it so funny, so goddamned ironic. He had been attracted to her the moment he saw her in hospital because she reminded him of Kathleen. Then he had had this magical afternoon with Kathleen, and lost her. Because she was married and had walked out of his life on high clicking heels as she had walked into it. And all he had felt for her was turned to Shelagh.

He thought of what she had said after she had dressed and tidied herself. As she had put on her hat she turned from the mirror to look at him, her eyes enormous, shadowed, and said, "You know, Jim, I wasn't ready. I mean—" she had paused— "you know what I mean. And you didn't do anything either. And I felt something I never felt before. Never felt with Freddy Oates." Her soft mouth, her lips full with love and bruised with kisses, smiled. "By God," she said, "that would be a joke! To pay him back with a bastard. He can't give me a baby. I'm sure he's sterile."

"Not impotent?"

"I only wish he was. Sometimes I'm afraid of him, Jimmie. Afraid of getting something from him. He goes with all sorts of women, girls. He drinks and then he doesn't care. A skirt's a skirt to him." Her eyes flashed. "I hate him! I only wish he'd get killed and I could marry you."

When Jim woke he wondered where he was. Battalion HQ— what the hell was he doing here?

336

Colonel Finch looked up from the table where he was writing a letter. "Awake, Jim?"

"Yes, sir. What am I doing here?"

"I kept you. You were a bit shaken up by Mulholland's death."

"Yes, I was. I still am but I'll be getting back."

"All right. Your man, King, is with the signalers. He was a bit worried and came down to look for you."

Jim said, "Thank you for letting me stay, sir. I shouldn't have liked to be alone." With that he went back to the line with King.

At his own headquarters he had a cup of tea and a sandwich. Then he called King.

"Come and have a look at Mulholland. I don't want to go alone. We were his friends."

"We could say something, sir."

"Say what?"

"Buggered if I know, sir. A bit of a prayer. Goodbye—something like that. I think he'd like it."

They went along the line to look at the body.

Afterward there was still Shelagh's letter to finish. ". . . a nightingale was singing. Another took up the song. . . ."

But when he had written that Mulholland had been alive.

45 : The Cutting

IT WAS not often that Goodby got a letter, so he was surprised when the post corporal called his name. He didn't know the writing. He opened the envelope and found that some anonymous friend had sent him a cutting—"Social Notes and Doings" —from the *Liverpool Standard*. Whoever it was had marked a short passage.

The Bramwells—Jack and Enid—have done it again. Winning the Tango prize at the Palais with a performance that was outstanding in its grace and beauty. A busy couple who, apart from stage and competition performances, go around all the camps in the north entertaining the troops.

So they billed themselves as the Bramwells—Jack and Enid. Bramwell was a superb dancer. Tall, handsome, rather heavy. But like so many heavy men, very light on his feet. With Enid for a partner there would be no stopping him. He and Enid had only beaten Bramwell in the competition because Bramwell's partner had not been in his class. A lovely brown-haired girl he was living with, a good dancer but lacking Enid's star quality. Enid, light as thistledown, graceful, with a beautiful figure, delicate as a child with a woman's form, almost breathtaking in her perfection. Christ!

He struck a match, lit the cutting and, holding it by the corner, let it burn slowly up to his fingers. Then he crumpled the black fragments and let them fall on the duckboards of the trench.

Who had sent it? Who would do a thing like that? Who hated him? Only Bramwell. He hated him because he had wronged him. Because he had stolen his wife, because he wanted to crow over him, because he hoped to reduce him to a state of desperation in which he would get himself killed. He understood Bramwell's mind, his brutal, cynical selfishness, his cold intelligence. He thought of him safe at home, physically fit in every way except for the loss of two fingers of his right hand in an accident that had rendered him unsuitable for military service. He couldn't even write a proper hand. It was this accident that had turned him from an amateur into a professional dancer. The lucky accident that had brought him a measure of fame and women. The brown-haired girl, Enid, and many others no doubt. Good luck and bad luck seemed almost interchangeable—a coin that never stopped spinning. Heads to tails and tails to heads again.

Well, he might succeed, Jack might. But it was strange: now

they had three things in common—dancing, Enid and a desire for Sergeant Goodby's death. That was funny. He really was doing his best to please Jack Bramwell and get himself killed. He had been doing it for quite a while. The cutting only added to his determination. It was such a simple solution.

That night he volunteered for a patrol. His party ran into some Germans in no-man's-land, killed several and brought one prisoner back. Two of the dead had been killed by Goodby, one with a club he had fashioned out of a pickhandle weighted with a ribbon of lead, the other with a knife in his guts.

"A very creditable performance," the brigadier said. That was how he got a bar to his MM. Very creditable indeed. Especially after the Mulholland rescue. But he had not achieved his objective, which was death. God must be saving him for some special purpose. Invincible. Invulnerable. The idol of his platoon. "Can't touch the bugger, can they?"

In a letter to Jimmie, Irene described the concert for the troops she had attended with the General.

"All professionals," she wrote. "Singers, conjurors, dancers. A girl with six performing dogs—fox terriers—that played a game of ball with their noses. But I wish you could have seen the dancers, the Bramwells, Jack and Enid, do the tango. She was so beautiful she took your breath away. People wondered why he wasn't in the army but he showed them. He held up his right hand. It had only three fingers."

The letter went on, two pages more of London gossip, of war news as they saw it, news of another zeppelin raid, of the General. He had given her a pearl necklace for her birthday.

Jim wondered how many beautiful dancers there were called Enid in the north of England. Somehow he was sure it was Goodby's wife. Poor Goodby. And he had forgotten his mother's birthday.

In their lodging at Harrowgate where they were doing a show, Enid said, "Jack, I'm worried about Arthur. What will we do when he comes back?"

"*If* he comes back, my girl, you mean. What can he do? Divorce you? If he does we'll get married. You don't think you're the only one, do you? Hundreds of women have done it. And I'm not afraid of him. I could lick him with one hand tied behind my back." He'd like to fight Goodby. To bash his face in. The bastard.

Enid began to cry so he left her. A silly little bitch who didn't know when she was well off.

But Enid wasn't at all sure about things, about the future. In a way she still loved Arthur, and she didn't love Jack. It was just that she was weak and had been so lonely. And he was such a beautiful dancer and she loved to dance. Then, one night after they came back he had come in with her and kissed her and said he was staying the night. She had said no, no, and he had twisted her wrist and hurt her. She could not stand pain. So he stayed, and that was the way it had come about. He satisfied one part of her and she was no longer alone, but she was frightened of him. He had stood over her when she wrote to Arthur. Made her write, told her what to write. Often she wanted to write again and tell him the truth, but she didn't dare. I'm not a bad woman, she thought. Just weak. I don't mean to do the things I do. Having absolved herself she washed her face, brushed her hair and made up. Jack would be back soon. He liked her looking pretty.

The General sometimes thought of the man who had said that if he could choose what he would be at various stages of life it would be, if he remembered correctly, a beautiful woman till she was forty, a general till he was sixty and a cardinal till he was eighty. An interesting cross-section of life. But he was very content to be a general of sixty with a beautiful woman of forty.

Shelagh wrote to Jimmie twice a week. Their relationship was still secret, although she was sure Irene Blakeney guessed it.

She had allowed him to take what her mother would have called liberties with her. The few that could be taken in a

London taxi. They could have gone to a small hotel—there were plenty that catered for that sort of thing—but neither wanted it that way. Cheap. But when he came back she'd sleep with him. She was a fool not to have done so before. And they'd get married as soon as possible. In every letter: "I want you; I want all of you. I want to hold you naked in my arms."

There were other men who wanted to marry her; plenty who wanted to sleep with her. But Jim was the one, only you had to let feelings ripen like fruit. Now that it was too late and he had gone, she wanted him. Her letters became as passionate as his. "I want you too, Jimmie. I am so lonely. Sometimes I cry myself to sleep. It's all so awful. All these wounded men. All the men who'll never come back." Like Francis, she thought. Not that she'd told him much about Francis. Only that she'd been engaged.

Jimmie's mother asked her to lunch several times. They'd talked about Jimmie. "I'm glad you're friends," she'd said, the "friends" sort of underlined as if it spelled "lovers." She'd said, "Jimmie needs a woman, a girl. He has that kind of nature." She knew what Irene meant: affectionate, passionate, needing love, needing it skin to skin, belly to belly. Crotch to crotch. That was where the ache lay, the emptiness. That was when the long white nights were born.

His mother's hazel eyes were like Jimmie's. She had the figure of a girl. She was wearing a gray coat and skirt and a small red hat with a short veil that came down to her small straight nose. She spoke of Jimmie's boyhood, of his school; of her late husband who had died when Jim was ten. She said, "There have been two other men in my life. They didn't come to anything. But it's very hard for a woman who has been married to live entirely alone. I don't think Jimmie knows, though he may suspect. I was always very careful." She smiled. She was saying, "Don't worry, my dear. I understand. Women aren't as different from men as they are supposed to be." Then she'd said, "I'd like to have you for a daughter, Shelagh. I have a husband to look after now and Jim needs someone."

But Irene Blakeney was right. A girl needed a man, needed

love. She found herself wondering where they'd make love. She was sure he'd find a way. A hotel in the country, perhaps. Or out of doors if it was fine. On some rabbit-mown lawn, with their dry marble pellets all around them and the sky above her over Jim's shoulders and head. There was no getting away from it. She wanted to make love. Sex. She knew what her mother would have said: that she was immoral. Loose. Her mother had not been an understanding woman. There had never been much love between them.

46 : Exit Miss Moon

AT LAST Mona had met a man who wanted to marry her. Not a member of the club which had almost ceased to exist, but a captain in the RASC—Royal Army Service Corps. He was very insistent on the "Royal." He was called Albert Smith and she had met him at Lyons Corner House where she was having a solitary lunch. He sat down at her table with a "I hope you don't mind, miss?"

She looked at him out of her big brown eyes, said, "Not at all," and went on eating.

"I saw you right across the room," he said. "You stand out. You're beautiful."

Mona said, "Thank you." She was still not used to these pick-ups. She hated having to talk about money, like a tart. But if she didn't, they thought it was free, because she'd liked the look of them or was patriotic or something. Of course she never solicited like a tart. She just sat and waited and they came. Cats to a saucer of cream, flies to a honey pot.

Now she waited for his proposition. It didn't come—not in the usual way at all.

He ordered coffee and a Bath bun. When they came he said, "I've had lunch but I had to order something, didn't I?"

Mona had tomato soup, a dear little veal and ham pie and a vanilla ice. She ordered coffee.

"Now you've finished eating we can talk," the man said. "My name is Albert Smith. It's a very ordinary name but one day a lot of people are going to know it."

"Are they?"

"Yes, they are. I'll tell you why later on. What I suggest is that since it's such a nice day you run down to Farnborough with me—I've got a business there—and then we'll come back to town for dinner and a show. That is, if you're not busy. If you are we could do it tomorrow, but it may not be such a nice day."

"I was going to do some shopping, but it can wait," Mona said. This man interested her. He spoke nicely. He seemed sure of himself. He was not a boy. He had a car and a business. "Does your wife approve of your taking young ladies on motor drives?"

"Wife?" he said. "I've got no wife. Never had one."

"Why not?"

"Working too hard. A wife costs money. I needed all the money I had to put into the business."

"What business?"

"A garage. I started as a mechanic fifteen years ago, but it's mine now. While I've been in the army my cashier runs it, but I go down whenever I'm on leave."

"Back from the war?"

"Oh dear no. I'm stationed at Scarborough. Repairs, reconditioning army lorries and so on. I've never been to the front. Terrible things they do to the lorries there, I hear. Very hard on them, war is. Been at Scarborough the whole war, almost."

"Then you must have a girl there?"

"No girl. Girls are too expensive. I'm saving my pay. I've got big plans for when it's over. I've bought land near my garage. I want to float a company and build my own cars."

When Mona had finished her coffee he put sixpence on the

marble table for the waitress and picked up her slip with his own. Before leaving, he bought her a box of chocolates.

The car was a black Sunbeam. He drove very well. He talked of his plans; repair works first. Buy wrecked cars—good ones, Rolls, Rovers, and so on—and recondition them. They passed a lot of horse transport. Carts, wagons, traps. He looked at them contemptuously.

"They're finished," he said. "Another ten years and there'll hardly be a horse on the roads."

"You know," Mona said, "if I was rich I might put some money into your business."

"If you were rich you might do worse," he said. "And what do you do, Miss Moon?"

She had known this would come. "Oh, Captain Smith, I do a lot of little things. My dad left me a little money—not enough to live on, but something. I do some war work, wrap parcels and so on. And then I was companion to an old lady but she died last month. I can't type or anything so I expect I'll have to be a saleslady. A clothes shop would suit me."

"I've got a month's leave, so don't do anything for a month."

"I have to work. I can't take a month off. And besides, what should I do with myself?"

"You'd spend it with me."

"I'm not going to live with you, Captain Smith."

"I never suggested it, Miss Moon. But you can work for me. I'll give you a salary."

"What would I have to do?"

"Go around garages. Tell them you need a car and see what they have for sale. Get prices, specifications and so on. Say your fiancé wants to buy you a car. Get addresses, names of the owners and so on."

"But why?"

"To get an idea of the market. The number of garages and salesrooms in the West End. Statistics. I can't do it in uniform, there'd soon be talk. A fiver a week, Miss Moon, plus expenses. Taxis, meals and so on. Think you can do it?"

"Do you think I can?"

"I wouldn't ask you if I didn't."

344

And all this time he had not so much as put his hand on her thigh. Mona made up her mind. She'd chance it. Close the flat, go to a boarding house where there could be no nonsense about "Let me just come in with you for a minute" or anything like that. She said, "I'd like to make something clear, Captain Smith. Although I let you pick me up and said I'd go for a drive with you, I am a good girl. My fiancé was killed on the Somme." And so he had been—quite a number of times. "We were going to be married on his next leave. He was going to buy a little house with a garden. Something to come back to," she said. She dabbed her eyes with a lace-edged handkerchief. It was easy enough to cry when you thought about them. "A little house," she said. "A garden. Babies. A nice fat dog, a cat and a canary. I've always loved animals but you can't have them in a boarding house, can you?" She pulled up her dress a little out of habit and to see what he would do.

He did nothing. "You needn't worry about me, Miss Moon. When I saw you at the Corner House I knew you were just what I needed. Pretty, smart-looking. Those chaps will like talking to you. Tell you all they know—about the cars they have, about business, about what they think will happen after the war. They may have some big cars stuck away that are too expensive to run now with a petrol shortage. Racing cars, specialities, foreign cars. That's what I want to get my hands on."

The garage was nice. It looked efficient and well run. Captain Smith showed her his workshops. She said she thought the country around here was very pretty. He said, "I'm glad you like the country." Why was he glad?

They had dinner at Quaglino's and went to see *White Horse Inn*. He put her in a taxi and she gave her address—"a friend I'm staying the night with." She had his fiver in her bag. She was to start tomorrow and meet him at the Troc at six.

"Good night, Miss Moon. And thank you for a very pleasant and profitable day."

"Good night, Captain Smith, and thank you for everything."

Tomorrow she'd pack a suitcase and move to a boarding house.

Mona found the work quite interesting. Captain Smith had been right. They were all ready to pass the time of day with a pretty girl whose fiancé was going to buy her a car. She dined with Captain Smith every night. Quaglino's, Frascati's, the Café Royal, the Troc, the Piccadilly, Les Gobelins, the Elysée. At weekends they drove around the country looking at garages. And all this time—a whole fortnight—he'd done nothing. Not kissed her, not even held her hand. And then one evening when she met him he put a little parcel into her hand.

She opened it—a gold wristwatch. "Oh Captain Smith!" she said. "I can't take it. I couldn't take such a present from a man. . . ." It was extraordinary. He said he avoided girls because they were expensive, and then he had done this.

"Not even if he wanted to marry you, Miss Moon?"

"What!" she said. "Are you proposing?"

"I'm popping the question, Mona. Will you marry me?"

Mona began to cry. Right there among the palms and all the people. "Yes, I'll marry you, Albert. I think I love you, but you never showed anything."

"I was afraid of scaring you," he said. "I thought you might think all sorts of things. I thought we could get married next week and go up to Scarborough together when my leave's over."

Mona began to cry again. All her dreams come true at last! Mrs. Albert Smith, with a little house and garden, a fat dog, a cat, a canary and babies. Mona Moon had disappeared off the face of the earth. Gone. Dead as the men on the battlefields of France. The widow of twenty lovers was a virgin again, respectable. And a month ago she had been on the verge of becoming a tart, asking for money. Bickering about prices. She'd never go back to the flat again. She wanted no memories of it. She'd post the key to the estate agent, tell him she was getting married and going abroad and that he could let it furnished to some tart. A real love nest.

She said, "Is that why you took me to Farnborough and asked if I liked the country?"

"Yes, darling. It was love at first sight. And tomorrow we'll buy the ring. I've got one picked out at Spinks'. I hope you'll like it."

Albert Smith had plans all right. He always had had plans. Mona was just part of them, fitted in like a split pin to hold the lock nut together. She'd found him several good cars—a Rolls, two Daimlers, an Hispano-Suiza. He could get them cheap. Nobody wanted them now. They all seemed to forget the war would end one day. They were going to be the nucleus of the Al Smith Hire Service. He'd get good-looking ASC drivers in smart uniforms to drive them. That was one little company; he had raised enough money for it already.

She had also found him three racing cars—monsters with big copper exhausts that ran like snakes along their sides. Those he would recondition and tune up himself. After the war there would be a shortage of racing cars. He'd find drivers for them, pay expenses and split the stakes. But they'd all be Al Smith cars, with Al Smith painted in big white letters on their sides. This was his private venture.

And finally, there was the big garage deal. A chain of Al Smith garages all over London and the home counties. He was going to use American plans, American methods. Clean windscreens, check tires, oil, battery. All for free. Rest rooms for ladies and gents. This was the biggest thing, and it would grow. No limit to the size. And of course there would be the army supply disposal sales. Lorries, trucks, staff cars. A fortune in that, too, and he'd be in on it. He had friends with hot money. Glad to let him use it. A piece of cake, that was what the war was for chaps with a bit of brain. The name of Al Smith was going to be known all right. His name would ring a bell. The name in big, simple letters. A plain name for an exceptional man. He laughed to himself.

And Mona? A neat little trick who thought she had fooled him. That first drive had just been because he wanted company, and then he'd seen she could be useful. After that he'd decided to have her investigated. Put a couple of boys on to it and they'd found out all about her. Good girl, indeed! A little tart. But it was something to hold over her. He'd marry her all right, and if she didn't toe the line she'd find herself where she belonged—on the bloody streets. But if she behaved and did what she was told, she'd be useful. Suppose he couldn't put a deal through, he'd make her seduce the chap and he'd catch them at it. "OK," he'd say. "OK. I'll not send the picture to your wife. I'll even give you the negative. All you've got to do is to sign on the dotted line."

No girls? Fancy her swallowing that one with a chap like me! And there was no doubt, what with one thing and the other, the war had been a bloody godsend. He'd done quite a bit of fiddling with the stores. Spare parts and so on. He'd made a lot of useful contacts and he'd had a fine time. Captain Albert Smith, RASC, had had a finger in a lot of queer pies and a hand up a lot of skirts since it all began in '14.

47 : Attack

THE 10th did two more tours in the line and then regrouped for a show on a three-divisional front. The day before they went up Jim gave Captain Green, the quartermaster, two dozen field service postcards for Shelagh and his mother, with everything crossed out on them except "I am well." They were postdated, one each for every day.

"Keep them from worrying," he said.

"Your women, Jim?"

"My women. My mother and my girl." He hoped she was still his girl—in spite of her letters he sometimes had doubts. She was so beautiful, all ivory and gold. Still, there must be so many men wanting her. Men. Not boys, like me. Twenty-five, twenty-eight, chaps who'd been around. Done things, seen things. And he knew nothing—school, the war, that was all. He'd never even been to Paris, much less Venice or the Argentine or the

Far East. Temples, pagodas, elephants. The South Seas. Rubber plantations. He'd listened to men talk often enough. They could tell a girl interesting things. All he could do was to love her and want her. Mona had told him things men told her. Wonderful yarns. Big game they had shot. Big ships, liners. Foreign parts, as she called them. How could you compete with chaps like that? Good dancers, who knew all about ordering meals, tips and the rest of the civilian drill. One day he was sure, absolutely sure. The next he was in doubt. He had heard so many men tell how they had been ditched.

There was something very moving the way men sang, marching toward the guns, to the orchestra of their throbbing fire. "Daisy, Daisy" . . . "You take the high road and I'll take the low road, and I'll be in Scotland afore ye" . . . "Pack up your troubles" . . . "Little Grey Home in the West" . . . "Tipperary" . . . all the old repertoire of marching men. Coming out of the line, they seldom sang. Too tired. They had been too near to eternity.

Marching at ease, weighted with packs, their feet mechanical, irrelevant. Singing music-hall songs in ironshod step, each pace a yard toward the war, a yard away from safety. So they sang as men whistle in the dark, boys in a churchyard at night. Praise to God when they sang a hymn, and straight from God to "Bollocky Bill the Sailor" and "Mademoiselle from Armentières." So it went, the deep-voiced songs, vulgar, rough, nostalgic, hanging above the moving men, a blanket of sound moving with them. An entity keeping them company, smelling of sweat, of white chalk dust, of leather and khaki cloth, of dubbined boots and dirty feet.

Jim opened a tin of Goldflake. Yellow, round, like a cocoa tin but shorter. Cigarette-length, in fact. The lid had a little triangular piercer attached to it. You pulled it back with your thumb, then put the lid on again and pushed it down. It went through the thin silver inner airtight lid. You felt it go, the air hissed in and you turned the cover, rotating it to cut the diaphragm. Then

349

you opened the box and the little silver circle of thin metal lay loose on top of the cigarettes. He picked it out; even in the predawn dark it shone like the bits of tin they all had fastened on their backs. Identification, so that the observer planes, spotting for the gunners, would know where they were and be able to plot their position on their maps.

He looked at his synchronized watch: four-thirty-five. A runner had come up from battalion with a watch. He had sent for the platoon officers and they had all set their watches. Hundreds of officers' watches all along the line were ticking away the seconds precisely. Time, machine-tooled, all set like a bomb to go off at four-forty-five ack emma. A bomb filled with men. Three divisions, twenty thousand men. At four-forty-five it would explode. They were ready, loaded for action. No packs or overcoats. Fighting order. Just haversacks on their backs. SAA—small-arms ammunition. Bombs, flares, rockets, Very lights, sandbags, spare bandoliers. The stretcher bearers' boxes of bandages and iodine had been checked. Iron rations.

Four-thirty-eight. The pegs were ready. Driven into the parapet for the men to hang on to as they climbed out. Everything was very quiet. The Germans expected an attack, they'd seen the material building up in the rear. The dumps of food and ammunition. Miniature mountains covered with tarpaulins. They'd seen more guns come up. Oh yes, they knew all right, but they didn't know when.

The men were still. Stood to. Standing with their bayoneted rifles beside them. The Lewis gunner teams had their guns and drums of ammunition packed up. What were they all thinking of? What was anyone thinking of? What was he thinking of? Why had the detail of opening a tin of Goldflake seemed so important? The tiny noise of the air going into the vacuum as he pierced it? Why? Because perhaps he had realized it might be the last one he ever opened. They'd had a rum ration fifteen minutes ago. Dutch courage. They didn't need it but it put heart into them and drove out the predawn cold.

Two men had given him letters to post—"just in case, sir." Why the hell did they think he had a better chance than they?

Quite the contrary. The Germans had snipers detailed to pick off the officers and NCO's. Anyone they saw leading troops. At least now they wore the same uniform as the men. In '16 they had gone over the top in riding breeches, boots and Sam Browne belts. In '14 they had carried swords. Christ . . . Swords! Now an officer was indistinguishable from a private soldier, his pips of embroidered khaki were on the shoulder straps of his tunic. He carried a rifle and bayonet.

Four-thirty-nine. It was amazing the ground the mind covered in a minute at a time like this. They said when you were drowning you saw your whole life. That a long dream only took a few seconds. Four-thirty-nine and a half. His eyes were on the luminous dial of his watch. In thirty seconds the barrage would begin. At four-forty it would fall—a hail of high explosive—on the German wire and front line. It would last for ten minutes. At four-forty-five they would climb out of the trench under its protective fire. Like an umbrella in the rain. Oh Jesus, how bloody silly could you be? At four-fifty the barrage would move on to the support line.

And there it was. It had begun. The whole line behind them had erupted with a roar. Heavies, field guns standing almost wheel to wheel. The shells—thousands of shells—were passing over their heads, screaming like trains, exploding in orange and salmon flame on the German wire. The light of the explosions lit up the smoke and cascading earth of their devastation. You'd think no one could live through it, through such a barrage. But they could. He had himself.

Suppose the wire wasn't fully cut? It had happened before. His eyes never left his watch face. How often he had looked at it, the round face of a friend. Nearly time to see Mona, Shelagh, to meet some chaps at the Savoy, to go to a show. Funny things, watches. Part of you. Ticking away like your heart. Going everywhere with you. To war, to women.

This was it. Five seconds to zero. He must be the first man out. He felt the pegs in his hands, he felt his muscles pulling him up. His rifle lay on the parapet. He bent to pick it up. All around him the men, darker shapes in the dark night, were climbing out, their rifles at the high port, their dulled bayonets' black points against the night sky. How strange to be out in the open with space all around you! The men followed him toward the exploding shells. An inferno, but comforting. As long as the barrage lasted they were safe. Relatively safe. The German gun positions were being plastered too. It was when the barrage lifted, moved on, crept toward the support lines, that you were left with it. Cut the wire, pound the front line till the infantry got there, and then up and on.

They walked on slowly, a single line of men at two-yard intervals. King and Nobby were beside him. Friends. They were very close to the barrage now. A short would hit them. Then neat as a whistle it lifted; the curtain of fire passed on, sweeping over the German front like a broom.

"Charge!" he shouted.

No one could hear him as he began to run through the wire. They'd done a good job. The men were shouting, cursing. Nobby and he jumped down into the German trench together. Both stumbled. Christ, they dug them deep! The first phase was over—the waiting, the crossing the open ground.

"Come on!" he shouted. "Rout the bastards out!"

No need. The Germans were coming out of the dugouts. Now it was man to man in the deep, narrow trench. No more than two men could fight side by side.

When the sun came up they finished the job, and moved on to attack the second line.

It was strange to be walking in almost unshelled country, in long grass, hay-tasseled with seed and flower, that would never know the scythe. Marguerites, white, yellow-centered, childhood flowers like long-stemmed lawn daisies. Blue scabious, red clover bent with furry bumblebees. The scent of it all, of meadowsweet, almost sickly, like the smell of the dead. Summer, caught like a butterfly in the net of war, with the shells going over it in both directions as if summer was a place and not a time. And the larks singing a requiem to the fallen dead. Disturbed by gunfire, they sang above their hidden nests, rising and falling vertically, yo-yos on their string of song. To the right and left, as far as the eye could see and beyond it, men were advancing, walking slowly, their bayoneted rifles at the trail through these fertile fields. Unturned for years, unloved by plow, they lay waiting for this war to end as older wars had ended; for the dead to rot and the cycle to start again under the slow hooves of the horses and turning furrow.

A covey of partridges whirred away and came down on coasting wings. A hare ran along the line of men till impaled by a bayonet lunge. The killing mood was on them. Boredom, fear, anger and the rum ration had done the trick. They'd kill anything that appeared in front of them. These good, quiet men; husbands, fathers, brothers, lovers. Who the hell had decided that a sixty-fourth part of a gallon was the right amount to dish out to a fighting man? Not too much and not too little.

How odd it was to be walking in a field hand in hand with death as if it was a girl! To see great trees of earth spout upward, seeded by shells into instant growth. To feel the ground tremble under the vibration of the explosions. It was all unreal, a dream rather than a nightmare. There was no fear in it, or so much that it had ceased to be fear as water ceased to be water in the ocean. Who thought of it as water, as drops and droplets? Droplets of fear were for civil life—this was the sea.

Jim saw men fall, men he knew. But it meant nothing, merely that they had fallen and were no longer there, not with them, not walking in this eternal field. A shell burst, red with brick dust. There had been a farm here once. A house with people in it, who had eaten and made love and worked the land. And still they went on, their own shells preceding them in a moving curtain of fire. One felt safe behind it, or almost safe, like a child in the night with a blanket pulled up over its head against imagined terror.

They would be in the wire of the next line soon. The shells should have cut the pricking strands into tatters and held the enemy down till they got in to make the kill, jumping into the trench with bayonet and bomb. Tossing grenades into the dugouts, hearing them bounce like iron balls on the steps. Mop up, fill sandbags, reverse the trenches. Set up the Lewis guns to defend them till the second wave of men came to leapfrog them and take the next line of defenses, and the third wave came to leapfrog the second. The red line, the blue line, the green line—all so clear and simple on the squared-off maps.

Jim was not there himself; he never was in battle. That was why he felt no fear, felt nothing at all. Once again he was a long way off, watching the action from a hilltop, seeing this young chap, Jim Hilton, going into action with all these men and taking it fairly well. All utterly objective. But his mind was wandering, at ease. He was thinking of Kathleen and Mona, of Shelagh, of Louise and Marie, of a hot bath, of the best way to get rid of the lice in his clothes, of horses, of the summer at Laurent Plage and his mother picking sweetpeas for the dining room. She liked the pale pastel colors best.

In his hand he held a rifle with one of the new oxidized bayonets that showed no sun or moonlight glint. It was at full cock and he carried it at the high port. They were in the wire at last. Cut, thank God. Iron brambles that could hold a man trapped. Even as it was, a piece ripped his boot and almost tripped him. They were there in the second line. They need go no farther. Take it and they were home. This was the 10th Wilts L.I. objective. The men were closing in on either side of him, like chicks around a hen. It was almost quiet, the gunfire had gone on again. The trench had been pounded. Now it was up to him, up to them, the infantry, and their hand weapons.

"Come on, you bastards!" he shouted, and jumped into the trench, hoping no one was waiting for him to land. On to the firestep and down. Not a soul except two dead men, still bleeding. A German came around a traverse. He put up his rifle and shot him. One of his men clapped him on the back, said, "Good shot, sir!" and began lobbing bombs over the fallen body from the bag he carried. With quiet precision he pulled out the pins, let the handles fly off and tossed them—like a child playing ball against a wall. They went up, black, pineapple-shaped, against the blue summer sky, and fell with a thud to explode a moment later.

Jim, with his bomb-thrower behind him, and the other rifle-men behind the bomb-thrower, advanced down the trench. When they came to the gaping mouth of a dugout they tossed a couple of bombs down it, waiting for them to explode before they went on.

"More bombs," Harris, the bomb-thrower, said. "Pass the word down. Send up some more bloody bombs."

Jim set up a Lewis gun at a communication trench, left a section with a bag of bombs and mounted sentries to see they didn't counterattack across the open. He heard English voices.

"Who's there?" he shouted.

"Sergeant Morris, No. Two Platoon. Mr. Birk is hit." Mr. Birk was a new officer.

He had made contact. Now all he need do was mop up and see if Corporal Hacker had made contact on the right. There were his casualties to count—the dead, the wounded, the missing. The wounded to get away. The line to consolidate. They were to stay here till relieved.

In London Irene was thinking about her life. When she married the General and moved to Albany she let the house in Melbury Road and put her furniture into storage. She didn't want to sell it, it was part of her life. It had come to her on her father's death. Stuff she had been brought up with at the vicarage in Little Galton, mostly old things that her parents had themselves inherited. Queen Anne, Georgian, Regency. Mahogany, pol-ished by a thousand hands, day after day, year after year. Her father, the Reverend Archibald Moxon, a good but ineffectual man, had left her very little. His assets had amounted to less than two thousand pounds, and the furniture. Her mother had died when she was a young girl. She had hardly known her and had been brought up by a housekeeper and a governess.

Mervyn Hilton, a consulting engineer just back from Peru, had met her at a garden party at Chaddon Park; had fallen in love with her and married her within two months. She had been eighteen. It had all seemed very romantic at the time. Swept off her feet by this big, impetuous, handsome man, twelve years older than herself. She had hoped to travel with him: Peru, Mexico, South Africa, India. But he never took her. Too rough. So he went and he came back, and went off again. Copper mines, diamonds, gold, emeralds. He reported his findings, took some leave and then left her again.

Her life with Mervyn had consisted of a series of honeymoons—none of them satisfactory, at least not to her. When he was killed after ten years of marriage in some riots in Bogotá—emeralds again—she mourned him in a conventional manner and concentrated on her son. Prep school at Tunbridge Wells. Denby. Then the war had come and he'd gone—a temporary second lieutenant at seventeen.

Mervyn had left her seven hundred a year. It was enough to live on quietly in the small house she had taken in Melbury Road: drawing room, dining room, bedroom; a bedroom for Jimmie. Bathroom and two servants' rooms on the top floor, and what were called the usual offices. She'd kept three servants—a cook, a parlormaid and a housemaid. The house even had a small garden with a pocket-handkerchief lawn, some rosebushes, a pink flowering cherry—how lovely it was in spring!—a lilac and five azaleas. Pretty. Very pretty for London. She'd bought a lead cupid for the middle of the grass and planted a laburnum beside him. A dear little naked lead boy. One day, when they moved to John's place in the country, she'd fetch him. He always reminded her of Jimmie, when he was about four, in his bath.

Her life had been a routine. The summers at Laurent Plage with Mervyn's brother George. Calls on Mervyn's sister Julia, also a widow but a rich one and childless, who lived in Berkeley Square. A few friends—women. Married couples of her own age. Theatres, concerts, games of bridge, little dinner parties. And then her lovers. Vernon McKnight, a widower, who wanted to marry her—or said he did. She had the feeling he just wanted a good home. And Ralph Fennerton, a married man with a wife in an institution. Asylum really, only they never called it that.

Love. No, it had not been love. She knew that now and had known it then. It was something else, a combination of things.

But looking back, she was glad of them. They had kept the mechanism going, prevented the clock of her life from running down, so when she had met the General and seen what he felt for her she had decided to marry him. Still not love. But he was handsome, well off, a baronet. A good match that would give her both sex and security.

And now she loved him. Madly, passionately, indecently. The way no girl could love, because nature was in a hurry. Not long to menopause. This was the full bloom of the rose before the petals began to wither and fall. He was in a hurry, too. Sixty. How many more years of it had he? Make the most of it. Hay while the autumn sun still shone.

It was curious that her life had been all honeymoons. First with Mervyn, then with Vernon and Ralph; now with John at Albany or his divisional headquarters. When the war was over she supposed they'd settle down at the Hall. County life. Hunting, shoots and so on. It would be wonderful to be on a horse again, sidesaddle. He promised to get her a nice quiet hunter. She had not been on a horse since she had been married. But he said riding was something you never forgot. He said this, that. The General thinks . . . Good God, she seemed to have no mind of her own anymore! But it took her thoughts away from Jimmie. It was no good brooding, the General said. There it was again! Just hope and pray. She did both. Her Jimmie and those girls—Mona something, a tarty little piece, and Shelagh, the pretty blonde nurse. Boys were marrying so young now. "If we're old enough to fight, we're old enough to marry." Who could argue about it?

She thought about the girl in France. Those few days at the outbreak of war. Kathleen. Blonde, too. A wild little thing, though she was sure her mother hadn't suspected it. She remembered George Hilton having a row with Jim because he'd caught him kissing her. If he'd kissed her and if she was right about the girl, he'd done more. Puppy love.

Boys, girls, men, women—wherever you went you saw it. The same old thing, but accelerated, made more urgent by war. It had the same effect on her. It was partly worry about Jimmie that drove her so often into the General's arms—John's arms where, for a while, she could forget her son. What a terrible thing to think! But it was true. Sex, the great anodyne. The men, home on leave, forgetting the war with their girls, the girls forgetting their men at the war with other men. It was like some kind of drug.

She must get fresh flowers. How wonderful it was to be able to buy all the flowers she wanted, and at a place like Solomon's too. She must send Jimmie another pacel. Fortnum's fruit cake lasted so well. Veal and ham pie, dates, chocolate, Gentleman's Relish, Hartley's marmalade, chicken and ham paste, herrings in tomato . . . And write to John—a love letter. How easy they were to write, and what else was there to say? "I love you, I miss you, I want you. Darling John."

There it was: on his thick, cream-laid, crested notepaper. She put on her hat to go out. Post the letter. Solomon's. Fortnum's. What a convenient place to live—everything within a few hundred yards of Albany. She might as well drop in at Hatchard's and send the boy some books.

Outside she saw the headings on the newsvendors' boards: "New Attack launched by British . . . German Third Line taken . . ."

Jimmie! My God, where was Jimmie? While she had been lost in dreams of the past and hopes for the future, she had forgotten the now. Today there was a new battle raging. . . .

48 : The Sniper

THE 10th had not been relieved after the attack. They had been reinforced and told to hang on. But things were quiet. Both the British and the Germans were exhausted, the position of troops uncertain. Both sides were licking their wounds.

But there had been some sniping. One sniper in particular was worrying Jim Hilton. He was behind them. Another man had just been shot. Blake, one of the new sergeants, had reported it. He said, "You'd better come, sir. He's going and he's asking for you."

"Who? Young Ginger? Bad as that, is it?"

"Yes, sir."

They went along the trench together. The men crowded against the parapet to let them pass. "Ginger's copped it." They knew. It was worse this way, with the line quiet in one of those curious lulls of a great battle that may last for days or only hours. A sniper. One shot. In the back again, like the others. Telescopic sight, the crossed hairs in the circle of the sights. Asking for me—what the hell can I do?

They came around a traverse and there he was: Ginger, lying on the firestep, his head at the feet of the sentry who was looking out through a little slit between the sandbags. His mates were around him, one of them holding his hand. A stretcher bearer was bending over him. Ginger looked up and shook his head. The negative motion. No go. No, I'll not go on with you. I'll not make love, not drink, dance, sing. Not do nothing. Not live.

The men turned. "Askin' for you, sir."

"Ginger," Jim said, "I'm here." He took the hand from the chap who was holding it. How cold it was.

"That you, sir?"

"It's me, Ginger."

"Thank you for coming. I did all right, didn't I, sir? I mean, for a kid?"

"You did fine. We're proud of you. Don't worry. We'll take care of you. Get you away as soon as it's dark."

"I've had my chips, sir. Copped it. Napoo, finis. I can feel it, sir. Tell my ma. Tell 'er I did all right—for a kid, I mean. Didn't I, sir? Didn't I?"

"I'll tell her, Ginger."

This was the first time Jim had actually watched a man die. The first time he'd had time to watch life taking flight. He tightened his grip on the hand he held. Ginger's face was getting paler, his freckles stood out like little brown islands, his red hair seemed to blaze. His cheeks were sinking in.

"It's 'is guts, sir," the stretcher bearer said. "I can't stop it. His guts must be full of blood."

How silent it all was—not a shot, not even a distant gun, as if the whole world had paused, waiting for Ginger to die. Just the bloody larks singing in the blue sky. Two of the men were crying quietly; everyone loved Ginger. But he was going. His life was going, like a bird taking wing. Jim felt it in his hand. It was no longer a hand. It was dead. There was no sound, no spasm. Ginger's jaw relaxed, his mouth opened. A fly alighted on his blue, staring eyes. He had gone.

"He's gone, mates," the stretcher bearer said. "Get a blanket, someone. Cover him up."

Jim felt tears in his eyes. He'd asked for him. For me. "Done all right, didn't I, sir . . . for a kid . . . tell my ma."

One of the men gripped Jim's wrist hard and turned away. By God, how close he was to them, even the new drafts! Like Ginger. He'd go down in his blanket with the limbers that brought up the rations. The stretcher bearers would carry him down the communication trench.

Shot in the back by a sniper. Another one. The Germans had the pull over them with their snipers. Jäger battalions. Hunters, gamekeepers, poachers, who always stayed in one part of the line. Expert shots who knew every tuft of grass, every sandbag, bush, tree, every brick in every ruined building. Like hunters, they waited to strike. But this one was behind them; he had to be.

Sergeant Blake detailed a fatigue party to go down the line to meet the limbers that were bringing up the rations. Dixies of thick stew, gallons of rum in stone jars, sacks of bread. Five-gallon petrol tins of chlorinated water, small-arms ammunition in wooden boxes with two rope handles; sacks of bombs, flares, rockets, extra picks and shovels; rolls of barbed wire, iron screw piquets, duckboards to replace those that were broken. A more mixed or harder lot of stuff to carry would be hard to imagine.

They went down empty-handed except for Ginger under a

blanket on a stretcher. The transport chaps would stick him in a limber and jolt him back to the horse lines. The brigade would bury him. When the parson had done his stuff they'd shovel the ground in on him and put a nice little white cross with his name, regiment and number on it over the piled earth. And that would be the end of Ginger.

Meanwhile Jim was writing to his mother. "Dear Mrs. Jones, I regret to inform you . . ." Another of them. Of course in a big battle you had no time to write them. "A brave boy whose last words were 'tell my mother.'" The candle, stuck in its own grease on the top of a Goldflake tin, guttered and he pinched off the wick. "I assure you he did not suffer . . ." What a lie, with a wound in the guts! ". . . and died in the arms of his friends. Etc., etc. Yours sincerely, James Hilton, Captain, 10th KOWLI." He wondered if Mrs. Jones had other children, other sons. It was a hell of a war for women. He wrote to his mother and Shelagh.

Then he went around the line again to talk to the sentries and look at his chaps resting beside their equipment hanging from live 303 ammunition driven into the wall of the parapet. Young Findlay was the officer on duty this watch. Not been out long, might be jumpy. Have a word with him too.

Foxy Barker was the fourth man shot in the back. He was killed two days after Ginger Jones. There was only one explanation. Among the scattered dead behind them—a confused mixture of English and German corpses—was a sniper playing possum. A dead man who wasn't dead, who, watching his chance, fired a single shot and then lay back, lost among the others, a needle in a putrefying haystack. What went on in his mind? How consumed with hatred he must be, lying there in that stinking battlefield! He'd move at night, getting food and water from the dead. But how did he expect to get away, to get back to the German lines? What hope had he? But he was clever. One shot, then nothing for a day. Easy too, in a way, because who was looking backward? Who wanted to? It was not a pretty sight. The whole of what had been open country—bare, clean, untrenched—between the German front and support lines, was now plowed up by shellfire and littered with bodies, lying this way and that, facing in all directions. On their faces, on their backs, staring with sightless eyes at the burning summer sun by day and the stars at night.

It would be impossible to examine every corpse even at night. The only thing to do was to have a man watch the dead for movement. Jim put Corporal Dent on the job with a pair of Zeiss glasses he had taken from a dead German officer.

"Watch for anything, Dent," he said. "Any movement. He's out there somewhere."

"Yes, sir. I'll watch for the bastard. But if he's lying in a shell hole we may not see him."

"If we don't see him, someone'll have to lie out there too. Go out at night and lie doggo."

"I'll do it," Dent said. "Foxy was my mate."

Dent, his face blackened with burnt cork, watched the old battlefield from behind some tussocks of long grass on the edge of a shell hole that had smashed the parapet. He swept the ground slowly from right to left and back again. Slowly. After a few times he knew the way every man was lying. He was sure if one moved while he was looking elsewhere he'd remember it. But not one moved. The bastard, he thought. The bloody bastard. Then his mind went to Foxy. Good old Foxy. Beer and eggs, that was what Foxy liked. Even French beer. Omelettes. He was different from Foxy. It was girls he liked. So there was never no trouble between them. He'd leave Foxy to swill beer and find himself a bit of skirt. They were both married, him and Foxy. But Foxy was new to it and wouldn't touch another. You will, he'd told him many a time. But now he couldn't. Never fuck another woman. Not even his wife. Nor drink another pint, nor eat another bloody omelette. The bastard. By Christ, he'd get the bloody bastard! One move and he'd have him. Not shoot. Not call the sergeant, nor young Hilton. He'd take a chance. Run straight out into the open and stick the bastard as he lay doggo. Never take his eyes off him.

Two hours later he was relieved. Jim came along with Smith. "Give him the glasses, Dent," he said. "Go and rest your eyes." He gave Smith the glasses and the stump of cork.

"Black your bloody face, mate," he said. "And lie still. The bastard's watching us too."

So they worked it, he and Smith in spells. Watching and laying off to rest their eyes. And then while Dent was watching for the third spell he saw a movement—a gray body rolled over onto its elbows. He was up and out as the shot was fired. Running. He heard the shout of stretcher bearers coming from the trench behind him. He ran on, his eyes on the man. The bastard was shooting at him. He heard the bullets crack past him. He jumped bodies, he dodged, he skirted shell holes, only half seeing them, and he was there, on him. The German jumped up but he hadn't got a chance. No bayonet. Just a rifle with a telescopic sight. He put up his hands and dropped the gun.

"Kamerad!"

"Kamerad, you bugger! I'll *kamerad* you!" Dent's bayonet took him in the throat. He gave him the butt. He went down. Dent drove his bayonet into him again, pinning him to the ground, and fired. Then he dropped beside him as the German machine guns opened up on him. They'd seen what had happened from beyond the British line and would get him if they could. So he lay still in the grass listening to the German die. Then he began to crawl slowly back to the line. The lads would be watching for him. Waiting. Mr. Hilton, the sergeant. They'd seen him do it. Kill the bugger, kill him dead. You weren't supposed to kill a wounded man. *Kamerad!* Not bloody likely, with Foxy and the others shot in the back. He crawled around shell holes, around bodies. He'd write to Molly. Pretty Molly, the wife Foxy'd been so mad about. When he went on leave—if there ever was any leave again—or he got a blighty, he'd go and see her. A redhead. Hot, they was. Foxy had told him how hot she was. Couldn't wait for it. He'd see her and . . . Who'd have thought it? When they were all together before they came out, he'd sat looking at her over the table and thinking about it. About her and Foxy. And now he'd have her. He was sure of it if he got back in time. He'd seen it in her eyes even then. That she liked him, like. But Foxy'd been his mate. So it was off.

Then, that was. Not now though. It was a queer thing, this crawling and lying to rest with all them bodies. And what a stink and mess—broken rifles, equipment, bandages, stretchers. Christ, the whole bag of tricks! They didn't lie orderly. Every which way. Our chaps and them all mixed up. Lonely, too. There wasn't far to go now. Twenty yards or so. He wondered how the hell he'd done it. And with that bastard shooting at him, missing him from a prone position. It was the surprise that got him. Seeing me charging down on him—running, jumping bodies, yelling. He saw him again, dropping his rifle and putting up his hands. He felt the bayonet go in just above his collar. In, out. He'd hit him in the face with the butt as he bent forward and went down. Then he'd stuck him in the back—into bone— and put his foot on him to withdraw, but the bayonet was stuck, wedged fast. So he'd fired a round to clear it. That was what he'd been taught to do. If the bayonet sticks, fire a shot, the instructor had said. Molly. A hot one. Molly with her red hair and her white skin. Ten yards.

"Come on, Dent! Come on in!" That was young Hilton. Christ, he was tired. The skin was off his hands and he was bleeding where he'd caught himself on some wire.

Hands reached out for him, dragging him over the parados. He heard young Hilton say, "I'll put him in for something." That should help with the girls, he thought. With Molly. They liked medals, girls did. He passed out.

49 : Mr. Death

THE SUNKEN road lay parallel with the line of advance. Jim could see the shells of the barrage plastering it. And a bloody lot of good that would do since it would be lined with dugouts and it had to be crossed. Down one steep bank, across the road, up the other side again. The second wave would finish the job and mop up.

They walked on. It was just as safe as running. Besides, they had a long way to go. A line of helmeted men, their bayoneted rifles at the ready, proceeding toward their objective. Those were the orders; *proceed,* the word. A good word. It was quite light now. The grass was long with a little self-sown wheat, blue cornflowers and red poppies among it—an old cornfield abandoned but also proceeding to sow itself and grow. The soil was chalk, white where the shells had broken open the ground, stripping away its pretty skin of grass and flowers.

There was always this sense of unreality about a battle, a dreamlike quality, until you got into it and were lost in it atavistically. Primitive fighting without conscious thought. All reflex action.

They were getting close, the guns had raised their sights. They'd done all they were going to do. They must get over the road before the bastards recovered, while they were still dazed. He blew his whistle—it was quiet enough for it to be heard—and began to run, his feet weighted with lead. Nearer, nearer. The edge. He could see into the road. It was white chalk with the hanging dust of direct hits like a mist in the still air. Christ, it was deep—twenty-five or thirty feet down, across and up again! Like a railway cutting. He saw the black mouths of the German dugouts; some had been hit, blown in, but not all. Besides, they were deep. The bastards dug them deep. There were stretchers lying on the sides of the road and a few dead.

He jumped. He felt rather than saw the men jumping with him. Landing on his heels, he ran forward, still down, the way kids like to run down hills. He was on the road and across it as the machine guns began to fire. Like shooting fish in a barrel. He was scrambling up the other side. Not hit yet, but a lot of men would be. They had to go through a solid stream of bullets. The machine gunners were safe. They could set up their tripods in the open and squat on the road behind them. He was hanging on to tussocks of grass, pulling himself up. Up and on and out of it. At last he was on the top, lying flat, as flat as a bloody pancake. There were some men with him; a handful, fifteen or so. He turned and looked down onto the road. No more to come. They were all here with him or down there. The machine guns had ceased firing.

"Come on!" he said, and got up. They had got over but hadn't taken the first objective, and the sooner they pushed on toward the barrage that seemed to be waiting for them, the better. There were groups of men on either flank moving forward. Just groups though, hardly a company. What had happened to the battalion? How many were left? They walked on and on. Next objective, the blue line. Were there enough of them to take it?

The groups were closing in on one another automatically, toward the center, as if for company. They'd be there in a minute. He saw the trench. With a cheer, their bayonets high, they ran forward slowly, in an almost dignified manner, toward it. The line of men was still straight, still ordered. As they reached the trench the Germans jumped out. Men with white bands to their gray porkpie caps and no rifles, their hands above their heads. *"Kamerad!"*

Cavalry. Dismounted cavalry in the support line. They'd made it. They began rounding up the prisoners. A funny sort of victory. Pyrrhic. How were they going to hold the line? How were they going to get the prisoners back over the sunken road if the second wave hadn't taken it yet? The Bedfords had got as far as this too, but hadn't been able to hold it. There'd been dead Bedfords all the way. Killed neatly in lines, three summer days ago. He'd tried not to look at them. Corpses, swollen with the heat. There had been Bedford bodies lying in the sunken road when they'd jumped down into it, and a few fresh-killed Germans caught in the barrage before they could go to ground. He'd lost a lot of men and both his Lewis guns. Three men with him had flesh wounds; they were sitting down putting on field dressings with the aid of the remaining stretcher bearer. The men looked tired but excited, their eyes bright. Jim supposed he looked like that too. He looked at his watch. It was seven A.M. They'd gone over the top in the dark at three. In four hours they had lost, from the look of it, a hell of a lot of men. He wanted to talk to the men but had nothing to say. They weren't talking either. They were all breathing hard. A sergeant he didn't know was herding the prisoners into a bunch. He went over to see what was left of the German trench. No wonder they had surrendered—the guns had almost destroyed it. Equipment and tattered dead laying strewn in wild disorder. Hardy was coming toward him. Major Hardy. He recognized his walk.

"Glad you're all right, Jim" he said. "We lost a lot of chaps. Only four officers left. Send your wounded back with the prisoners. We'll go on." He looked at his watch. "In five minutes. We're ahead of the timetable."

The attack had succeeded. They had crossed the sunken road. Some of them had, anyway. This country was almost unspoiled by war. There seemed to be very little wire and no proper trenches. Beyond them Germans were still coming toward them with their hands in the air. *"Kamerad! Kamerad!"* His men were closing in on them. My God, how few were left! He signaled to the Germans to go to the rear and they went on in extended order, their rifles at the trail.

Then the Germans dropped a barrage on them and the whole world seemed to go up in bursting flame, smoke and noise. Crumps, whizzbangs, woolly bears. King was down, killed within two yards of him. Both his runners—Nobby and Fanshaw the new one—a direct hit got them both. But the rest were still going on. Another crash—on top of him almost—and he was flung on his face. This was it. He was badly hit this time. The men were going on. They looked much smaller from where he was lying. He looked at his watch—nine-twenty-five. He tried to crawl to a shell hole; he couldn't move his legs. For a moment he thought they had been blown off. He didn't dare put his hand back to feel. If this was death there was nothing to it. What a lot of bloody balls the parsons talked! Easy as rolling off a log. He thought of the Australian who had died next to him in hospital. The red screen. Well, Mr. Death, so we meet at last. He'd had the two biggest things in life—love and war. He wished he'd had more girls. Mona. Kathleen, just once more.

There'd be no Shelagh now. He looked at his watch again—nine-thirty-one. In six minutes he had reviewed his life. But if his legs were off—even one leg with the femoral artery cut—he would have bled to death. He was delighted with his logical thinking, with this meeting with Mr. Death. Not a bad chap at all. What you had to be afraid of was Mr. Pain. He'd come along later—if there was a later. He put his hand back. His legs were there. He could feel his bottom and his legs, but they couldn't feel his hand. Bloody odd. Must be paralyzed.

He saw two magpies in some elms. Lucky, two magpies were. Lucky! The shelling had not disturbed them. It was a beautiful day. He was glad it wasn't raining. The sky was blue, full of larks going up and down on the string of their song. It had been the same last time in '16. The Somme was a great place for larks once you got into the grassland. Couldn't expect the little buggers to sit in the chalk and mud, could you? "Oh, for the wings of a dove . . ." Of a bird. Birds flew out of it. But there were always birds in no-man's-land if there was grass. Larks, partridges. No one interfered with them there. The shells from both sides passed over them. Only an occasional shot ever burst in no-man's-land. What a good name for it that was! He'd never thought about it before. Mona—Shelagh—Kathleen. Kathleen —Shelagh—Mona. How did you arrange them? Two fair and one dark. Soft-skinned, soft-bellied. Trimmed with fur, their bellies and their armpits. Little tufts and triangles. Created by God. God ruling off lines on the bellies of the girls—all the girls in the world. Gold, red, black. And the in-between colors—like horses: browns, bays, chestnuts. He was wonderfully lucid. Bleeding like a bloody pig, though. It ran hot and then cold. Like Hargreaves had said it did. He thought of the Australian again. That was the way to die—cursing, fighting, laughing. Not another bloody woman, not another bloody drink. "Never put me legs over a good horse again." Parson, sky-pilot. He had no time for them. They had it too cushy. Never saw one in the line. Only the Catholic padres. They often went over with the boys to help them when they died. To introduce them to Mr. God and Mr. Death. He wondered how people could still believe in God.

But it wasn't too unpleasant, dying here like this in the sunshine with the larks singing overhead. Because he was dying all right. Bleeding his life away. If no one came to put a dressing on his wounds, he'd die, and no bloody error about that. But he didn't feel a thing. Too bruised. Nerve centers and all that. Bruised, numb. Horses. By God, he'd ridden some splendid horses. Girls. He wondered if a man ever got tired of sleeping with girls. Of ramming his hard root into the softness of their bodies. Bloody funny thing to want to do when you came to think of it. Bloody odd. But there it was, stiff as a poker. Just a girl or your hand. That was the way you were made. And they wanted it, too. What did they feel? What did they get out of it?

A little breeze began to make the marguerites and poppies nod their heads. Flowers, grass. Men were just manure. He thought of the graves commission boys on the old battlefields, digging where the grass grew greenest, tallest. Pushing up daisies. Horses, girls, his friends. Maurice and the others at Loos. He'd never made new friends like those chaps. What a bloody waste. . . .

He saw a wounded soldier making his way back. Walking wounded, hit in the leg. He was limping badly. Jim shouted to him and waved his hand. "Hi! Hi, there!"

The man changed direction and came up to him. "Hit bad, sir?"

"Buggered if I know, White." It was one of his own men. "See if you can get a dressing on me. What happened to you?"

"Hit in the calf, sir. Not too bad, but the sergeant told me to go back. We got it bad, sir. Not many of us left. It was that bloody sunken road, sir. Now," he said, "I expect this'll hurt. I'm going to take your arms and drag you. A nice hole over there."

"Can you do it, with your leg?"

"Bugger my leg. Now, sir. One, two, three!" He had him under the arms and pulled him over the grass to the edge of the hole. "Can't move your legs, can you, sir?"

"No, White."

"All right. I'll shove them in. Hold on to the grass with your 'ands. Now we're all cozy," White said. He lit a cigarette and put it into Jim's mouth. "Going to take your trousers off. Bloody mess you're in, if you'll excuse me saying so."

He reached into the front of Jim's tunic for his field dressing. All this had happened before. He got his trousers down. "By God!" he said. "Both cheeks. But they're not bleeding too bad. Fat," he said.

"I can feel the blood running, White."

White raised his jacket and shirt. "Got it in the back, too, sir. I'll put a pad on it and wind the bandage around your stomach." White wound the bandage around and around him.

"Is it in the backbone?"

"Pretty near it, sir."

So that was why he could not move or feel his legs. Paralyzed. A frightening thought. He lay on his belly again. He was still bleeding somewhere. "I'm still bleeding, White. Better have another look."

"Where, sir?"

"Front, I think."

White rolled him on his back again. "Christ!" he said.

"What is it?"

"An inch from your balls. An' we've got no more dressings. I'm going out, sir. Get some from the dead. Then I'll do your bottom too. Three dressings."

Machine-gun bullets were hitting the wire now. Zing, zing.

"Be careful, White."

"I will, sir."

He crept out. Ten minutes later he was back. "Got four. An extra one for luck. Don't look sir. It'll upset you."

But Jim looked; he couldn't help it. Right in the left groin, not two inches from his privates. He saw his femoral artery like a bit of gas piping. Jointed, like the pipe that Mona had on her gas ring by the fire that was filled with little white skulls that turned blue and then red. Mona . . .

White broke another iodine ampoule over the wound. It didn't sting. He put on the pad and the bandage. Then he turned him over again and did his bottom. "It won't hold, sir, if you move much."

"I can't move."

White rolled him on to his belly again. The bullets were still hitting the wire, making it sing.

Jim said, "Thanks, White. You'd better get out of it now. If they counterattack there'll be another barrage."

"I'm not going without you."

"You're a bloody fool. Get out while the going's good. You can't get me out alone."

"I'm going to stay, sir."

"Thank you, White. I must say it's a bit lonely here by oneself."

White said, "Sir! Sir! There's some Jerries coming. *Kamerad* chaps. We'll take 'em, sir. Make 'em carry you back. 'Ere!" He dragged Jim to the edge of the shell hole so that his head and shoulders were out. He took his pistol out of his holster and put it in his hand. "They won't see you're hurt bad," he said. "And I've got me gun."

When the Germans got close, White stopped them. There were four of them. Just right. " 'Alt!" he shouted, as he stood up and pointed his rifle at them. They halted.

Jim pointed his pistol in a menacing manner. If they only knew, he thought. White indicated a German groundsheet, brown, with aluminum eyelets, that lay with other battle debris near them.

"Bring that 'ere!"

They seemed to understand and brought it.

"Spread it out!"

They spread it out. White rounded them up like a sheepdog, his rifle cocked, his bayonet near the kidneys of the tallest one.

"Get him out and set him on it," he said.

It was evident they understood some English or that it was just common sense. The Germans picked Jim up and put him on the groundsheet.

"Now one at each corner and up!"

Three of them got into position. The fourth stood still. *"Offizier,"* he said, pointing to his shoulder straps.

Jim said, *"Offizier,"* pointing to his own. White's bayonet

371

came close to the German's throat. He moved to the corner of the sheet.

"Now up!" White said.

They picked up the four corners.

"March!" White said.

They 'set off, White behind them, his rifle at the ready.

Larks. All the bloody larks in the world were singing. Over the grassy fields, down the side of the sunken road. Steady, White. Steady, you bastards, across it. Jesus, just look at the dead! How the hell had anyone got across alive? Up the other bank and into the long grass again. More dead. On to the railway embankment. Croiseulles. There was a roaring sound of shell and a 5.9 burst in front of them. The Germans dropped him from shoulder height right on the line. That didn't do me much good, Jim thought, and wondered what would happen next. Objectively, not there. Like last time, an observer. He heard a rifle shot. White had put up a bullet near one of the running Germans. He fired a second round. They came back and picked him up.

At last they got to their old front line. A gunner officer was there, observing the fire.

"Badly hit?" he said.

"Pretty bad."

"You're the first officer in. Give me the news and I'll telephone it back."

"Tell them we got there. Tenth Wilts L.I. Very heavy casualties. In among the German cavalry. White cap bands. Tell them we're holding on. Must have lost three hundred men. Four officers left. The sunken road," he said. "Tell them to reinforce. Give some artillery support to stop a counterattack."

"Who are you?" the gunner said.

"Hilton, James. Captain, Tenth Wilts L.I." That was the last thing he remembered till he came to on a stretcher lying in a road with hundreds of others by the main casualty clearing station.

He lay there two days in the open with a blanket over him. Someone gave him water. They injected him with morphia. Too many wounded. They couldn't cope with them. He passed out again. Dope. The next thing he knew was the hospital train with the stink of the wounds that had turned rotten—gangrenous— and urine and shit and Jeyes Fluid.

All of them in a bad way. Left too long without attention; only the field dressings that their mates had put on. The orderlies and nurses were doing their best. "Bloody scandal," someone said. They hadn't been ready for such heavy casualties. Another shot of morphia. "This boy won't live, sister." That must be the doctor speaking. This boy? Christ, that's me. . . .

50 : Bad News

MAJOR-GENERAL Gore Blakeney was worried about that damn boy of Irene's—a good lad. New generation, of course, and not much in common with him . . . Forty years and a woman between them. However, they had got on even better than he had hoped. But having a soldier son was playing hell with her. She tried not to show it but he knew the boy was always on her mind. Damn it, he needed Irene. Send her a wire. Only a woman could take the edge off a man. What was the good of her staying on in London? Do her good, a few days in the country.

"Fitz!" he shouted. "Send Lady Blakeney a wire."

"What shall I say, sir?"

"Tell her we need a little feminine society at this HQ."

"Tell her to get fell in, sir?"

"That's about it, Fitz. Love, John, and all that."

"Yes, sir."

He got on with Fitz. Ninth Lancer. He'd been knocked out on the retreat but he'd wanted to stay in the army. ADC, anything. Lucky to have him.

Fitzherbert went off to send the telegram. He was smiling. So

373

the old man was randy again. Couldn't blame him. She'd improved him a lot. Much easier to get on with since his marriage. Everyone said so. A fine old boy, popular with all ranks. And what a seat on a horse—a bloody centaur! A bugger for spit and polish, but there was something in that too. No guts without pride, and a proud man had to be a clean one. Brasso was a kind of secret weapon. Fitz composed his telegram.

"Please come up to headquarters. A great deal to discuss. Love, John."

'A masterpiece. "Discuss" was really a wonderful word. He was smiling when he sent the signal.

Irene held the telegram in her hand for several minutes before she dared open it. Then she began to laugh and cry at the same time. With relief, with fury that he could have been so stupid as to wire at a time like this. Then she became very happy suddenly. It was all right. Jimmie was all right. It would be good to see John. The General. He always took her mind off things—things being Jimmie. Worrying wouldn't help him. She was quite excited as she packed her two suitcases. She had a letter from Jimmie she'd show him.

When the General came to her room at the hotel Irene kissed him and said, "What do you want to discuss, John?"

"Discuss, Irene?"

"That's what the wire said: 'Come to HQ. A great deal to discuss.' So I came at once."

The General began to laugh. "That's Fitz. I told him to send you a signal. The young devil! Still, I suppose discuss is as good a word as any. We can discuss things after dinner, darling."

"I was pleased to get it, John, because I have something to talk about. I was going to come up and see you anyway."

"You know, Irene, you were up here ten days ago. It's very flattering for an old man to have a pretty woman running after him."

"Even if it's his wife?"

"More so."

"Order some drinks, John. I had one while I was waiting for you but I want another."

The drinks came. The General squirted soda water into the whisky. They raised their glasses, looking into each other's eyes.

"I've got some news, John."

"Not bad news, I hope."

"I don't think so. I went to see the doctor yesterday morning."

"The doctor? You're not ill, are you?"

"No, darling. But I shall be in a few months' time."

"What d'you mean—months? Got to wait for an operation or something? And you say that's not bad news! My God, girl . . ."

"I waited to be certain. It's not cancer. It's a growth, John. But I'll be all right."

"You're a brave woman, Irene."

Irene began to laugh. "Oh, John," she said, "how can you be so stupid? You've done it. To use your own coarse expression, you've put me in foal. I'm pregnant."

"You're sure, darling?"

"I'm sure. That's why I waited to tell you. It's what you wanted, isn't it?"

"I've prayed for it, Irene." He dabbed his eye with a white silk handkerchief. Then he was on one knee beside her chair, kissing her hand. She hoped he wasn't pricking his bottom with his spur, and then remembered that dress spurs had no points on the rowels. They were just made for show. The General got up and sat on the sofa. "Good God!" he said. "A son, after all this time. Sixty-two years. Pity I'll not see him into the army. Sandhurst, perhaps, with luck."

"John," Irene said, "I should like to remind you that babies come in two kinds."

"Not mine, they don't. Family always breeds boys. I'm the last of four. Only got nephews." He came over to her, his spurs clinking. He held her in his arms. "Got to take care of you, my girl. No drinking, no smoking, no late nights, no dancing."

"No lovemaking, John?"

"I didn't say that." He sat down again. "My God!" he said again. "In foal."

Irene laughed. "You know," she said, "once I thought you were very coarse, but now I think it's funny and rather sweet. I think I must try it on my friends. I'll not say I'm pregnant, darling, I'll just say I'm in foal to the General. Sounds like a horse, doesn't it? A Derby winner or something. The General."

The General patted her. "I like it when you pull my leg. I was pretty stodgy, set in my ways, till I met you. . . . Old Gore Blimey of the Greys."

"Yes, dear, you were. But you'll always be cavalry. Making much of me, patting my quarters. But I adore you. I love you, John. All of you. Your smell of cigars and whisky and shaving lotion. Of Kiwi polish and Brasso. I love your two rows of medals and the way you clink about like a horse in harness. And now how about ordering another drink for the girl you've put in the family way? You know, I feel like a girl with you. . . ."

"Champagne," he said. "I'll ring. The Widow. Girl?" he said. "Of course you're a girl. Young enough to be my daughter. Practically incestuous."

A waiter came in and he ordered a bottle of Veuve Clicquot 1900.

"And the boy, Irene? Have you told him about his brother yet?"

"There's plenty of time for that, John."

"Won't put his nose out of joint, will it?"

"I don't think so. And I shouldn't be surprised if he got married and had a baby of his own before long. I wish he would. To Shelagh."

Jim married, she thought. My baby with a baby, and me a grandmother with a baby of my own. It was all very odd.

The waiter came back with the wine. "Shall I open it, sir?"

"Of course. We want to drink it."

The cork popped.

"Pour it, sir?"

"Yes, pour it." The wine bubbled in the flat, long-stemmed glasses. The waiter went out.

Irene said, "Lock the door, John."

They raised their glasses. "To the boys," the General said. "My sons."

When Irene got the General's telegram her heart had almost stopped. He shouldn't have sent a telegram. She thought, I'll give him a piece of my mind when I see him. Telegrams weren't for mothers with sons at the front. But she hadn't said a word. What would be the good of it? Him with his sons. Jim and the one that was on the way.

She had packed her nicest things. Camiknickers—fragments of chiffon and lace—chemises, nightdresses, silk stockings. She packed petticoats with accordion-pleated hems. She packed her evening shoes with the highest heels. She packed a tea gown, her laciest peignoir, her perfume. Two evening dresses, her long white gloves. She would go up to the shires in her brown tweeds. That would be enough daytime outdoor clothes. Brown brogue shoes. She didn't want to look tarty, no matter what she felt. She laughed as the few days she would spend with her General unfolded before the eyes of her mind. They were always the same and she wanted no change. Honeymoon escapes between weeks of anxiety.

For five days Lady Blakeney forgot everything. There was the little dinner in their suite—oysters, because there was an R in the month, trout, whitebait, roast chicken, salad, zabaglione and a cheese savory. Two wines—Barsac because she liked it, and champagne. Port, coffee, liqueurs. She wore her pink tea gown, and very little else. When the waiter had cleared away, she let her hair down in a blonde cascade onto her shoulders.

There was a semiofficial dinner at the Blue Boy with the General's staff and his four brigadiers. There were formal *tête-à-têtes* in the public dining room, and then back to London, her woman's mission accomplished. Almost shamefaced about it, she kissed her major-general goodbye.

In the train she went over it all in her mind. The days and nights at headquarters and what the doctor had told her when she had gone to him with her suspicions. Prendergast. Her vet, as John called him; he had said, "Yes, I think you're pregnant, Irene. You're still in the full flush of your womanhood. You've

377

nothing to worry about. In spite of being widowed you've kept yourself young. Young at heart. Come back and see me in a month." That was when he had confirmed it.

After Irene had gone the General lit a cigar and poured himself a brandy. Her news had shaken him up. Pregnant. What a woman! How lucky he was! Take her to the Hall when it was all over. Settle down. Breed a few horses, get some good blood mares. Dogs. Start the home farm again. Family place for four hundred years. Wanted to be buried there. Roots. By God, a chap couldn't get away from his roots. They caught up with you when you started breeding yourself. Take care of myself, he thought. Live to eighty, see the kid into the army. Boy—of course he'd have a boy. By God, he missed Irene. And she hadn't been gone an hour. A baby. A baby at Blakeney Hall. He'd been the last one. That left a sixty-year gap. Dogs. Ponies. Nurses. Good God, a bloody miracle! Servants' dances. Christmas dinner for the tenants. Christmas trees. Shooting parties. Presents. And all of it due to Irene.

He'd been on a three-day Cook's tour to the front, but he hadn't told her. There'd been several other generals. Dugouts. The mud. Shelling. And we thought we knew all about it in South Africa. The dead on the barbed wire. He'd got away from the party and gone on his own to the Serre front. Men still lying there, rotting. Scarecrows. Terrible.

When Irene got back to Albany it was there in the letterbox with the bills and invitations. The telegram she had feared so long had come at last. "Regret to inform you Captain James Hilton 10th Wilts L.I. has been severely wounded. . . ." While she had been making love it had been lying there with the rest of the mail.

She went out at once and wired John, "Jim severely wounded." He'd be with her by morning. How severely was he wounded? Where was he? What was the wound? He might be dead. . . .

378

51 : Justice

"Sergeant Goodby, sir," the sergeant-major said.

Sergeant Goodby stood hatless at attention in front of the colonel's table in the orderly room.

"You wanted to see me, Sergeant Goodby?"

"Yes, sir."

"What about?"

"My leave, sir."

"What about your leave?"

"I don't want to go, sir."

"Why not? You've been out since the beginning. You've never been home. You've never been sick. You've been in every show. You've been awarded the DCM, MM and bar. . . ."

"Yes, sir."

"Well?"

"I don't want to go, sir."

"Want to or not, you're going." The colonel began to laugh. "I've never heard of anyone going on leave under escort, but . . ."

"I want to stay with the battalion, sir."

"My God, Goodby," the colonel said, "if I could do it, I'd let you. We're short of good NCO's."

"Yes, sir."

"And you refused a commission?"

"Yes, sir."

"You've got to go, Goodby. It's come down from Corps. I got a rocket for not sending you before in spite of saying you'd refused all leave."

"I want to refuse it again, sir."

"This time it's no good. But why don't you want to go?"

Goodby looked around the orderly room. The sergeant-major was there. The orderly sergeant. The adjutant. A clerk typing out some buff-colored forms. "Can I speak to you alone, sir?"

"All right," the colonel said. "We'll go to my quarters." He pushed his chair back and put on his cap. Goodby put on his helmet and followed him.

In the colonel's hut he halted and took off his helmet again.

"Sit down," the colonel said. "And now what's this all about?"

"My wife, sir. And a man."

"Yes?"

"If I go back, sir, I'll kill them."

"She left you?"

"He took her away, sir."

"My God," the colonel said.

"Yes, sir."

"Can't you keep away from them?"

"No, sir."

"Well, you've got to go."

"Yes, sir. If it's an order, I don't have any choice, do I, sir? But please remember what I've told you, sir. I can't hold myself responsible."

"I'll remember, Goodby," the colonel said. "But don't kill 'em. Beat 'em up."

Goodby felt himself smile as he said, "I'll try, sir. I'll try." My God, if once he started where would it end? He put on his helmet, saluted and turned about.

Two days later he was on his way. "Have a good time, sergeant! Love to Blighty! Love to the girls, the lights, the booze. . . ."

The trip from Boulogne was calm, the sea a millpond. At Folkestone the train, as usual, was overcrowded, but a brigadier general insisted that he share his compartment with some staff officers. "It's his first leave," he said. "Been out since 'fourteen. Imagine it!"

Then London and the Bond agency. They'd know where they were. As he climbed the stairs he wondered how often he'd been here with Enid. Twenty times. Thirty, perhaps. Dirty little stairs in a dirty little alley off Shaftesbury Avenue, but they'd been good agents and with luck no one would know him. He'd been away a long time. He'd changed. He was in uniform.

The girl at the desk was a blonde. A stranger.

"And what can I do for you?" she said. "You look as if you'd just come back from over there."

"That's right, ducks," he said. He knew the kind. Kid her along and he'd get what he wanted. Anything he wanted, if he wanted it.

"Well," he said, "I'm looking for a cousin of mine. Jack Bramwell. I've lost touch with him, and he said . . ."

"Oh," the girl said, "the Bramwells. They're on our books all right and doing pretty well. They were in the north. Yorkshire and all that. But they're here now."

"In London?"

"Sure, in London. At the Palladium."

"Can you give me their address? I'd like to surprise old Jack."

"You a relation?"

"That's right, miss. A cousin, as I said, but we were always very close. Had a lot in common."

"OK," she said, getting out a file. "Here it is. Forty-seven Gardby Crescent. That's in Earls Court. If you went at once you should catch him before they go to the theatre. They're on at nine-thirty. But he's always home at four in case we telephone. Likes to rest, he says. Shall I call him, sergeant?"

"No, don't do that, ducks. I want to surprise him."

"OK," the girl said. "But come back and tell me about it. Long lost brother and all that."

"Cousin, ducks."

"Same thing. But come back and we'll have a cuppa. It's bloody dull here now with all the men away."

"I'll do that," Goodby said. "Same time tomorrow."

"I'll be waiting for you."

"Cheerio," he said. "See you tomorrow."

He took a taxi to Gardby Crescent, paid it and knocked on the door. It had a knocker shaped like a hand.

An elderly woman opened the door. "Yes?" she said.

"I'm looking for my cousin, Mr. Jack Bramwell. He lives here, I believe." He saw her looking at his pack and rifle and said, "I'm just back, madam."

"Back from the war?"

"That's right."

"Come in, then. I'm sure he'll be pleased to see you. First floor front."

He climbed the stairs and knocked on the door.

"Who is it?" That was Enid's voice. His heart stopped a beat.

"Telegram," he said.

The door was unlocked and a hand came out. He pushed the door open.

"Good God! Goodby!" Bramwell said.

"Oh! Arthur!" Enid gasped.

Goodby turned, locked the door and put the key into his pocket.

"What are you doing that for?" Bramwell asked.

"Don't want to be disturbed, do we, Jack? We've got a lot talk about."

"Have we?"

"Oh yes. Her, for instance." He nodded at Enid. She was looking lovelier than ever. Half dressed. She had been changing and stood frozen, her hand in front of her mouth. As he stared at her she reached for a dressing gown.

Bramwell looked belligerent. His fists clenched. He took a step forward. A big powerful man in good condition from dancing.

When he came into the room Goodby had rested his rifle against the wall. With a quick movement he drew his sidearm. The bayonet came out of the scabbard with a rasp. "Don't try anything, Bramwell," he said. "It's sharp. Point like a needle. And you wouldn't be the first man it's gone into. . . ." His voice changed. "And now where were we? Oh, yes. The little talk we are going to have."

"I've got nothing to say, Goodby."

"I can believe that, Jack. Nothing about seducing a man's wife and living with her while he's fighting."

382

"You can divorce her."

"Yes, I can divorce her and give you not only a beautiful girl but the best dancing partner you ever had. I expect you hoped I'd be killed."

Bramwell glared at him.

"I tried, Jack. That's how I got these things." His hand touched his medal ribbons. "Pretty, aren't they? I killed a lot of men to get them. So in a way their blood is on your hands."

"Germans," Bramwell said.

"Men. Men who if I had not been trying to get myself killed might have lived."

"Pity you weren't."

"Well, at least you're honest, Jack." He went on. "I had some miraculous escapes."

"You were lucky."

"Yes, Jack. That's what I thought at first. Then it went beyond luck. I felt the hand of God over me. I knew I was being preserved for some special purpose." He paused and then said, "You must have made a lot of money, Jack. You and Enid."

"I'll give you five hundred quid . . . a thousand. . . ."

"Do you think God preserved me so that I could sell my wife? No, no, Jack. That's not the way of it." He reached back for his rifle, held it between his knees and fixed the bayonet. It clicked home. In a fluid movement the rifle came up, like a living thing, to the high port, and Sergeant Goodby was transformed from a soldier on leave into a fighting man.

"No, Jack," he said. "That isn't why God preserved my life. Or why, despite my protests, I was sent on leave. The hand of God was in that, too. God said, 'Now is the time, Goodby. Go and do My work.'"

Bramwell had gone pale. He tried to laugh. "Put that bloody thing down and don't talk nonsense about God. Look," he said, "be sensible. She was lonely. She wanted to come. I took care of her."

"Yes, Jack. You kept my bed warm for me."

"He forced me," Enid screamed. "He raped me. He wouldn't let me go."

"I don't suppose you tried very hard, Enid," Goodby said.

383

"You're just weak and silly. Beautiful devil-bait. A crooked little whore."

She collapsed, sobbing, face downward on the bed.

"No, Jack," Goodby said, "that cock won't fight. It won't wash. You can't fool about with God's work, His laws, His justice. God sent me to kill you, Jack."

"No, no! You'll hang for it, you fool. Hang for a woman that's no good. If it hadn't been me it would have been some other man."

"Yes indeed, Jack, I may hang. But at least it will be for killing a man I wanted to kill instead of a stranger."

His right foot and his arms came forward in a thrust. The bayonet caught Jack Bramwell in the throat; as he withdrew it and Bramwell pitched forward, Goodby brought up the butt and smashed it into his jaw. Goodby stood looking at Bramwell twitching on the floor, at the blood running out on the carpet. Then he unfixed his bayonet, wiped it clean on Bramwell's shirt, returned it to its scabbard and again leaned his rifle against the wall. He turned to Enid cowering on the bed.

He dragged her to her feet by her hair. Her beautiful long hair. As she stood swaying, staring at him with wild wide eyes—her beautiful eyes—his hands closed on her beautiful slim neck. Closed and closed. Her eyes protruded, her pink tongue came out between her beautiful lips. Still holding her, he raised her off the ground and shook her as a terrier shakes a rat. Her head lolled on her shoulder. She was dead. He thought of the words of the song they so often sang at the war—"A Broken Doll"—as he threw her onto Bramwell's body.

He sat on the bed—their bed, where they had made love—till his heart stopped beating so fast. Then he picked up the telephone and called the agency.

The girl at the other end of the wire said, "Bond's Theatrical Agency."

He said, "This is Sergeant Goodby. I called to say I shan't be in for a cuppa tomorrow. And also to tell you that the Bramwells will not appear at the Palladium tonight or, for that matter, ever again."

"Why? What's the matter? Are they breaking their contract?"

"In a manner of speaking they are, miss. You see they are both dead. I have just killed them. . . ."

Then he called the police. He said, "I wish to report a double murder. Mr. Jack Bramwell and Mrs. Enid Goodby, sometimes known as Mrs. Bramwell."

"Who is speaking?"

"Sergeant Arthur Goodby . . . Forty-seven Gardby Crescent . . . She was my wife. . . . I killed them . . . dead . . . of course they're dead. I bayoneted him and throttled her. Yes, I'll wait for you." He lit a Woodbine. Suddenly he was at peace for the first time since he had got Enid's little note telling him she had gone to live with Jack Bramwell. Of all the men he had killed with rifle and bomb, only Bramwell had deserved to die. Plans for the future were forming in his mind. If they didn't hang him, that is.

52 : Hospital

JIM DID not remember being taken to hospital. When he woke up he was there. A nurse, seeing him move, came over to the bed.

"Where am I?" he said.

"This is the Queen Victoria Hospital for Officers in Grosvenor Square."

So he was in London. He noticed there were five other beds in the ward and went to sleep again.

Downstairs General and Lady Blakeney were talking to the matron. She was a small birdlike woman wearing a diamond and ruby Red Cross brooch. She said, "Yes, your son is badly wounded. It is impossible to say how badly until after the operation. It will take place at five-thirty. I shall be there. I

385

attend all operations." She looked at the card in her hand. "Gunshot wounds back, both buttocks, left groin. I'll call you as soon as it is over."

Irene noticed how beautifully her hair was done. For some reason this tiny woman gave her confidence. John knew all about her. Sister Blanche was a rich woman who had devoted herself to the care of wounded officers. She had begun nursing in the Boer War.

"Can I bring a girl, Shelagh Moran, to see him, Sister Blanche?" Irene said. "I think they are engaged. She's staying with me. A VAD. She got a few days' leave."

"By all means, Lady Blakeney." Sister Blanche put her hand on Irene's arm. "I know it's no use telling you not to worry, but remember we'll do our best." They said goodbye.

Jim knew his mother and Shelagh when they came. He saw them vaguely in a morphia dream. Tears came into his eyes. Shelagh wiped them away. He didn't speak.

"He's under sedation," the nurse said. "He was on the table for two hours. The wounds are clean now but there's still a piece of shrapnel in his left buttock."

Then they left him. They'd be back tomorrow, and tomorrow. . . . Such a lot of tomorrows. Sir John had gone back to his division. Shelagh was in the spare bedroom with the horse pictures and the weapons. Two women. A general and a young soldier who might die. They were the actors. The young soldier the center of the stage, doctors and nurses a moving frieze about him. The mother and the girl symbolic figures representing the past and the future. The future only if he lived. Not to die was to live. That was all they prayed for at first. And he didn't die. He improved. He had another operation and showed Shelagh the bit of shell casing they had taken out of his bottom. He had it lying on a bed of cottonwool in a small white box by his bed. He spoke very little. At first he had just held Shelagh's hand and cried, but talking was difficult. What was there to say? Not the war. Not his friends. Not even the weather.

He and his mother just smiled at each other. She would say,

386

"How are you today, Jimmie?" and he'd say, "I'm getting better."

Then when he had been in hospital about a month and could sit up they did have something to talk about. Irene saw him looking at her curiously. He said, "Aren't you getting fat, Mother?"

"Yes, darling, I am, aren't I?"

"You used to be so careful of your figure. Diet and all that."

"I wasn't married then, Jimmie."

"You don't mean . . ."

"Yes, I do. I'm going to have a baby. Do you mind? Will you be upset?"

"Good God, no! Why should I be?"

"Some boys would be."

"I bet the old boy's pleased. The General, I mean." Jim laughed.

It was the first time she'd heard him laugh. "Yes, he's pleased, Jimmie. He's got great plans for him. Put him down for Eton already. The army. Whole career mapped out."

"Suppose it's a girl?"

"I daren't have a girl."

They both laughed. Irene thought: fancy telling him here in a ward with five other men. How unnecessary the worry about breaking the news to him had been! She said, "John says he'll have two sons now—one grown up and one a baby. He thinks of you as a son, you know. You don't mind, do you?"

Mind his mother having a baby? Mind the General thinking of him as a son? What the hell would be the good of minding? But he didn't. "No, Mother," he said. Somehow this baby business and his being hit again had changed things. Anyway, his mind was full of Shelagh. Something he wanted to ask her when he had the guts to do so.

Shelagh came to see him whenever she could get off. The matron gave her special privileges to come out of visiting hours because she was a nurse. But he was still as weak as a kitten and could never get comfortable, even on a water-bed. A rubber mattress filled with water was only a help, not a cure for discomfort. The dressings twice a day were agony. He used to cry when the trolley came. They didn't rip off the sticky bandages as they did in some places; they put them on with liquid paraffin so they didn't stick. But still it hurt and it took so long and he had to be moved so much. Turned right over.

His mother came every day. He was mildly amused to see that her pregnancy was really beginning to show. Sometimes he thought about it—a baby half-brother. The General had been to see him twice. Bluff, soldierly. "Proud of you, my boy. Regular commission in the field. Been gazetted temporarily. Major. Military Cross." Yes, that had come through. A second one. A bar. That meant a little silver rose on the ribbon. Fine old boy. Not his cup of tea but his mother's. Yes, Mother's cup of tea. He was glad she was happy and the General impressed him with this little-brother business. Talked about him as if he was already there. Eton, Sandhurst, the Greys. If the General said so it had to be so. In orders, so to speak. Mother'd find herself in the guard room if she gave birth to a daughter. He could not help thinking of their sleeping together, of his mother's liking it. And she must or she wouldn't look so contented. He thought a lot about that. About men and women. About Kathleen who'd married a bastard, about their afternoon together. By God, he might have given her a kid! A young Oates who was a Hilton. Mona. No news of her for months. That didn't surprise him. He expected she'd changed her way of life and got married. She'd told her she wanted to. Just cut off the past, turn a new leaf and all that sort of thing. But this thinking wasn't real thinking. It was superficial, a kind of mental blanket he had thrown over his main thought. His groin wound. Damn near got my bollocks. But had it damaged them? There'd been the awful time when he couldn't make water and they'd had to stuff a catheter up his tool and into his bladder when it was full. That was over. He could pee now. But the other? His anxiety was building up. Just suppose . . .

He'd been given a ward to himself when one became vacant. There was a bedside table, another table, a chair for visitors. When Shelagh came that afternoon, he said, "Shelagh, will you do something for me?"

She looked very pretty in her pale blue uniform with a dark blue cape and white starched cap. Very pretty, very desirable, very like Kathleen. In his mind they had merged into one blonde, beloved girl, two parts of a whole, and if he'd lost the one he had the other.

"Of course, Jimmie."

"Then give me your hand under the sheet." She did so; it was soft and warm. He led it down to his belly. "Touch me," he said. "Touch me. See if it . . ."

She understood him. At her gentle touch, life sprang into it. It grew hard. She withdrew her hand. Someone might come in.

"Oh, Jimmie!" she said. There were tears in her eyes. "It's all right. Were you afraid?"

"My God," he said, "I've not been able to think of anything else. I tried myself but it was no good. So I thought you might. Because . . ."

"Oh, Jimmie," she said, "I love you!" She stooped over the bed to kiss him and went out, back to her own hospital, without another word.

She really loved him. He needed her. The feel of his flesh, proud in her hand, had shown her the truth. He was her man. And women had to be needed. Of course it would probably never be what had been with Francis. The wild passion that melted her all over at the very sight of him. He didn't even have to touch her. How they had wasted their time together—with only six hours of real love at the end of it. Kissing, touching, holding each other. Trying to get closer to each other, ever closer. Striving, sweating. And all with one eye on the illuminated face of the bloody clock. Once more, if they could. If he could. A love-race with time that had turned into a race with death, which they had lost. And Jimmie had been in the same battle. Two years ago now. There had been other men, kissing her, messing her about, but she'd not let any of them get very far except Jimmie. And he'd never tried to force anything, not even to seduce her when he'd had the chance. He'd said, "I don't want it like that. We'd be sorry afterward." That, as he called it, was for girls with whom there'd be no afterward.

Lady Blakeney had gone to see Mr. Horstal, the surgeon in charge of her son's case. She had made an appointment with him. A tall, thin, ascetic-looking man of sixty in the uniform of a major in the RAMC.

"Please sit down, Lady Blakeney." He pointed to a chair. "You've come to see me about your son, I expect?" he said.

"Yes, Mr. Horstal."

"A lot of mothers do. Some of them demand miracles." He smiled. "We can't perform miracles. We can only do our best."

"How is he?"

"Considering how badly he was wounded, he's doing very well, and if you will allow me to say so he'll owe his life to you."

"Why do you say that?"

"Because you breast-fed him. How do I know, dear lady? I know because if he'd been bottle-fed he'd have been dead by now. A breast-fed baby has a seventy percent better chance of living through a crisis like this. More resistance. That is why women have milk. I know it's not fashionable today, but it's the truth."

"I breast-fed him for nine months. My husband was away a great deal. He was all I had. I only stopped because he seemed to want a meat diet. I couldn't stop him biting." She felt herself smiling. She trusted this man. He'd save her Jimmie.

"So I was right, Lady Blakeney. It was just a guess but I was sure in my mind."

She got up and held out her hand.

"Don't worry," he said. "Come and see him as often as you can and send that girl. That nurse. He watches for her." He covered her hand with his own. "Tell her," he said, "tell her if she stopped coming I think he'd stop fighting. She gives him his will to live. Sex," he said, smiling into her eyes, "is the life force. It has a lot of faces."

To her surprise, when she got home there was a telephone call from Dr. Davis, the psychologist. He said Nurse Moran had suggested he come to see her. She said she would be delighted to see him. Would he like to come and have tea or a drink tomorrow?

He said, "Tea. I'll be there at four-thirty."

As she prepared tea Lady Blakeney wondered why Shelagh had asked Dr. Davis to come and see her. It was two years since she had seen him in his office. A charming man, who had been a great help to Jim and indirectly to herself, since Jim had passed on the books he had told him to read.

When they had had tea, he said, "You know Shelagh and Jim are in love?"

"I hope so. I hope he marries her."

"I'm glad you are pleased. I was afraid you might think he was too young. She is a year older than he is."

"I like her. She's a very pretty girl."

"Your son, Lady Blakeney, is not an ascetic type."

"That's what his doctor told me yesterday."

"Women are an important factor in his life. Please do not misunderstand me, Lady Blakeney, but men are not all the same. Some need women more than others."

"I think I understand, Dr. Davis. The life force."

"That's one word for it. To tell the truth, it's something we still don't know a great deal about, except that it is a variable in both men and women."

"And Shelagh?" Lady Blakeney asked.

"She is normal. She will suit him. She has talked to me. There is nothing frigid about her. She has had one love affair. The man she was engaged to was killed. She wanted you to know she is not a virgin, but didn't want to tell you yourself."

"I don't think Jimmie'll mind. Anyway, that's their business. I'll never mention it." She saw the doctor looking at her and laughed.

"Yes, I am pregnant. Isn't it ridiculous at my age? It's really rather embarrassing. Of course Jimmie noticed it when I went to see him. And my friends. They hold up their hands in horror. I don't think many of them even sleep in the same room as their husbands. But the General, my husband, did so want a child." She was getting quite flustered.

391

"An admirable desire, Lady Blakeney, and one which will keep you young. There can be no love without sex. Though sex is possible without love. Your son needs love."

"That's what the surgeon said. He said it was Shelagh's visits that were keeping Jim alive, giving him the will to live. Will you tell her?"

"I will. She loves him. It is a classic situation. The young hero whom she nursed. The fighting man dependent, helpless as a child, needing her. I don't think you need worry, Lady Blakeney." He passed his cup for more tea. "How odd that we should be sitting here talking about them. I bring a message from her. You give me news of him."

"He owes a lot to you, Dr. Davis, and so do I. The books you told him to buy have helped me. You know, till I read them I was sometimes ashamed of my feelings for my husband. They are most unladylike."

"There is no such thing as a lady. There are only women. I think you are fortunate in having a husband who appreciates your beauty. For you are a very beautiful woman. Not a girl, but a woman in the full flush of your maturity. You may easily have another child and the menopause will not end anything for you except your ability to bear children." The doctor rose. "I cannot tell you how happy I am that Jim is getting on so well. From what Shelagh tells me it was a near thing."

"Very near. He lived because he was breast-fed, the surgeon said, and now he is living because of Shelagh. Two women."

"It is women who give men both life and a cause to live. Goodbye, Lady Blakeney. Thank you for seeing me. But I was worried about Jim. He's always been more than just a patient to me."

When Dr. Davis had gone Irene wondered if morals had really changed so much with the war, or was it just that, having a grown-up son, she had suddenly become aware of them? Young men taken away from their own environment, homeless, lonely, naturally sought the companionship of girls. And the girls were excited by the admiration of so many strange young men. She was glad Dr. Davis had come. He had relieved her mind about both Jimmie and herself. He had said they were alike, and it was true. They both had a desire for life and love, which were in a sense the same thing. She was looking forward to having her baby, a baby of her own, when so many of her contemporaries were grandmothers. She would suckle this one too. That was what the General would want. A madonna. One couldn't visualize a madonna with a bottle.

Shelagh still wondered about the other women in Jimmie's life but she wasn't worried about them or even jealous. If she'd had a flat of her own and let him make love to her there would have been no others. It's me he wants, she thought. And then, because he wanted her and couldn't have her, he went to someone else for his greens. What a curious phrase! But you couldn't live among soldiers without learning some of their expressions. She had got sick of taxis or of being whizzed away on his red monster on her day off if it was fine. How did poor people do it? Out of doors, she supposed, and perhaps they were less inhibited. By some kind of convention courting couples became invisible except to policemen and the prurient old women who reported them for indecency.

She had become very fond of Irene. They talked a kind of shorthand, saying and asking things by suggestion, talking beside a subject, around it, leaving the middle, the core, unstated but fully understood by them both. When Irene talked about her first husband she was really talking about Jimmie. She said he certainly hadn't been faithful to her in his long absences abroad. But all this by implication, by suggestion. Albany became a kind of second home to Shelagh. She even kept some of her clothes there. She could see Irene wanted her for a daughter-in-law but never pushed things. She had showed her Jimmie's letters but had never even asked if he had written to her.

Before he went back to France Jimmie had said, "What about your people, Shelagh?"

"What about them?"

"I suppose I'll have to meet them some time."

"They're dead, Jimmie. I've only got Aunt Janie for a

family—Aunt Janie and Uncle Flash—he's her bookmaker friend. And they're common, Jimmie. I suppose I'm common, too, in a way. At least not upper class. Dad was the headmaster of a horrible boys' school. He pretended, Jimmie. I was brought up to pretend, but Aunt Janie's real. She's genuine. Her dad, my grandfather, was a greengrocer. Do you think they'll mind—your mother and the General?"

He'd said, "Why should they?" Again this transformation into a man. He had put on what she had come to call his "war" face, hard, ten years older in the twinkling of an eye. Then he changed back again. "They'll love them. They like anything genuine. And I'll lay six to four after they've met that Flash does all the General's betting for him. He'll talk about 'my bookmaker' at the club." He began to laugh. "And Mother will love your Aunt Janie. Who could help it? What a character! What a pair! I'm looking forward to meeting them." That was after she'd told him more about them.

Aunt Janie had never married. Having been on the stage made her seem romantic, though nothing could have been worse from Shelagh's mother's point of view. But she was still pretty —at least you could see she had been—and she had various men friends, Flash in particular. Her hair's dyed, Shelagh's mother used to say. Touched up a bit, anyway. Shelagh smiled. Fair, like me, with big gray eyes and a soft mouth. A good person to stay with at a time like this. She'd like Jim and ask no questions.

As soon as Jimmie told her he was being sent to Hove she'd written to her. "My friend, Major James Hilton, is going to hospital in Hove. Can I come and stay with you?" The answer had been a telegram: "Any time love, Jane."

Love affairs were going on all over England, and they were going to get married. Soldiers and girls everywhere. Officers and men with girls all like her, ready for life, on their toes, stretching up for it, trying to grasp it before it eluded them. And over there—she looked out of her window—men were still dying. How lucky she was. . . .

She thought of her parents' remarks about Aunt Janie. Had

she married one of those men yet? Did she still have those awful cats? What a dear little house she had, and in such a good position too! They'd no idea anyone could do so well on the stage. How unkind, how cruel they had been in a nice suburban way! By innuendo. By loosing the bagged hares of scandal on the downs of conversation.

How wonderful it was that Irene and the General had accepted her! The General thought she was pretty and he liked her name because once he'd had an Irish mare called Shelagh on the Curragh. He'd thought that a great joke. A dear old man who was as fond of Jimmie as if he had been his own son. And Irene going to have a baby. That was really rather sweet, and at last the war was almost over—and Jimmie safe. What a wonderful world it was!

53 : Aunt Janie

THERE WERE twenty other officers in the convalescent home at Hove. Jim shared a room with a major in the gunners who had lost a leg. Major Charles Wilson, RFA, was easy to get on with. He was a Canadian with a wife and two children in Toronto. Their conversation, like that of most soldiers, was about the war, which might be over any day. The Germans were on the run.

"Pity we're not in at the death, Hilton."

Jim agreed with him. It must be exciting to be moving forward at last. There were stories of the booby-traps the Germans left behind them: *Pickelhaubes* that triggered a bomb if touched, doors and pictures wired to explosive charges. But Jim's mind was on Shelagh, who had written to say she'd be with her Aunt Janie in Brighton next week. He was getting stronger every day. He could walk quite a long way—a couple of miles—without difficulty.

But there was one thing he must do before she came. Finding a jeweler he liked the look of, he went in.

"Yes, sir. Can we help you?"

Jim said, "I want an engagement ring. A nice diamond."

A tray lined with black velvet was put on the counter in front of him. He picked out a three-carat solitare, rose cut, set in platinum.

"And now," he said, "I want a wedding ring."

Smiling, the jeweler said, "If you will permit me to say so, sir, I think you're right. No point in a long engagement when your mind is made up, is there, sir?"

"None at all," Jim said, putting the little parcel in his pocket.

When Janie got her niece's letter she was delighted. So she had a young man in a convalescent home in Hove and wanted to be near him. Very sensible too. Shelagh was the only relative she had. Pretty girl. Turned out very well, but not as shapely as she had been at her age. But girls weren't anymore. No more shapely girls. But it would be nice to have her stay and meet her young man. Courting. Walking out. A soldier boy. She wondered if she'd slept with him. She'd have to tell her the facts of life if she didn't know them. That was something good girls never found out—and how could they? You only found out one way. But they'd got to have it, the young ones had. And older ones, too. If you wanted to keep them they had to have it. The bastards always wanting to go to bed and slip it into you. Nothing like a man to keep a girl young. She knew.

Very comfortable she was. Feathered her nest. Cozy. Comfy. Room full of pictures of her friends in the theatre, on the boards. Paper fans, a sword you could swallow if you were a sword-swallower. Sad to think that was all that was left of Ferdinand. Famous, he'd been. Swallowed swords, ate glasses. Framed programs and billings. Posters. A lifetime on her walls and money in the bank. And it would all be Shelagh's one day. When I turn my toes up, she thought. Love. Young love. How bloody wonderful it was! All that excitement. And much easier now that girls didn't wear stays, not proper ones. Times changed. That they did. But it didn't. It never changed. Never had and never would.

Real old madam, that's what I am, she thought. Planning to get 'em into bed. And I've never even seen him. Fun and frolic, eat, drink, sing, dance, be merry—and then hop into bed. Funny the things that happened in beds. You loved in 'em, you were born in 'em, you died in 'em if you were lucky. Thousands, hundreds of thousands dead in the open in the war with no one to wash 'em or put pennies on their eyes. No coffins. Lord, she'd been to some lovely funerals! Beautiful, with black horses and plumes.

There was Harry, for instance. What a one he had been for it! At all hours, drunk or sober. But he'd died. So many wreaths and flower crosses she'd not been able to count them. A mountain of flowers. Winterbotham, who ran the show, had sent a whacker. Old cold-arse, the girls had called him, and some of them knew; they said it really was cold. Tears came into her eyes. She filled up her glass and raised it to a photograph of a man in a leopardskin holding a bar above his head with bulging muscles.

"Harry," she said, "here's luck, Harry, wherever you are."

Then she got up to feed her cats. Astonishing what a cat could eat. Surprise you if you didn't know. Both toms: Timmy and Whiting—Whiting because as a kitten he'd always had his tail in his mouth.

But times had certainly changed. Girls with no shapes, motorcars coming down from London every day, paper money. Paper money wasn't like gold. No weight to it, no feel. Lord, how she'd loved seeing them shoveling golden sovereigns at the bank with their brass scoops, like sugar at the grocer's! Nothing would ever be the same again, but she'd had the best of it with the old Queen and Teddy. George was all right, she supposed, but he was no ladies' man. Not like Teddy with his girls, race-horses and rich Jews. She liked Jews, very generous she had always found them. And Ireland wanting to go it on her own. Home Rule indeed! And women with a vote. Who the hell wanted a vote? That Pankhurst. Called themselves ladies.

Kicking the coppers and chaining themselves to lampposts. Wearing bloomers. They'd be wearing trousers next. Why, in her mother's time, no respectable woman even wore drawers.

There was no doubt about Aunt Janie being common, Shelagh thought as she drove up to her aunt's little Regency house. Her weight lifter had never married her. "Had a wife already, ducks, if not two. But he left me a nice little bit of lolly, and look at the fun I've had, the places I've been to, foreign parts and all. And the friends I've got. Good old Janie, everyone loves her. Always have, only not so passionate now, ducks. All friendly, like, no slap and tickle, but I've got me memories. Memories and lolly—what more can an old girl ask, I ask you? Kids—who wants 'em? Just a bloody nuisance when they're little and a pain in the neck when they grow up. Much harder not to have 'em. Any bloody fool can have kids."

Now Aunt Janie met her at the door.

"Welcome, love," she said. "Glad you came. Not seen your young man yet, I suppose?"

"Not yet, Aunt Janie. I'm meeting him this afternoon."

"Well, bring him here soon. I want to meet him. I'm a good judge of men, and ought to be, too, with all them I've known. There was that conjurer friend of mine. I worked with him for a bit. Bloody great ripsaw, ducks, and him saying, 'Now, ladies and gents, I am about to saw this beautiful young lady in half. And if you are afraid of blood, just cover your eyes.' That's how the patter went. Of course it's a trick; it never hurt me, but I didn't like it. What I liked was the white pigeons and rabbits and things. There I stood in my spangles and tights. Beautiful legs. Me beautiful, principal boy legs. Ought to have been in panto, dear; many's the time I've said that. Three sets of tights: red, blue and purple. One on, one off and one at the cleaner's. Handing him things, I was: silk hats, little boxes, tables, jugs, glasses. Straight as an arrow I stood, sticking out me tits and making eyes at the gents in the front row. Sooner look at me than a white rabbit, I promise you, my girl. I had a shape, I did, then, like an hourglass. Not skinny like girls are today." Her

398

eyes were dreamy as she stared back into the past. The boards, the footlights, the clapping hands. Then she came to.

"Yes, bring him to see me. I hope you're being good to him. Giving him a good time, if you know what I mean? Men need it. They're not like us—take it or leave it. Enjoy a good roll in the hay, of course, but just for fun. Not like men, poor bastards. They've got to 'ave it."

While he was waiting for Shelagh, Jim sat on the front looking out to sea. Things were going well now. The Boche was really on the run. He'd been in at the beginning of their retreat but he'd have liked to have been in at the end of it, advancing with the victorious army, seeing the hordes of prisoners and marching through villages with the band playing. Cheers. Girls kissing the troops. Girls.

The round pebbles of the Brighton beach washed up with every wave and ran rattling back as it retreated. Advance, retreat—like war. The waves came in so bravely, beat vainly against the shore and went back, leaving the pebbles like the dead behind them; others, the walking wounded, finding their own way back—rolling, staggering.

He thought of Shelagh. That day in hospital when he had said, "Give me your hand." Why had it been so important? Was that all there was in life? Suppose he'd lost his balls, what then? He'd still be alive, well. Was that all a man was, a complicated arrangement set about his organs of generation? All a girl was, something set in a body that might be pretty or might not? Men wanted the pretty bodies, but it was the same in them all. A blind man wouldn't care. He could fool himself. But it was there in them all, decorated or not decorated, like food. The need of it a hunger. And rich men got the best as they got the best food. The richest, the creamiest, with the most highly flavored sauces.

The waves still came in, rolling their pebbles, bombarding the shore in their endless battle against the land. They had been doing it when Julius Caesar landed in England; when William the Norman brought his cavalry ashore. The white cliffs had been there too, and the seabirds crying. For thousands of years men had sat watching the sea. Warriors, waiting for invasion. Lovers with their women. All interchangeable with the same emotions, hopes, fears, passions. Waiting to kill, waiting to make love.

Idly, to pass the time, he picked up a newspaper someone had left. Something caught his eye: "War Hero Held for Murder." He read on.

Ex-soldier held for murder—Sergeant Arthur Goodby, DCM, MM and Bar, 10th Wiltshire L.I., has been arrested in connection with the deaths of the well-known dancers Mr. George Bramwell and Mrs. Enid Bramwell (or Goodby). Mrs. Bramwell was the wife of the accused. She had been strangled. Mr. Bramwell had been killed by a bayonet-thrust through the throat. . . .

So this was the end of the story. The love idyll that had begun, so far as he was concerned, with reading Goodby's Song of Solomon letter. Poor Goodby, who had refused all leave because he had been afraid he would do this if he got home. He had tried to get himself killed and all he had done was to become a hero. What a strange story of love, adultery, courage and murder! Goodby had worshiped that woman. Was this the judgment of a jealous God? The God who said, Thou shalt have none other gods but me? Was the Christian God like Siva, who was also the god of war, the god of the creative force in nature and at the same time the god of all violent death, of destruction and murder?

He was still thinking of Goodby when he saw Shelagh walking toward him. His heart beat faster. She was wearing the blue coat that matched her eyes. They would have tea at the Ship or the Metropole. Crumpets, dripping with melted butter. Goodby was forgotten.

Shelagh saw Jimmie waiting for her. It was the first time she'd seen him up and dressed. He'd only been in a dressing gown in London. The sea air had done him good. He was coming toward her with the shingle noisy under his feet. She was going to introduce him to Aunt Janie and Flash Jack. As soon as they found some place alone they would kiss . . . and . . . and what? And everything.

He said, "Hullo, Shelagh!"

She said, "Hullo! You look better."

"I am better. And look at this—I call him Charlie." He held up a round red air-cushion with a hole in it like a lifebuoy. "That's what comes of being hit in the arse. Running away." He laughed.

She laughed with him.

He said, "Come and sit down." They sat on a seat with glass windbreak sides. "I've got a present for you, Shelagh," Jim said, putting a little leather box in her hand.

She snapped it open. "Oh, Jimmie!"

"Engaged, Shelagh. Official. But just for us. We'll keep it dark till after we're married. Marriage is a private affair."

The ring flashed in the autumn sun. "What shall we do, Jimmie?" she said.

"Go and have tea at the Metropole. Crumpets dripping with butter." His mother loved crumpets. His mother. She wouldn't be able to come to the wedding, the baby was due any day now, but he'd write and tell her, of course. Her and the General . . .

Shelagh began to laugh. Dripping crumpets, a circular air-cushion, hit in the arse: romance. But there was the ring on her finger to prove it. This was a difficult moment. The wounded boy had turned into a man and they both knew they would do something about it soon. It was in their minds as they ate the crumpets and licked the butter off their fingers. There were other officers with girls at tables around them, each couple a little world of their own.

Shelagh said, "How about taking me home after tea and meeting Aunt Janie?"

"I want to meet her."

They went out, Jimmie smiling at the people who looked at his cushion.

"So this is your soldier boy?" Aunt Janie said. "Pleased to meet you, young feller."

"Shelagh's told me about you."

"Not all, I hope. Not that she knows all. But she's a good girl."

Shelagh held out her finger. "Look!" she said.

"Jesus, that's a nice ring! Cost a packet I'll bet, but you can always pop it in if you're in a hole."

Jimmie laughed. He liked the old girl. Quite a character. He was glad Shelagh had prepared him for her. Two cats walked into the room and rubbed themselves against him.

"That's a good sign," Janie said. "Them liking you, I mean. Don't like everyone." She got up. "You'll stay to supper, I hope?"

"I'd like to."

"Then I'll go and make it. Take about half an hour. I expect you can entertain each other so I'll exit." She winked and went out.

"Well?" Shelagh said.

"She's wonderful." He took her in his arms. Their first real kiss since he had got back from the war. He undid her blouse and found her breasts. Half an hour. Tomorrow if it was a nice day they'd go into the country. Take a bus and walk on the downs.

There was a knock on the door. Janie popped her head in, laughing.

"Like old times," she said, "knocking on doors, and in me own parlor too! Supper's ready, so come on. Bangers. Sausage and mash, and a nice trifle. Whisky if you want it. Port wine. Brandy."

It was a gay meal with stories of Janie's adventures on the boards. "Bed and boards more like," she said. "Much sought after I was in them days."

Jim said very little. He just watched the two women. He felt at home here.

The next day was fine, quite exceptional. Special, as if God was on their side. Jimmie picked Shelagh up and they went to Lewes. They had lunch at the White Hart and then came out onto the downs. The sun was almost hot, the wild thyme aromatic beneath their feet. It wasn't long before Jim found what he wanted: a little grass lawn mown by rabbits, as smooth as a golf green, set in a maze of gorse. He kissed her, then took her left hand and before Shelagh knew what he was doing he had slipped the wedding ring onto her finger.

"I'm not going to wait any longer. We've been engaged for a whole day and I'm going to marry you now, in the eyes of God, the larks and the bloody rabbits."

When they had sat down Shelagh had known what would happen. He was going to make love to her. She wanted him to. Somehow it seemed right on such a beautiful day. Some gorse was still in flower, its sweet fecund smell joining that of the wild thyme. A lark high in the sky began to sing. A seagull swept by quite low. Jimmie was kissing her. He had pushed her back on the grass carpet of this little room with its walls of dark green gorse. She could feel the new ring on her finger. How romantic he was! She had never guessed he had this side to him. Her head was on his round cushion, on Charlie. She saw his face close to her with the blue sky behind it. She felt his weight on her. She had thought she would never feel again what she had felt for Francis, but she'd been wrong. She felt the same for him as she had for Francis. More, perhaps, because she had snatched this man from the jaws of death—what a cliché that was! But clichés were true. She thought of what the doctor had said. "So much depends on that girl"—that was her—"he watches for her."

She smoothed her clothes, tidied her hair, made up her face and said, "I want to tell you about Francis, Jimmie. He made love to me once just before he went to France."

"Thank you for telling me, darling, but that's all over and done with long ago." And he didn't care. No more than if she'd been a widow.

Shelagh was thinking that it had happened the way she had thought it might, on a little rabbit-mown lawn, with their dry marble-sized pellets all around. The flowering gorse, the blue sky, and the larks and the gulls as witnesses to the consummation.

At Brixton Prison Mr. Joseph Quinlan, KC, was talking to Sergeant Goodby of the King's Own Wiltshire Light Infantry.

"In France I could get you off. Crime of passion. War hero. DCM, MM and bar. Betrayed by wife while fighting for his country."

"I only got the medals because I was trying to get killed. I took no leave. I was afraid I'd do this."

"Well, don't say that in court for God's sake."

"No, sir." Goodby paused. "What'll I get, sir?"

"Ten years, I'd say."

"A nice rest. There's a lot of reading I want to do."

An extraordinary man. "What kind of reading?"

"About God. About religion. You see, I have made my plans; when I come out I'm going to join the Army."

"The Army?"

"Yes, sir. The Salvation Army. I've got a letter, sir. They say they'll have me. You see," he said, "I think I could do a lot of good with the hard boys. Having done time for murder. War hero." He smiled apologetically. "With my ribbons and so on. They'd listen to me. I see the hand of God in this. His instrument. They were bad, sir. Wicked. Three years' hell, sir, ten years' purgatory, and then into the arms of Jesus. Hallelujah! The ways of God are strange, are they not, sir?"

54 : Flash Jack

JIM WAS up early next day. He went down to the sea. That was the place to think. He wanted to be alone till he went to fetch Shelagh at Aunt Janie's. She'd give him breakfast. He couldn't have faced it with all the chaps. Not today, which was the day after yesterday. How lucky he was with Shelagh! She was so pretty, as pretty as Kathleen. What a coincidence that she should have nursed him! He thought of how they had made love—proper love, in that little dell on the downs. They had been one flesh. Joined, coupled. He had gone into her.

But he wanted her in a room, on a bed. Naked. That strange man-part of him that had a will of its own. That was the extraordinary thing. Impotent when it was tired, or a man was old. The mind wanted to and it wouldn't. A man had very little control over it. But all this excitement, all this fuss, worry, pain, over something that took less than a minute. As if this minute was the culminating point of life. Perhaps it was. The visible and outward sign of it. The seed of life that had to be planted, or at any rate got rid of. Insistent.

He looked at his watch, the watch he'd worn in battle. The same little second hand still ticking the seconds away. Ticking away when he was bleeding to death, when he was making love to Shelagh, to Mona, to Louise, to Kathleen. But Kathleen was just a ghost now. Dead, reincarnated in Shelagh. It was time. Zero. Time to go to Aunt Janie's.

Shelagh opened the door to him. "I thought you'd be early," she said. "I couldn't sleep either."

Aunt Janie came bustling in, her peroxide hair tied up in a blue check duster. "Early, aren't you, Jim?"

"I thought you might give me some breakfast."

"Want your eggs scrambled or fried? Tea or coffee?"

"Fried, Aunt Janie, please, and tea."

"Three eggs and two rashers, toast, marmalade. The bloody lot, my soldier boy. I take it you're going to make an honest woman of the girl?"

"Oh, Jimmie," Shelagh said, "I forgot to take my wedding ring off when I came in."

"An' I didn't half laugh," Aunt Janie said. "Dragged it out of her. But I'd have known anyway from her eyes. *Al fresco,* as they say. Well, it was a nice day for it."

"We want you to be a witness when we make it legal," Jim said.

Romantic, that's what it was, her little Shelagh getting herself

405

married to that beautiful boy. Hero, that's what he was. Two wound stripes, a Military Cross and bar, and still shy as a girl. She'd bet he wasn't shy with Shelagh though. Full of blood and spunk. Aye, lay her bottom dollar on it. Make her happy if she'd let him. Wanted her to be a witness.

"We need two, Aunt Janie. Next Tuesday."

"Tuesday's a lucky day, ducks. Two, eh? Who's the other one?"

"I don't know. We'll have to find someone," Jim said. "What about your bookie friend?"

"I'll call him up." She picked up the phone and asked for a number.

"Flash Jack speaking. Flash Jack Welshman, the Welshman who never welshes. Wot do you want? I'll give you the best odds . . ." His voice could be heard all over the room.

"It's me, Jack. Janie."

"Oh, it's you. What do you want?"

"I want you over here at once. It's urgent."

"Urgent, eh?"

"Yes, it's urgent. So hurry."

"I'll be around in fifteen minutes."

"If you'll excuse us we'll push off," Jimmie said. He wanted to be alone with Shelagh and was in no mood for introductions.

"Well, what's all this about that's so bloody important?" Flash Jack had let himself in with his own latchkey.

"It's a wedding."

"Well, I'm bloody well not going to marry you, Janie. I like living in sin. Makes me feel young when I look at all the married coves dragging their balls and chains. But I'll tell you what I'll do, Janie. We'll get engaged. An' that's as far as I'll go. I got a pawnbroker pal wot's got a bloody great flasher, blue-white. It would look good on your 'and. Bloody great diamond," he said again, "going cheap because it's an old-fashioned cut and got two flaws. But who's to look for 'em? Need a glass to see 'em."

"All right then, we'll get engaged. And about time too. Flash Jack—never welsh, indeed. Welshed on me, didn't you?"

"What do you want to bring that up for now when we've just got engaged? But no wedding on Tuesday."

"It's not ours, you bloody fool."

"My God, so you fooled me! Got a sparkler for nothing." He began to laugh and slapped her bottom. Janie slapped his face. They collapsed, laughing, in each other's arms. "Now tell me," he said. "Who is it?"

"It's Shelagh, my niece. Going to marry her soldier boy. We're to stand up with 'em. Witnesses. Make it nice and legal."

"All right, my girl. You can flash your ring at 'em. Knock their bloody eyes out."

"Christ, I love you, you great big bastard, even if you won't make an honest woman of me!" They started laughing again. Jack poured out two three-finger drinks.

"To us!" he said.

"To us, Jack."

"Well, as I'm over here, we might as well, eh?" He started upstairs.

"Romantic, aren't you, Jacky-boy?"

"Randy," he said, "Every time I see you."

Flash Jack Welshman, a big, red-faced man, weighed about fourteen stone. He wore a high brown bowler that he never took off except in bed, check suits like horse blankets, yellow shoes; a flower in his buttonhole; a big gold hunter and a gold chain as thick as a cable across the equator of his belly.

But she'd loved him for years. Not so passionate now, she'd told Shelagh. Well, not quite perhaps. But you could get a good tune out of a couple of old fiddles if they knew the music. Blue-white, he said. Engaged. Sixty years old and God knew how many men between the ventriloquist and Flash Jack. The first and the last of 'em, with all her life like a ham sandwich between 'em.

When Shelagh came in Janie said, "What about clothes, ducks? Trousseau?"

"No trousseau, Aunt Janie. No time."

"We'll find time, ducks. A wedding present from Auntie. Silk,

407

satin, lace insertion, silk stockings. The bloody lot. Want to send him mad, don't you?" She winked and gave a ribald laugh. "Good God, pretties are half the battle, darling. Chemises . . . knickers . . . nighties. Not shy, are you, ducks? I mean, now you've 'ad it? Saw it in your eyes. I didn't even have to see the bloody wedding ring. Saw it in the way he looked at you and touched you when he thought I couldn't see. Those hands know you, ducks." She pulled down a lower lid. "See any green in my eye, ducks?"

Shelagh began to laugh.

"It's nice to have you here, dear," her aunt said, "and not have to mind my P's and Q's. But I've got something to show you, and I've got the other witness."

"Who is it?"

"Flash Jack. And look!" She took the diamond ring from her reticule. "I'll put it on now. I wanted to surprise you. Engaged, ducks. Yes, your Aunt Janie's engaged. Has been, in a manner of speaking, for ten years. But now it's official."

Shelagh kissed her. "I'm so glad." Oh dear, she was thinking, what would Jimmie make of all this? He and Aunt Janie got on like a house afire, but Flash Jack might not be so easy to explain.

"You know, Shelagh my girl, we're really married already except for that little bit of paper, an' seeing you do it on Tuesday may make him see how easy it is."

"So that's your plan, Aunt Janie?"

"In a way. You see I worry about him catching cold, coming and going at all hours, and in winter too. He's not a boy anymore. Needs a woman's care. Love. Cherish. Just a big baby, that's all Flash Jack is. And I want my rights, a woman's rights. I want the right to sleep with him regular, and nurse him when he's sick. That's what I want." Tears formed in her eyes.

Shelagh kissed her again. What a good, kind woman she was! What if she had had lovers? She certainly hadn't harmed any of them, and one day she'd give Flash Jack a bit of her mind. She saw Janie with new eyes. A beautiful woman for her age, who must have been lovely once. She saw her in spangles, her

408

principal boy legs in silken tights. The bone was still there in her face, and bone was the peg on which all beauty hung. And how sweet she was about the trousseau! She saw herself wearing it for Jimmie.

55 : November Honeymoon

WHEN JIM got to Aunt Janie's on his wedding day he was surprised to see an enormous Rolls outside. Shelagh, who had been waiting for him, ran out.

"Whose car's that?" he said.

"Flash Jack's, Jim. He says a Rolls gives people confidence. It's known on every racecourse in England. Now come in and meet him. I hope you like him. Remember, he's been very good to me."

But she needn't have worried. When Jim and Flash Jack met, they hit it off. Flash Jack was dressed in his best. New high brown bowler, new check suit with checks the size of those on a chessboard. An enormous pink carnation in his buttonhole. His face scrubbed and polished till it shone like an apple.

Janie presented him. "My fiancé, Mr. Welshman."

"Flash Jack Welshman," he said, bowing with his hand on his watch chain. "The Welshman who never welshes. At your service, sir and madam." He slapped Jim on the back and said, "Wouldn't mind being in your shoes, young man. Mind if I kiss the bride?" Powerful as a gorilla, he swept Shelagh up in a horse-rug arm and kissed her loudly. "Very honored, I'm sure," he said. He fished in one of his enormous pockets and brought out a small parcel. "Present," he said. "Hope you'll accept it. Friend of the family. Open it!" he said.

Shelagh tore off the paper and opened a small flat leather case. A pair of gold and diamond cufflinks and a string of pearls.

"We can't take them, Mr. Welshman. They're too valuable."

But before she had finished speaking, Jack had clipped the necklace around Shelagh's neck and slipped the links into Jim's pocket.

"Don't worry," he said. "I can afford it."

What a wedding present! What could they do that wouldn't hurt his feelings? All the way to the registry office in the Rolls Jim kept wondering what to do. When they got out of the car he said, "You know, Mr. Welshman, we can't take your presents; they're too valuable."

"Don't talk nonsense, boy. You're me new relatives, and don't mister me. Flash Jack's the name. Known far and wide." He fingered the diamond stickpin in his fawn Ascot tie.

Jim continued to protest till Aunt Janie said, "Come on! We can't stand in the bloody street outside the registry office as if we hadn't made up our minds. You both have, I suppose?"

It did not take long. "You, Shelagh, take this man, James Charles Edward Hilton, to be your wedded husband. . . . James, you take this woman, Shelagh Muriel Moran, to be your wedded wife . . . in sickness and in health . . . till death do you part. Put on the ring."

Shelagh held up her hand. Jim said, "Mrs. Hilton," and slipped on the narrow band of gold. It had only been off since breakfast.

"Kiss her," the registrar said.

Aunt Janie began to cry. Flash Jack pulled an enormous purple handkerchief from his pocket and dabbed at his eyes. Janie took his hand.

The registrar had seen some queer marriages but this one took the cake.

Lunch at the Metropole. Flash Jack said, "All ordered. Magnum of fizz waiting in the bucket."

"Got 'em on, ducks?" Janie whispered to Shelagh. "All of 'em?"

"Yes, thank you, Aunt Janie." She spoke like a little girl saying "thank you" for the party.

"Then for Christ's sake stop all that blubbering. You're supposed to be happy."

In the hotel Jim slipped away from them to buy some cigarettes.

As he turned from the clerk, he heard a woman's footsteps behind him. They stopped and a voice said, "Jim?"

It was Kathleen.

"What are you doing here?" he asked. Shelagh had joined him. How alike they were! Like sisters.

"I told you," she said. "My husband's people live near here."

He said, "Shelagh, this is Kathleen Gowan." Her husband's name escaped him.

"Oates," she corrected.

"My wife, Shelagh."

The two girls looked at each other. Kathleen said, "He was killed last week. My husband." They had not shaken hands.

Shelagh said, "I'm so sorry."

Then Kathleen said, "My son is eight months old."

Jim echoed her. "Eight months old."

She said, "Do bring your wife over to lunch. I'd like you to see him. It's not far and I often come to Brighton to shop." Then she added, "What a bloody waste!"

What was a bloody waste? The war?

Shelagh excused herself, but Kathleen was still beside him. Her eyes followed Shelagh as she walked away.

Jim watched her go down the lobby, her hobble skirt tight above her black silk stockings, her gold bobbed hair on her shoulders. It might have been Kathleen but it wasn't. Freddy Oates had been killed too late.

"It might have been me, mightn't it, Jim? It would have been me if my mother hadn't bitched us. If Freddy had been killed sooner." If . . . If . . . If. Kathleen dabbed her eyes with a handkerchief. "You loved her because she was like me?"

Jim said nothing. She was right. . . .

Kathleen said, "The boy's name is Frederick James—James after Freddy's father, of course. It's such a common name, isn't it, Jimmie?" Then she turned and went out.

It could have been Kathleen. And the kid's birthday was in April. Jim was counting months on his fingers. . . .

Kathleen was not the only one of Jim's past loves to be widowed. The same paper that had contained the news of Goodby's arrest had also carried a small item referring to the death of Captain Albert Smith, RASC, who had been crushed against a wall by a five-ton truck being backed onto him. "His widow is resuming her maiden name of Miss Mona Moon and returning to London," announced the paper. "It is understood that she has been left well provided for."

But Jim didn't see it. He was thinking of Goodby.

Al Smith's death had not been quite so accidental as it appeared. He had himself laid the foundations of the structure that led to his end. The foundation stone had been laid when he told Mona to allow herself to be seduced by a town councillor from whom he wanted certain concessions. This man had a casting vote. She refused and he thrashed her with a dog-whip; then she submitted. The scene was classic, simple, and often to be repeated. A man was asked to dinner. After dinner Al was called away. Something had happened at the depot. He'd say, "I'm afraid it will take some time to iron things out, but don't rush away. Mona will entertain you." She did. Fat, vulgar, old men, not at all what she had been accustomed to.

More beatings. Badger game tricks. Men photographed in bed with her, the blackness illuminated by the explosion of Al's flashbulb.

His next move was to want to insure Mona's life.

"So you want to insure my life, Al?"

"Yes, darling, for ten thousand smackers. You'd be a great loss to me, you know."

"I'll say, you bloody double-crossing pimp."

"Say that again and you'll get it."

"Oh no, I won't, not today. You don't want me marked up for Mr. Bloody Johnson, do you? I mean, when you're called away on business after the nice little dinner I'll cook for the three of us?"

"Well, just take a look at it, dearie." He went to the top drawer of the chest of drawers and took out a short nilgary covered in brown leather, an officer's swagger stick, and whistled it through the air.

Mona controlled a shiver. The bastard. She'd kill him one day. Stick some rat poison in his food. It had always surprised her that more girls didn't kill the men who knocked them about. Poison them or kill them in their sleep. Stick a knife into their gizzards. Every man, even a strong man like Al, was as helpless as a baby in his sleep. But now she knew why they didn't do it. They were afraid. Suppose it didn't come off, suppose they messed up the job? And besides, there was a kind of respect for the sheer brute animal force that they couldn't resist. They belonged to these men, the way a dog belongs—a bitch.

"Ten thousand, Al? That's a big premium."

"You're worth it, honey. Every penny of it. You'd be hard to replace. Not that hard, but it would take time. I need you—you know that. Just be a good girl and you won't get hurt."

Good girl. Sleep with fat old town councillors, contractors, play the badger game. Might as well be on the bloody streets. She, who'd only slept with the best in England. All introduced. A kind of club. How he had deceived her, betrayed her!

"Insure me so you can get some of your strong-arm boys to knock me off when you've done with me?"

"Don't be such a bloody little fool. Sign here." He stuck his finger on a line of the policy.

She said, "I've got a better idea."

"What sort of idea?"

"That you insure yourself for ten thousand too—in my favor. Look much better."

An expression of cunning came over his face.

So she was right and he had had no intention of paying that premium for long.

"All right," he said, "I'll get another policy made out."

"OK, Al. Then we'll sign them together."

He had given in. It would look better if they were both insured.

413

And then Staff Sergeant Harris came into the picture. She had seen him look at her when she went to Al's office in the ASC depot. A good-looking, redhaired man. He always seemed to be about. He saluted her. He spoke, "Good morning, madam. Good afternoon." She replied, "Fine day. Wet day." Their eyes met. She knew the expression on his face. After all, she had seen it often enough. A few days later she said, "I think I shall go for a walk in the park tomorrow after lunch if it's fine." It was fine. They met.

"Fancy meeting you here, staff sergeant!"

"Just fancy, madam."

They walked side by side. Mona let her thigh brush his. His hand found hers. He said, "You don't love that bastard, do you?"

She said, "I hate him!" Oh, how she hated him! He had degraded her.

"Don't you wish something would happen to him, Mrs. Smith?"

"I often do."

"Then you'd be pleased?"

"Delighted." Mona smiled. It was a wonderful thought.

"And you'd be prepared to have a little celebration, if you know what I mean?"

"I know what you mean, staff sergeant."

It was all very easy. Harris hated the captain. Everyone did. So one day when he was covering some stuff he'd put in the back of a five-ton truck with a tarp, it happened. The stuff was stolen government property. Engine parts. Harris had been ordered to drive it because no one would question a staff sergeant. He'd done it a good many times before because Smith had something on him. That was his trick—to get something on people and turn the screw. The bastard. Practically everyone had done something at some time, and that was what he ferreted out.

The lorry had just been cranked up. Running smooth, she was. He'd put in the clutch with the engine in reverse. An accident. Could happen to anyone.

That afternoon he'd gone to call on Mrs. Smith. Mona.

"Mrs. Smith," he said to the maid. "I came to offer my condolences."

She heard his voice and called, "Come in." She was in black, a handkerchief in her hand.

"Mrs. Smith," he said, "I came to offer my condolences. A terrible accident. It's good of you to see me, seeing as 'ow I was responsible for it. Careless. But 'ow was I to know he was behind the lorry?"

Mona said, "I know how fond you were of him. He often spoke of you. I think he'd like me to give you something of his, a little souvenir. Cufflinks, perhaps? Come upstairs and choose something." She led the way to the bedroom.

"There's no time to undress," she said, as he closed the door.

"Who wants to undress?" In his walk of life, undressing was considered indecent.

Five minutes later Mona, standing at the door as he went out, said, "I'm glad you chose the cufflinks." She put them into his hand.

"Thank you, madam," he said. "It's nice to have something to remember him by. A souvenir I'll never forget."

The wedding lunch was wonderful. Oysters, salmon, grouse game pie, roast beef, a special trifle for Uncle Jack, ice cream, champagne, brandy . . .

Jim's mind was in a whirl. Goodby in prison for murder. Kathleen free and wanting him to come and see his son. He'd been counting on his fingers again under the tablecloth. In an hour they'd be off on their honeymoon, and he'd write "Major and Mrs. James Hilton" in the hotel register. The thought of it fascinated him. That's what it would always be now. He had done in twenty-one years what many failed to do in the whole of their lives. He had love, grasped like a bird in his hand. He had survived the greatest war the world had ever seen. His friends, his contemporaries, almost all of them, were dead and nothing could ever frighten him again. Nothing could be as bad as what he had come through. One phase of his life was over and another was about to begin.

He thought of the women he had known. Gwen, Mona,

Kathleen, Louise, Marie, Shelagh. All women. All woman. His wife. He thought of the time they had made love on the downs. *Al fresco,* as Aunt Janie had called it. Of all the taxis in which they had made half-love. Of everything that had led up to this.

"Dreaming, my boy?" Flash Jack said.

He was right. He had been, and now was the time to give them the news. Jim stood up.

"I have a telegram," he said, fishing in his pocket. "It's from my stepfather, Major-General Sir John Gore Blakeney." He smoothed it out and read, "Congratulations and best wishes from us both. Regret inability to attend wedding and lunch but you now have a brother. Mother and son doing well."

Now there was another toast to the baby . . . to the young couple, God bless them, and then they were out of the swing doors and in the street again.

Flash Jack put his arm over Jim's shoulder and signaled the waiting Rolls. "She's yours for the honeymoon, my boy. And here's something to go with it." He put an envelope into Jim's hand. "Twenty fivers. Everything costs more if you have a Rolls."

"My God!" Jim said. "I can't . . ."

"You can, my boy. It's for England. Hero," he said, blowing his nose. "And remember, I'm your rich uncle now. Yes, uncle in a kind of way. Come on, stop buggering about and get in!"

With his foot on the running board, Jim stopped to listen. A newspaper boy was shouting something as he ran dishing out papers. People were giving him silver, paper Bradbury's, and not even waiting for the change.

"Armistice signed. . . ." The was war over. "Extra . . . extra."

Flash Jack was kissing Aunt Janie. Strangers were shaking hands. Women were crying. What a day to begin a honeymoon! The 11th of November, 1918. There was peace on earth. God was in His heaven. Jim laughed. God must just have looked down, noticed what was happening on earth and stopped it.

The Great War was over. There would never be another. Everyone said so. And Shelagh was his wife.

416